
THE LOOKOUT'S GHOST

A. KNIGHTLEY

The Lookout's Ghost
by A. Knightley

This book is a work of fiction. Names, characters, places, and incidents are the product of the author's imagination or are used fictitiously to provide a sense of authenticity. Any resemblance to actual events, locales, or persons, living or dead, is coincidental.

Copyright © 2025 A. Knightley

All rights reserved. No part of this book may be reproduced in any form or by any electronic or mechanical means, including information storage and retrieval systems, without written permission from the author, except for the use of brief quotations in a book review.

Cover art by WendiBones | @wendibones
Interior art by Ego Rodriguez | @egorod
Chapter header art by Milo de Moss | @milodemoss

The author does not support the use of genAI in books or art. No genAI was used in the creation of this book or its contents. To the author's knowledge, no genAI was used in the creation of the cover and interior art.

First paperback edition | October 2025
First hardcover edition | October 2025
First Ebook edition | October 2025

ISBNs | 979-8-9906541-7-4 (paperback), 979-8-9906541-6-7 (hardcover), 979-8-9906541-8-1 (Ebook)

AUTHOR'S NOTE

This book contains descriptions of graphic violence and murder, brief, passing references to self-harm/suicide (not considered or committed by any characters in the story), chronic illness/disability representation (multiple sclerosis, migraine, Raynaud's Syndrome), descriptions of struggling with depression and anxiety, brief description of violence against an animal (neither Rocky nor Randy is harmed in this story), cheating (one MC is cheated on in a past relationship, not between MCs), and parent loss (in the past, not on page).

It also contains descriptions of consensual, sexually explicit content that is only appropriate for readers who are 18+ years of age.

If you have any questions regarding the content warnings, or you identify additional content warnings that should be included, please reach out to the author on Instagram (@author.aknightley), or via email (author.aknightley@gmail.com), and I would be happy to discuss.

When you're ready, look the Thing in the eye.
Hate it.
Rage at it.
Grieve it.
Hold it.
Love it.
When you recognize it again,
when you see you again,
live with it—because you're so worth the living.

— A. KNIGHTLEY

PROLOGUE

My entire life changed on a cold Tuesday in January.

"Why weren't you there to pick me up from the airport, Josh?" I asked, throat scratchy.

He clenched his jaw. I used to think it looked sexy. "Reece. Let's not do this right now. You should rest."

I couldn't really rest, though—not after all the steroids I'd just swallowed. And I wanted answers.

Weight braced against the kitchen counter, I threw back the last of my pills, grimaced, and chased them down with a big gulp of water. God, if they didn't kill me directly, the taste sure as fuck would.

No, I thought. *I refuse for that to be the last thing I eat before I croak.*

My last meal should be something good, like pasta. Or tacos. Or beef tips and gravy over mashed potatoes.

Fuck, when was the last time I ate mashed potatoes?

My stomach roiled. Too bad I was far too queasy at the thought of consuming anything more than a handful of saltine crackers right now.

Double vision was a bitch.

Steroids were a bitch.

My boyfriend forgetting me at the airport because he was probably fucking someone else was a bitch.

Finding out I had multiple sclerosis at thirty-four years old was a *mother-fucking* bitch.

I set the glass on the counter and watched as an identical ghostly image drifted up toward the right before I blinked, snapping it into place.

It drifted again... *Blink*. Back into place.

Two water glasses... *Blink*. One.

Progress. A day and a half ago, I couldn't even do that.

I should go lie down.

"Tell me why you weren't there. I need to hear you say it." Why was I so calm? I should be crying, or maybe screaming. I'd already done both, but not because of him.

The room spun when I turned. Both Joshes stood in the kitchen doorway, shoulders up around their ears.

Blink. One Josh.

He didn't reply. He stepped aside when I shuffled by, one hand braced against the wall while I made my way toward the stairs. I took one step up and stopped, leaning heavily on the railing while the carpeted floor tilted beneath me.

Woah. Too quick.

Josh rushed forward and grabbed my arm. "You always do this. You steamroll in at the worst possible moment. We don't need to talk about this right now. You don't need to talk about this right now."

I let out a humorless laugh. "And you always do that. Dance around the fucking question. Now just give me a minute."

Forehead braced in the hand not supporting my weight, I suddenly felt very heavy.

I wanted to sleep. The kind so deep that for just a few seconds after I woke up, I wouldn't remember who I was, where I was, or any of the awful shit life had thrown at me in the last forty-eight hours.

That sleep would evade me for a while, though. My body vibrated as the steroids kicked in. Twelve hundred and fifty milligrams worth. Twenty-five pills a day, for three more days. Enough to kill a horse.

Well, not really. Or not enough to kill me, anyway, and while I was a big guy, I didn't weigh more than a horse.

They would, however, stop the double vision. The neurologist had said so, anyway. *"But you might experience trouble sleeping,"* she'd followed up regretfully.

Like that was the extent of the hellscape I found myself in.

When I felt steady enough, I slowly climbed the rest of the stairs with Josh's help and shuffled into the bedroom. With a heavy sigh, I sat on the edge of the mattress, mussing the perfectly made duvet.

Josh leaned against the doorframe. The wood creaked under the weight of the guilt twisting his symmetrical face, cast in deep shadow.

"Well? Where were you?" I asked, already tired of this conversation.

Josh pinched his brow and sighed, shaking his head. "Reece…"

That was answer enough.

I already knew—before I left for the conference. Before I ended up in the hospital. Before my entire future imploded —scattered in the wind by a diagnosis I still hadn't even begun to wrap my head around.

I'd suspected he was having sex, and maybe a relationship, with someone else for a few weeks. Lying awake in the dark, staring up at the ceiling while he slept soundly next to me, I'd seethed that it was never actually the ones who did something wrong that struggled to sleep—it was the rest of us, left to deal with the fallout.

Imaginary scenarios fueled by resentment and rage played like a movie in my head.

I'd shake him awake, confront him, and make him confess. I'd eviscerate him with my words, watch the sharp rebuttal die on his tongue, and kick him out of our home in the middle of the night—*my* home, he'd moved in with me after I bought the place, goddammit. I'd feel so smug and self-satisfied as I slammed the door in his face.

I never actually did any of it.

Instead, I'd ignored the signs—the showers after he returned from *running errands*, taking his phone into the bathroom with him so I wouldn't be able to snoop through his texts. The updated password when I finally had sneaked a hold of his phone. The fact that I couldn't remember the last time he asked me to fuck him, and that he rebuffed me anytime I felt inclined, which was seldom.

Maybe that was what Josh meant when he said my timing was always shit—I pushed now, but I hadn't then.

Had he wanted me to? Would he have preferred it if I fought for him? Begged him to stop sleeping around and stay loyal to me? Promised I'd be a better man, a happier person, a more attentive boyfriend, if only he'd stop letting the guy he met God knows where stick his dick inside him?

Truthfully, I wasn't ready to know, then. I wasn't prepared for how disruptive a breakup would be to my life.

I was self-aware enough to recognize how unfair that was —to know we were a ticking time bomb waiting to go off, postponing the inevitable only for when I was ready for the explosion.

It's also unfair to fuck other people when we were meant to be in a committed relationship.

Well, yeah. There was that.

"How'd you meet him?" I asked dryly, genuinely curious.

Another sigh. "We work together."

The confirmation made me feel nothing. Empty. *Huh.* "Wait, was he that blonde who eye-fucked you all night at the holiday party? What was his name? Brad? Brett?"

"Brock. And yes, that's him."

I snorted. Brock. My boyfriend of a year and a half cheated on me with a guy named *Brock?* Had my life suddenly transformed into a season of *The Young and the Restless?*

Although, in my defense, I *had* pushed a little, then. Not

in front of the guy—I wasn't that thick, as Josh liked to call me.

My big, chubby, forest man, he used to say.

I couldn't remember if I'd ever liked the endearment. Actually, I wasn't sure it'd ever really been one, coming from him.

I *had* liked reminding him I had three degrees—one more than him. He may be the fancy Range Rover-driving corporate lawyer who fucked guys at work named Brock and judged my Great Clips haircut, but people called me Doctor West.

Not the kind that was any help on a plane, though. Only the kind that knew too much about trees.

No, I'd waited until after the party to question the heated looks between them. But Josh had dismissed it, so I did to. I'd never understood the point in worrying over whether someone would steal my partner. If they wanted to go, then I didn't want to be with them anymore, simple as that.

Although maybe if I had pushed a little more, none of this would've happened. Maybe if I'd confronted him right away and ended a relationship that ran its course long before that night, the anger, hurt, and anxiety over what came after a break-up at thirty-four years old wouldn't have bottled up so much.

Maybe it wouldn't have triggered my immune system to attack itself, eating away at the protective layer around the neurons in my brain.

Maybe it wouldn't have caused me to wake up two mornings ago after three grueling days of networking at a conference, only to find the hotel room slowly spinning around me.

I'd had a pretty low-key evening the night before, choosing to grab a couple of po'boys—*when in New Orleans*—to eat alone in the room rather than suffering through another group dinner. I'd washed them down with a Coke and a bottle of water.

Blearily rubbing my eyes the next morning, I'd blinked, only for the hotel furniture to stubbornly remain in duplicate.

Chalking it up to stress from travel and the conference—my two graduating master's students had given great talks on their thesis research—I'd fumbled through packing and arranged transportation to the airport, hoping the double vision would go away on its own.

It only grew more intense.

By the time I'd landed back home in Missoula, Montana, the spinning made me nauseated. I'd stumbled around the small terminal—decorated more like a Great Wolf Lodge than an airport—and did my best to avoid looking like a fucking security threat, sat down, and called Josh.

Over and over. He never answered.

Panicked, I'd called my dad. When he picked up, I'd shut my eyes, pressed the heels of my palms into my sockets, and cried.

"Reece? Reece! What's wrong? What happened?" he'd asked, frantic. Something shuffled around in the background, like he'd tossed aside whatever he was doing.

Through shallow inhales, I asked, "Will—you—come—get—me?"

"Where are you? Do you need to call an ambulance?"

"No." I heaved a deep breath and collected myself enough to speak in full sentences. "No, I don't need an ambulance. I'm at the airport. Josh was supposed to come and get me, but he's not answering. I just can't *see*, Dad. Everything's double. Spinning. I don't know what's wrong. I don't know what's happening to me."

"I'm on my way."

My father, Michael West, the law-abiding, Eagle Scout troop leader, never drove above the speed limit. It'd made me want to claw my face off as a teenager. Still did, on occasion. But he'd sped through the mountain pass that morning, trekking north from his house three hours over the Idaho-Montana state line in record time.

The rest of the day was a blur of panic, a small emergency room filled with too many healthcare workers all at once, an MRI, a rushed spinal tap, more needles in my arm than I could count, and finally, a hospital bed.

By the time the neurologist strode into my room later that evening, I was exhausted and had forgotten all about Josh leaving me stranded at the airport.

Dad held my hand when she'd told me I had multiple sclerosis.

"This isn't the typical pathway to diagnosis," she'd said gently. "Usually, people wait weeks to see a specialist, and even longer for insurance to approve the diagnostic tests. I won't tell you you're lucky—but at least we were able to spot it quickly."

I'd just stared at her.

I knew people with MS. It was one of those words

people said with a grimace, a whisper. Like they'd catch it if they spoke too loudly.

Did you hear Jerry has MS now? So sad.

That was it.

The beginning of the end.

You're on the prayer list now. Only the first of a tragic series of updates until people you used to know merely smiled at you in passing because they didn't know what to say anymore.

"But... Like, are there more tests? Could this be something else?" I'd asked, stunned.

Dad wrapped his arm across my wide shoulders. He was stony-faced.

The neurologist gave me a sympathetic look and pointed at the pictures of my brain up on the computer screen. "We can see lesions here, here, and here. Different areas of the brain. These two are active, increasing. We're starting you on a course of IV steroids immediately to knock them back. This one, here," she'd pointed to a vague blotch on the screen toward the center, "could be what's causing your diplopia. The steroids will help. You'll be protected from further relapses—flare-ups—for a month or so. You should schedule an appointment with the treating neurologist right away to figure out what course of treatment is best for you moving forward."

I didn't remember much of the conversation after that. I cried, too, once she'd left. Holding on to my dad like I hadn't since I was a boy, we both wept.

Josh had found my hospital room sometime later, clothes

rumpled and disheveled, and just stared when I stumbled through an explanation.

He didn't give one of his own.

I was discharged the next afternoon and given a prescription to continue the steroids orally.

Josh's voice brought me back to the present. How long had I sat in silence, mind drifting?

"Reece. You're a fucking mess. Once you finish the steroids, we can talk more. Talk about what we both want. Go to couples therapy. Until then, you need to try and relax," he said, crossing and uncrossing his arms.

Ah, there was a feeling other than exhaustion. Anger burned my cheeks. "Tell me," I said, teeth gritted, "what about any of this is relaxing?"

I breathed through the rising tide of rage, the neurologist's words banging around in my skull.

Intense stress can trigger a flare-up, yes. But we have no idea of really knowing what caused this one, or how long the pre-existing lesions have been there. MS looks different on everyone. It's good that your symptoms presented so early, so we can start you on a course of treatment.

"Well, it's not like anything can happen right now," he said, dismissing my question with a wave. "You shouldn't be alone. We can research diet plans together after you've rested. I did some reading, some people say the carnivore diet is great for MS. It might help you with—"

"Get out." My words cracked like a whip between us.

Josh looked up, surprised. "Excuse me?"

I studied his features. When was the last time I really looked at him?

His freshly highlighted hair was perfectly styled, short, with one strand falling just over his brow so naturally I was certain he'd placed it there on purpose. Wide, hazel eyes gaped at me in shock, soft, moisturized lips parted in disbelief. His cheeks reddened.

He was objectively gorgeous. A foil to my messy light brown hair, sun-weathered face, and five o'clock shadow that appeared around eleven in the morning. My pulse used to quicken every time he glanced my way, baffled that someone who looked so perfect could actually want me.

None of that existed between us anymore.

"You heard me. I don't need your help. I don't want you to tell me what I should do, or eat, or how I should deal with this. I can't stand looking at you. Maybe Brock will let you sit on his dick in exchange for a spare room. Leave."

"What the fuck, Reece? You're sick. You're sweating, you look half-dead, and you nearly choked on your own spit, swallowing all those pills a few minutes ago. You can't—"

"GET OUT!" I roared. Suddenly upright, I strode toward him, lurching as I reached for one of the bedroom doors to slam in his face.

He recoiled.

I was bigger than him. He reminded me of it often. I was taller, over six feet, and had one of those guts that never stopped looking soft, no matter how much I strode up and down mountains and swung an axe and heaved heavy packs of field gear through the forest.

He'd tried to high-protein, gym-bro-macro it off me ever since we met.

It never budged.

Still, looking at me in fear was a low blow. I'd never raised my voice at him before, never touched him with anything other than gentleness. Love, once. Maybe.

It was a reminder of how much we'd grown apart. How little we actually understood each other.

"I'm sorry for yelling," I said, blowing out a breath. I kept my voice low, with one hand braced on the door. Exhaustion wrangled my anger back in as quickly as it'd lashed out. "I would never hurt you. But you do need to leave my house. We can sort out a time for you, or whoever you want to hire, to move your things. This is over."

Something sharp sparked in his eyes, and I wondered if he had wanted my rage, after all. If he'd poked and prodded for it, all this time. "I don't understand you. Aren't you going to ask me why? Aren't you going to ask me to stay? To go to counseling together? Show me you feel something, Reece, for fuck's sake."

Genuinely confused, I shook my head. "Why would I do any of that?"

The pleading in his eyes fell away, replaced by the cool mask of the corporate lawyer. "I'll have someone call to arrange picking up my things."

He turned, padded down the stairs, and walked out the front door, keys jingling in his hand. I crashed back onto the bed, rolling so I could pull the covers over me, sweatpants and all.

Great. Life-changing diagnosis and long-term breakup done, within forty-eight hours of each other.

The last few days had been an *efficient* bitch.

I stared at the ceiling. Who was I kidding? This wasn't

my house. I'd bought it, sure, but even if I stripped the place of everything *Josh*, it would still be full of reminders of him.

Even more than that, though, it would be full of reminders of me, from before.

This bed was for the Reece who didn't know his future might be significantly more difficult and painful than he'd thought. This room was for the man who didn't worry about things like MRI results, phantom limb pain, stumbling over words, and hands that stiffened and ached.

He planned research fieldwork trips around things like weather, terrain, and the gear he'd need to pack. I couldn't even imagine planning one at all. What if I panicked, shoved myself into a flare-up, and couldn't hike to safety?

I didn't know how the Reece I was now, the Reece *after*, fit anymore.

In this house, or in this life.

You don't, the Thing hunched at the end of the bed rasped. *You don't fit anywhere anymore, with anyone.*

I turned away, unable to look at the truth in its words. It'd crawled into my life the day I was diagnosed, plucked the fears from my deepest, darkest hidden thoughts, and whispered them back to me at my lowest.

I hated it. I hated it so much.

My phone rang from where it charged on the nightstand. Pulled from my dark spiral, I checked the caller ID and silenced it upon seeing the unknown number. Maybe Josh had forgotten something and called from Brock's phone, hoping I'd actually pick up.

Probably whatever product he used to style his hair in that annoyingly, perfectly imperfect way.

He could wait.

But when the voicemail notification chimed, I reached over to check again. Who the fuck left a voicemail instead of just texting?

Brows creased, I hit the speaker button on the recording.

"Reece," a familiar voice said. "It's Leonard, your Dad's buddy back in Ponderosa. Got a new number a while back. I tried calling him the other day to get hold of you, but I haven't heard back. Anyway, there's a fire lookout position open in the national forest, and I thought I'd see if you're available for the season. I'd need you here by the last week of May. It's been a dry winter so far, and the summer weather pattern predictions are making everyone nervous—could be fiery, so we're filling all the towers. Give me a call if you're interested."

"What the hell is going on?" I mumbled, slowing my truck to a crawl.

Carefully, I avoided side-swiping the long line of parked vehicles that stretched along the narrow shoulder of the highway in front of me. On the opposite side of the road, dozens of people milled around in groups, many of whom were dressed in bright pink shirts and congregated around signs staked into the ground.

"ZONE A", "ZONE B", and "ZONE C" flashed by as I passed. I lost track of how far down the alphabet the signs went before media vans overtook the narrow patch of grass.

Odd. It didn't look like a protest, but I couldn't think of what else it would be.

A police officer wearing a bright yellow safety vest stood in the center of the road up ahead, directing passing cars through the congestion. Several other police vehicles were parked along the highway, and a handful of officers appeared to be calling out directions to the people gathered farther back.

I nodded at the cop and rolled by, picking up speed again. Thankfully, traffic wasn't backed up. Not that there was anything close to real traffic on the winding highway into Ponderosa, Idaho.

It was called the *Gateway to Nowhere* for a reason, after all.

I'd worked and lived in Missoula, Montana, for the last six years, and as rugged as it was compared to most cities in the country, it paled in comparison to the terrain surrounding my hometown.

Really, Ponderosa looked more like a moody off-road SUV commercial than anything else.

Tunnels of fir, spruce, and pine so thick and tall they blocked out the sun grew on either side of the pavement. Abruptly, a sharp bend in the road plunged vehicles out into the open, winding around the sheer mountain face, unveiling dramatic vistas of conifer-covered valleys and steep canyon drop-offs blanketed in fog.

"Douglas fir, Lodgepole pine, Western redcedar!" I used to call out, pointing at each cluster of trees Dad and I drove by on the way home from school. My Forestry Merit Badge was the one I'd been most proud of.

"Very good," he'd say, chuckling and ruffling the hair on my head. "How about that one?" he'd ask, slowing down to point so I could get a better look.

"*Um...* I don't know that one," I'd said, brow furrowed. That was ok, though, because Dad did, and he'd never once made me feel bad for needing help.

"It's a Ponderosa pine," he'd said with a smile. "Don't usually get them up this high, despite the namesake."

The forest was magic, then. Ethereal. A never-ending vastness I couldn't comprehend beyond *infinity*, filled with trees and birds and bears and mountain lions. As a child, it'd been exciting.

Now, I saw it for what it really was.

Stark and harsh, the landscape still took my breath away, but in the way a siren song lured an unsuspecting sailor. The forest would swallow me whole if I weren't careful, caught staring for too long, and not watching my step.

Beautiful and dangerous.

Maybe I would let it, one of these days.

An incoming call rang through the truck speakers, briefly pulling my attention away from ensuring I wouldn't steer off the side of the mountain road into *Nowhere*.

That would *not* be the way to go out.

I checked the caller ID and answered. "Hey, Mom. I'm just coming into Ponderosa now."

"Oh, good. How was the drive?" she asked. A water faucet shut off in the background, followed by pots and pans banging around like she'd called mid-dinner preparation.

"Uneventful for the most part. I'll be at Dad's in ten minutes or so. I think we're meeting Leonard and Bobby for a bite tonight, so I can grab the keys to the lookout."

"Are you driving out tomorrow?"

I flicked on my blinker and turned off the paved highway just before coming into town. The deep ruts in the dirt road jostled me as I slowly wound down the steep drive. "Day after. I need to finish supplying up in town tomorrow. I'll head out Sunday morning."

She sighed. "Well, just be careful. Keep your phone with you all the time when you're out there, you know I worry. Call me if you need anything at all, that's all I ask."

I knew what she wasn't saying.

I wasn't *before* Reece anymore, so I had to be extra careful. I wasn't the man who'd practically grown up in a fire lookout.

When I wasn't visiting Mom in Tennessee, I'd spend at least a few weeks every summer with Dad when he'd fill in as a lookout for the U.S. Forest Service. I could operate an Osborne Firefinder in my sleep and knew how to mentally manage the extended periods of isolation.

That was the whole reason I'd agreed to take the job this season. The thought of leaving everything behind and disappearing into the forest for a few months was music to my ears.

"I'll be fine, Mom, please don't—SHIT!" I yelled, slamming on the brakes. My tires skidded, sliding on loose gravel and dirt until the truck lurched to a halt.

A large tree limb lay across the road and blocked my path. It was hidden around a bend, my view of the road obscured by the thick brush growing on either side until I was nearly on top of it.

"Reece! Oh my God, are you alright? Reece? Reece!" Mom yelled, voice pitched high.

"I'm alright!" I answered, probably louder than I needed to. "It's just a fallen branch in the road, that's all. Nothing to freak out about."

Great. Another worry for her to suffocate me with.

Heart still pounding, I unplugged the phone, cradled it to my ear, and stepped out to move the obstruction aside.

"Are you sure you should be out there all by yourself?" Mom asked, just like I knew she would.

I rolled my eyes and gripped the snapped-off end of the branch to drag it back into the encroaching tree line. "I'll be *fine*," I repeated with a huff. "The scariest thing at a fire lookout is the lack of indoor plumbing. As long as there's enough toilet paper, I'll be set."

She wasn't assuaged by my sparkling sense of humor.

"What if you have another flare-up? Or something else goes wrong? It could take hours for someone to get to you. I'm just not sure you're ready—*what?*" She hollered the last part away from the phone, her voice echoing like she spoke to someone across the house.

"*Oh!*" She continued, talking to me again. "Keith wants to say hello. Hold on, let me put you on speaker."

I took advantage of the brief pause and heaved the other end of the branch to the side of the road. Dad would probably have to deal with it later, or else it'd roll and block the drive again, but I'd at least get through for now.

Back in the truck, I connected the phone to the speakers again and crept along the bumpy road the rest of the way to the cabin. The various meal-prep noises suddenly grew louder, followed by my step-dad's booming voice. "Reece! How's it going? How'd your, *uh*, what's that medicine you're on, now? How'd that go?"

Thank God for Keith.

He was always attentive to Mom's penchant to worry,

and had been a life-saver the last few months in dissolving the tension between us when it began to grate.

My parents divorced when I was ten, as amicably as that sort of thing could be. Mom remarried Keith, a computer programmer who worshipped her and his lawn—in that order—a few years later and moved to Tennessee. She and Dad had decided it was best for me to stay in Idaho with all my friends during the school year, and visit her for a month or so over the summer.

Short and soft-looking, with a round face and a laugh that could be heard a mile away, my mom had gone full Tennessee bleach blonde when they moved, complete with a twang in her voice. She dressed like she was headed for the country club every day.

"Hey, Keith. My infusion went really well. It's supposed to be highly effective in preventing flare-ups, so crossing my fingers it works."

Crossing my fingers it works!

Hopefully, this takes care of it for now!

Just gotta keep trucking on!

I really fucking hated every single word that came out of my mouth when I updated family and friends since I'd been diagnosed back in January. Almost five months later, and I still wasn't sure what I was meant to say. How could I explain the snarling, tangled mess of fear, denial, and anger that simmered every time I thought about it?

I had a potentially life-changing chronic illness that I'd manage for as long as I was alive. I'd already been a grumpy, emotionally unavailable asshole on a good day; now I'd have to explain to anyone I dated that a future with me could be fine, or it could be a slow, sad, painful descent into losing my independence.

A real fucking catch, I was. Not that I was looking, after the way things ended with Josh.

So, I really didn't know how I felt about the infusions. My neurologist had outlined several treatment options that ranged from low efficacy with minimal risk to high efficacy with increased risk, and asked which I'd prefer.

"You can take a few days to think about it, don't rush a decision," she'd said.

In the end, I didn't need to think about it. I *was* a fucking risk factor. My lottery ticket from Hell had already been cashed in. "Give me the effective stuff," I'd said, decision-fatigued and weary.

Actually, I knew exactly how I felt about all of it.

Resentful.

I resented that I was forced to accept an increased risk of cancer and an impaired immune system in exchange for the hope my disease progression would slow down.

I resented the appointments and the phone calls and the well-intentioned but invasive as fuck advice from everyone I knew.

I resented that I couldn't work late into the evening like I used to, when my brain felt most alive, because I was so exhausted I couldn't keep my eyes open.

I resented the fight with my insurance company, and that I'd had to convince them my doctor and I should be the ones who made decisions for *my own health*, not some medical-malpractice-ridden gremlin squatting in a windowless office somewhere, hitting the *deny* button over and over.

Most of all, though, I resented that I'd become a resentful person.

So yeah, I was doing more than *crossing my fingers* these infusions were effective in preventing another flare-up any time soon. The only way I could sleep at night was by knowing I was doing *something* to prevent my eyesight from going wonky again. Sometimes I couldn't breathe from the overwhelming hope that I'd be one of the lucky ones—or the luckiest of the unlucky—who made it to sixty or seventy without major hindrances to my health and mobility.

Saying all of that out loud made people uncomfortable, though.

Me, especially.

"That's just fantastic," Keith said with genuine enthusiasm. "I'm so glad to hear it. Isn't that good news, Pop?"

My mom's real name was Paula, but she'd been *Pop* since she was a girl. "Of course it is. How will you know it's working, though? More blood tests?" she asked, her worried tone grating on my last nerve.

I could see the warm light pouring from Dad's cabin windows up ahead, just visible through the dusk-darkened trees. I pulled around the circular drive in front of the house and parked my truck behind his. "I won't know if the infusions are working until my next MRI, but she said as long as I don't get too sick from my suppressed immune system, all should be well."

"Your next MRI isn't for another year, though! That's too long. You should call your doctor. I'm sure she can get you in sooner if you ask."

I gritted my teeth. "Insurance doesn't work like that."

"But—"

"Look, flare-ups rarely punch through this treatment, Mom. For once, I'd appreciate it if you could just be happy about that and stop stressing me the fuck out with your what-ifs."

The line was silent for a beat. My eyes burned.

Keith cleared his throat. "Well, it's a good thing you'll be out there all on your own, then, so we don't have to worry about someone getting you sick," he said gently. "Keep your mother and me updated, please. Now, I smell something really great happening for dinner."

Mom couldn't hide the wobble in her voice. "I'm sorry for worrying you. Yes, we'll let you go, Reese's Pieces. We love you so much. *Be safe.*"

Every bit of the anger and bitterness that'd built up melted away, swiftly replaced with guilt that I'd felt it at all. "I will, Mom," I said gruffly. "Love you guys, too. Bye."

I sat in the ensuing silence with the truck turned off and listened to the early summer song of the forest come alive. Insects hummed. Nightjars called to find their mates. The trees felt closer all the way out here, like they leaned in. I wouldn't be surprised to turn and find one had crept up behind me when I wasn't looking to peer over my shoulder.

Judging me.

You're the worst sort of son, the Thing said from the passenger seat.

"I know," I whispered back, staring straight ahead.

All of my mom's grating worry and questions were just love, expressed in the only way she knew how right now. Maybe if I were more forthcoming, more honest, more present, I wouldn't feel so exhausted and angry all the time by putting on a brave face.

Well, not brave. More like an *I've got this under control* face.

That's a fucking joke, it quipped.

My nostrils flared. "Go away."

It did.

With a deep breath and a quick swipe at my eyes, I stepped out and shouldered my backpack. The rest of my gear and belongings were packed tightly into the backseat and truck bed, awaiting the drive up to the lookout.

Dad lived in an A-frame cabin that comfortably housed one person. He'd built it himself from rough-hewn Western redcedar—*naturally insect and decay-resistant, lightweight*—after the divorce, and we'd used it as a weekend retreat growing up. He'd sold our house in Ponderosa and moved in permanently when I went off to college.

A true loner at heart, Dad thrived in the solitude of the forest. I was lucky he was forced to have a cell phone for work; otherwise, I'd probably go weeks at a time without hearing from him.

He'd started his career as a helicopter pilot for the U.S. Forest Service, making supply runs for lookouts, scouting smoke plumes, and dropping firefighters into the middle of *Nowhere* to contain the flames.

He'd needed a more predictable schedule after Mom moved, though, so he transferred and became an EMS helicopter pilot. Even though his shifts were more manageable, he could still be on call for several days at a time, so I'd spent many nights sleeping over at my friend Bobby's house.

I strode up the porch steps and tried the handle, but it was locked.

Huh. He should've heard me pull up.

Peering through the large front window, I tapped on the glass. "It's me!"

No answer.

Probably working around back.

I left my bag by the door and circled behind the house. "Hey, Dad?" I called.

Still, nothing.

The lights weren't on in the detached shed, but I thought I'd check anyway, just in case. "You in there?" I called again, a little louder. Grabbing the handle of the manual garage door, I yanked up, but it wouldn't budge.

Was it stuck? I heaved again, but it stubbornly remained shut.

I frowned. Why would he lock this? He didn't have a neighbor for miles.

"Dad? Where are you?" I called again, glancing back toward the house. The only windows on the backside of the cabin were up high, positioned over the loft where he slept.

Snap.

I whipped around at the sound of a broken twig somewhere off in the woods, eyes tracking the tall, thin, tree-shaped shadows.

I squinted. Had something just moved, there, to the right? Or was the rapidly dimming evening light playing tricks on me?

The insects quieted, and the birds hushed.

Everything stilled.

The hair on the back of my neck stood on end, like slow, creeping fingers trailing up my spine. I'd spent enough time in the wild to recognize the feeling—being a few pegs down on the food chain, I'd be dead if I didn't.

A predator was near.

I froze, breath caught shallow in my chest. My entire body tensed, poised, listening, ready to run.

Idaho grizzlies had been over-hunted in the last century, but there were rumors of a few far-ranging bears wandering down through the Snake, Clearwater, and Salmon River drainage basins in the last ten or twenty years, reclaiming what was theirs.

Black bears were common, and so were mountain lions—but I probably wouldn't ever see one of the latter up close unless it was already ripping out my throat.

Well, that's a nice thought to have right now.

My pulse pounded. Again, *not* the way I wanted to go.

Snap.

Another twig, this time closer. I took a slow step backwards, afraid to turn away from the trees pressing in, even though I couldn't discern anything in the near dark.

I tried to make sense of the shapes.

It's probably nothing, I thought. The trees can't actually move or whisper to each other; nothing waited for me to drop my guard, ready to pounce...

A firm hand gripped my shoulder from behind. "Reece."

CHAPTER TWO

"*A*HH!" I screamed, jumping about ten feet in the air.

Ruggedly. I screamed and jumped in a very manly and rugged way.

I certainly didn't yelp.

"Hey! It's just me! Just me!" I turned to find Dad staring at me like I was a spooked horse, with his hands up as though to calm me.

Fair. I wasn't certain I hadn't knocked a few screws loose, myself.

His light brown hair was wet like he'd just showered, and he smelled like Irish Spring soap and beard oil. "Sorry I didn't answer right away. I was in the shower and forgot to unlock the front door for you."

I clapped a hand over my heart. "S'fine," I said, catching my breath. "Just couldn't find you. I came to check if you were back here and thought I heard something," I said, gesturing vaguely toward the trees.

His gaze found the shed over my shoulder. "C'mon, let's get inside."

I glanced back one more time, scanning the tree line. It was fully dark now. Even if something had been there, I wouldn't be able to see it anymore.

"Something wrong?" Dad asked, clapping me on the shoulder to lead us back around the house and up the porch stairs.

I snagged my backpack on the way inside. "All good. Gave myself the willies, that's all." I threw the bag down by the couch—my bed for the night—and turned to give Dad a proper hug.

He was my height, but narrow-shouldered and wiry. Where he looked like he could pick up and run a marathon next Tuesday, I looked like one of those European men who threw logs around for entertainment. Mom always said I got my brawny-man build from her side of the family.

My blue eyes were all his, though.

"So good to see you," he said gruffly, patting my back before releasing me. "How was the drive?"

I settled into the couch while he flipped the lock on the front door again—*odd, he never locks up like that*—and sat in the armchair across from me.

The living room was cramped, with only the two items of furniture crowded around a coffee table that sat in front of a small wood stove, longer than it was wide. A breakfast bar countertop separated the living area from the kitchen, and a tiny mudroom led out back. The stairs built off the left wall led to a loft area where he slept, and a stand-up shower bathroom tucked under the stairs.

One-man cabin, indeed.

"The drive was fine. There was a whole group of people up on the highway just before the turn-off. Oh, and I had to move a limb that blocked the road. I was on the phone with Mom at the time, it nearly gave her a fit," I said.

If anyone understood how suffocating her anxiety could be, it was him. Dad had clearly yearned for a smaller life, but her stress and worry over his job fighting fires in a helicopter was probably the biggest reason for their divorce.

Still, he'd never, not once, spoken ill of Mom in front of me.

"Be kind to your mother," Dad said gently. "It's not been easy on her being so far away from you with everything that's happened."

I sighed. "I know."

She'd flown in the morning after I kicked Josh out, and was a godsend in the hectic days that followed.

I'd been so exhausted from the flare-up and steroid withdrawal that I barely stumbled from the couch into bed before passing out without even pulling the sheet over myself first. She'd kept me fed, ran errands with me when I was still hesitant to drive, and kept me sane—all of which was no easy feat.

When Josh's hired help came to wipe the house of his existence, she'd stood in my living room wearing white ankle pants and a maroon University of Montana Grizzlies sweatshirt. Hands on her hips with her nose in the air, she'd surveyed the last of Josh's things as they disappeared out the door.

"I'm glad you're done with him," she'd sniffed. "There was always something about you he wanted to change. He never stopped picking."

She'd reached up and patted me on the cheek. "You deserve someone who wants *you*, Reece. You're not an HGTV special."

In hindsight, that was actually hilarious, given I was on day four of those joggers and could barely stand.

"Right, we should take off," Dad said after a few moments of silence. It wasn't easy for him to talk about my health, either. "We're meeting Leonard and Bobby at seven thirty. I'll drive." He stood and grabbed his keys off the counter.

I heaved a sigh. "Alright. Let me pee first, and I'll meet you out there."

"Did you lock the door on your way out?" Dad asked when I stepped up into the passenger seat of his truck a few minutes later.

I pulled the door shut and buckled in. "Yes. Why are you being weird about that?"

"What do you mean?" he asked, glancing at me before he pulled out, headed back up the road I'd come down just a few minutes earlier.

"The garage door to your shed was locked—I don't ever

remember you locking that. And you checked the front door about fourteen times in the five minutes we were inside. What's going on?"

He heaved a sigh and ran a hand down his face. The headlight beams bounced along the encroaching tree line. "Someone broke into the shed a few weeks ago."

I whipped my head around to look at him. "What? Did you see who it was? Did they take anything?"

"No, I didn't see anyone. They must've come while I was on a shift. And..." He shot me a look I couldn't place, knuckles white where he gripped the steering wheel. "Do you remember those old bear traps I kept hanging up in there?"

A shiver ran down my spine. "Yeah."

Of course, I did. They'd freaked me out for my entire life.

"They're all gone. Every single one," Dad said quietly, almost disturbed. He turned onto the highway toward town. The pavement was smooth compared to the dirt road we'd just come from.

A beat of silence passed between us.

"Did you report the theft?"

He shook his head. "No. They were illegal and never really mine to begin with. I didn't turn them in because... well. They're gone now."

"Is that all that was stolen?" I asked, tiptoeing across the decades-old eggshells of this conversation.

"Yeah. Nothing else was disturbed. It's like that was all they were looking for, and knew where to find them." He gave a nervous shake of his head. "It's got me a bit shaken up, is all. I don't like thinking about someone snooping through my things when I'm not there. Plus, everyone in town's all worked up over those missing hikers, and—"

"Wait," I interrupted. "Missing hikers?"

He nodded. "Three solo hikers have disappeared this month. The last one was reported just a few days ago. That was probably a search party meet-up you saw on your way into town."

My pulse picked up, brow furrowed. "People go missing all the time in the national parks, though," I replied cautiously, leaving the rest unsaid.

So why do people think these three are different?

I didn't ask, because I was afraid I already knew.

While most outdoor enthusiasts were responsible and entered the wilderness well-prepared to fend for themselves for several days or weeks at a time, it was difficult to comprehend the sheer scale and remoteness of the area, even for those born and raised there.

If something happened—an unexpected storm, a fall, a slight miscalculation in mapping a route—it could very easily turn into a life-or-death situation in which a helicopter was the only way out alive.

Dad knew that all too well.

So it was fairly common for worried family members to report hikers missing, only for them to turn up tired but otherwise unharmed a few days later. Most of the time, there was nothing to worry about.

Except in Ponderosa.

The whole town collectively held its breath every time

someone went missing, waiting to see if there'd be another—and another. Especially when they were solo hikers.

He'd preferred those.

"I think it's way too soon to be worried about anything," Dad said. "It's not even June yet. We're still early in the season; people get ahead of themselves and aren't prepared for the weather to turn or how rugged the terrain is. The rest is just fear and gossip."

"So, it's not like...the others?" I asked.

Dad slowed as we came into town. Off to the right, we passed a wooden sign carved in vintage lettering, lit up so it could be read even in the dark.

Welcome to Ponderosa—Gateway to Nowhere!

"No," he said resolutely. "It's not like the others."

CHAPTER THREE

A bell chimed over the door announcing our entrance to the bar and grill.

It was busy, with most of the tables and booths already occupied by a sea of bright pink shirts. It seemed the search party had called it a night and retired for dinner.

"Reece!"

Heads turned toward me at the call out, the steady murmur of conversation momentarily hushed. I felt their eyes take me in, cautiously assessing before flicking away.

It always took a few days to readjust to that small-town gaze, now compounded by the simmering unease of those pink shirts.

The joys of coming home.

Despite feeling exposed, the heaviness that hung in the air evaporated at the sight of Bobby, my best and oldest friend, waving us over from across the room.

"Hey man," I said after we weaved our way between tables. "Good to see you."

"Ditto," Bobby replied as he pulled me into a hug. "I'm stoked you'll be around for the season." He clapped me on the shoulder and went to hug Dad.

Bobby and I'd been friends since Cub Scouts. Our dads were leaders together in the local troop, their friendship dating back to Dad's Forest Service days.

"Is Leonard coming?" Dad asked as Bobby and I slid into the booth across from him.

"He's meeting us here in a few minutes. He stayed late to finish up a few things at the ranger station."

Now seated, I was finally able to look closer at the pink shirts without outright staring. Along with a large picture of a young, beautiful, blonde woman, they read:

MISSING: Haley Thomas
    AGE: 27
    Height: 5'7"
    LAST SEEN: Dead Man's Creek Trailhead,
Salmon-Challis National Forest

A tip hotline was printed underneath the photo in big, bold numbers.

"Can I get you boys anything to drink?"

The question pulled my attention back to our table. "*Uh*, a water, please," I said when it was my turn to order, smiling at the server.

"What do you think? Mozzarella sticks?" Bobby asked before she left, waggling his eyebrows at me.

Josh's pinched face flashed through my mind, the very look he'd given the menu the last time we ate there. He'd pestered me to add more cottage cheese to my meals for weeks afterward. "And spinach and artichoke dip," I answered, my stomach growling its very own *fuck you* to the image of my ex's carb judgment.

Also, fuck cottage cheese.

Bobby grinned. "God, I missed you. It's great you're here without... *uh*, anyone else. I mean, then too, of course." He cringed and studied the menu like we hadn't eaten there once a week for most of our lives.

Like Mom, Bobby never really warmed to Josh.

"All good, man," I said with a half laugh. The muscles in my face hadn't stretched like that in a while. It ached in a good way. "And I missed you, too."

"How's Jade doing? And the baby?" Dad asked once we'd placed our drink and appetizer order.

Bobby's eyes twinkled. "They're good. I never did know how to say no to her mother. I don't know how I'm gonna learn with Molly."

Fuck, my friend looked happy. He married the girl he'd loved since high school a few years back, and they'd just had their first child in February.

"Sorry we're stealing you away," I said.

Bobby shook his head. "Jade's mom is watching Molly for the evening, and I was all but pushed out the door after them. She mumbled something about an hour-long shower and chips and queso in bed. I don't think she's had a night to herself since the baby came. We both needed a break."

Dad smiled. "How're Leonard and Joan taking to grand-parenthood?"

Bobby's smile faltered a bit. "Ok, I think. Dad's been stressed with work, though. Sounds like it could be a hectic fire season."

The bell over the front entrance chimed again.

"Speak of the Devil," Dad said, waving the newcomer over with a smile. "Glad to see you made time for us!" he hollered over the din.

Still clad in his park service uniform, Leonard shot a cocky grin our way. "Not before beer," he called back, earning a few weary chuckles and a muted '*cheers!*' from one of the patrons sitting at the circular bar in the center of the room.

I almost missed the man who slipped in just behind him.

He was also wearing a uniform, except his had a distinct *law enforcement* look, all black with a service weapon on his hip rather than the more relaxed brown and green of the park ranger getup. When I looked past the uniform, though, I realized I recognized him.

"Is that Tate Morris?" I asked Bobby, keeping my voice low and angling my head in his direction.

"Yeah," he said. "Weird, right?"

Sure is.

I was pretty certain the last time I'd seen Tate, he was a short, scrawny freshman smoking weed in the back of the high school parking lot. His hair was dyed black, then. Other than his face, the kid I remembered looked nothing like the filled-out, boy-next-door blonde quietly making his way to a corner booth.

"I guess we all grow up," I commented, taking a drink of water.

"Wonder if he still has a crush on you," Bobby teased, elbowing me.

I shot him a deadpan look. "Yeah, that's likely." A freshman mooning over the only out senior in a teeny, tiny mountain town was hardly groundbreaking. I wasn't interested then, and I certainly wasn't interested now.

Not in anyone.

As if he'd heard our whispered conversation, Tate peered up, eyes immediately finding mine and widening in surprise. Before I could react, though, the waitress arrived with our appetizers, followed by Leonard scooting in next to Dad with a sigh, a pint glass of whatever was on tap in hand.

Just as he settled in, a grim-faced man wearing a pink shirt approached our table. "Hey, Mike. Leonard," he greeted. I vaguely recognized him from around town. "Just wanted to say thanks for your help the other day. It means a lot."

Dad nodded. "No problem, Ray. Wish we could've helped more. How'd the search go today?"

"Nothing yet," he said with a shake of his head. "But we'll keep looking. They deserve to be found."

Found. Not saved.

The man thanked Dad and Leonard again and left, rejoining his group.

"What was that about?" I asked.

"Somehow, Leonard swung it so I could fly out a couple of people to do an aerial search using the Forest Service helicopter a few days ago, after that last hiker went missing,"

Dad said lowly, aware of how many people might be listening in.

"What about the others? Weren't there two more before her?" I asked, confused.

Dad grimaced. "There wasn't as much attention before her. You know how these things go."

"That's fucked up," Bobby commented through a mouthful of fried mozzarella.

"There are a lot of people out looking for the three of them, now," Leonard said. "If it was foul play, they'll find something. Hopefully, they were just caught in bad weather and will come stumbling down the trail in a few days."

I was skeptical of his optimism.

The wilderness surrounding Ponderosa boasted the largest stretch of uninterrupted forest in the lower forty-eight —and the most remote. On its own, the national park was massive, and it was only a piece of the vast expanse of *Nowhere* that stretched for millions and millions of acres. Whatever—or *whoever*—had happened to those poor people, the chances of finding them were slim to none.

Unfortunately, that was already proven by the other six missing hikers who'd never been found nearly forty years ago.

Bobby and I dove into the chip basket while they were still hot and fresh, practically elbowing each other out of the way for that first steaming scoop of cheesy goodness. I'd always thought calling it spinach and artichoke dip was sort of like saying pizza was a salad.

"Well," Leonard said, smiling and shaking off the weight of the previous topic, "it's great to see you, Reece. I'll admit I was relieved when you agreed to help us out for the summer. I know your Dad'll be glad to have you nearby, too."

I nodded. "No problem. I'm taking a sabbatical for the academic year anyway, so it's good timing. The truck's all packed and ready to drive up to the lookout on Sunday."

He blinked at me and then swore. "I'm so sorry, I forgot to tell you."

Dad frowned. "Forgot to tell him what?"

"I've had a hell of a time lining everything up for this season, and it completely slipped my mind. We've got double the amount of volunteer firefighters on call in case we need them—scheduling the training alone has been a nightmare—and all of the towers in our district are in service, even the ones usually on standby."

"What does that mean?" I asked, eyebrows creased.

Had he forgotten about me? Or realized I wasn't needed, after all?

I didn't have a house to go back to in Missoula. I'd sold off quite a few things—whatever was left after Josh gutted the place of his belongings—and put the rest into storage. My realtor had hired landscapers to add a little curb appeal before I put it on the market later this summer. I depended on the next few months to figure out my future living situation.

There was nowhere else to go.

"You're in a different lookout than we first discussed," Leonard said, grimacing.

"Oh," I said, relieved. "But there's still somewhere for me to stay, yeah?"

"Yes," he said emphatically. "We've hired a few new

people who weren't comfortable with such a remote posting, so I've assigned them to the drive-up towers. Yours is a hike-in only. I should've told you sooner."

"Wait, how's he getting all of his stuff out there, then?" Bobby asked through another mouthful of mozzarella.

I joined him, first dipping the breaded cheese into the marinara sauce before taking a bite.

Fucking delightful.

"You'll need to drop everything off tomorrow at the ranger station—all of your belongings and supplies. The Forest Service still provides your water and firewood, like usual, but you've gotta do your own grocery shopping. It'll all be helicoptered in on Sunday afternoon. You should plan to be out there in time to meet them at the landing pad. The crew will help you carry everything up to the tower."

"Is there power?" I asked, suddenly nervous. I'd prepared to be physically alone for most of the summer, aside from the days I'd drive into town to restock my groceries, fuel, and water, but I hadn't prepared to be completely inaccessible from June through October.

Mom is going to freak out.

Honestly, I might, too. So much of this trip was about proving to myself that I could still handle all of the time outdoors my research required—that I could confidently enjoy camping and hiking again without the fear that a flare-up would interfere with my ability to survive in the wilderness.

Also, I wanted to do these things while I still could. Just in case.

"Propane fuels a refrigerator and freezer in a shelter

attached to the outhouse, plus a couple of outlets up in the lookout," Leonard said. "You'll have to hike out every few weeks to restock your food, and a helicopter will bring it all up along with your water again."

"Can't I just ride in the helicopter, then? How far is the hike to the lookout, anyway?" It'd been nearly five months since I did any serious physical activity—I didn't relish the idea of a spontaneous trek in.

Leonard shook his head. "No. They'll be fully loaded with supplies and are on a tight schedule to service several towers at a time. They can't take additional passengers. You'll be able to drive out to the trailhead using the park service access road, and from there it's about a four-hour hike up to the lookout."

I blew out a deep breath. In my prime, easy. Now... doable. Maybe. I'd have to set out early and keep an eye on how I handled the elevation.

The image of my old, empty house flashed through my mind. I pictured myself wandering aimlessly from room to room, a ghost of who I was, who I wanted to be.

I shuddered. No. I couldn't go back to that. "I mean, it's a change of plans for sure, but it'll be fine. It'll be good," I said, mostly to convince myself.

"Which tower is he assigned to now?" Dad asked, a sharp edge hidden somewhere in the question.

Leonard stared into his already half-empty pint glass. "We got it all fixed up last month. Cleaned out the inside real good, installed new windows and shutters. Cleared out the chimney, made sure the frame's structurally sound. Got the propane and power all hooked up. Hell, we even replaced the shitter. He'll be better off in that tower than anything closer to town."

"Which tower?" Dad repeated, emphasizing each word.

Leonard grimaced. "Seven."

There was a beat of silence.

"Wait," Bobby said. "Tower Seven? You mean Dead Man's Lookout? The *haunted* one? I thought no one had stayed there since, well, *you know*, way back in the eighties."

Leonard scoffed. "Careful, you almost called us old. And it's not haunted, we just haven't needed it until now."

He didn't sound convinced.

"No," Dad said.

"Mike—"

"*No.*"

"It will be fine."

"Did they see any ghosts?" Bobby cut in, snickering, clearly too focused on his mozzarella sticks to clock the serious turn the conversation had taken.

Dad glared at Leonard. "I don't give a fuck about made-up ghost stories. I'm worried because *it's not safe*," he said, not lowering his voice. A few people turned to look. "The last time someone stayed in that tower, they disappeared. That girl who just went missing was hiking Dead Man's Creek trail. I won't have Reece up there all alone without a vehicle."

"Don't pretend we don't know what really happened to that lookout, Mike," Leonard growled.

A hush fell over the restaurant. The tinkling cutlery and quiet murmurs ceased, pushed to the edges of the room by the giant elephant that'd just trundled in.

People in Ponderosa don't talk about Tower Seven's last lookout.

Dad's eyes flicked over to me, full of an emotion I couldn't quite place. I saw the denials he'd so confidently proclaimed on our drive fall away, shattered by the reality that *I'd* be the next person to walk into those woods without an easy escape, not some nameless stranger. "We don't know that for sure," he said, turning back to Leonard. "Especially now, with more missing—"

"*It's not the same thing*," Leonard hissed, real anger in his voice. "Don't you start with everyone else in this paranoid fucking town. It's an unfortunate coincidence, that's all. We need all the eyes we can get this season, or there might not be a town if the fires get out of hand. *I'm* the one who's responsible for that."

"You don't need—"

Leonard cut Dad off. "I tried to keep Tower Seven empty. I did. But we can't risk a fire getting out of hand before it's spotted, and that lookout's viewshed has the least amount of overlap with any of the others. Besides, Reece is an adult. He can decide for himself whether he stays there or not."

They both turned to me.

Tower Seven, colloquially known as Dead Man's Lookout, weaved through the fabric of Ponderosa as tightly as the six missing hikers that haunted the psyche of everyone who lived there, almost forty years later.

Tucked high up on the peak of Nowhere Ridge, it'd sat empty after its last lookout, Charles Randolph, disappeared one late summer night in 1986, never to be heard from again.

Shortly thereafter, the police declared the six missing hikers deceased, and the investigation was suspended indefinitely. There was never an official statement, but the rumors quickly spread anyway.

Some speculated he'd skipped town and changed his identity after the pressure of the investigation into the disappearances became too much. Some whispered he'd thrown himself from the tower onto the jagged rocks below, the guilt over what he'd done vanishing along with his body in the bellies of roaming wolves.

In the end, it hadn't mattered. A mysteriously missing man can't be prosecuted, even if he was guilty.

The very real horror of that summer morphed over the years into a ghost story. Whispered under lantern-lit sleeping bags and across crackling campfires, it resurfaced in the paper every few years when a group of foolhardy teenagers ventured into the woods and came out screaming about a knife-wielding ghost chasing them down.

Sometimes it was a hatchet.

The weapon of choice changed depending on who told the story, mostly because no one knew how the hikers had actually died.

A chill ran down my spine, not unlike the one I'd felt earlier at the thought of a predator nearby. I was meant to live in that tower for the next five months. Would I be chased from my bed by the ghost of a hatchet-wielding murderer?

Get yourself together.

Ghosts weren't real. No one haunted that lookout—it was just old, a little run down, and needed new life breathed into it.

I could fucking relate.

"It's not the same thing," I said, parroting Leonard's words. "I'll be fine. It'll be good for me."

Dad looked ready to argue.

"I'll be *fine*," I repeated. "There's power. I'll have the signal booster for my phone and the radio. If anything happens, I'll call you. I promise."

Leonard nodded. "Then it's settled."

Dad didn't acknowledge him. "Anything out of the ordinary, and you call me. I can get a bird out to you in half an hour," he said, gripping the edge of the table hard.

"Anything out of the ordinary, and I'll call," I agreed.

Hopefully, I wouldn't need to.

The late-May evening breeze was cool against my skin when Bobby and I stepped outside, full to bursting after all the food we'd eaten. I zipped up my jacket against the chill.

Cheery bistro lights lined the awnings stretched along Main Street. Colorful window art advertising sales and specials decorated each storefront, ready and eager for peak tourist season. Gas-lamp style street lights were dotted along the brick-paved road and sidewalk, brightly lit and welcoming against the inky night.

It all looked different, though, once I noticed the missing persons posters.

Alex Alonso, 39, male, 5'10", last seen at Sockeye Trailhead on May 3rd

Tony Donalds, 23, male, 5'8", last seen at Salmon-Challis National Park Visitors Center on May 14th

Haley Thomas, 27, female, 5'7", last seen at Dead Man's Creek Trailhead, May 22nd

If you have information regarding these missing persons, please call NOW. No tip is too small!

Now, the quaint, touristy mountain-town backdrop looked less inviting and more desperate. *"Nothing bad ever happens in Ponderosa—Gateway to Nowhere! We promise!"* it said with a clenched smile.

The spring evening wasn't cozy, but cold, like the difference between watching a blizzard through a window, warm and safe inside, and being lost in it.

Dad and Leonard left a few minutes before us and stood a few blocks down, talking. Hopefully, settling the tension between them over my lookout posting. Bobby and I meandered a few paces before we leaned against the corner of the building.

"It was great to see you. Tell me when you're heading into town for a supply run and we'll get together," he said.

"You, too." I pulled him into another hug. "Really, I'm glad to be around more, at least for a few months. Thanks for coming out tonight. Give my love to Jade and Molly."

Bobby stepped back and smiled, his eyes soft. "Will do. And how about you? Anyone catch your eye lately?"

I scoffed. "I think that's a long way off for me."

"Why do you say that?"

It was hard to explain to Bobby. Jade was his high school sweetheart—neither of them had ever really had to confront the horrors of adult dating.

"It's difficult," I went with. "I'd rather walk into traffic than download another dating app, and as shitty as Josh was in the end, I wasn't great to be around either. And that's before the, well," I waved my hands around vaguely, "complications."

"Complications?" he asked, voice pitched in anger. "Did that sack of dicks say you were *complicated* after your diagnosis?"

I laughed. God, I fucking loved my friend. I *had* been an emotionally unavailable ass to Josh, but Bobby was ready to kick down his door and pour all of his hair products down the drain when I'd told him how things had ended anyway.

"No," I said with a chuckle. "I'm still working through shit leftover from that relationship, but that's not where this comes from. I just don't know how I'd ever feel like anything but a burden with everything that comes along with me now. *I* can't even stand it most days, how can I expect someone else to?"

Talking to Bobby was so easy. Sometimes I shocked myself by the things I said and how true they really were.

His eyes were glassy. "You're my best fucking friend. You're hilarious when you're not being a grump, you work hard, and you take care of the people you love. When you're up in that tower all alone, you remember there are so many people who need you here. You're not a burden. And you never know when you'll meet someone who sees everything you are and loves you more for it."

Well, shit. How was he the same kid I'd watched eat a worm on a dare when we were eleven?

I looked at my boots, scuffing one against the ground. "Being a dad has turned you into a walking Hallmark card," I said, wiping at my eyes.

Hey, we couldn't both completely fall off the deep end.

He chuckled. "Your farts after eating all that cheese tonight are going to burn a hole in your dad's couch, and you snore like a freight train. Is that better?"

I laughed. "Better. But I don't snore."

He rolled his eyes. "Alright, I really gotta go. Oh," he lowered his voice to a whisper, leaning in. "I think he wants to talk to you. He's been standing there this whole time."

He jutted out his chin, gesturing behind me. "We'll talk soon," he finished, before heading for his car.

"Yeah, talk soon," I said before turning to see who he meant.

Tate Morris stood waiting about four parking spaces down. He leaned back against the door of his police cruiser, one of those rugged, full-size SUVs with *Canine Unit* stamped all over. He stared right at me with his arms crossed.

Huh. Where's the dog?

"Reece West," he said when I made my way over. "Been a few years."

Ponderosa High wasn't a big school, so it wasn't odd he remembered me. It was odd he'd wait up to talk to me, though. Especially in uniform.

"Guess being a pot head in high school doesn't preclude

you from becoming a cop," I replied, a second before I realized what an absolutely shitty idea that was.

It took every ounce of control I had not to slap my hand across my mouth. Guess I'd thrown any chance at a normal greeting out the window. Hopefully, he had a sense of humor.

His cheeks flamed, and he straightened, uncrossing his arms. "Like I said, it's been a while."

Right. Not even a chuckle. Time to shut the fuck up.

"Where's your dog?" I asked instead.

That's not shutting the fuck up, Reece. I cringed. Surely that was safe territory, though, right?

There, he smiled. Only a psychopath wouldn't smile while talking about their dog. "Dropped him off at home before coming out for dinner. He had a long day at work."

I nodded, finally shutting up so he could get to the point. Clearly, I couldn't be trusted with law enforcement small talk.

"I wasn't trying to eavesdrop, but I couldn't help but overhear you'll be around for the season. Stationed out at Dead Man's Lookout?" he said, surprising me.

Was he also trying to make small talk? Why?

"Yeah, sounds like they've opened all the towers in the park this year. Leonard needed someone who's done this before in one of the more remote locations."

"Hmm," he said, thoughtfully. "I hike up in that area quite a lot on my days off. Maybe I'll stop by, see how you're getting on."

"*Um*, ok?" Fire lookouts were a popular hiking attraction, and visitors would occasionally stop by to take in the views, especially at the more accessible locations. It was rare, though, at a tower as remote as mine.

"It's late, I should get home and let Rocky out," he continued before I figured out a polite way to ask why he was saying all of this. "I just..." he paused, casting a glance behind us as if to make sure we wouldn't be overheard. He lowered his voice. "If you see anything out of place out there, let me know."

He dug around in his pocket and pulled out a business card and a pen, scrawling something across the back. "That's my personal number. Anything weird, call me, yeah?"

I frowned, but took the card from him. Surely, he wasn't flirting over some missing, maybe-dead hikers? Also, the number of people who assumed I'd see something strange at the lookout was becoming uncomfortable. "Should I be worried? Is this about those missing hikers?"

He hesitated a moment before he shook his head. "We're still investigating those as individual cases. Unfortunately timed missing persons, that's all. Hopefully they'll turn up. But..." He looked around again. "Keep your head on a swivel. Be careful. And call *me*, not the station, yeah?" he pointed to the card clutched in my hand.

Danger flashed through my mind for the third time that night. What the hell was in the water in this town?

"Sure thing," I said, stepping away. "I'll do that."

I sure as fuck will not be doing that.

Why would a police officer ask me to report suspicious activity via his personal phone number?

Leonard was right. Everyone was paranoid, and I'd been

back in Ponderosa all of three hours before it'd seeped its way into my mind, too.

"See you around," I said, backing away farther. That predator-aware voice whispered in my ear not to turn my back, just yet.

"I'll see you soon," he responded with a wave. "And welcome home, Reece."

CHAPTER FOUR

"Got everything you need?" Dad asked, stepping off the front porch of his cabin in the pre-dawn dark. He tracked the solitary backpack I tossed into my truck's backseat. I'd opted to pack light for the hike in, carrying only the essentials.

Everything else, including my laptop, clothes, toiletries, towels, bedding, blankets, books, sketch pads, cookware, and more groceries than I'd ever purchased at one time, was at the ranger station, stacked neatly in plastic storage bins, waiting to be flown up to the lookout.

"I sure hope so, it's too late now if I don't," I replied, shutting the back door. "I can always grab what I need when I come back down for supplies."

"In three weeks." His tone was a reminder of just how long that was.

"In three weeks," I echoed, my own assurance that I *would* be back.

He nodded and reached out, pulling me into a hug. "You keep that bear spray on you all the time," he said gruffly, releasing me and scruffing a hand through my hair like he had when I was a boy. He shuffled, eyes casting around. "I understand how important it is to you to do this yourself. But there's nothing I wouldn't do to be there for you when you need me, Reece. Please remember that."

I sighed. What did I have to say to convince the people in my life that I would be fine? Was I burdened by the weight of being alive? Maybe. Did I look forward to finally being alone to sulk guilt-free and grieve the carefree future I'd hoped for? Sure.

But I was *fine*, all the same.

"Thanks, Dad. Really. I'll see you in no time," I said, giving him a smile that would've felt disingenuous anyway, given the hour.

I climbed into my truck, anxious to get going. It was early, before sunrise, but I had a two-hour drive ahead of me on minimally maintained Forest Service roads. Once I reached the trailhead, it was another four-hour hike up to the tower, and I needed to be there in time to meet the helicopter.

I waved at Dad before driving off. His silhouette faded quickly through the trees, backlit by the warm glow of his cabin until he was just a dark shape in my rearview mirror, unrecognizable in the gloom.

I *am out of fucking shape.*

Heaving for breath, I swung my backpack off my shoulders and pulled the bottom hem of my already-damp shirt up to wipe my brow. I'd become one with my couch entirely too much over the last five months and thoroughly regretted it now.

I grabbed my water bottle from the side pocket, took several big sips, and relished in the light breeze cooling my skin beneath the hot midday sun.

And I drank in the view before me.

Stunning.

Two hours into the hike to my lookout, a sharp curve northward led the trail through a break in the dense trees, spilling onto the shoreline of one of the most beautiful places I'd ever seen.

Lake Sapphire plunged deep along the heavily forested ridgeline, marking the true start of my ascent to the tower's peak. As the crow flies, I wasn't very far at all from my destination, currently obscured by the towering treetops, but it would take me another two full hours to cover the remaining distance.

Carved by shifting ice-age glaciers thousands of years ago, Lake Sapphire earned her name from stunning postcard-worthy blue water, reaching depths of over a thousand feet.

In fact, it was one of the deepest bodies of water in the whole country.

Longer than it was wide, it snaked down through the mountain pass, flowing past the neighboring tower and out of the national park. Only the farthest western edge, where I now stood, was visible from my lookout.

I wouldn't complain, though, because it was the *best* part of the whole lake. Why?

No one was in it.

To my great pleasure, motorized vehicles of any kind were prohibited within the national park, except for the scant government vehicle or necessary employee, like look-outs stationed at drive-in towers.

Otherwise, no cars, boats, or jet skis were allowed.

Or ATVs, I grumbled to myself, noting the very-illegally made tire tracks running through the dried mud along the lake shore.

Assholes. I'd report those.

There was a whole section of the massive lake outside the national park where people could boat and ski and drive around until they were blue in the face if they wanted. The point of the motor ban in the national park was to preserve the natural landscape and avoid disturbing the wildlife.

Fucking teenagers, probably.

Turning away from the cerulean waters, I swung my bag back onto my shoulders, ready to continue. I wouldn't let it bother me—not when I had five glorious months without someone's fucking leaf blower to listen to at all hours of the day.

Whoever invented them deserved a special circle of Hell all to themselves. Why were they so loud? How much debris did my neighbors need to blow around all the time? Didn't they know the wind would undo their hours of work in just a few minutes, anyway?

Sometimes I felt like I was in a comedy sketch where they took shifts constantly running a leaf blower, just to see what I'd do.

Would it be considered destruction of property if I *accidentally* ran them all over?

I think a jury would understand. Even if they didn't, it would probably be worth it.

"What's he in for?"

"That's the leaf blower basher."

I'd be a king in prison with that title.

I snorted out loud at how ridiculous my thoughts sounded.

Shifting focus from the distracting noises I wouldn't hear, I took another sip of water, tilted my head back, and relished the sounds I would.

Woodpecker. Song Sparrow. Some sort of small animal shuffling through the fallen pine needles—a squirrel, maybe? Or a chipmunk? It could be a marten. I hadn't seen one in ages.

The forest was both pleasantly quiet and buzzing with sound, in the way only remote wilderness could be. The cry of a Red-tailed Hawk, unmistakable and often incorrectly attributed to Bald Eagles, sent a Stellar's Jay squawking. The Black-capped Chickadees joined in with their alarm *chick-a-dee-dee-dees*.

And accompanying all of it, like the percussion section uniting an orchestra as one, the trees.

Tall and thick with minimal understory growth, this section of land was filled with groves of old-growth pine, conifer, juniper, and fir. The wind rustled their needles, a quiet *shhhhh* that made my shoulders drop from their permanently clenched position around my ears. Their broad trunks creaked and groaned as they swayed.

Yeah, I'd accepted the lookout job for *this*.

I needed sound that wasn't noise. I could already feel my blood pressure lower the longer I listened.

As rested as I'd ever be, I slipped my water bottle back into its pocket and started off on the final leg of my hike. Already looking forward to a great night's rest, I couldn't wait to crash into bed once all of my things were tucked safely in the tower or the utility shed.

I could even take it easy over the next few days, unpack slow, and relax. I had nowhere to be, no one to see, and nothing to do but watch over the forest, high above the trees.

Hopefully, it'd be a slow start to the season.

I hadn't realized how dark the trail up to the lookout was, tucked under the forest canopy, until the tree line abruptly ended.

Striding into the open, I squinted against the bright afternoon glare of the sun and brought a hand up to shield my eyes. Shouldering off my bag to catch my breath, I blinked, eyes adjusting to the overabundance of light until I could properly take in the view.

Breathtaking. Absolutely breathtaking.

If I thought the view of Lake Sapphire was something special, this... this was otherworldly.

An ocean of green treetops as far as the eye could see swayed in the breeze, only disrupted by sheer rock faces and cliffs jutting out haphazardly.

Birds of prey circled above, and a scattering of pillowy cumulus clouds hovered over the next ridge, pale against the bright blue sky. Off in the distance, I could see more moving in—massive looming thunderheads threatening the picture-perfect vista below.

Indeed, the western edge of Lake Sapphire hooked around the far eastern slope, disappearing into the next tower's viewshed. The blue appeared even deeper from this height, almost as if it were painted into the landscape. With binoculars, I might even be able to see a small stretch of the Forest Service road I'd driven in on in the far distance.

Somehow, everything was smaller and so much bigger.

Views from a peak like this had always made me emotional, even as a boy. I couldn't describe why, other than to say it was *too much*. As if I couldn't fully comprehend the vastness of everything before me, my mind scrambled to take it all in at once, grew overwhelmed by the intensity, and all I could do to process was cry.

Most of the time, it was embarrassing. Now, though, I let my tears fall.

Although the tectonic plates of my own life had shifted, altering the topography of my future into something unknown, not yet recognizable, maybe even a little broken, at least this remained.

I turned, taking in the hulking structure of the lookout itself.

Reaching even higher into the clouds, Tower Seven,

Dead Man's Lookout, perched on reinforced wooden stilts forty feet above the rocky ground. A staircase zig-zagged up the center, ending in a wrap-around porch at the top. One door led into the square, fourteen-by-fourteen-foot cabin, located on the opposite corner from the stairs—probably so that lookouts wouldn't step out onto the deck and immediately tumble down the narrow staircase.

Not the way to go.

I'd thought entirely too much about death lately.

I circled the tower, headed for the stairs while scanning for anything out of place. Like Leonard had said, the support beams looked sturdy, and the copper grounding wires—built in lightning rods—appeared secure. The stairs were solid under my heavy boots.

Back and forth, I climbed the switchbacks. I paused on the fifth landing, heaving for air and thighs burning, before ascending the final flights.

If my ass doesn't look fantastic after five months of climbing all these stairs, I'll pitch a fit.

Finally, I reached the top and paced along the wrap-around deck, noting the safety railing barely came up to my hip. I'd have to be careful during inclement weather or high winds—the worn planks under my feet would be slippery, and I wouldn't trust that railing enough to even lean on it, let alone tumble into it.

Windows wrapped three hundred and sixty degrees around the cabin, currently shuttered and secured against the elements.

Well, all except for one.

Huh, odd.

I stopped and inspected the exposed glass. It was a westward-facing window, overlooking what I imagined were stunning sunsets over the far ridgeline.

I pulled on the secured shutters on either side, noting they didn't lift easily. Glancing up, I saw where the open wooden plank had been lifted and hooked onto the overhanging roof via a metal latch. I reached up and flicked it off the hook, startled by how quickly the whole thing swung down and slammed over the window, landing with a loud *thud*.

Ok. So they're really heavy. Good to know.

I'd chalk one or two loose shutters up to the wind, but I doubted one could blow and lift in such a way that it latched itself open.

Someone, or *something*, appeared to have done it intentionally.

My pulse quickened. The hairs on the back of my neck stood on end, and again, I had the overwhelming sensation that I wasn't alone.

All of the strange stories I'd heard of Dead Man's Lookout over the years flashed through my mind.

Hikers who'd claimed someone stood at the cracked and disrepaired windows, watching them as they passed. Teens who'd broken into the cabin, dared by their friends to spend the night, told stories of objects flying around the room, followed by loud banging coming from the walls until they left, screaming.

People who'd said they were chased through the surrounding woods by a knife-wielding maniac.

I'd scoffed at all of it growing up. Of course, ghosts

weren't real. It was a combination of a horrific history and an overactive imagination—that was all.

Also, there was probably a lot of alcohol involved on the part of the rowdy teenagers.

But I wasn't scoffing now.

Casting a look around, I realized I'd left my bag—and my bear spray—forty feet below, on the ground near the trees.

Fuck.

Fuck, fuck, fuck!

I couldn't make mistakes like that. Every gut instinct I possessed told me I was being watched, and all I had was the small pocket knife hooked to my belt.

They probably just forgot to close the shutter after it was renovated a few months ago, I thought, trying to calm myself.

Yes, that was it.

Leonard said they'd made repairs to the tower to prep it for the season. I was sure one of the workers simply forgot to close the final shutter.

I shook off the creeping sensation. I'd be a complete mess all summer if I allowed every paranoid thought to rule me. I needed to get hold of it now, before it became a problem.

After a deep breath, I swung the shutter open again, reached up, and latched it. I gave it a good shake to ensure it was secure and took a step back.

Satisfied there would be no more nonsense surrounding the mysteriously animate shutter or the stubbornly persistent feeling that I wasn't alone, I peered through the open window into the tower I'd call home.

Only to find a man staring right at me.

CHAPTER FIVE

"**D**on't close my window!" he shouted through the glass.

I screamed. Lurching backwards, I landed heavily against the safety railing.

Too heavily.

It shuddered and groaned beneath my weight. My arms spun almost comically, desperately trying to shift back over my feet.

Except I couldn't.

It happened slowly. *I'm falling,* I thought. *This will kill me.*

There was no way I'd survive a forty-foot tumble onto the jagged rocks below—my head would crack open like an egg.

Fuck. I don't want to die.

The realization shot through my body like a bolt of electricity. I'd spent the last few months on autopilot, resentful that my life had become complicated with doctor appointments and infusions and medications and exercises and worrisome parents, and, and, and...

Hanging over the edge of that goddamn tower, I realized I'd take all of it.

Every single complication.

Please. I don't want to die.

Hands, firm and cool, circled my biceps just as my weight fully tipped over the railing and yanked me forward, hard. I cried out in pain when my shoulder hit the deck and rolled onto my stomach, angling my body away from the death-drop I'd nearly plunged from.

Even that short fall stole my breath. Coughing, I propped my body up on one forearm and looked around, wide-eyed.

"What the fuck?" I panted, desperate for some sort of explanation.

"Are you okay?" a voice asked from behind me.

I quickly rolled onto my back and scrambled away from the man standing at my feet.

He wasn't solid. He wasn't a whole person, like I'd thought he was when he first startled me through the window. Patches of him were missing and see-through, while others appeared corporeal, but fading fast.

His face remained, though.

Thick brows knitted together in concern, and his nose, upturned just-so, had the lightest dusting of freckles. A curl of dark hair fell across his forehead, and his warm brown eyes pleaded with me.

For what, I had no idea.

He looked... *handsome.*

Maybe I really had fallen, my brain splattered all over the ground below, and this was some sort of death-induced hallucination.

"Who are you?" I asked, voice trembling.

My whole body shook, actually, as the fear from my near-death experience—*or my actual death experience, I'm still not certain about that*—flooded my veins with adrenaline.

"Are—y—k?" he asked again, ignoring my question. His words were broken up this time, like a radio just out of signal range, not nearly as clear as they'd been a second ago.

In fact, his whole body flickered in and out of my vision now.

Oh, no.

I blinked rapidly, frantically looking around.

No, no, nononono!

Nothing else flickered, though, or split in two. There was only one cabin. Only one railing. Only one hand I held in front of my face.

Only one barely visible man.

"I—*sorry,*" he gasped, like he'd used his final breath to do so, before he disappeared entirely.

And I was left alone, alive, and so, so confused.

What the actual fuck just happened?

I was dazed for the rest of the afternoon.

The helicopter arrived on schedule, landing on the gravel pad halfway between the tower and the tree line.

The two pilots probably thought I was an asshole, or experiencing some sort of mental break over how far I really was from civilization, because I barely said a word to them.

I stared at the first pilot as she hopped out and greeted me, waiting for her to... I don't know, act like I wasn't really there? Run over to where a body I couldn't see sprawled on the rocks beneath the tower? Scream and run? Whisper, *"I see dead people,"* maybe?

I'd really prefer to know as soon as possible if I'm actually dead, rather than haunt my loved ones like some chump.

Thankfully, she didn't do any of that, but she did shoot weird looks my way for the rest of their visit, when instead of greeting her with something normal like *"Hello,"* or *"Thank you for helping me,"* I said, "Oh, thank God, you can see me."

In hindsight, that would probably just fuel the rumors that weird shit happened at Dead Man's Lookout.

Weird shit does happen here, though, clearly.

I'd only been there for an hour at most, and I'd already seen a... Well, I wasn't sure what to call it. Call him?

A man who could mysteriously disappear, I went with.

Admitting I saw a ghost was a step too far right now, especially given that I'd nearly become a *disappearing man* myself.

Fantastic.

A slightly crazed chuckle bubbled out at my own thoughts. The pilot side-eyed me again.

Even though I was a little unhinged, they helped me carry the heaviest of my boxes up to the tower. Together, we checked that the propane in the utility shed functioned properly and the fridge, freezer, and outlets up in the lookout had electricity.

Lastly, we unloaded a good amount of firewood, which they'd hauled in using a mesh sling attached to the helicopter via a rope, for the wood stove—the only heat source in the cabin.

I thanked them and waved goodbye as they flew off.

Maybe I shouldn't have let them go without me after what I'd just experienced, but honestly, the thought of explaining what'd happened was just as terrifying as the event itself.

As I climbed the stairs back up to the lookout, practically hugging the cabin to stay as far away from the railing as possible, I remembered Dad's words from the other night.

Anything out of the ordinary, and you call me.

Was being nearly scared to death by a ghost, followed by being rescued by that ghost, considered out of the ordinary?

*A*re ghosts real? I asked, typing the question into the web search bar on my laptop later that evening.

The load time was only a few seconds longer than it would've been at home, so the signal booster and cell phone hotspot I set up that afternoon must've worked.

I'd already tried to talk myself out of believing I saw a ghost. But as much as I wished I'd merely been dehydrated or exhausted from the hike, I couldn't reason away the disconcerting wobble of the railing, the ache in my shoulder, or the free-fall sensation that still spooked me to think about.

I would've died, had *someone* not pulled me back over.

And if a person had saved me, they wouldn't have disappeared right in front of me.

So. Ghosts.

"Expert consensus suggests ghosts may be real, depending on your location and time of day..." read the AI summary above the search results.

"Fucking hell," I mumbled. What a wonderful example of cutting-edge technology, completely worth the inevitable collapse of society.

I scrolled, hoping to find an article titled something like, *"Do you consider yourself a fairly level-headed, if not boring person, except that you're pretty sure you just saw a ghost? Click here for validation it was real before you check yourself into the nearest mental health facility."*

Because how else was I supposed to process what'd happened that afternoon? Talk about it with someone?

Absolutely not.

Instead, I found articles like *"How Science Could Enlighten the Paranormal,"* *"Is it a Poltergeist or Are You Just Afraid of How Much an Electrician Will Cost?"* and, my personal favorite, *"How to Check if You Have Ghosts."*

As if they were a typical household pest.

I bookmarked that one for later.

How to know if I saw a real ghost? I tried next. The results were similarly ridiculous and uninformative.

Sighing, I shut my laptop. My wooden chair creaked when I leaned back to stretch. It was old, but sturdy, and matched the small desk pushed up against the north side of the lookout. I'd already stacked a few books along the wall, and my sketch pad lay open next to my computer.

A small nightstand sat to my right, where I kept a rechargeable lantern, followed by the full bed tucked into the corner. An ancient-looking wood-burning stove crackled in the corner to my left, and the tiny, four-burner gas range and oven hugged the opposite wall close to the door, along with several wooden shelves and storage counters.

I'd shaken out the mattress, which had thankfully been replaced, dusted, knocked down a few cobwebs, and swept before unpacking that afternoon. Overall, the lookout was in far better shape than I'd anticipated for being out of commission for so long.

Ready for bed, I stood. My heart skipped a beat when my reflection, lit up by the soft glow of the lantern and wood stove against the pitch black night, stood with me.

To my relief, it was *only* my reflection this time.

I'd uncovered all the shutters before I locked myself inside for the evening and wiped down the glass. Now, though, I wished I'd waited until morning as I fought the urge to cover the window with a blanket so I wouldn't feel so exposed.

Except I couldn't hang just one blanket, because the uncovered windows wrapped all the way around the damn tower.

Like a glowing fish bowl, my new home lit up like a beacon against nighttime dark so deep I wouldn't be able to see my own hand in front of my face if I took two steps out the door.

Anyone—or any*thing*—could be out there right now, and I'd have no idea. That ghost could be out there. Or a wolf, mountain lion, or even a bear.

Or whoever's been murdering hikers and hiding their bodies so deep in the woods no one's ever found them.

I shuddered.

In the safety of Ponderosa, a small mountain town filled with normal, unassuming people, it was easy for Dad, Leonard, and Tate Morris to spread their assurances that there was nothing to worry about. But out in the wilderness, alone in the dark, I didn't believe those hikers were lost or missing—not when ghosts came calling and the killer could be right outside my door.

Watching.

Right. That's enough thinking for tonight.

I strode over to the door, circling the heavy wooden table at the center of the room where the Osborne Firefinder sat, ensured the lock was engaged, and tucked myself into bed.

The temperature had dropped significantly after sunset. This high up, I'd probably need the wood burner to keep the cabin comfortable overnight for at least another week. So, I snuggled beneath the heavy down duvet plus a flannel-lined quilt and shut my eyes, ready for some much-needed sleep.

Except it stubbornly wouldn't come.

The wind picked up, and lying down, I could feel the way it blustered against the wooden panels, rocking the tower ever so slightly. A chill crept in, and I stuffed a pillow between me and the outer wall for added insulation.

Scritch scratch scritch scratch scritch

What was that?

I sat straight up, holding the covers to my chest while I tried not to breathe too loudly in the dark, ears strained.

Scritch scratch

Scritch scratch scritch

The sound came from outside.

I stood and snatched my bear spray and a flashlight off the counter, holding them at the ready. My boots waited by the door, but I didn't waste time lacing them up, slipping into my fleece-lined Crocs instead.

I was self-aware enough to know they were a heavy-weight contender in the *World's Ugliest Shoe* competition, but the thought of Josh's disgusted face if he saw me wear them earned an instant purchase.

Plus, they were practical. My kind of shoe.

SCRITCH SCRATCH SCRITCH SCRATCH SCRITCH SCRATCH

Fuck! It was closer now, and sounded big. Was it climbing the stairs?

A gust of wind, stronger than the others, rattled the north-facing windows. I couldn't see movement outside, but that didn't mean much when it was this dark.

Or when your intruder was see-through.

SCRITCH SCRATCH SCRITCH SCRATCH SCRITCH SCRATCH

Flipping the lock, I slowly opened the door and braced

for something to attack. My exhales trembled out, and the flashlight wobbled in my grip.

What if the ghost came back?

Or, what if it *wasn't* a ghost this time? What if it was something worse? A murderer? Or a bear?

I had no hope of outrunning a bear on a good day, let alone in Crocs. Or a hatchet-wielding serial killer, for that matter.

Please, God, I cannot die in Crocs.

I quickly flipped the straps into sport mode so they were secure on my feet before tip-toeing outside, bear spray first.

My vision narrowed to the flimsy beam of the flashlight —*I should order one of those crazy bright torches to pick up on my next trip into town*—but after a quick sweep around the deck, I could at least breathe easier that the immediate vicinity was clear.

SCRITCH   SCRATCH   SCRITCH   SCRATCH SCRITCH SCRATCH

I whipped around, shining the light through the cabin windows and out the other side.

Eyes gleamed at me in the dark.

"Oh, fuck," I whimpered, true fear setting in. *What the hell is that?*

Like an idiot, I froze in place, unable to tear my gaze away from the bright, blinking eyes. I couldn't see its body or how big it was, as the glare of the windows obscured it. I made another pathetic sound, and its head tilted this way and that, deciding which parts of me would be the tastiest.

Then it made some sort of...*chattering* noise, as if to scold *me* for disturbing *it,* instead of the other way around.

You're the intruder here, it seemed to say.

My turn to blink, and then squint, straining to see its shape. I took a step to the left, and it skittered across the railing to the opposite corner, like it was coming around to chatter at me some more. Or rip my throat out.

Hard to be sure.

I scooted backwards. Was it going to eat me? I held out the bearspray, ready to aim and pull the nozzle...

"Tower Seven, this is Tower Eight. Come in."

I screeched.

This time, I couldn't pass it off as anything remotely rugged. The bear spray fell out of my hand when I jumped, startled, and rolled.

Right off the edge of the deck.

"Fuck!" I yelled and scrambled after it, only pulling back right before I crashed through the dangerously loose railing.

SCRITCH SCRATCH SCRITCH SCRATCH SCRITCH SCRATCH

The terrifying creature pitter-pattered away and shimmied back down one of the tower's wooden stilts, frightened off by my scream.

Or maybe I'd asserted dominance.

Yes. I'd go with that.

The flash of its tail just before it disappeared stole any of my remaining dignity, however, as I was finally able to identify the life-threatening predator that'd nearly eaten me on my first night in the middle of *Nowhere*.

"Goddamn raccoon," I grumbled.

Fuck. Now I had to schlep all the way down the stairs to retrieve my only method of defense. Although I wasn't sure what good it would do, when the tower seemed more intent on chucking me over the railing than anything else.

"Tower Seven, this is Tower Eight. Do you read?"

I jumped again, reminded of the voice that'd startled me in the first place. Now that I wasn't about to leap out of my skin, I noted the feminine voice was kind, and maybe a little worried.

The two-way radio crackled again as I hurried back inside. "Tower Seven? Are you there? You didn't check in on the main radio channel, and we're getting worried. Do you read?"

I sat at the desk, reached for the small handheld device, and held down the *talk* button. "Hi, I'm here. *Uh.* Copy. So sorry, no one was on the main channel earlier, so I thought we weren't checking in until tomorrow morning. I must've switched to a different channel by accident. Over."

I cringed. I didn't want to start off being the problem child of the group, and I was rusty on my radio chatter etiquette.

She responded a few seconds later. "Copy. No problem. There are still a few who haven't checked in yet. You're not the last. I mostly just wanted to make sure everyone was situated, so I surfed a few channels to find you. Call me an old worrywart, but you just can't be too careful. We all need to look out for each other. Over."

I softened. She sounded mature. Matronly, even. Some in the park had been lookouts longer than I'd been alive. "Copy. Thanks for checking in. Yes, we all need to be careful, especially with... You know. I'm Reece, in Tower Seven.

Uh, I guess you know that. You said you're Tower Eight? Over."

"I'm Janine," she answered. "Yeah, Tower Eight. Hello, neighbor. Aren't you a hike in location? I've always wondered what that tower's trail is like. You get settled in okay?"

So *she* had the full lake view. I mirrored her relaxed posture on the radio-speak. "Congrats on the assignment," I said, a tinge of jealousy in my voice. "What a view. Yeah, I hiked in and am all settled, but the trip nearly killed me, *heh*."

I cringed again. That joke wasn't funny anymore. For a lot of reasons.

She chuckled anyway. Good. I didn't want a stuck-up coworker. Neighboring lookouts often communicated and worked together to lock in the position of a fire for a speedy response. It would be best if we got along, or it could be a long five months.

"Don't have to tell me," she said. "I had a hike-in for nearly two decades. I'm an old biddy now, though, so I've spent the last few years at a drive-up location. Practically feels like retirement! *With* a view!"

"Sounds well deserved," I said with a smile.

"Oh, we'll get along just fine. So you're all good, yeah? No ghosts?"

I burst out laughing. Fucking hell, if only she knew.

I wasn't going to be *that* guy, though. Who knows what she'd think if I spouted off a bunch of nonsense about a ghost frightening me over the railing and then saving me before I tumbled to my death.

"All good," I went with once I'd collected myself. "Everything's great."

There was a long pause. Had she heard the slight hysteria in my voice? "Alright. Well, I'm going to move on to another channel to check for the others before bed. You keep an eye out, and if you need anything, let me know. We can always switch over to this channel so we don't clog up the feed. It was nice to meet you, Reece. Over."

"Wait!" I said. "*Um.* You wouldn't happen to know how to keep raccoons away, would you?"

She laughed. "Depends on if it's decided you're the toilet, or the den."

I dragged a palm down my face, shuddering at the thought of waking up to find raccoon scat all over the deck. "Great."

Janine talked me through a few things to try before we signed off for the night. Tying plastic bags to the railing seemed like the most promising start. Hopefully, they'd scare it off for good.

Would that work on ghosts, too?

Braving a chance encounter with the killer raccoon, I trekked downstairs one more time to retrieve my bear spray and use the outhouse. Back in bed, I realized speaking with Janine had made the lookout feel a smidge less scary than before.

Maybe I didn't want total isolation, after all.

Scritch scratch scritch scratch scritch

Except for that goddamn raccoon. "GO AWAY!" I shouted.

It skittered off again, scolding me as it went.

I dozed, thoughts of predators, ghosts, and serial killers circling round and round. Right before I drifted off, I was struck by something so obvious I should've considered it hours ago. I'd spent the day dwelling on whether or not I'd seen the Ghost of Dead Man's Lookout, but had completely overlooked a question that was even more important.

Who was the Ghost of Dead Man's Lookout? Could it be the maybe, *probably* serial killer, Charles Randolph?

CHAPTER SIX

He came back two days later.

Despite my wild start, I quickly settled into a work routine. Roll call over the radio started at nine in the morning, and with thirteen towers in commission this season, scattered throughout the park, it took a few minutes for everyone to check in and share their morning precipitation reports.

Thankfully, all were accounted for.

Janine was the most senior lookout and naturally fell into a leadership role. Technically, we all reported to Leonard, but several of us had already asked her to switch to a separate channel to talk through various aspects of the job.

Most of my time consisted of completing full, three-hundred-and-sixty-degree sweeps of my viewshed at least once an hour. We checked for signs of smoke, or in the case of inclement weather, lightning strikes. However, we also collected weather data at each lookout, which could be just as important for predicting fire and red flag warnings. When a hazard response team was deployed, we guided them to the correct location and kept an eye on other potential dangers.

I recognized a couple of the lookout's voices as Forest Service employees who'd lived in Ponderosa for a long time, but most were strangers to me. Everyone seemed nice, though, and radio chatter was polite and succinct.

Technically, our shift ended at six in the evening, but considering we lived in the towers, off-the-clock smoke reports weren't uncommon. Eventually, I'd like to use the hour I had free over lunch to hike the nearby trail, but truthfully, with all the stairs between me and the bathroom—*and the refrigerator*—I was already far more active during the day than usual.

I'd never been congratulated more by my FitBit.

So, by my third evening at the tower, I was completely exhausted and tucked into bed by nightfall, far too tired to worry about things like ghosts or bears or annoyingly persistent raccoons.

Or whatever else might be lurking outside my door.

Listening to the now-familiar creaks and groans of the tower shifting in the wind and the rhythmic sound of my breathing, I pulled the duvet up and quickly slipped into that soft, barely lucid place just before sleep.

Thunk.

With a sharp inhale, I bolted upright, yanked awake.

Had something fallen off the counter? Had the raccoon found a way inside? It wasn't shitting on my deck, nor was it sleeping there. I'd deduced it merely wanted food and would go away once it realized I wasn't going to feed it.

Not again, I inwardly groaned. Every time I investigated an unknown noise, it turned out to be something harmless.

That'd sounded close, though, like it came from inside the lookout. I waited a few minutes, breathing steadily, but just as I was about to lie back down, I heard something else— much, much closer.

Riiiip.

I scrambled for the bear spray I now kept on the windowsill above my head while I slept and shuffled back into the corner. My eyes darted around the room, looking for movement in the shadows cast by the still-glowing wood-burning stove.

But there was nothing.

No striped tails or mischief-filled little masked faces. One of the positives of living in a small space was there was nowhere for an intruder to hide.

Unless they were a ghost, of course.

Air shifted in the space next to my bed, and a scrap of paper fluttered in front of me, landing in my lap as if dropped out of thin air. It looked like a corner had been torn from the sketch pad lying open on my desk.

Was that the sound I'd heard?

My heart pounded as I reached for it, fingers trembling. I squinted in the low light before flicking on the lantern next to my bed, blinking down in disbelief that there were words —real, tangible words in handwriting that wasn't my own— scrawled on the note.

Definitely not the raccoon, then.

Hi. I don't want to startle you again. Can I sit by the fire? I won't bother you.

My voice caught when I tried to respond. I gulped down water from the bottle I also kept on the windowsill next to me, and cleared my throat. *What the fuck do I say to a ghost?*

"Are you in here?" I asked, throwing my 'normal person' card out the window. My heartbeat pounded in my ears.

"Yes, but I'll leave if it bothers you." The soft reply came from across the room, still empty.

I swore. "Who are you? Why are you here?" I asked, unable to stop the tremble in my voice.

The wood floor creaked under invisible feet, slowly treading closer before they stopped halfway to where I sat in bed.

Suddenly, he appeared.

I sucked in a breath. He was more whole than before. I could see all of him, enough to note that while some parts of his body were see-through, others appeared solid. He wasn't as tall or imposing as I'd remembered. In fact, if I stood up, I was certain I'd be taller. Broader.

He was just as handsome as I remembered, though. Not in a well-groomed, perfectly symmetrical kind of way, but more like, I could look at him for a very long time, maybe even sketch him, and never quite capture him fully.

"Can I sit here?" he asked, gesturing to the wooden desk chair.

I nodded dumbly.

He scooted it across the floor so it was in front of the fire and sat with a heavy sigh. "Thank you."

There was so *much* in those words I wasn't sure I'd ever parse it all, but they had me releasing the deep breath I held. I pushed the comforter off my lap—thankfully, I'd worn sleep shorts to bed—and turned to lean back against the windowsill, facing him.

He wore a vintage, brown leather flight jacket with a Sherpa collar over a white shirt and faded blue jeans. His hiking boots looked worn, the laces undone and frayed.

"What's your name?" I asked again. It was less of an accusation this time.

He didn't look up. The orange glow behind the stove glass made his eyes look like honeyed whiskey. "Charlie."

Charlie, I mouthed. Yes, he looked like a Charlie.

My scalp prickled. "Is that short for Charles? Charles Randolph?" I asked, holding my breath again.

For a reason I couldn't give if my life depended on it, I didn't want Charlie to be Charles Randolph. Maybe it was purely self-preservation—I had invited him to sit, after all.

He looked up. "Yeah," he said, eyes curious and warmer than I'd expect from someone who'd probably murdered a bunch of people. "How'd you know?"

"*Um...*" How the fuck was I supposed to explain that? He'd been terrorizing visitors for nearly forty years, though. He'd *shouted* at me when I first arrived. Certainly, he was aware that he was a local urban legend.

"Well, I mean, you were the last lookout up here before me, right? You're sort of known for that?"

"Was I? How long has it been since I... Since?"

"That was 1986. It's 2025. Thirty-nine years."

Emotion flashed across his face. Shock, pain, and something else. He sucked in a breath and faced the fire again. "Oh."

It was quiet for a long time, the air heavy and aching. I

wondered if I shouldn't be there to witness this private moment of grief for lost time, if I should step out onto the deck to give him space.

He hadn't asked me to leave, though. He hadn't disappeared.

Maybe he just needed someone to sit with him. I had, when the neurologist strode into my hospital room and changed my life. Dad sat with me without saying a word after she'd left, and it'd helped more than I'd ever be able to tell him.

So I sat with Charlie, and no matter what came next, or what else I found out about him, at least I'd given him this moment of humanity.

"I don't remember most of it," he whispered after a while. "The passing time. It doesn't feel like it's been that long. It was just...cold. Very cold." He scooted the chair closer to the fire and held out his hands as if to warm them. "I tried to talk to a few others who came, but they couldn't see me or hear me. And then more came all at once, and they were too loud, so I threw things around until they left. I'm sorry for yelling at you. I didn't think you'd know I was there. I wasn't trying to frighten you. I just didn't want you to close my window. I didn't want it to be dark in here again."

I tried to imagine that—desperately wanting to communicate with someone, anyone, only to go unheard and unseen. What would it feel like to be trapped in the dark for decades?

"I'm sorry," I said, with feeling. No one deserved that.

"Do you talk to dead people a lot? Are you like a, what do they call those, a psychic? Or a medium?" he asked.

I snorted. "Definitely not. I was firmly in the camp that ghosts were for the beaded curtain people. Having a bit of an identity crisis over it, actually. You scared me to death when I first saw you."

He raised an eyebrow, and I realized how badly I'd just put my foot in my mouth.

"Shit. Not to *death*, obviously. I mean, I considered that I had died and made you up, but then the pilots spoke to me like normal, so I figured I wasn't actually splattered all over the ground outside."

His eyebrows were practically in his hairline by now, and a small smile appeared on his face.

"*Fuck.* I didn't mean to make that sound insensitive. I don't know how you, ya know, *went out*, but I'm sure it was with more dignity than that. And if it wasn't, that's fine, too. It's all fine. Or, not *fine*, but—"

"I didn't jump off the deck," he said with a laugh.

He was *laughing*.

I sighed. "Oh, thank fuck. You'd be the fourth person I said something off-putting to in a week, and I don't have another recovery in me."

He chuckled before his face turned serious again. "Do you know... Did my parents get to bury me? That was important to Mom. She'd drag us all out to clean up the family graves every year and put out new flowers."

He wiped at his face. Did ghosts cry? Or was it a reflex to brush away tears that would never fall again?

"No one knows what happened to you," I answered quietly. Peripherally, I was aware of the bear spray sitting on the bed next to me. Would it be effective against a ghost if he grew angry and attacked me? Or would it pass right through him?

Focus.

"You disappeared. They never found you," I finished.

Fresh shock and then horror marred his face. Irrationally, I preferred it when he smiled. "Never? What do you mean, *never*? I was... Wait..." he cast around as if to solve a puzzle I couldn't see.

"But I was here. Right here," he said, waving his arms around the cabin. "How could they have missed me? I met with someone earlier that day, that police officer who hiked out to talk to me, then I went to bed, and..."

He shook his head and stood, pacing the length of the lookout and wringing his hands together. "I was *right there!*" he shouted, pointing at the bed I now slept in.

Fucking hell. I scrambled up and leaned back against the desk to avoid running into him.

Whether it was intentional ignorance or my subconscious protecting me, I wasn't sure, but I had honestly never considered I now slept in a dead man's bed.

"Police officer?" I croaked, desperately trying to think of literally anything else. "You met with a police officer that day?"

He stopped right in front of me and peered up just so, to meet my eye. "Yes. He came to ask if I'd seen..." Impossibly, his face grayed even more. "Is that what happened to me?" he whispered. "Did I end up like those missing hikers? We were meant to be looking for them, for campfire smoke, or abandoned tents. The officer asked if I'd seen anything. Did I go missing like they did? Did someone *murder* me?"

"Oh my God," I said under my breath.

"Well?" he demanded. "Is that what happened? Was my face plastered on a bunch of missing persons posters? Is that why you knew my name? Did my family wonder if—if I'd ever come *home*?" he finished, voice cracking.

I gingerly sat back down on the bed and cupped my head in my hands. "No," I said lowly, desperately wishing, as awful as it was, that I could say yes. "That's not what happened to you. Or not what people think happened to you, anyway."

His brow creased in confusion. "I don't understand."

I peered up at him. "Please sit down," I said, the way they do in movies before telling someone their loved one was dead. Suddenly, I understood it was more for the comfort of the giver of bad news than the receiver.

He sat back in the chair by the fire. "What happened to me?"

I blew out a long breath. He deserved to know. With each word, it became increasingly clear just how wrong and fucked up and awful the situation was, but he deserved to know.

Plus, I needed to gauge his reaction to what I was about to say to be sure whether my horrible realization was true.

"I don't know any of this for sure," I started, "but I'll tell you what I've heard. You didn't check in at roll call one morning." I stopped, realizing I didn't know the exact date he went missing. How insulting was it that I couldn't even tell him that much?

"Someone came out to check on you," I continued.

"They never found you, or your, *uh*, body. The police were called in, and..."

"And?" he prompted.

"They never released an official statement or anything. I only know what's been speculated about. But after they came out here, they pronounced all of the missing hikers dead. They suspended the investigation into their murders indefinitely. No one was ever charged," I said, hoping he'd understand what I meant without having to say it outright.

He shook his head. "If they didn't find me, how could they say I was dead or murdered? What did that have to do with the rest of them?"

Right. I'd have to spell it out.

"Everyone thinks *you* murdered them, Charlie. The police must've found something that made them think so, to call off the investigation."

He blinked, stunned into silence.

One heartbeat.

Two.

"Some people thought you ran away," I continued, needing to fill the silence. I couldn't stand the slow horror creeping over his features. "Others thought you committed suicide out of shame. They closed down the lookout, and except for trespassers, no one's been out here since. Until... Well, now. Until me."

More silence.

"They think *I* killed those people?" he asked in disbelief.

I nodded.

He stood, and the outline of his body flickered and surged again, like too much and too little electricity ran through him all at once. "But, why? I didn't hurt anybo—!" he said, voice rising. "I would never hu—how—me?"

I stood too, attempting to calm him. "Hey, I can't hear you when you get worked up. It's okay, we can—"

"IT'S N—OKAY!" he yelled, real tears falling. Several items scattered across my desk rattled, as if lifted and dropped in unison. "I—D—N'T!"

He became increasingly hard to understand, and the lack of communication made him frantic and angry. He reached out and grabbed my shoulder, hard. "YOU HAVE—B—LIEVE ME! MY FAMILY—Y SISTER—MOM—THINK I KIL—THEM? THAT'S NOT FAIR! THA—OT FAI—!"

I took hold of his wrist. "Charlie? Hey, calm down! I can't hear you when you panic."

That only wound him up further.

The chair sitting by the fire skidded across the room and slammed into the cabinets along the opposite wall. Small objects zipped through the air. He took hold of my other shoulder and shook me a little with each statement. "NO! NO! I DI—N'T HURT ANY—!"

His body pulsed and flickered. Pieces of him faded until he was only a faint outline.

"NO!" He continued, the only word I could understand anymore. "NO! NO!"

Silence, sudden and hollow, swallowed the cabin.

The flying objects clattered to the floor.

Charlie vanished.

CHAPTER SEVEN

I left the chair by the fire for the next seven nights.

It warmed up, and I didn't need to light the wood stove anymore. In fact, I opened a couple of windows when it became uncomfortably stuffy in the evenings, but I still lit a fire.

I couldn't shake the sight of Charlie holding his hands out over the hot stove.

On the third night since he disappeared, I draped a blanket over the back of the chair.

Just in case.

Our conversation consumed my thoughts. I went through the motions of the job and relished the stunning views and slow pace, all the while cataloging everything I thought I knew about what'd happened at Dead Man's Lookout all those years ago.

I cycled through what he'd said over and over—that a

police officer had hiked out to discuss the missing people, and that he last remembered being in the lookout before he died.

The police had always remained tight-lipped about the investigation, so the fact that it wasn't widely known that someone met with Charles Randolph—*Charlie*—the day before he went missing wasn't surprising.

But then why hadn't they found his body? And what had they found instead that convinced them of his guilt?

A simple answer to those questions was that he'd lied to me, and he was, in fact, guilty.

It just didn't feel right, though. The potent combination of disbelief, desperation, and rage that'd poured out of him would be difficult to fake. And why lie in the first place?

He was already dead.

Plus, his first thought hadn't been for himself, or the legacy of fear he'd left behind. It was for his family, and whether they'd suffered in hope that he'd someday come home.

I refused to believe someone who loved their family that much could murder six innocent people in cold blood.

Storms rolled in at the end of my first week. When the forecast called for lightning after hours, we were paid over-time to continue our watch. Honestly, as live-in lookouts, most of us kept an eye out anyway, but the overtime was a nice bonus.

The towers themselves were safeguarded via a system of lightning rods and copper grounding wires, which attracted and dispersed electrical currents without harming the struc-ture or occupants, but still.

There wasn't anything quite like experiencing a lightning storm in the clouds.

It made for a tense couple of days, and a welcome distraction from my tumultuous thoughts. I'd settled into the job just fine, but really stretched my legs those first stormy nights. I called in three strikes, rotating the Firefinder until I centered the smoke plume between the front and rear sites, and reported the reading over the radio.

A few more reports came in from neighboring viewsheds, but so far, no fires.

"Lightning's a tricky beast," Janine said during our debrief on a private channel just before bed.

I was exhausted and sore from being on my feet so much, but it was a good kind of ache.

"It can simmer in a root system for days. I had a fire once that popped up nearly two weeks later! So keep a close eye on those strike sites."

"Yeah, will do," I replied before crashing into bed.

"Everything alright over there? How's your standoff with the raccoon going?" she asked.

It was nice to talk to someone who didn't know about my diagnosis. Normal, even. I spoke with Mom, Dad, and Bobby regularly, of course, but it grew tedious to feel like I had to reassure them all the time that I was fine.

Janine didn't know about any of that, and it was freeing.

"Just tired, it's been a long few days. And I can't figure out what the damn thing wants from me. It's not defecating, and I've never fed it. Hell, most of my food is down in the utility shed, anyway. Why would it climb all the way up here?"

She laughed. "Maybe it just wants to be friends."

I rolled my eyes. "I get the impression it wants me to *leave*."

We also had an unspoken agreement to avoid the topic of the disappearances as much as possible. At least for now, anyway. Until we were told otherwise, it genuinely didn't help to worry and stress over it.

It lingered, though. Every day that passed without a lost hiker turning up safe and sound, it grew harder and harder to ignore.

"Alright," she said. "I'm exhausted. Time to get some shut-eye."

I looked at the time. It was nearly midnight. "Same here. You have a good night. Over."

"Oh, hey, before you go," she cut in just after my transmission went through, "someone's been driving an ATV along the trail near my lookout the last few days. I've reported it, but you should keep an eye out, too. I'm here for peace and quiet, not to hear some jackwagon drive around at all hours of the night. They need a big, fat, *stay-the-fuck-away* fine."

Suddenly, I remembered the tracks I'd noticed down by the lake. "I saw tracks, too," I told her. "On my hike in. Completely forgot about it until now. Probably just idiot teenagers with nothing better to do."

"I hate kids," she grumbled.

"I hate raccoons," I grumbled back.

She laughed again. "Talk to you tomorrow."

Janine didn't report for roll call the next morning.

It was the eighth day since Charlie disappeared, and I spent hours cycling through radio channels, trying to reach her, the way she'd done for me at the start of the season.

Empty static was the only response.

I'd just finished my midday smoke sweep, jotted down the weather collection data on the daily observation log, and hooked the radio to my belt before I headed down to the storage building to grab a few things for lunch.

There'd been chatter about her absence all morning. The ranger station called the police right away, and as far as I knew, they were on their way to her lookout for a wellness check.

While we waited for news, people offered up perfectly valid reasons as to why she wouldn't have checked in.

Maybe her radio died.

She could've left for an early morning hike and fallen.

A family member might've called and needed help.

I hoped it was simply a case of a family emergency that she'd rushed to respond to without alerting us to her absence, but I had a sick gut feeling it was much worse than that.

She wasn't the type to just up and leave.

I sorted through my quickly dwindling supply of food—I'd need to plan my groceries better next time—and thought about the horrifying conclusion I'd dwelled on almost obsessively over the last week.

If I believed Charlie was innocent, then his death had somehow, by manipulation or happenstance, allowed a serial killer to get away with murder for almost forty years. Three more people had disappeared in the last month.

And now, Janine was missing.

There was a surge in radio chatter, as if several people tried to speak over each other at once. I turned up the volume, ears strained to catch what they said, before it ceased altogether.

Had they switched channels? Were they at her lookout? Had they found something?

On the way back up to the tower, my phone buzzed in my pocket. Worried it had something to do with Janine, I quickly shifted the grilled cheese accoutrements into one hand, pulled out my phone with the other, and answered without checking the caller ID.

"Hello?"

I recognized Bobby's voice immediately. "Oh, thank God," he said.

Judging by his tone, something was very wrong. "Bobby, are you okay? Is Jade alright? And Molly?"

"The girls are fine."

I let out a sigh of relief.

"I called to make sure *you* were okay," he continued quickly. "I heard a lookout went missing and panicked."

"Fuck, I'm so sorry. I should've called. I was caught up in keeping tabs on the radio this morning. I haven't even talked to Dad yet." Back up the stairs, I tucked the phone between my ear and shoulder, struggling to balance my lunch and open the cabin door at the same time.

"You'd better do that right now, or he's going to hear and have a goddamn heart attack. They said the tower's empty, but they weren't saying who. We haven't texted in a couple of days, and I thought—*fuck,* I'm so glad you're okay," he said, voice thick with emotion.

"I'm really sorry. Let me call Dad, and then I'll call you back, okay?"

Before he could reply, though, I shouldered open the door to find Tate Morris standing in my lookout.

"**B**obby, I've gotta go. Tate Morris is here," I said, making direct eye contact with the man who'd sneaked into my tower.

He had the sense to look contrite.

"What the fuck?" Bobby asked.

"I will call you back in an hour." *And if I don't, you know who to call the dogs out for.*

Speaking of dogs, a very large German Sheppard sat at Tate's heel, tongue lolling and nose in the air, as if I'd brought the cheese in just for him.

"*Half* an hour," Bobby said before hanging up.

I really had no idea what I'd done to deserve such a good friend.

I set the phone and food on the counter. "Right. I don't want to bear-spray your dog, so you'd better have a good fucking reason for creeping into my tower behind my back."

He raised an eyebrow. "But you do want to bear spray *me?*"

I didn't answer. He wasn't in uniform, but I figured threatening a cop even off the clock wouldn't go over well. "Why are you here?" I asked instead.

He patted the dog's head. "Down, Rocky," he said softly.

Rocky listened, heaving a sigh as he plopped onto his belly and stared up longingly at the bag of cheese.

Tate looked back toward me. "You didn't text me, so I had no way of contacting you. I came to see if you were alright."

I shuffled to the side, centering the Firefinder more securely between us. "I didn't realize it was a social invitation."

Honestly, I was only evading his questions until he explained what the hell he was doing there, but the blush that flamed his cheeks took me by surprise. "Wait," I said, "*was* it a social invitation?"

He looked away. "It was both. You're back in town again, and I thought, well. A friend would be nice. But I also needed you to know you can contact me if you see anything suspicious while you're out here. Which is why I'm here. The second part, not the first," he finished, blushing again.

"And you had to break in to accomplish that?"

He sighed. "First of all, it's not your property. It's the government's."

"That really doesn't make it better," I mumbled.

"*Second,*" he spoke over me, "I wasn't trying to sneak in. I thought I saw you up here and called out when I reached the top of the stairs. When you didn't answer, I got worried. The lookout in Tower Eight is—"

"Missing, yes, I'm fucking aware. I reported for roll call, though. Why did you assume something was wrong with me? Also, you would've had to head this way," I checked my watch, "right after the call came through to make it by now. Why?"

He sighed. "Look, some weird shit is happening in these woods. People are going missing. After the call came in, I came to see if you're alright, and to ask a few questions about what you may or may not know about the missing lookout."

Something about the way he assessed me, and then glanced around as if only casually interested in my belongings, made my scalp prickle. "Her name is Janine. And you're here to *question* me about her."

He didn't confirm. Rocky whined into the silence, still eyeing the countertop with longing.

I sat on the edge of my bed and looked to the chair in front of the wood stove—the only other chair in the lookout. "Have a seat."

It felt wrong, somehow, offering him that chair. It wasn't *his* chair.

And that was when I noticed the blanket wasn't draped over the back anymore. Rather, it was sprawled on my bed, as if thrown off in haste.

Tate could've moved it, or...

I thought I saw you up here, he'd said.

It could've been Charlie.

I sensed it, then. Not exactly the feeling of being watched, but not alone, anymore. A week ago, that would've terrified me. Now, with a cop poking around asking questions, it was comforting.

Time to hang up the beaded curtains.

ate's casual interrogation was interrupted by my phone ringing not once, or twice, but *three* times.

The only reason it wasn't four was because Dad had the sense to check on me first before calling Mom. He'd been on a tarmac somewhere, shouting, *"ARE YOU ALRIGHT?"* over the loud rhythmic beat of helicopter blades in the background.

I'd texted Bobby to say I was fine and he didn't have to alert the National Guard, but he'd called to hear me confirm it myself.

Leonard had checked in, too, to make sure I was alright. He couldn't share much other than what I already knew; they hadn't found Janine at her post. As the direct supervisor of all the lookouts, I couldn't imagine the mess and worry over one going missing while on the job.

"So, how well did you know Janine?" Tate asked after I hung up.

"I've never met her in person, but we talk quite a bit over the radio. She helped me settle into the job. She's been doing this for a long time and is a great neighbor. Observant as hell. She catches a lot. We don't talk much about non-work stuff, though."

"By neighbor, you mean the next lookout over? Can you

see her tower from here? Did you notice anything amiss overnight?" He peered out the windows as if searching for a faraway lookout.

I shook my head. "No. We have a slightly overlapping view of the lake, but her tower is just over that far ridgeline. We can't see each other."

He hummed. "How long would it take you to hike there, from here?"

I glared at him. "Are you seriously asking me if I hiked over there in the middle of the night, did something to her, and trekked all the way back here to make it in time for the morning check-in?"

"No. I asked you how long it would take to hike there. You jumped to your own conclusions."

I rolled my eyes. "You wouldn't come all the way out here to ask for my best guess on timing a route."

He just stared.

Then, I realized. "*That's* why you're here so quickly. You came to see me without calling first to catch me off guard—to see if I'm hiding something."

More staring.

"Well, I'm not. It takes four hours to hike from the trailhead up to my tower, one way. Hers is a drive-in, so I'd have to take the service road that circles all the way around to reach her. Another hour, maybe two? I didn't sign off until close to midnight last night. She and I spoke for a few minutes on a private channel before I went to sleep. There's no possible way I could've made it there and back for our nine a.m. shift."

"What did you two talk about on the private channel?"

I gave him my best *fuck you* eyebrow. "Raccoon shit."

A book, which had been propped up against the wall on my desk, tipped over. If I didn't suspect there was a ghost lurking nearby—*a cheeky ghost, apparently*—I wouldn't have thought twice about it.

Rocky stood and padded over to sniff the fallen book, before placing his head in my lap for pets.

I took a deep, steadying breath. "Hi, buddy," I said, scratching behind his ears.

"Everyone always prefers him over me," Tate said with a sigh.

"He didn't imply I had something to do with Janine going missing," I grumbled.

Tate dragged a hand through his hair. "This is a shitty situation, alright. But I wouldn't be doing my job if I didn't ask."

My shoulders dropped. "Sure. Look, could she have just taken a day off and forgotten to tell Leonard? Or maybe she went on a hike and fell? Or got turned around?"

Neither of those was a great possibility, but it'd be better than the alternative.

Tate shook his head. "I can't say much, but there's reason to suspect she didn't intend to be away from the tower for very long, if she left of her own free will at all. Have you seen or heard anything unusual in the last forty-eight hours? Or at all since you came out here?" he asked.

"*Um...*" *Of the alive person variety?*

And then I remembered.

"She saw someone driving an ATV on the trail near her lookout. Or maybe she only saw the tracks? Not sure. But I also saw tracks down by the lake on my hike in, a week and a half ago."

Tate's gaze sharpened. "When did she see them?"

"Yesterday? The day before? I can't remember."

"Do you think she would've confronted them, if she saw them again?"

I shrugged. "I don't know her well enough to say, but she was pissed about it. She may have."

"Have you seen any since your hike in?"

I shook my head. "No. I've seen a few hikers pass by on the stretches of trail lower on the mountain. I think I noted them in my observation logs. You can look, if you want. Otherwise, it really has been calm. We only had our first storms in the last couple of days."

"Yeah, if you wouldn't mind, I'll take a look at your logs so I can cross-reference where the hikers went with other towers."

"Sure thing." *And then you can leave,* I thought.

I stood and shuffled through the folder before passing him the completed stack. "I have to keep those to turn in at the ranger station on my next supply run, but feel free to take pictures."

"Thanks," he said, and pulled out his phone to do just that.

My stomach growled. "Mind if I start making lunch?"

He waved me on. "No, not at all."

I pulled out a few pieces of bread and buttered a side of each while a pan warmed on the stovetop. When I opened the cheese bag and peeled off a few slices, I looked down to find Rocky sitting at my feet, giving me the biggest, saddest puppy eyes I'd ever seen.

"You'd think you've never been loved a day in your life with those eyes," I said down at him.

Tate chuckled. "You can give him a bit of cheese if you want. He'll love you forever."

"Well, we do have to pay the cheese tax, don't we, buddy? Yes, we do. It's important," I cooed, holding out a small piece.

He slurped it up and grinned at me, tongue lolling.

"Good boy," I said, patting his head again.

"Thanks for this," Tate said, waving at the papers. "And if you'd actually give me your number, it'd be a lot easier to get a hold of you, instead of hiking all the way out here."

I mentally side-eyed that comment. He could've asked Dad or Bobby for my number if he really didn't want to make the trip.

"Alright," I said anyway, grabbing my phone.

After we exchanged numbers, he pulled a long, hands-free leash out of his bag and hooked it to Rocky's harness. "I'm glad you're alright. Really. If you like, let me know when you're back in town. Maybe we could grab lunch."

I honestly didn't know how I felt about that. He seemed genuine in his offer of friendship, but also, I was clearly on a list somewhere of people to keep an eye on, and I didn't like that at all.

Especially not with what'd happened to Charlie so fresh in my mind.

I laid the assembled sandwich in the pan. God, the smell of bread toasting in butter was unmatched. "My supply runs are pretty quick, but I'll let you know. You sure you don't want to stay for a sandwich?" I asked when I was confident he'd already committed to leaving.

"No, I won't take your food," he answered, smiling like he knew exactly what I'd been thinking.

"Be safe hiking out," I said, and meant it.

I may not fully understand his motivations, but I didn't want the guy to end up *missing,* too.

CHAPTER EIGHT

"He likes you," a voice said behind me. "The way he looked through your things before you came up here—it wasn't just out of suspicion, he wanted to know what books you read. He flipped through your sketch pad."

I watched out the window until Tate disappeared into the tree line below. "He's also not sure whether I had anything to do with the missing lookout next door."

"You didn't."

I turned to look at Charlie.

He didn't startle me this time, but it was jarring to see him appear exactly the same. From his outfit, to the way his hair fell just so across his forehead, and the way his boots were unlaced—he never changed. "No, I didn't. And I don't believe you had anything to do with the missing hikers all those years ago, either."

His shoulders fell. The cautious hesitance on his face melted away, like the weight of the world had been lifted. I marveled at the power of being seen, of being understood, even if it was by just one person.

"Thank you," he said. There were multitudes in those words all over again, before his face turned grave. "It's happening again."

I nodded. "Yeah. I think so."

"I'm really sorry about your friend. The other lookout."

"She could still be found. She might be lost or injured."

He didn't squash my hope. Maybe he saw how much I needed it. "You have to be careful." *Or you'll end up like her. You'll end up like me*, his eyes said.

"I will be. Besides, I'm not the only lookout keeping watch in this tower anymore, am I?"

The outline of his body pulsed with light, like a flare of electricity. More pieces of him filled in, and he appeared less fuzzy and more whole than I'd ever seen him. "No, I'm here too."

"Good."

I meant that. I couldn't explain why, but I did.

He cast around as if searching for something else to add, before his eyes widened. "Oh. What's your name?"

"Reece West."

I liked seeing the smile back on his face. He had dimples, and his cheeks stretched wide, as if unused to accommodating joy. "Hi, Reece."

All of a sudden, I felt like a nervous teenager, unsure of what to do with my hands. "Hi, Charlie."

His gaze caught over my shoulder. "Your sandwich is burning."

"*Shit.*" I turned back to the stove and grabbed the spatula, quickly flipping it over. Sure enough, the first side was less toasted and more charred.

Oh well, I guess that meant I had to make two. I'd still eat the first, of course, but you know. At least one should be properly cooked.

This kind of thinking is why you are already running out of groceries, you animal.

I opened the window over the stove to air out the smoke. "Can you grab the other window?" I asked over my shoulder. We'd need a cross-breeze to get rid of the smell.

"I can try," he said.

Fuck, I hadn't even considered. Sometimes he interacted with objects as though he were solid—he'd grabbed me firmly by the shoulders twice now—and other times he looked more like, well, a ghost.

"My bad, I got it," I said, flipping the sandwich onto a plate before the other side joined the first, and it became completely inedible.

"No, I want to try." Hesitantly, he took hold of the handle and cranked it a few times until the window cracked open. "That's as far as I can go for now." He sounded out of breath.

"Thank you." I padded over to open it fully. I wasn't sure how the physics of his corporeal body worked, but that seemed like progress. "That's pretty amazing, you know. For a..." I cringed.

"For a dead guy?" he finished.

I guffawed. "I was going to say ghost, but same thing, I suppose. Have you always been able to touch things?"

He shook his head. "Not always. It's hard for me to be physically present in a space, especially when I get worked up or upset." He grimaced. "I'm sorry for the other day."

"No. Don't apologize to me for that. I've become more upset in my life over less. You *should* be angry, and I'll listen whenever you need me to."

I'd needed someone to vent my anger to, without feeling as though it burdened them. Even the ones who loved and cared for me very much just wanted me to feel better. To be okay. To be healthy.

Carrying their hope *and* mine was exhausting.

Overcome with the urge to comfort him, I reached out as if to pat his arm, but hesitated.

What would he feel like? Would my hand fall right through his body? Or would he be solid, like the other day?

I gently rested my palm on his shoulder.

He felt surprisingly... *normal*. My hand slid easily over the cool leather of his jacket. His soft sherpa collar brushed against my fingertips. Rather than one amorphous apparition, his clothes retained their original textures. They weren't *ghostly* at all.

Fascinating.

His shoulder was firm, and this close, he smelled faintly of cotton. Like warm sheets drying on the line on a hot summer day.

He sucked in a breath and jolted, blinking up at me.

I yanked my hand back and cleared my throat. "Sorry."

"It's ok," he replied quickly. "It's just been a long time, that's all."

Thirty-nine years. Thirty-nine years without a comforting touch, without any human connection at all. I'd be jumpy, too.

"*Um,* how long was I away?" he asked, glancing around again as if to gauge the time.

"Eight days."

His brows creased. "I've only just felt strong enough to come back and show myself like this."

"Does it always take you that long to get your energy back?" I couldn't place why that bothered me so much. Maybe I was just worried about Janine or missed her company.

He shrugged. "Like I said, time is different there. It doesn't feel like I'm gone as long as I am, but I think..." he scuffed a foot along the ground.

"You think?" I prompted.

"I think it helps to be around someone." His cheeks darkened. "To feel like a person."

There were a few moments of silence. I thought back to when he'd shouted at me for closing the window, and how I'd misinterpreted his anguish for rage. "I left the chair and blanket out for you," I said gruffly. "You don't have to ask me to come. But maybe let me know when you're here, so I don't get naked or something."

I washed every other day out on the deck using a portable shower I warmed in the sun, and I wouldn't want to startle him.

Heh. Wouldn't want to startle the ghost.

He blinked rapidly. Did he already know that? "You mean, you want me around? I don't freak you out?"

I laughed. "At first? You absolutely terrified me."

He smiled a little.

"But now, no. You don't freak me out." My stomach growled again, louder this time.

His smile widened. "God, I miss food."

"Do you want to try eating something?" I asked, matching his grin.

He grimaced. "I don't know what would happen to it, and I don't want to waste your groceries."

"I'll finish what you don't eat, and I need to make a trip to town to restock soon anyway. Come on, what's the worst that could happen? It won't kill you."

The words were out before I could think. My jaw dropped at my own stupidity.

Foot. In. Mouth.

Charlie burst out laughing, clutching his belly. When he could take a breath, he wiped at his eyes and said, "You're right. It won't kill me to try. But eating that burnt husk of a sandwich might, so I want a fresh one."

I grinned.

S earch parties and scent dogs combed the forest for a week after Janine went missing.

The radio chatter was constant. Everyone was on edge, passing around information and rumors they'd heard like wildfire. It got so bad, we were told to take the non-work talk to a group text, rather than clog up the channel in case someone had to report a fire.

On the third morning since she disappeared, rumors spread that the dogs alerted to a possible crime scene in the woods near Janine's tower, but no one knew what they'd found.

The two lookouts closest to me on the west side, Tower Six and Five, quit the next day.

"That happened the first time, too," Charlie commented. He'd appeared a few minutes ago, right as I prepared lunch. "Most quit after the fourth person went missing. But I was the only one left on the west side of the park, and I'd moved out here to be a Ranger. I thought staying was the right thing to do, and could put me ahead when they were hiring full-time."

"I hate that," I said. "I hate that you stayed because you thought it was right, and still..."

My words trailed off. *Still died.*

He looked out toward the forest, pensive.

I plated up two bowls of ramen, because we'd discovered Charlie could eat. He liked grilled cheese sandwiches—*unburnt,* he'd unnecessarily commented—tomato soup, canned ravioli, and hot dogs.

Granted, his palette was severely limited by my remaining food supply. I'd finished the last of the fruit and vegetables days ago.

"Want an egg?" I asked into the quiet.

"No, plain is good for now. Thank you."

I added a fried egg and hot sauce to my bowl before

sliding the other down the counter for Charlie. He wasn't confident enough yet to hold something that might break or spill if he dropped it.

Bending over, he sipped at the hot broth and sighed. "You really don't have to share with me, you know. You can't have much food left."

"Meh, I was already going through my groceries too quickly. I'll ask if it's ok to leave in a few days to restock early." I leaned back against the counter next to him and slurped at my own noodles.

He peered at me, hesitant and questioning. "So you'll come back?"

Charlie looked so normal in moments like this; sometimes, I forgot he wasn't. That he'd been alone in this lookout for decades. Was he trapped here? Could he leave the tower if he wanted to?

Or if I wanted him to?

"Yeah, I'll come back. I don't really have anywhere else to live right now anyway, except for my Dad's pull-out couch. And trust me, you *don't* want to sleep on that thing for more than a night."

The quietly pleased look on his face made my stomach feel funny, but he didn't press further.

I cleared my throat, swirling the bright orange yolk around the seasoned broth. "What's your favorite food?"

"Roasted chicken, I think. When the skin gets all crispy, *mmm*. With mashed potatoes," he said, eyes dreamy and distant. "Oh, and warm peach cobbler for dessert. With vanilla ice cream."

"Obviously," I answered. "The ice cream is critical. The melt—"

—The melt," we said together.

He laughed. Charlie laughed a lot for a ghost. It made his whole body glow brighter, like for a moment, a surge of whatever energy or force kept him here ran through him a little stronger. "I always requested that for my birthday meal. Mom would make the chicken and mashed potatoes, and Frankie made the cobbler." He had such a fond look on his face, I didn't want to interrupt his happy memories with more questions.

I had a lot of them. Mostly about how and why he was stuck in ghost form and not wherever people went after they died.

He probably wouldn't have the answers to those, though. Or wouldn't *want* the answers, maybe.

When he was done, he pushed his bowl toward me to finish off what he hadn't eaten. He mostly pecked at things like a bird, afraid of what would happen if he ate too much at once, but wherever he'd go when he disappeared, and whatever happened to his corporeal form when he went there, made the food disappear.

I called it blinking.

He'd blink in and out throughout the day, chattering away at me before he left to rest again. He'd always return in the evenings, though, to watch the sunset and relax by the fire.

Later that night, when sleep crept closer and I could barely keep my eyes open, he reappeared.

Scooting his chair closer to the wood stove, he draped the

blanket over his lap and settled in, like a night watchman. "Go to sleep. I'll keep an eye on things," he said with a smile.

I couldn't explain why, but I trusted he would. So much so, I tucked beneath the duvet, eyes slowly blinking shut, until only the barest hint of his outline remained.

"Goodnight, Charlie," I rumbled.

"Goodnight, Reece."

CHAPTER NINE

Mom called the next day.

"A lookout goes missing, and you don't *tell me?*" she screeched in greeting. Impossibly, her voice grew more shrill with each word.

I guess we skipped right over hello, I thought, and cringed.

She had a right to be angry. I'd gone back and forth on whether or not I should tell her, knowing all she would do was worry herself and everyone else into an early grave.

I hadn't decided yet either way, but clearly, I'd waited too long.

"I'm sorry, Mom. I was distracted by keeping up with everything and didn't want to worry you."

"She was in the next tower over!" she shrieked. "And she's the fourth person to go missing in two months!"

She must have wrung those details out of Dad.

I didn't have her on speaker, but she was loud enough

that Charlie turned from where he stood at the window, binoculars dangling from his neck, and gave me a look that said *she has a point.*

"Don't start," I mouthed at him, gesturing with my hand for him to turn back around and mind his business.

He rolled his eyes and continued with the hourly smoke check.

"The search parties are still out looking for her. She may have gotten lost or injured—they could still find her alive."

Truthfully, I didn't believe that anymore, but it was a knee-jerk reaction to soothe Mom's nerves.

"Just promise me you're being careful." She sounded tired.

"I promise," I answered, staring at the back of Charlie's head.

We chatted for a few more minutes before saying our goodbyes. "I've got to take these cookies over to the church before this afternoon, so I'll let you go. I love you, Reese's Pieces."

"Love you too, Mom."

When I hung up, Charlie faced me again, his mouth kicked up at the corner. "She seems nice."

"She is. Her worrying gets on my nerves, but I can't complain, all things considered," I said, joining him at the window.

"Does she..." he trailed off, blushing. "I mean, the way that cop acted, it seemed like he might've wanted to be more than your... friend." He began nervously twisting the strap of the binoculars. "Are you and he, like, well, I mean, have you—"

"Charlie?"

"Hmm?" His voice was about four octaves higher than normal.

"Are you asking if I'm gay?"

"*Uh-huh.*"

I bit my cheek to keep from smiling at the way his voice cracked. "Yes, I am."

"Yes, you're seeing the cop, or yes, you're gay?"

"Yes, I'm gay. No, I'm not seeing Tate."

He cleared his throat, outline flickering a bit. "Oh."

I raised an eyebrow. "You good?"

"Yeah. Yeah, I'm good. So, does she—I mean, she said she was taking cookies to church. Does she know?"

My heart broke a little. The more I learned about Charlie, the more it felt like I'd *always* known him, but then I'd suddenly remember he grew up decades before me. Of course, there were still people nowadays who couldn't come out to their family, but a lot had changed since he was alive.

"Yes, she does. My dad knew well before Mom, I think. But the summer I turned sixteen, my step-dad, Keith, caught me making out with the neighbor boy by the pool. So, you know, that sort of blew the door off that secret."

His eyes widened. "What did he do?"

I chuckled. "He told me I should talk to my mom about a few things, and then invited him to stay for dinner."

I'd probably never forget the sight of Keith standing in front of us, grill tongs in hand, looking like he'd rather be anywhere else.

"And they were ok with it?" Charlie asked quietly.

"More than ok with it. They've always loved me for who

I am. After that, Mom found a church down the street that flew a rainbow flag in the parking lot."

He looked a bit misty-eyed. "That's really nice. I didn't— I mean, I had girlfriends. I liked women. But I also liked men. I just never had a chance to act on it, or maybe it was easier to ignore it. I'll never know what my family would've thought, but I'll always wonder."

He shrugged and peered through the binoculars again, as if he hadn't just said something important. The clenched muscle in his jaw spoke differently.

"How old were you when you died?" I asked quietly.

"Twenty-nine."

Fucking hell. Twenty-nine. He'd been on the cusp of settling into his life; enough experience to have an idea of what he wanted to do, who he wanted to be, only for it all to be snuffed out.

I reached out to pat his back. He was cooler this time, and while my hand didn't fall through his body, it felt more like that just-barely-close-enough magnetic pull right *before* touching someone, than actually making contact. Like he was there, and not there. "I'm really sorry you never had the chance to find out."

His light flared, and his back solidified beneath my palm. "It feels good that I got to tell you."

I studied his profile. "Do you want me to look up your family for you? To reach out?" I doubted his parents were still alive, but hadn't he mentioned a sister? Maybe he had cousins?

At the moment, I couldn't imagine something I'd rather do *less* than cold call a stranger to tell them I was living with the ghost of their dead family member, whom everyone assumed was a serial killer, but I found myself offering anyway.

Who the hell am I? I regularly ordered delivery online so I wouldn't have to speak to another person.

But if it helped ease the sadness in his eyes, I'd do it.

"No," he responded quickly, shaking his head. "No. Not yet. I'm not in denial that Mom and Dad are probably... That they've probably passed away." He cleared his throat. "But I don't want to know about Frankie yet. Or what she thinks of me, if she's still alive."

I nodded. "Is Frankie your sister?"

"Yeah. My older sister. We lived together before I moved out here for the lookout job."

I took a step back, dropping my hand. "Where are you from?"

"Iowa. I wanted a career in the Forest Service, so when I got this job, I jumped on it, hoping it'd be my way in. Mom and Dad were sad I was moving so far away, but Frankie knew it was where I wanted to be. She was so excited for me."

Charlie smiled a little, like he could still feel how happy she'd been for him.

Was she still alive? Did she mourn him, or had she done her best to forget her brother-turned-serial-killer had ever existed at all?

"She gave me this for my birthday," he continued, holding his arms out to indicate the flight jacket he always wore. "It was the last night I saw her. My birthday wasn't for another month, but she knew we wouldn't see each other again for a while, so..." Eyes far away, he drifted off in thought.

"When's your birthday?" I asked softly, pulling him back.

He blinked out of his memories. "June twenty-seventh."

My mouth popped open. "That's only a few days away. We have to celebrate."

"Celebrate?"

"Yes! I'll get what we need on my supply run. You only turn thirty once," I said with a sly grin.

He shot me a deadpan look. "I'm well over thirty by now."

I waved it off. "We'll celebrate anyway, yeah?"

Charlie got that small, quietly happy look again, as if too afraid to actually look forward to something. He shrugged. "Sure. If you want to, that'd be nice."

"I want to."

I really, really did.

I called Bobby a few hours later, after Charlie left for his afternoon rest.

"Hey," he answered. A baby wailed in the background. "Everything going alright?"

"Sounds like I should be asking you that," I replied, talking through my wireless earbuds. Just about finished with my hourly smoke sweep, I paced around the outer deck to double-check the lightning strike sites I'd reported in the last storm, like Janine said I should.

"Ear infection. Poor girl's been up three nights straight."

I cringed. "I'm sorry. Is she okay? How are you two holding up?"

Bobby sighed. "Doctor said it's normal. Jade and I are alive, but that's about all. Anyway, how are things there?"

"As good as they can be. Janine's still missing. Another lookout quit this morning. Everyone's worried. Oh, and Mom called. She knows. I should've told her myself, but now she's not going to leave it alone."

Bobby made a dejected noise. "Can you blame her? Have you thought about getting out of there?"

I stopped short. "What do you mean?"

"I mean quit, like the others."

"I can't do that."

"Why not?" he asked, confused. "It's not about the money, is it? I'm sure you could figure out somewhere to live for the summer. I can talk to Dad and see if there's a position for you at the ranger station in town. Anything other than staying out there all alone."

I turned to go inside, but stopped short when I saw Charlie had appeared. He shook out his blanket and carefully folded it before draping it over the back of his chair. When he looked up, he grinned and waved hello.

"I can't leave," I answered, more harshly than I intended to.

"Okay..." Bobby said. Molly's wailing pitched higher.

"I'm the only lookout left on the west side," I added, softer. "I don't want to leave your dad hanging."

Bobby sighed. "I get that. But—"

"I feel better out here," I cut in. With sudden certainty, I knew it was the truth. "I haven't thought about the shit that's wrong with me in days, Bobby. A lot of that is about what's going on, sure. And I'm worried for Janine. But it's also just being out here. I enjoy this."

My eyes caught on the way Charlie tentatively picked up the binoculars, his hands tangling in the straps. "I'm not ready to go back to real life yet. I feel like I'm just finding it again, if that makes sense."

He shushed the baby in the background. "You do sound lighter. And I'm happy for that. I just don't want you to get hurt, that's all."

I looked at Charlie again. "I'm being careful."

Scritch scratch scritch scratch scritch

"You've gotta be kidding me," I groaned, tossing my sketchpad aside.

It was late, well after dark. I sat in bed sideways, with my back to the wall, facing Charlie. As usual, he hovered near the wood stove, and the way the firelight danced along his cheekbones had inspired me to practice my shading.

For no particular reason.

He peered up from the book in his lap. "What's that noise?"

"This goddamn raccoon won't leave me alone," I grumbled, shuffling over to slide on my Crocs. "I've tried everything I can think of to make it go away, but it keeps coming back."

"Oh, is it Randy?" he asked, excited. Darting over to the window that'd been uncovered when I very first arrived, he peered out. "Hi, Randy!"

SCRITCH SCRATCH SCRITCH SCRATCH

"Who the fuck is Randy?" I asked, tromping over to join him.

"The raccoon!"

And there it was, in the flesh. Fat as it could be, the furry little creature squatted on its haunches in front of the window, chattering excitedly.

It *never* sounded like that with me.

With its black mask, beady little eyes, and striped tail wrapped around its middle, the little shit waved its tiny hands out, whiskers twitching as if in hello.

The railing wobbled precariously beneath its weight.

"You named the raccoon *Randy*?"

It stopped chattering and hissed at me.

Charlie glared. "Do you have a problem with that name?"

I blinked at him. "You're fucking with me, aren't you?"

He reached for the window latch. "Not even a little bit. Now move, she wants inside."

I grabbed his hand and pulled it away. "Absolutely not!"

He glared at me again. "She gets cold at night. She used to live in the old mattress before they came and replaced everything. I couldn't get the window open when they left and have been worried sick about her ever since."

I gaped at him, at a loss for words.

Charlie yanked his hand out of mine and undid the window latch, cranking it open. "Come on, girl," he cooed, reaching his hand out. "I bet you've been so cold and hungry out there all on your own. I'll cut you up a hot dog, how's that sound?"

"Doesn't look like she's been hungry," I grumbled.

The raccoon hissed at me again and scurried farther down the railing.

"Don't be mean," Charlie scolded.

Despite his coaxing, five minutes passed, and he hadn't cajoled her any closer. "She doesn't like you," he huffed, hands on his hips.

"Would you like *me* to sleep on the deck, instead?"

He peered up at me as if debating it, before he sighed. "I suppose not."

"You *suppose* not?" I asked, offended. "You'd rather live with *her* than me?"

He smirked. "Spot the difference."

I laughed so hard my stomach hurt. "How do you know it's a she?" I asked when I could breathe again, wiping my eyes. I hadn't been light-headed from laughing in... Months? Longer?

"She brought her babies here a few years ago," Charlie said fondly, as if reminiscing. When I looked over at him, though, he was staring at me.

I heaved a defeated sigh. "We'll put a cut-up hot dog out for her tonight. But *only* for tonight. Will that make you happy?"

Charlie's eyes twinkled. "Yes. It would."

And that was how I became a beaded-curtain-believing man who fed a raccoon named Randy.

CHAPTER TEN

A few nights later, well after the fire dimmed and I fell into a restless sleep, I sprang awake from a vivid dream.

I ran through the forest, fleeing from a wall of people that made up a quickly approaching search party. Dad was linked arm-in-arm with Bobby, Tate, and Leonard, along with several other faces I recognized, all dressed in bright pink shirts.

Were they looking for Janine? They weren't calling out her name, though.

They were shouting mine.

I sat up. Panting hard, my sleep shirt clung to my chest, soaked in sweat nearly down to my belly button. I wiped at the moisture on my upper lip.

"It's too hot in here, it's giving you bad dreams," Charlie said, speaking quietly into the dark. He was curled up in the chair by the fire, exactly where he'd been when I fell asleep.

"Are you still cold?" I asked, voice thick.

He smiled softly. "No, Reece. I'm not cold anymore. No more fires after tonight. Let's open the windows for a breeze."

I reached for the one next to my bed, and he opened the opposite across the cabin. "You're getting good at that," I remarked.

I swore I saw the faintest blush darken his cheeks. Was that even possible? It made me want to reach for my sketch pad again.

His eyes tracked the *V* of sweat down my chest, honey-bright in the gloom. "I want to try leaving the lookout tomorrow."

My eyebrows rose in surprise. "Can you do that?"

He shrugged, still staring at my chest. "I don't know. I couldn't before. If I tried, I'd only end up going back to that other place. The only time I've ever managed it was when you nearly fell. But..." His eyes darted up to mine. "I think I want to try again."

"What does it look like? That other place?" I asked.

He turned toward the smoldering fire, face hidden in shadow. "It's like I'm here, and not here," he whispered. "I'm in the lookout, but it's full of shadows. There's no color, or light, or warmth. The windows are all boarded up. There's no door. I don't think it's really death. Or, it is, but not the final place you go when you die. It feels more like... Waiting."

What have you been waiting for?

Instead, I asked, "So then how do you find your way back?"

Charlie looked at me again, eyes molten. I felt *seen* by him. Like all the layers separating life from death peeled away, and he gazed at the truest heart of me. His lips parted in answer, and my breath caught.

A piercing scream interrupted the moment, cutting through the forest all around us.

I shot out of bed, wide awake. "What the fuck was that?"

"I don't know," Charlie replied, striding over to look out the windows. His voice shook. "I can't tell which direction it came from."

We heard the scream again, and again. Three, four, five times. They were short, wordless staccato wails, like someone crying out for help. Charlie grew increasingly distressed with each.

"Reece, what do we do?" he cried, spinning around, as if searching for a way to make the sound go away.

Abruptly, they stopped.

Panting, we stared at each other in the near dark, panic-frozen in fear.

And then Charlie pointed at something over my shoulder. "There," he whispered.

I spun around. A light, bright against the inky darkness, bobbed and darted around below the tower. It was far enough away to be well into the trees, had we been able to see where they began.

And then I realized.

"That's a flashlight," I said, frantically tugging on my boots. I didn't bother lacing them. "It could be Janine."

"Reece, wait—" Charlie said, but I was already out the door.

"Janine!" I yelled, eyes darting around to find the light again as I rounded the tower toward the stairs. "Janine!"

I realized I'd forgotten my own light source when I reached the landing, the glow from inside the tower too dim to make out the steps ahead.

But then Charlie was there. "You'll trip and fall again, you idiot," he huffed.

We didn't have time to marvel that he'd done it—he left the tower.

Handing me the lantern I usually kept on my nightstand, he followed me down the stairs before we booked it for the tree line, barely illuminated ahead of us.

I'm definitely buying that high-powered torch.

The flashlight still bobbed ahead of us, too far into the trees to make out properly. "Janine, is that you?" I hollered.

As if in response, the light switched off.

Charlie put a hand on my shoulder and pulled me to a stop just before we entered the forest. "Wait," he said, panting. His face paled, and his outline flickered, pieces of him turning hazy and see-through. "Something's wrong, Reece. I don't like this."

"We have to help her," I answered, also struggling to catch my breath.

"We don't know if it *is* her. And I think I know—I mean, I think I *remember* what ha—pened—"

His eyes widened as his words became choppier. Frantic, he gripped my shoulder tightly, looking more and more frightened as he tried to communicate. "I can't—R—ce. You can't—*alone!*"

Fuck! He must not be able to get this far away from the tower. Or maybe it was the adrenaline?

Either way, I couldn't let him leave. "No, wait, Charlie—please, don't go. It's ok, we'll go slow. I'm sorry, please stay," I begged, trying to hold on to him.

But it was too late. He blinked away.

And I was left alone, in the dark, with whoever—or *whatever*—wandered through the woods in the middle of the night.

My panicked breaths were too loud in the hushed quiet.

A leaf crunched somewhere ahead of me, just outside the glow of the lantern. I swung it wildly, hoping to catch sight of whoever was out there, watching.

Predator, predator, predator, my instincts screamed.

"Janine?" I asked tentatively. My voice cracked. *I really fucked up.* I hadn't stopped to consider what I'd do if it *wasn't* Janine I found all the way out here, defenseless and alone.

And Charlie was gone.

He might not return for hours, or even days. I'd reacted without considering him at all, and whether he could handle the running and stress.

Another rustle of leaves, this time to my left. My heart pounded in my ears. I took a step back, and another. If it were Janine, lost and hurt, she would announce herself. She wouldn't do this... Whatever this was.

She wouldn't *stalk* me, like a predator.

Suddenly, footsteps pounded the ground, fast and loud as they charged.

Stumbling backwards, I turned and sprinted for the lookout, barely able to see anything. I could hear someone behind me, breathing heavily.

I kept running.

Reaching the stairs, I took them two at a time, uncaring of whether I slipped on the damp condensation. My boots crashed along the wrap-around deck. I slammed the door of the lookout shut behind me and threw the bolt into place.

Flicking off the lantern, I grabbed the can of bear spray.

Fucking useless, I thought. *What's bear spray going to do to a homicidal maniac?* Crouched down with my back against the opposite wall from the door, I waited.

Listened.

Everything was quiet. I was almost certain they hadn't followed me up the stairs, and the *thud* of their steps along the deck would give them away before they reached the door.

Wouldn't they?

Maybe they left.

I strained my ears, searching for any sound at all.

Crunch, crunch, crunch

There. Boots on the gravel behind me.

Then on my left.

In front, now.

On my right.

Behind me again.

They circled the tower.

Why would they do that? Why not come up here?

Maybe they weren't willing to risk it if I was armed? Or maybe, they'd realized I wasn't a small person and weren't confident they could overpower me?

I held my breath as they circled again, and again, and again. Boots crunched on gravel, steady, sure, and deliberate.

It felt like a message.

I know you're up there. I know you're all alone. I know you're afraid.

Frozen, I sat there. I should've found my phone, should've called someone, but I was stuck in place, terrified of making any noise in case it prompted them to climb the steps and attack.

Just as I convinced my muscles to unclench and stretched one leg in front of me to crawl across the small cabin in search of my phone, the sound of their steps shifted.

Scratch, scratch, scccraaatttchhhh

What the hell were they doing? I froze again, afraid to even breathe, terrified I'd drawn their attention with my movement.

Scratch, Scraaaatttchhh

For once, being high above everything else didn't make me feel comforted and safe—it made me feel trapped.

I wasn't sure how long I waited, listening to the shifting gravel before the cadence of their steps changed again and grew distant. Slowly, breaths shallow and trembling, I raised my head just enough to peek out the window. As I'd noted so many times before, I couldn't see anything in the dark.

Then, as suddenly as it'd gone out minutes or hours ago, the light appeared again.

It was a ways away from the tower already, moving at a steady clip back into the trees. I watched as it drifted farther and farther away, until it finally disappeared, swallowed by the inky blackness of the night.

I still couldn't move.

For whatever reason, they hadn't followed me up, and I didn't want to turn on a light to draw their attention and cause them to change their mind.

So I sat on the floor of the lookout for hours, praying they wouldn't come back.

And that Charlie would.

When the sun appeared over the ridge, burning away the damp condensation and fear glueing me in place, I stepped out onto the deck. The knots in my stomach clenched further at what lay waiting for me below.

LEAVE

Scratched into the dirt and gravel beneath the tower, dried, rust-colored streaks decorated each large, jagged letter like grotesque calligraphy. Splotches of the deep red liquid pooled in divots where a boot must've dug in too far.

Is that blood?

By the time I made it down the stairs, my hands shook so

violently I could barely grip the railing. This close, I could smell it; a warm, tangy rot that coated the back of my throat. I approached just enough to see bits of animal hair and viscera caked in the dried blood.

Lying nearby was the torn-up carcass of a bobcat.

The screams.

I turned away just in time to throw up all over the rocky ground.

Wiping at my mouth with the bottom hem of my shirt, I climbed back up the stairs away from the awful smell, took a few deep breaths to collect myself, and called Tate.

He swore when I briefly explained what'd happened last night. It was still early, and he sounded exhausted. "Are you alright? Are you sure you're alone? They didn't come back?"

I paced along the outer deck, scanning the trees and avoiding the gruesome sight below. "I'm sure. They could've broken in and didn't. They... left a message."

"A message? How? What does it say?"

"Check your texts," I said, snapping a picture of the scene and sending it his way.

There was a moment of silence, and then, *"Fuck."*

"Yeah."

"Is that a dead animal?"

"Yes. I think I heard them killing it last night. I thought it was a person screaming, but in hindsight, I've heard that before. I just panicked." My words caught in my throat. "I thought it was Janine crying for help."

He blew out a breath. "I'm sorry. Are you armed?"

"Only the bear spray."

He grunted. "That's right, how could I forget?"

Under different circumstances, it would've been funny.

His tone shifted from processing to planning. It was very *cop.* "You shouldn't hike out alone, and definitely not unarmed. I'll call the station to let them know what's happened and get search parties back out in that area. They'll have to come and process the scene. I'll ask Leonard how soon a helicopter can be available to pick you up. We'll come back for the rest of your things later, but you'll need to give a statement, and—"

"No, I can't leave. I'm not leaving," I interrupted, panic rising in my chest.

"What the fuck do you mean, you aren't leaving? You were attacked last night, Reece. Someone chased you out of the woods. You were *threatened.*"

"I know," I said. "I just..." I looked down at the awful message. I hadn't yet been forced to confront the true depths of their cruelty, but there was no hiding from it, now. If this was any indication, *missing* was too gentle a word to describe what those hikers had suffered.

"Look, you didn't hear this from me," Tate said before he paused, as if waiting for a response.

"Okay," I prompted.

"No, I need you to say you didn't hear this from me. You can't repeat this to anyone. Not Bobby, not your dad, *no one,* do you understand?"

I blinked, staring out at the low-lying clouds moving through the pass. "I understand."

He sighed. "What you just described, we think something similar happened to Janine, too."

Chills skittered down my spine. "What do you mean?"

"We know she used social media just after midnight, and didn't report for roll call the next day. We searched her tower and found her boots missing, but nothing else. Her phone was still on the charger, and her jacket was hung up inside. Nothing was disturbed. We think she left the tower willingly —to use the bathroom, or maybe she was lured out the way you were, I'm not sure, but it's too fucking similar for comfort. You *need* to leave. You can't stay out there, Reece."

I ran a hand along the beard I'd let grow out. Turning to pace back along the deck, I was startled to find someone standing just behind me.

Charlie.

He was gray and see-through. His face and hair were ashen, devoid of all color, his clothes the same as they always were.

Even down to his unlaced boots.

I blinked. The realization washed over me. I looked at my own shoes, still undone from our frantic flight to help Janine. The answer to Charlie's mysterious disappearance was right in front of me. It always had been. Charlie tried to stop me from leaving the lookout last night, and I didn't listen. He'd grown frantic and panicked, but disappeared before he could tell me why.

And I think I know—I mean, I think I remember what ha —pened—

Last night, had he remembered his final terror-filled moments? Was he so upset because he already knew what was about to happen? Was he lured out of the safety of the lookout, just like I was, only to be killed?

The brokenness in his eyes said yes.

"Reece? You there?" Tate asked.

"I'm not leaving," I repeated. I spoke the words into the phone, but they were meant for them both.

I couldn't leave. Charlie would be cold without a fire. We hadn't even celebrated his birthday yet.

Tate grumbled something under his breath that sounded suspiciously like *idiotic asshole.* "Did you hear what I just said? You might not have a choice!"

Charlie stared down at the scene below and turned away, passing through the wall and back into the lookout without acknowledging me. I'd only ever seen him do that once before, the very first time I saw him, when he'd pushed through the window to catch me before I fell.

The sight of it now knocked something loose in me.

"Listen to me," I growled at Tate, my lip curling in anger. "I was scheduled for an early supply run. I can either hike out on my own or wait for a helicopter to pick me up, but you can't tell me I'm not coming back here. I'm not listening to some fucked in the head freak. The next time they try to play games with me, I'll shoot them. I'm being paid for the whole fire season, and I'm staying for the whole fire season. Bring your search parties out here, scour the whole goddamn mountain for all I care. But *I'm not leaving.*"

He was quiet for a beat. "I'll call Leonard. Hopefully, a crew can pick you up this morning. Work out your return with him. I know you think I'm being an asshole, but I really am just worried, Reece. You shouldn't be in danger or stressed out over a job. It's not worth it."

I dragged a hand down my face. "I *need* to be up here, alright?"

"Why?"

I peered into the lookout to find Charlie sitting on the bed, with his head in his hands. "I just do."

I stayed outside long enough to call Dad and explain what'd happened, and let him know that I'd be back today. His stance was about the same as Tate's, but I said we'd talk about it later to avoid an argument.

Anxious to see Charlie, I paced back down the deck toward the door, looking for him through the windows. "Charlie?" I called, rushing inside. I scanned the room, as if there were somewhere for him to hide. "Charlie!"

The lookout was empty.

My sketchpad lay open on the desk, familiar handwriting scrawled across the page. In two strides, I crossed the room and picked up the note.

Reece,

It's not safe for you here anymore. I'm very sorry I wasn't there last night to help. The last thing I want is for you to end up like me. Thank you for being my friend and for making me feel human again. I'll stay away so they can help you move out. Please leave a window open for Randy when you go.

Charlie

I crumpled the note in my fist before smoothing it back out, tracing my finger over his words as I read again and again.

Thank you for being my friend and for making me feel human again.

Jaw clenched, my eyes welled up. "I don't know if you're still here," I said out loud, throat scratchy. "But you don't have to thank me for anything, because you've made me feel human again, too. You've made me laugh and remember what it feels like to look forward to things. I'm making you roasted chicken with crispy skin and peach cobbler when I get back. And it's your birthday dinner, so you'd better not stand me up."

The silence after weighed heavily. With a sigh, I readied to depart.

An hour later, I squeezed into the back of the helicopter with my trash and recyclables and watched as Dead Man's Lookout grew smaller and smaller the farther away we flew. Just before it disappeared from view, I swore I saw a flash of movement—like someone stood at the window, keeping watch.

I thought of the message I'd left behind, scrawled in big, bold letters along the bottom of Charlie's note.

IM COMING BACK

CHAPTER ELEVEN

Dad stood at the edge of the tarmac when we landed, arms crossed and face grim. He pulled me into a fierce hug the second I was far enough away from the helicopter blades, eyes blazing. "Are you okay?"

"Yeah, I am."

And I was. I mean, exhausted, sure, but in the harsh light of day, with the image of Charlie holding his face in his hands haunting me every time I closed my eyes, I wasn't afraid anymore.

I was angry.

Angry I hadn't listened to him and caused this mess.

Angry I'd sat in fear for hours instead of confronting the person who'd taken so many lives. Who, if my gut feeling was correct, had taken *Charlie's* life.

Angry all of this had been pinned on an innocent man whose laugh was far too bright to belong to a killer or a dead man.

Angry he thought it was better to say goodbye rather than risk my safety.

Most of all, though, I was angry he was dead at all.

"Come on inside," Leonard hollered over Dad's shoulder. He and Tate stood just outside the back entrance of the ranger station, waving us over.

"Are you sure you're up for this?" Dad asked as we headed their way. "You look upset. I'm sure Officer Morris will understand if you need to rest first."

The vein in my forehead throbbed. "I was treed like a fucking mountain cat last night. Yes, I'm upset. And no, I don't want to do this, but what choice is there? Let's get it over with so I can get to the grocery store to resupply."

His steps faltered. "You're going back?"

Dad had never pushed me into a decision. Becoming a Boy Scout was my choice, even though he was a troop leader. I'd decided to study Forestry in college because he shared his love for trees and the importance of protecting and managing public land with me; he'd never forced me into a career path of his choosing.

Maybe it was a holdout from trying to counterbalance Mom, but he'd always let me come to decisions on my own.

I could tell it was a struggle for him now, though.

"I am," I said firmly. We'd made it to where Tate and Leonard waited, so I directed my words at them all. "Please don't try to talk me out of going back. I won't let some creepy fuck keep me away. I feel... *good* at the lookout. It feels right to be there."

It shocked me to find that, despite my utter exhaustion and simmering anger over the night before, it was entirely true—I felt good. How long had it been since I'd thought about my health, or diagnosis, or fears for the future? Days? Maybe longer?

The lookout was good for me. *Charlie* was good for me, and I needed to go back as quickly as possible.

Dad studied my face before his forehead smoothed. Could he also sense the truth in my words? "You'll need to be in contact with someone every day. I can't go longer than that without knowing you're safe."

Leonard gaped at him. "Are you serious? You chewed my ass off for assigning him to that tower, and now you're fine with it?" He turned toward me, eyes pleading. "Reece, please, it's not worth it. I'll find work for you here at the station so you can stay in town."

"It's not about finding work," I said, agitated. "I want to be there. I *need* to be there. I finally feel—" I cut myself off.

Alive. I finally feel alive again.

Dad must have sensed the words I didn't say. "They won't return to the lookout with the search parties and police crawling all over."

Tate raised an eyebrow at him, but remained wordless. Observing.

"You have no other lookouts left on the west side of the park," I said to Leonard. "Can you really spare me?"

He ran a hand down his face, just as exhausted as the rest of us. "I don't want you out there if you feel threatened or unsafe. Anytime you need to go, call me, okay?"

"Thanks," I said. "I just need my supplies flown out tomorrow. I can hike in and meet the helicopter in the afternoon like I normally would."

He shook his head. "They won't have multiple lookouts to service, so you can catch a ride with them again. No sense in hiking through the woods alone if you don't need to."

"You can't go back out unless you're armed," Tate cut in firmly. He was quiet up until now, and again, I had the sense he was assessing, searching for something. "It's idiotic. I'm not saying you've gotta carry everywhere you go, but you need to be able to protect yourself."

I nodded. I'd feel better knowing I had something stronger than bear spray to defend myself with if they came back.

"I'll sort you out in that regard," Dad said, clapping a hand on my shoulder.

"Glad that's settled," Tate said. "Now, we're set up in a conference room in the back. Are you ready to give your statement?"

Brow furrowed, I asked, "Why not at the police station?" It was only a few minutes away, and I'd assumed Tate would prefer it over the ranger station, which was fairly busy in the summer months. It served as a main hub for Forest Service workers as well as tourists and backcountry hikers logging their routes through the national park.

Tate's face did something funny before he quickly schooled his features. "You'll be busy prepping to fly back out tomorrow, and we're already here. Might as well."

"Excellent. Glad I arrived just in time, then," a deep voice boomed behind me.

I whipped around to find a stranger sauntering our way.

A *huge* stranger.

He had dark, close-cropped hair and wore heavily tinted

sunglasses. His fitted black T-shirt only highlighted just how many muscles coiled around his broad shoulders. A sleeve of tattoos wound up his left arm, and his dark green ripstop pants clung in all the most interesting places.

Goddamn.

Tate scowled at him. "Oh, good. So glad you found the place."

He did not sound anywhere near *glad.*

The newcomer gave him a cool smile. "The directions you sent had me nearly out of town before I realized I must have read them wrong."

"It's easy to get turned around out here. Sorry about that," Tate replied.

I almost snorted at the dripping sarcasm.

"Luckily, there's a GPS in the SUV," Sunglasses said, before he turned to me. "Now, you must be the guy who got chased out of the woods last night. You had Tate here all worked up about it this morning. I'm Luke Waters, Special Agent."

I shook his offered hand and raised an eyebrow. "*Uh,* Special Agent?"

"He means FBI," Tate grumbled.

"The FBI's investigating?" Dad asked sharply.

Luke waved a hand. "I'm just here to scope out if we could be helpful first, before there's any official involvement. Shall we?" He finished, gesturing for us all to file inside.

I had a feeling there was more to it than that. The FBI was a lot of things, but *casually involved* wasn't one of them.

Shouldering past Special Agent Waters, who merely

smirked at his retreating backside, Tate led the way in. "Let's go," he grumbled.

I raised an eyebrow at Dad.

"I wouldn't get involved in that pissing match if I were paid to be there," he mumbled.

Jaw clenched, I sighed and followed them in. "Great. This'll be a blast."

Thirty minutes into the interview, their subtle digs and passive-aggressive snipes at each other were bordering on unbearable, right about the time my lack of sleep and hours spent crouched on the floor, frozen in fear, hit me like a freight train.

"After you ran back to the tower, how long did they stay outside? Did you confront them? Or get a look at them? A general height or sex, maybe?"

Yawning, I prodded my index and middle fingers into the spot at the base of my skull that throbbed like an ice pick chiseled into the soft tissue, trying to massage away the rapidly blooming migraine. "I've already said, I'm not sure how long it was. An hour? Maybe more? It was fully dark when they chased me from the woods, and they left before dawn. But their footsteps sounded heavy, like mine. I'm pretty sure it was a man."

Tate nodded, jotting down way more than I'd actually said in his notebook. He'd angled his body between me and the exit, and I couldn't shake the sense my words were being assessed as more than an eyewitness account of the killer.

"Right. He's told you all he can remember for now. It's time to go get some rest," Dad said, cutting off the next question. He eyed where I massaged my neck.

Special Agent Sunglasses narrowed his eyes. He hadn't been thrilled Dad joined me for the interview—*or interrogation*—but honestly, I was glad for the support. "Sure. If you can think of anything else, give me a call," he said, rummaging for a card before passing it to me.

Tate eyed the card. "He already has my number, ya know, since I'm the one on this case."

Sunglasses merely raised an eyebrow in answer.

The pain in my head shot down my left shoulder blade, pulling my neck tight like a rubber band. I'd struggled with terrible migraines in the first month or so after my diagnosis. *"Probably onset by stress,"* my neurologist had said, but they were less frequent now with the help of preventative medication.

I knew this one would be a bitch, though, with how fast it'd settled in. "I think I need to lie down for a bit."

Dad stood. "Do you have your meds with you?" he asked quietly.

Shit. I shook my head. "Left them back at the tower."

"We can see if the pharmacy here will fill the prescription for you. I'll give them a call on the way home."

Nodding, I made to stand.

"Just a sec," Tate said, putting a hand on my shoulder to keep me in place. "Can I ask you something in private?"

Sunglasses stared at Tate's hand before he sighed. "I'd

like a quick word with Mr. West, anyway," he said, gesturing for Dad to exit the make-shift interview room.

"You good?" Dad asked, glancing between me and Tate.

Not really, but I said, "Yeah, I'll be right out," anyway.

Dad followed the Special Agent out of the room, but left the door open behind him.

My head pounded. The overhead light was too fucking bright, and I grew nauseous in the stuffy room. Closing my eyes against the glare, I asked, "What do you want?"

Migraines and pleasantries didn't mix.

"Would you be willing to volunteer a DNA sample?" Tate asked, peering at me in that searching way again. I was fed up with how those looks made my skin itch.

"What the fuck is your problem?" Facial expressions hurt, so I tried to stay calm. "I told you the truth about last night. I didn't have anything to do with Janine's disappearance, and I haven't hurt anybody. Take my fucking DNA if you want it, I don't care. But why are you so insistent I've lied about something?"

He leaned away, eyes wide with surprise, as if he were shocked by my tone. "I'm doing my job. It will help us rule people out, more than anything. Do you *want* the person responsible for this to be caught?"

"Doing your job," I parroted with a humorless laugh. "If you were doing your job, you'd be out there, finding the real killer—not accusing innocent people. But that's happened here before, hasn't it?"

"What are you talking about?" he asked, eyebrows knit in confusion.

My head pounded, but once I'd opened the floodgates, I

couldn't stop. The rage that'd simmered since I left the lookout bubbled up and boiled over.

"The police were so goddamn sure Charlie—Charles Randolph, I mean—was the killer, but here we are! It's all happening again! And he was nice! Kind! What could he have possibly done to make them think he murdered six fucking people? Why couldn't they find him? Did they even look? Did they just leave him there, cold and alone, a convenient scapegoat? I know he spoke with a police officer that day—why wasn't he offered protection?"

"What the hell is going on in here?" Leonard asked, rushing in. "Maybe you should take this to the police station, instead of—"

"Do your fucking job," I said, cutting him off and pointing at Tate, "and figure out who the real killer is! Stop blaming me. Or else it's going to keep happening, all over again!"

I stood to leave. *Too quick.*

The floor shifted under me, nausea roiling in my gut.

"You're not thinking clearly. Are you ok?" Tate said, grabbing my arm to steady me. Leonard took hold of the other.

"I'm fine." I jerked out of their grasp and stumbled away. It felt like the ice pick was lodged through my head and out my left eye. The whole back of my skull throbbed. "I just need to lie down."

The floor shifted again, and suddenly I was on my ass, legs sprawled out and back braced against the wall. I could smell the warm, spoiled blood from earlier.

"Mike!" Leonard called out. "Something's wrong!"

His voice was garbled and far away. I couldn't open my eyes anymore—the overhead light was piercingly bright. "Turn it off, please," I groaned, shielding my face with both hands.

Dad appeared in the doorway. "What the fuck did you do?" Dad snarled. I felt him kneel next to me. "Reece? Are you alright? What's going on?"

I heaved in a deep breath so I wouldn't cry. "I don't know. I think it's happening again."

I didn't remember the drive back to Dad's. Once inside, he handed me a glass of water and some pain relievers before sending me upstairs to sleep in the dark, cool loft.

Lying under the blankets with an ice pack on the worst of my throbbing head and neck, I sent a handful of frantic messages over MyChart to my neurologist and then fell into a fitful sleep, tossing and turning the whole time.

She called me later that day and calmly explained this was more than likely just a migraine attack.

"Pseudo-flare-ups aren't uncommon, though. Patients with MS are particularly prone to temperature sensitivity, and symptoms lasting less than twenty-four hours after exposure to extreme heat should go away on their own without further intervention."

"So I could get double vision all over again if I get too hot?"

"Yes, but flare-ups aren't always the same as you've

previously experienced. You could experience new symptoms as well."

Great. *"It could be brand-new!"* wasn't exactly comforting.

"But I don't think that's what's happening, now. Hydrate, eat something filling and nutritious, and get some rest. We'll send your prescription to the pharmacy in Ponderosa. Take care, Reece."

Turned out she was right—it wasn't happening again.

The migraine knocked me out for three full days, though. In my dreams, I'd wake up hot and sweaty in the lookout, eyes scanning for Charlie. I'd wander through the woods, searching for him behind blood-coated trees and in dense piles of leaves. Chunks of animal hair clung to my hands as I dug through them, but I never found him.

His chair remained empty, and the blanket he usually had draped around his shoulders was sprawled at the foot of my bed, lifeless and unused.

CHAPTER TWELVE

ow, it's time to remove the spine.

Using your kitchen shears, start at the parson's nose and cut up through the ribcage along either side. Don't throw it out—save this yummy piece for stock!

"What the fuck is a parson's nose?" I mumbled, glancing back and forth between the video demonstrating how to spatchcock a chicken and the whole, raw chicken sitting on the counter in front of me.

None of it looked like a nose.

Now that we've got that part out of the way, flip the bird over, and...

"Slow down!"

The cheery British woman in the video did not slow down and began smashing the chicken flat against the counter with an alarming *crack!*

I reached for my phone to hit pause, only remembering my slimy salmonella hands at the last moment.

With a sigh, I gave in. "Hey, Siri, what is a parson's nose?"

The video paused while Siri considered. *"A person's nose is the organ that extends outward in the middle of the face between the eyes and the mouth. It is the first organ of the upper respiratory system..."*

"Jesus fucking Christ."

After cleaning my hands off with disinfectant wipes, I Googled what the fuck a parson's nose was, thoroughly studied the outright dismemberment involved in spatchcocking, and followed suit with my own raw chicken.

The whole process gave me the heebie-jeebies—*especially* after I'd returned to the tower to find the last of the crime scene investigators packing up their things, leaving me to kick rocks and dirt over the bloodied message that remained so I wouldn't have to look at it anymore.

I shuddered. What a terrible thing for any creature to die for. Hopefully, it'd at least been quick.

LEAVE

I shook my head, brushing off the weight of what it meant that I'd given the middle finger to the message and returned against literally everyone's wishes except my own.

But I'd promised Charlie a birthday dinner of roasted chicken with crispy skin and peach cobbler, so there I was, *spatchcocking*.

With the unpleasantness out of the way, I thoroughly seasoned the whole bird and popped it into the small oven before moving on to boil potatoes. The cobbler was already baked, set aside on the small kitchen counter to cool, and the ice cream waited in the utility shed freezer, along with all of my other groceries.

"How many weeks are you going to be out here before your next supply run?" the pilot had asked, looking somewhat perplexed at the sheer amount of food I loaded into the helicopter.

"I eat a lot."

She'd especially eyed the packs and packs of hot dogs, which I had *not* purchased for a mangy, beady-eyed raccoon. Charlie liked them, that was all.

She'd merely shrugged and prepared to fly out after we unloaded everything. Just in time, too, because it'd begun to hail a few minutes after she dropped me off. A slow-moving storm was forecasted to pass through over the next few days, with freezing rain, ice-cold wind, and even snow at this elevation.

Charlie could sit in front of the stove again this evening.

If he showed himself, that was. Which he'd better, because today was his birthday.

With a few minutes left until the chicken was ready, I dug his presents out of my bag. I had no idea what a good gift for a ghost was. He couldn't take anything with him when he left, so I wanted to give him something he could use in the lookout. But when I stopped thinking of ideas to give a ghost, and thought of *Charlie*, instead, I knew exactly what to get.

It only took a handful of thumb tacks and a bit of creative jerry-rigging to mount the small solar charge panel, and then the cabin was lit in a magical, soft glow from the fairy lights I strung above the windows all around. These wouldn't require power to operate and would stay lit well into the night.

I set the other small box on the desk for him to open later. "Are you here?" I asked into the quiet. The potatoes were mashed, and the broccoli was sautéed. All that remained was to carve the chicken.

No answer.

"Charlie, please come back. I've lit a fire and made dinner."

I paced back over to the note, unmoved from where I'd left it.

I'M COMING BACK

Had he even read it? Had he stood me up?

A half-laugh, half-groan burst out of me. "I will not be ghosted by a *ghost*. Come out! I spatchcocked a chicken for you."

"You did *what* to a chicken?"

I spun around. Charlie stood next to the fire, one hand fingering the blanket draped over the back of his chair. He was mostly all there, in the same flight jacket and pants he always wore, but the color in his face before I left was gone, leaving him gray and see-through.

"Hi," I said awkwardly.

"You came back," he replied, shy and quiet. A statement, yes, but also something more.

"I told you I would."

A promise.

He threw himself at me. Ghostly arms wrapped around

my middle, head tucked just under mine. Stunned, it took a few seconds before I realized what was happening, and then I gripped him tightly in return.

He was so cold, but his torso solidified in my arms until he felt real again, and I smelled the faintest hint of sun-warmed cotton sheets.

"I can't believe you came back," he repeated, voice thick with tears. "What a stupid, *stupid* thing to do."

I chuckled, but held him close. "I'm sorry it took a few days. I got held up."

The longer we clung to each other, the more solid he became, until I swore I could feel the barest hint of warmth radiating from him.

"I remember," he whispered into my damp shirt. "Not all of it, but enough. You really shouldn't have come back."

I pulled him closer, as if I held on tight enough, he wouldn't disappear again. "Do you want to talk about it?"

With one last squeeze around my middle, he stepped back and wiped his cheeks. "No. Not right now. I want to be here right now. I don't want to go away again so soon, if I can't—if it's hard to talk about. Later, though?"

He looked up at me, his brown eyes warm and soft and no longer gray. Fuck, he was beautiful with a bit of pink back in his cheeks and tears clinging to his long lashes.

Was it weird to think someone was a pretty crier?

"Sure. Later. Whenever you're ready." I cleared my throat, ignoring the confusing way my stomach swooped when he slowly blinked up at me, all vulnerable and needy. "*Um*, happy birthday!" I said, gesturing to the twinkle lights. "They're for you. So you're not stuck in the dark anymore."

He peered up and slowly spun around to take them in, something like awe on his face. His brown eyes glowed amber in the warm light. "You got me... lights."

I crossed my arms and uncrossed them, suddenly nervous. "They're solar powered, so they won't go out. You can turn them off if you want."

Charlie surveyed the messy disaster sprawled all over the small counter from my dinner preparation. I palmed the back of my neck. "*Uh*, yeah. Sorry about the mess. I'll clean up after. We should eat while it's warm, though. If you want."

He turned toward me again, eyes glassy. "You roasted a chicken for me?"

"*Spatchcocked* and roasted."

His eyes danced. "You've gotta stop saying that."

I nudged him forward, crowding him toward the stove. "Go on and fix your plate before I spatchcock you."

He grinned over his shoulder. "Don't threaten me with a good time."

I rolled my eyes. His responding laughter was bright and clear and warm against the sleet pelting the windows, and despite the danger lurking outside, I felt more at peace in this lookout than I'd ever been.

Or maybe it had more to do with the man who lived there.

"Favorite color?" I asked, spooning up what was left of the ice cream from my bowl.

"*Bwue,*" Charlie replied through a mouthful of cobbler before swallowing. "Song?"

"Impossible, I couldn't pick just one."

He narrowed his eyes and knocked his foot against mine. We sat side by side on the bed, leaning back against the wall. "It doesn't work like that. You have to answer."

"Fine. The *Braveheart* soundtrack."

"Is that a movie? *Braveheart?*"

My mouth dropped open. "Holy fuck, you haven't seen *Braveheart.*"

His eyebrow quirked. "In case you forgot, I was busy being dead for a while."

I could tell he was just trying to get a rise out of me. "I meant there's so much you haven't seen yet. So many good books and songs and television shows and movies you could read and watch and listen to now."

He fiddled with the duvet we sat on before peering up at me through his lashes. "Would you show it to me? If it's your favorite?"

My stomach swooped again. "Yeah."

"What about..." He blushed. "My sister and I went to see *Top Gun* in the theater together. She was the only other one who knew that I liked men, too, so it was fun to just enjoy it with her without worrying over whether it was obvious I was drooling the whole time. We went three nights in a row the week before I moved out here. Could we watch that one too?"

I cleared the catch in my throat. "Of course, I'll watch

Top Gun with you. After we're done, we can watch the sequel."

His eyes lit up. "They made another? With the same people?"

"Some of the same. It came out just a few years ago, so they're all older now. Goose's son is in it."

"Oh, Goose..." he sighed dreamily, sinking further down the bed. His legs dangled off the side. "That mustache did things to me."

I laughed and found myself running a hand over my beard. My eyes caught on the way his jacket and T-shirt rode up, exposing a strip of soft skin.

What did Charlie look like without all those layers on?

I coughed, reached over to grab our bowls, and carried them to the counter, busying my hands with cleanup before I embarrassed myself. What the fuck was I thinking?

My MS flare-up left me feeling like a lot of my body wasn't my own the last few months, and the boatload of steroids they'd given me hadn't helped.

I stressed over whether I'd simply slept on my arm wrong and caused my hand to fall asleep, or whether the fleeting numbness was a sign of something more serious. Sometimes I searched for a word for too long, wound up stumbling through a conversation, and dreaded that it wasn't just exhaustion or distraction.

I'd lost all interest in my career, even though this past Spring semester marked significant milestones I'd worked my ass off to achieve. My two master's students successfully defended their theses and graduated, and my tenure application was approved.

And I'd felt nothing.

My neurologist had warned me the stress from an MS diagnosis could impact my life in unexpected and significant ways, but with catching it so early and their swift action to begin treatment, I hadn't expected to still feel like so much was taken from me.

So, whether it was stress, a lingering effect of the flare-up, steroids, or because depression was often co-morbid with MS, I wasn't sure, but I hadn't had a sex drive in months.

Until now, apparently, at the sight of Charlie, happy and relaxed in my bed, with just a hint of skin peeking out. I felt a bit like a teenager all over again, desperately trying to hide an involuntary boner.

"So, *Top Gun* was your favorite movie?" I asked, readying the leftovers to take down to the fridge. I tried to think of anything that would make my half-chub go down.

Like health insurance, maybe.

Ahh, yes, works like a charm. Finally, something it's good for.

Charlie shrugged. "At the time, yeah. It's why Frankie got me this jacket. *It's cold in Idaho,* she'd said." He laughed. "I told her it wasn't cold in the summer. And now look," he gestured to the sleet-crusted windows. "Guess she was right."

His gaze grew distant, lost in his memories again, but the soft smile on his face told me they weren't sad, this time.

I left him to it and finished up the dishes before gathering everything we needed to store in the outbuilding. "I'm going to take this down and use the restroom. I won't be long," I said quietly, afraid to interrupt his introspection.

He blinked up at me before a serious look came over his face. "I'm coming with you. You shouldn't go alone."

Reaching for the shoulder holster Dad lent me, I looped one arm through and then the other, clipping it in place before holstering the gun he'd *also* lent me. "I wanted to be armed with something more powerful than bear spray, after what happened. This keeps my hands free," I said. I felt safer knowing I could protect myself if the killer came back, but I didn't want to freak Charlie out.

He stared at the gun for a beat. "Good," was all he said before he stood and grabbed a stack of Tupperware. "Let's go."

Our trip out of the tower was uneventful, but cold. Flurries of snow danced and shifted along the ground as violent gusts of wind bit at my nose and cheeks. My fingertips were chilled and aching by the time we hustled back up the stairs and into the warmth of the cabin.

"Fuck, it's cold," I said, holding my hands over the fire to warm them.

"I remember we had a snowstorm in June, too. It melted quickly, though. Sounds like this one might hang on for a few days longer."

"Mmhm."

Charlie settled back on the bed. I glanced over to find him watching me, staring at the holster still around my shoulders.

I pulled out the gun, ejected the clip, and ensured there wasn't a round in the chamber before padding over, tucking it into my nightstand drawer. "It's only for if they come back."

"I know," he said, still watching me.

"Does it bother you?"

His eyes tracked the holster as I shrugged it off, a dusting of pink across his cheeks. "No."

I was already in joggers and a cozy long-sleeve Henley, so I threw another log on the fire before joining Charlie back on the bed. Together, we breathed for a while into the quiet, listening to the ice and sleet pelt against the windows.

My eyes fell on the wrapped box sitting on my desk. I reached for it and handed it to him. "This is for you, too."

His eyebrows darted up. "Another?"

"It's not big, but I thought you could use them."

Tearing into the paper, he read the description on the box out loud. "Hand warmers?"

I bit my cheek, suddenly self-conscious of how small a gift it was. "Yeah. All you have to do is take the wrapper off, and they'll warm up." I shrugged. "Just in case your hands get cold."

Charlie was quiet for a moment. "Thank you, Reece," he whispered. "For these. For the lights, too, and dinner. It's all so thoughtful. And..." he wiped his eyes. "And for coming back."

My arms ached to wrap him in another hug. "Happy thirtieth birthday, Charlie."

His grip tightened around the box of hand warmers.

"Are you leaving again, after this?" he asked without looking at me.

Fuck. That wasn't at all what I intended the gifts to mean. I just wanted to give him things he could use without help. I took the box and wrapping and set them on the nightstand before angling my body to face him. "I'm staying for the season, Charlie. I'm not leaving anytime soon."

His eyes darted up in surprise. *Pretty crier.*

I stared at his soft, pouty mouth. "I have enough groceries for at least another three weeks, depending on how many hot dogs Randy eats," I grumbled to get my mind off the way those big, brown, doe eyes shot straight to my cock.

He shook his head, like he didn't believe it. "I don't want what happened to me to happen to you, too," he whispered.

"Are you ready to talk about it?" I asked gently.

He wiped his nose. "No, but I think I should. Now that I remember a little more, I think I need to. I just don't want to get worked up and disappear again." His voice trembled a little, but he remained solid next to me.

I shook out one of the blankets and threw it over his lap before scooching in next to him. "Then let's do what we can to keep you here. Get comfortable. Whenever you want to stop, we'll stop. And tell me how else I can help."

Charlie's brow creased. He leaned forward, and slowly, hesitantly, holding his breath as if he wasn't sure what would happen, slipped the jacket from his shoulders.

Together, we watched him drop it on the floor next to the bed.

"Wow," I said. I shouldn't be surprised; he'd eaten nearly

an entire meal tonight, but seeing him remove his jacket, the one he'd appeared in and worn for weeks now, was jarring.

"Yeah, wow," he breathed. "I didn't know I could do that. I thought I was stuck in those clothes forever, like some weird action figure."

"What happens to it when you disappear?"

He shrugged. "We could find out?"

I nodded, and before my eyes, Charlie blinked away, taking the jacket with him.

I hated the seconds he was gone. Every time he left, I couldn't shake the quiet, slithering voice that said he wouldn't come back this time.

One, two, three...

Blink. There he was again, standing next to the fire.

"It went with you," I said, gesturing to the jacket as if he wasn't wearing the proof of that fact.

"It did. How odd."

"Can you take it off again?"

He grinned at me, sly and coy. "Already? I just got here; the least you could do is offer me a nightcap first."

I rolled my eyes and pretended his light-hearted teasing didn't make my heart skip. "C'mon, enough experimenting for the evening."

"Your mixed signals are giving me whiplash."

"You're impossible."

"Not impossible. You just haven't tried hard enough yet."

I groaned and threw my head back in defeat. "You win. I'm shit at banter."

Charlie winked at me. "Practice makes perfect." But he did finally take off the jacket again and draped it over the back of his chair, before delicately toeing off his boots, as if afraid he wouldn't have feet inside.

"Cool," he breathed, wiggling his socked toes against the hardwood floor.

My mouth went dry at my first look at him without the extra layers. His T-shirt sat higher on his hip bones than the jacket did. Irrationally, I wanted to press my thumb into the just-visible divot above his waistband. More svelte than I'd realized, he was toned like a long-distance runner rather than my *let's make it through winter* build.

His forearm brushed against mine when he sat back down next to me, tucking the blanket around his legs, and I could actually feel his wood-stove-warmed body through the thin material of my shirt without the thick leather in the way.

Goosebumps danced along my skin.

"Comfortable?" I asked when he'd settled in, dutifully ignoring the slight crack in my voice.

"Yeah."

"Good." I panicked a bit in the ensuing quiet. Did he expect me to prompt him? How does one ask a ghost to talk about the way they traumatically died?

I reached over and took his hand so he'd have something to hold onto, in case he started to disappear again. "You don't have to say anything, but I'll listen if you're ready."

All of our carefree teasing gone, Charlie squeezed back and didn't let go. "I don't remember how I died, but I remember what happened right before," he began quietly. "I was asleep. Something woke me up..." his eyebrows creased, as if remembering. "It was just like a few nights ago, when we saw the light in the woods. There was someone outside the lookout, in the trees, and I went down to check who it could be. I thought maybe it was one of the missing hikers."

Icy chills skittered up my spine. "What happened?" I whispered.

"I called out to them, but they didn't answer. I kept walking toward that light, though. I thought they were lost, or hurt, or couldn't hear me. I didn't realize how far into the woods I'd gone until it suddenly shut off, and I couldn't se— anything." His breathing sped up, near hyperventilating. "I couldn't *see*, Reece. I wa—ost. I ne—ed to find my—back— tower. I heard—"

On instinct, my arm went around his shoulders and pulled him into me. "It's okay. Hey, it's okay. Take a deep breath. We can take a break."

He clung to me, cheeks wet again with tears. "Don't let me leave," he begged. "I can't be alone again. Not now."

My heart cracked open at the brokenness in his voice. How long had he gone with only those awful memories for company? "You're not leaving. You're staying right here. Ground yourself, Charlie. You're here. You're real. They can't hurt you anymore. I won't let anyone hurt you again."

After a few deep breaths, Charlie relaxed in my arms, but he didn't release his grip. "I only wanted to help," he breathed into my shoulder. "I didn't hurt anyone. I have no idea why the police said it was me, or what they found to make them think so."

I wanted to shred into every single person who'd allowed that farce of a narrative to spread, and scream that it wasn't true. This beautiful, warm-hearted man had been painted a villain for far too long. "I know. I know you didn't."

He wiped at his nose. "I don't want to talk about it anymore tonight. I can't really remember anything else, anyway, and I'd rather stay here, if that's okay."

I pulled him in closer. "Of course it's okay. It's been a long few days. Let's sleep on it, you'll feel better tomorrow."

Frankly, I didn't want to know how his story ended. If he remembered who'd been responsible, he would've said so. But without that, what difference did it make?

Charlie would still be dead at the end of it.

I shuffled around so I was lying with my head on my pillow, and pulled Charlie down so he lay next to me, pressed up against each other.

"Is this okay?" I whispered.

"Yes," he breathed.

It was intimate; more so than I'd been with anyone in a very long time, even before Josh and I broke up. I wasn't sure exactly when we'd crossed the line from platonic into something that brushed up against *more*, or when I'd allowed myself to admit I *wanted* to hold him like this, rather, but there was none of the awkwardness that usually came along with it.

It felt like Charlie was always meant to be tucked right next to me, curled into my warmth while the wind lashed sleet and snow against the windowpanes.

"Reece?" His words tickled the soft skin of my neck.

"Hmm?"

"Do you think that's why I'm still here? Because I haven't... fully faced it yet? What happened?"

Reflexively, my arm tightened around his shoulders. "I'm not sure. Truthfully, I don't even understand how you're here at all, let alone what might be keeping you. Is that what it feels like? That there's still something you have to do?"

He was quiet for a long while. So much so, I'd contented myself that he wasn't ready to answer, but then he said, "For so long, it felt like I couldn't leave this lookout. It felt like I was trapped. Now, though, I wonder."

"What do you wonder?" I whispered into the space between us.

"I wonder if I was only waiting."

I couldn't vocalize the burning ache that bloomed in my chest at his words, but I could hold him close, and I could keep him warm.

So I did. All night long. Because there was a part of me, one I was too afraid to even silently acknowledge, that wondered if I'd been waiting, too.

CHAPTER THIRTEEN

"Who is *that*?" Charlie asked as he shoved a handful of popcorn into his mouth.

"Glen Powell," I grumbled.

"And him?"

"Miles Teller."

"Wow..." he sighed dreamily. "It really is that damn mustache, isn't it?"

I rolled my eyes and hid a smile. It would've rankled more if Charlie wasn't scooched right up against me, tucked into my side under our shared blanket.

We were off lookout duty for the day, and probably tomorrow, too, due to near-whiteout conditions throughout the mountain pass. We radioed in our weather data reports as normal, but there was no sense in being on the clock when I couldn't see a foot past the railing.

This storm would probably go down in the record books for June snowfall, but I'd always remember it as the day

Charlie and I watched a movie together for the first time. He'd loved seeing *Top Gun* again, all these years later. We'd stayed in bed all morning, snacking on popcorn and M&Ms before I made ramen for lunch.

Once we moved on to the sequel, though, I could tell something bothered him. As the ending credits rolled, he side-eyed me. "Does it bother you that I'm like, old?"

"Huh?" I asked, taken aback.

"While it was fun to actually celebrate my thirtieth birthday with you yesterday, in reality, I'm old enough to be your dad. I would look like them," he gestured to the aged pictures of the original cast.

I blinked a few times. "Honestly, I've never considered it before," I answered. "I mean, I wondered if you knew my dad. He was a pilot for the Forest Service during your summer out here."

"Oh? What's his name?"

"Mike West. He's never mentioned knowing you, but ya know..."

"He might not want to own up to being friends with a serial killer?" he finished with a raised eyebrow.

I cringed. "Something like that."

Charlie waved his hand. "It's okay. I understand. No, really," he said, noticing I was ready to cut in and apologize. "I'm not angry at the way people responded to those accusations. I can't say I would've done differently in their shoes, especially to a stranger."

I pulled up a picture on my phone of Dad and me, side by side with matching grins on our faces. Charlie took hold of it gingerly, in that awkward way that suggested he had no idea how to use modern technology.

"No," he said after a few seconds. "He doesn't look familiar. I wasn't really friends with any of the pilots."

Nodding, I took it back. "I'm sorry if the movie upset you. If it makes you feel better, technically, I'm four years older than you. So really, I'm the old man here."

"Grumpy enough to be," he faux-grumbled, eyes twinkling. "So it doesn't bother you, then?"

I let my arm drop around his shoulders, soothing his opposite shoulder. "No, Charlie. It doesn't bother me. I wonder sometimes..." I stopped, unsure whether he'd want to go there.

"What?"

"I wonder what you would've done with your life; if you would've stayed in Ponderosa, maybe had a family. I wonder if our paths would've crossed differently."

His face grew soft and pensive.

"I'm sorry," I said quickly. "I shouldn't have brought it up."

"No, it's okay. I can't really picture that other life. I was very angry for a long time that I didn't get to have it, whatever that unknown future was, but..." he shrugged and fussed with the blanket sprawled over our laps. "I'm not angry anymore, Reece. And I think you and I were always going to meet each other, somehow."

I stared at his mouth. "I think so, too," I whispered.

Charlie eyed me as well, lingering on my shoulders and chest before he dragged his eyes away. "So," he said, clearing his throat, "can we watch *Braveheart* now?"

I grinned and dug into the popcorn bowl perched on his lap. "Buckle up, baby. It's a doozy."

"I can't believe you can watch any movie you want, whenever you want. How are they all in there?" Charlie asked after we finished, pointing at my laptop suspiciously.

"Well, they aren't like downloaded onto the computer. They're on a streaming platform you subscribe to, or you can rent one."

He looked at me like I'd spoken a new language. "How, though?"

"*Uhh...* That's a good question. I have no idea how the internet works. Satellites, I think? It just does," I answered, shrugging.

"Is that how the other thing you have works, too? The one that's also a phone?"

I nodded. "Yeah, that's the internet, too. It doesn't usually work so well this far out in the middle of nowhere, but I have a signal booster and a hotspot set up, so I have internet access. Mom would've flipped out if I couldn't communicate with anyone all summer."

"I couldn't," he said with a shrug. "I mean, we had the radio to communicate with the ranger station and other lookouts, but otherwise we didn't talk to anyone unless they hiked out."

I shuddered. "I don't know how you handled that. I'd

probably go crazy without being able to talk to anyone for that long."

"It was nice for a little while," he answered quietly.

Time to change the subject. "It's not just movies and shows we can find, though. There are books, articles, and other videos people make that aren't movies, like entertainment and funny home movies, and stuff. You can email or message people, like sending letters through the internet," I added, at his confused look. "There's, well, there's *everything*. It's the internet."

He cocked his head. "How do you know who you're sending messages to?"

"Well, if you know their email address or you're friends on social media, you can message them directly. Otherwise, you look them up."

"Social media?"

I groaned. "I'm really bad at explaining all of this. I'm sorry. It's like, you have a page, a *place* that's yours, where you can put pictures or messages, and you can interact with other people through their page."

Charlie squinted at me. "Hmm. I think that's enough technology for today," he said before yawning. "And I need to go rest, anyway."

He'd slept next to me the night before, or whatever version of sleep he was capable of, but it was clear so much time in this form wore him out.

"Okay," I said with a stretch, feeling surprisingly exhausted myself for not moving all day. "How long will you be away?"

"Not long, I don't think. I just need to recharge. I don't

feel time passing in the normal way when I'm like that. It's like things just shut off. But I don't think it'll be long before I feel good enough to come back. Maybe tonight," he finished hopefully.

I watched him get out of bed. "Alright. Tonight."

Smiling warmly at me, he waved. "See you soon, Reece."

And then he was gone, leaving me to count the seconds until he returned.

For the rest of the afternoon, I took advantage of Charlie's absence by scrubbing myself clean with some hot water and a washcloth, and then I pulled out the shaving kit to tame my beard.

Moving in slow, practiced passes, I lathered my face up and shaved my cheeks clean, thinking about Charlie all the while.

I considered what he'd said about not missing the life he could've led anymore, and the way his cheeks had flushed the barest pink when we'd woken up next to each other earlier that morning, warm under the shared covers.

The dimples that'd appeared the first time he threw his head back laughing flashed through my mind, and my skin heated at the memory of how soft and inviting his lips looked when he'd sucked a bit of melted chocolate off his thumb.

Cheeks and chin done, I paused with the razor hovering over my upper lip. Tilting my head from side to side, I peered at my reflection in the small shaving kit mirror.

It really is that damn mustache, isn't it?

Rinsing off the razor, I set it aside and picked up the trimmer instead, shaping the scraggly mess into something that made me look even grumpier than I already did. I'd never tried a mustache before, but despite it solidifying my old-man status, I didn't hate it.

In fact, I didn't hate the man staring back at me at all. The Thing remained quiet in confirmation.

Between all the stairs I climbed every day and the light tan I'd gained from being back out in the sun, I looked healthier than I had in years. It wasn't just a sharper jaw and some color back in my face, though. There was almost... recognition.

Hello, old friend.

Maybe I'd avoided looking in the mirror for so long because I was afraid I wouldn't know the person staring back at me.

Sighing, I rinsed and brushed out my new mustache, leaving it for now. I could always shave it off if I decided I didn't like it later.

Or if Charlie doesn't like it.

Feeling a bit raw, I called and talked with Mom for a few minutes. I texted Bobby, too, and ignored a phone call from Tate. We hadn't spoken since the disastrous way the interview ended, and I had a feeling he was following up on that DNA sample.

I didn't give a fuck if he had my DNA or not, but I wasn't particularly keen on talking to the guy just yet. Besides, it'd be a while before I was back in town.

Busying myself with tidying up the cabin, I realized I

was already jittery for Charlie to return. It was an odd thing, really. I wasn't antisocial by any means, but there'd always been a limit to how much time I could spend with others, even friends and family.

And that was still true. I had time to myself when Charlie was away. I even felt like I had time to myself when he was in the same fourteen-by-fourteen-foot room with me —we worked remarkably well just existing near each other.

So when I tumbled back into bed with a huff, cabin clean and wondering what else I could do to fill the time, it hit me.

I *missed* him. I missed him so much; it was ridiculous for only having been apart for a few hours.

I wanted to feel him next to me again, pressed close while our chests rose and fell in sync. I wanted to watch his pupils dilate while he stared a little too long at my shirt pulled tight around my arms and pecs. I wanted Charlie.

I *wanted.*

Suddenly heavy-lidded and hot, I was finally glad to be alone as I fumbled underneath my bed one-handed in search of the lube I'd stashed away before tugging off my shirt and lying back against the sheets.

It'd been forever since I felt desire so strong—it hit me like a ton of bricks. I chose not to look too closely at why my body was finally reactive to pleasure again after being dormant for months and months, and just enjoyed it.

I ran a hand along my chest and belly, catching in the hair that covered me. Would Charlie's hands feel soft against my skin, or calloused and rough?

It didn't matter; the thought of him touching me at all made me hard, regardless.

Slowly, I pushed my pants and boxer briefs down. Palm slick and warm, I took my cock in hand and pumped until my breath caught, relishing the syrupy ache.

"Fuck," I groaned softly.

Mind empty, I let my body feel the sensations that were out of reach for so long. Thumbing the tip, I gently squeezed and pushed up into my tight grip, my other hand tweaking a nipple. I held the pressure, then pulled back.

My head buzzed, warm and fuzzy. *Thrust. Hold... Release.*

Over and over, faster and faster. My nipples grew too sensitive, so I reached down to massage my balls instead, tugging on them every few thrusts.

"*Mmmph.*" I'd never been much of a bedroom talker, but I was vocal, and even more, I loved hearing the sounds I could push out of a partner.

What would Charlie sound like, grinding up against me, with my tongue down his throat?

"Oh, fuck." I was close. I debated edging myself for a while longer, wanting the pleasure to last forever, but I also wanted to come.

Now. Right now.

Head tipped back into my pillow, I tunneled into my grip even faster. Briefly, I considered pulling up an old, reliable porn scene I'd watched more than a handful of times, but my cock was too hard and my slick hand felt too good.

Good. I finally felt *good.*

Pleasure quickly peaking, I rolled over, braced my weight on one forearm, and reached back down to fist my cock again.

I couldn't go slow anymore.

Grinding into the sheets, I shoved my face into a pillow to drown out my grunts and pictured Charlie's lips wrapping around my thumb instead of his own, sucking on my fingers while I milked the most delicious moans out of him.

My face scrunched up with each thrust of my hips, rutting into my slick fist while I imagined the gasp he'd make if I had his cock in my hand, too, jerking us together. I bit into my pillow, wishing it were his shoulder instead.

So good. So, so good.

I felt like... myself. Muscles loose and relaxed, I'd forgotten how much *fun* it was, and Charlie would be back soon, and I couldn't drag it out anymore, couldn't stop fucking into my hand even if I wanted to, and—

"*Ah!*" I cried out, cum spurting all over the sheets. I gripped my length hard while the shockwaves rolled through my body, wobbly-kneed from the force of it.

Panting, I collapsed to the side, avoiding the mess as much as possible, and threw an arm—the one that wasn't covered in cum and lube—over my eyes to catch my breath.

Holy shit.

Loose-limbed, sated, and brand new, a chuckle bubbled out of me. I was sweaty, sticky, and the whole cabin smelled like sex even though I'd just cleaned.

It was wonderful.

I spent the rest of the afternoon in a daze.

The storm hadn't eased; if anything, the wind only picked up speed, throwing sleet and snow harder against the lookout exterior, rattling the windowpanes. I debated closing the westward-facing shutters, but the deck was a slippery hazard even without the near-straight-line winds threatening to throw me off.

I was used to the sway and rock of the tower by now, but the creaks and groans coming from the support beams in this storm were concerning. It provided a sense of security I was thankful for, though. The chances of surviving this storm out in the elements were low, so I could breathe easy, at least for a day or two, knowing that if anyone had been lurking in the trees, they weren't anymore.

It also meant Janine was most certainly dead by now, even if her disappearance hadn't been foul play. It weighed heavily on me.

To keep my mind off it all, I curled back up in my freshly changed bed and lazily sketched some of my favorite things from memory.

A Cedar Waxwing perched on a juniper branch, with a berry in its beak.

The way raindrops cling to pine boughs after a cold, autumnal shower.

That smudged shadow just beneath Charlie's cheekbone.

I drew that one a lot.

I could excuse my newly reinvigorated libido as a series of lifestyle changes and the time that'd passed since my flare-up—even if the last few days hadn't exactly been stress-free.

What I couldn't ignore, though, was the tidal wave of *Charlie Charlie Charlie* my thoughts had become since I returned to the lookout.

As if the floodgates had flung open, he was nearly all I could think about.

I wanted his name vindicated, wiped clean from the mouths that had slandered him for so long.

I wanted to find the one who'd hurt him, who'd killed him. I wanted to punish them, to make them feel the decades of pain and loneliness he'd felt.

I wanted to protect him and shield him from any additional hurt.

Even more, I wanted him to smile again, every day. I wanted him to laugh and jest and tease me. I wanted to be on the losing end of his quick wit and watch his eyes go soft with words he wasn't ready to say just yet.

I wanted him to see every movie, read every book, and listen to every song he'd missed. I wanted him to have the park ranger job he'd moved here for, or anything else he decided he wanted. I'd fight and claw through whatever obstacle presented itself to give it to him.

What I wanted most, though, so much my soul burned with it, had been hidden in plain sight for far longer than I realized. Maybe even since that first conversation, when he'd asked if he could warm himself next to my fire.

I wanted Charlie to be alive, and I'd do just about anything to make it so.

CHAPTER FOURTEEN

The storm wailed its last breath a few days later, leaving behind dirt-crusted, melting ice and a skating rink on the deck.

"I fucking hate scraping snow," I growled, unlacing my boots and kicking them off by the door. "Especially when it's nothing but a sheet of ice. I get all worked up and sweaty, hot as hell under my coat, but my hands freeze."

Charlie glared at me. "Then why did you go do it by yourself?"

"I had to clear a path to the stairs."

He rolled his eyes. "I've already saved you from falling off that deck once; it was rude to make me do it again."

"I didn't fall. I slipped, that's all."

"Which would've led to *falling* had I not shown up right when I did. You should've waited for me, I told you I'd be back this morning."

I raised an eyebrow, sliding into my Crocs. "I had to take

a shit. What else was I supposed to do? Squat over the wash basin?"

He spewed the warm tea he'd just gulped down, some of it coming out of his nose. "You're an animal," he choked out, coughing.

I winked at him, sauntering closer. "You like it."

"I should've pushed you over instead of saving you," he grumbled, crossing his arms.

Ok, so maybe it wasn't smart to antagonize the guy who'd stopped me from sliding into the railing a *second* time that summer, but he was so cute when teased, I couldn't help myself.

"You'd miss me too much. And my mustache," I said lowly, leaning down into his space just a touch more than strictly necessary.

My flirting skills may have been rusty, but it hadn't taken much to warm up. I couldn't really help myself where Charlie was concerned, which should've bothered me more than it did.

Honestly, I didn't care. I just wanted to see... *There it is.*
He blushed.

It looked so real, so *alive,* I wanted to press my thumb into the color and feel the heat bloom across his cheek.

He'd nearly swallowed his tongue when he reappeared a few nights ago to find that I'd shaved, and had barely been able to stop looking at me since. His eyes were a near-constant, welcome weight wherever I went.

"I'd still prefer Randy," he sniffed, staring at the *V* of sweat at the collar of my shirt. "What's for lunch?"

I snorted, grinning. "Someone woke up on the wrong

side of the bed. Let me warm up my hands, and then I'll figure that out, grouchy pants."

He sucked in a breath and leaned into the contact when I brushed past on my way to the kettle of hot water.

The last few days were tension-filled torture. I'd already admitted to myself I wanted him, and if it was just a physical thing, I probably would've made a move by now and asked if he felt the same.

Judging by his heated glances when he thought I wasn't looking, he did.

It wasn't just about releasing pent-up tension, though. There was so much more to what I felt every time he reappeared after being away for a few hours at a time, and it was terrifying.

Realistically, though, I wasn't even sure if we *could* be together.

Setting aside the giant gaping canyon of, well, "*How do you have a relationship with a dead person?*", what were the logistics of intimacy with a ghost? Did he feel desire? Pleasure? Would his body respond as it would've when he was alive? Could he orgasm? Would he ejaculate?

He could eat and cry, so there was some sort of bodily function situation going on. Everything else, though, was a mystery.

I'd already stopped myself from looking it up. I didn't need "*Can ghosts have sex?*" haunting my digital footprint.

I'd searched whether they could come back to life, though.

Nearly light-headed with an emotion I couldn't place and out of my mind, I scoured the internet for credible information on whether anyone else had befriended a ghost, fallen in—*nope*—deep companionship, and figured out a way to bring them back.

As if a Stack Exchange thread existed for the minor inconvenience of death.

"Hi, I received an error message when I tried to bring my dead friend back to life. Any help solving the issue?"

It was ludicrous.

Millions, no, *billions* of people throughout history had lost husbands, wives, children, siblings, parents, friends, pets, and wished they could bring them back. Some would've given everything, even for a chance to speak with them, one last time. Why did I think our situation would be any different?

I'd slammed my laptop shut, tossing it aside.

Because Charlie is different, I thought. *Because he shouldn't even be here the way he is now. Why can't I bend the rules just a little more?*

Still, I couldn't shake the questions, weaving in and out of my periphery in a near-constant tangle.

Would Charlie want to come back if he could? How would it work? Where would he want to go? Who would he want to spend his time with?

I poured a bit of the hot water from the kettle into a bowl, lost in thought. Bringing the temperature down just enough to be comfortable with a splash of cool water, I submerged my hands, sloshing them around.

"Why do you do that?" Charlie asked, padding up behind me.

He'd changed into a pair of thick wool socks, joggers he'd

cinched around his waist, and a shirt that was way too big for him. He clearly enjoyed changing out of the clothes he always appeared in, and I wasn't ready to admit how much I loved seeing him in mine.

"When my hands get cold, they slow down, and it's harder to move them like normal. The fastest way to warm them up is hot water."

He cocked his head. "What do you mean, slow?"

I hadn't told Charlie about my MS. Mostly because it'd never come up, but also because it made me feel ungrateful to complain to a dead person about a disease I wasn't dying from, and would hopefully remain in remission for a very long time.

Even if it didn't, moaning about being alive to someone who wasn't felt in poor taste. He'd asked, though, and it wasn't like it was a secret.

"I was diagnosed with multiple sclerosis back in January. It seems to be under control for now, but ever since then, I get terrible migraines if I don't sleep enough or get too stressed about things. And it takes my hands longer to do things when they get really cold. The doctor said it's probably just stuff associated with MS that I'll live with," I said, indicating where my hands sloshed around in the warm water. They already felt better.

"Oh..." he said. Grief marred his face. He leaned hard into my shoulder, mirroring the way I might've comforted him if our positions were reversed. "My uncle had MS. Reece, I'm so sorry."

"It's not like it was before," I said quickly, staring down at the bowl in front of me while I slipped into the usual pattern of conversation. "The progress that's been made in the last ten—hell, even *five*—years is remarkable. I'm on a strong treatment plan. It's not what you're probably picturing. I'm lucky they found it so quickly; it should help slow down the progression. Maybe. Hopefully."

I kept rambling, feeling his eyes on my face. "I mean, I could go years without anything bad happening again. And even if it does, there are options."

Quiet yawned between us, the *woosh* of water running through my fingers the only sound besides our breathing.

"Look at me?" he whispered.

By now, I recognized I'd do just about anything he asked.

"I'm glad for all of that," he whispered when my eyes met his. "That there are options and treatments and doctors and all of it. And I hope it works for you as best it can. But I'm still so sorry."

I nodded. The genuine sorrow on his face was difficult to look at. "Thank you."

Almost. I almost left it, but the words were right there on the tip of my tongue, and instead of swallowing them back like usual, my shoulders dropped, and I let them out.

"I hate talking about it," I said with a huge sigh. I already felt lighter.

Charlie nodded, understanding. Always understanding.

"I resent that I have to," I continued, emotions I'd struggled to put words to suddenly clawing to be set free. "And I resent that it's my burden to fucking process now. To tell people about. I didn't ask for this. I can't look back at a past action and assess how to do it differently in the future for a better outcome. I can't change it, so why do I have to make it mine? To let it consume every thought I have of the future? It taints everything, and I *hate* it."

Tears streamed down Charlie's face, and I realized I was crying too. I gritted my teeth and continued. "I hate burdening others with it, but sometimes, when my migraines get too bad, I literally can't do things. And then I think I'd actually prefer to have a gaping wound in the back of my head instead, so I at least wouldn't have to explain why I feel like shit or can't do my job or feel like I hate everything."

Charlie's arms wrapped around me in a hug, squeezing tightly.

For a moment, I tensed, stepping away. "I'm sorry. I shouldn't complain to you about it. It's not—"

"Please complain to me about it," he interrupted, breathing into the crook of my neck. "I want to hear it. I want you to let go."

Without my permission, my own arms came up to hug him back, holding just as tightly. A sound I'd never heard myself make wrenched from my chest, like re-breaking a botched and badly-healed fracture—raw and angry and vulnerable and hurt, but necessary to set the bone.

"I *don't* hate everything," I sobbed. "That's the worst part. I don't resent my family's care and love; they mean more to me than I could ever say. It's like... It's like this *Thing* wandered into my house and sat down in my living room, and now I have to take care of it. Even when it treats me like shit, and gets in the way of my relationships, and keeps me from ever feeling like I'd be someone somebody could want— because who would? Why the fuck would you sign up for me *and* the Thing I'm forced to carry around everywhere? I hate it. Why wouldn't you? I wish it weren't there. I wish I didn't have to manage it and explain it away and make excuses for it. And I wish I wasn't worried *all the time* I was going to take one wrong step and set it off all over again."

My chest ached from giving life to the feelings I'd shoved away for so long, and speaking aloud about the Thing I'd felt squatting on my shoulders for months and months. I wasn't sure how long we stood there, holding each other while I cried out my demons.

"C'mon," he eventually said, leading me to the bed. "Sit down. I'll make lunch."

"No, it's fine. I already feel better after getting that out. I can do it."

"I know you can, but it doesn't mean you have to. Let me take care of you."

And so Charlie made us ramen, while the Thing and I sat in bed and watched.

I felt a bit like a wet towel that'd been wrung out and run over, but there was a peace in my soul I hadn't felt since long before that awful day I was left in the airport.

The Thing was still there, right beside me. It always would be. And I'd continue to battle it, probably for my whole life. But watching Charlie pad around, softly humming to himself while he stirred the noodles and fried eggs and drizzled just the right amount of hot sauce into my bowl before handing it to me, I realized something.

The curtain of my fear and resentment had been pulled aside just enough so a tiny sliver of light peeked through. Finally, I could see what I hadn't before, stumbling around in the dark for so long.

The Thing was scared and lonely, too, and looked an awful lot like me.

"I make better ramen than you," Charlie said, slurping up the last of his broth.

Hiding a smile behind my own near-empty bowl, I pretended to scowl. "It's ramen. What'd you do, boil the water differently?"

Charlie rolled his eyes. "You have to let the eggs fry long enough to get good and crispy around the edges. You rush them, you impatient man."

I couldn't hide my grin anymore. "Yes, Chef."

"Huh?"

"We have *so* much television catching up to do," I sighed.

He took our dishes and set them on the counter, shaking his head in amusement. "Favorite place you've ever been?"

We played this game a lot—trading each other's favorites back and forth with no rhyme or reason for when the questions began or ended.

"Besides here?"

He cast a look back at me like he'd thought I was kidding and then softened. I still felt raw and flayed open from earlier, like every vulnerable thought I had would come spilling out as soon as it crossed my mind, but when he looked at me like that, I didn't feel like I needed to seal myself back up.

"Yeah. Besides here," he whispered, wandering back over to where I sat. He stood just out of arm's reach.

"New England in the fall, just as the leaves turn. The orange—it's shocking to see in nature, almost like it's not real—is my favorite color."

He sighed wistfully. "I've never been there. And that's two favorites."

"Then I get two questions of my own, don't I?" I asked, that unnamed emotion fizzing up and making my stomach swoop.

He scooted forward a step, just enough so our knees brushed. "I suppose."

I searched his face, brightly lit in the midday sun, and hale. Whole. *Real.* "Would you want to go with me if you could? To see the leaves turn in the fall in New England?"

He sucked in a breath. "*Reece.*"

We hadn't done this yet; we hadn't directly addressed what I'd dwelled on for days. Weeks. "Two answers, Charlie."

Eyes glassy, he swallowed, and his outline glowed just a touch brighter than normal. "Yes," he whispered, "I'd go with you to see the leaves change. I'd go with you anywhere. New England, California, even *Missouri.*"

I snorted and reached out to hook my fingers in the waistband of his pants, pulling him closer between my legs. "Now, that's pushing it. Missouri? Really?"

He smiled and cupped my face. "Really. And I might even enjoy it, too. You're pretty fun to be around, you know?"

"You're just saying that."

His face grew serious. "I'm really not." He swallowed, his form flickering the tiniest bit before solidifying again. "I don't have the words or ability to fix the things that've happened to you, or to assure you nothing will ever go wrong again. It might, or it might not. But I do know, Reece, I wouldn't change anything about you. Not a thing. Not ever."

Intentional or not, his words were the softest, most gentle blow to any remaining restraint I still possessed. I stood, tightly banding an arm around his waist because I couldn't stand the thought of not touching him anymore.

Chest to chest, firm and warm, I peered down at him. "I'm going to ask my second question now."

Charlie swallowed. "Okay."

I cradled his face in my free hand, tipping his jaw up so his mouth was right there, a scant breath from mine. I ran my thumb along his bottom lip ever so gently. "Can I kiss you?"

His lips pursed into the pad of my finger, eyes heavy with want. "Yes."

Slowly, I leaned down and brushed my lips against his in a featherlight touch. A zap of energy shot through me, sharp and bright, and I pulled away just enough to look at him, searching. Had he felt it, too?

His eyes darted between mine, honeyed whiskey turned syrupy with arousal.

Our mouths crashed together.

He tasted like the first refreshing glass of iced tea on a hot summer day, and I drank him in, parched and needy. I dug my fingers into the small of his back to keep him close. It was electric, like energy flowed between us in a closed current of conduction and need so hot it burned. I swore I could feel the faint beat of his heart through my shirt.

"Reece," he breathed when we parted, shoving his fingers into my hair. "I want—"

"I know," I panted. "Me too."

I hauled him against me, crowding him backwards until he bumped into the far wall of windows with a *thud*. His hands were wild, gripping my back and ass and yanking me hard against him.

When he dropped his mouth open, inviting me in, I *took*. With one hand braced against the glass, I wrapped my other palm around the front of his throat and tipped his chin up for the perfect angle.

He groaned into the kiss, gripping the sides of my face in return, and I went light-headed with need.

I couldn't help but paw at him, roaming my hands over his shoulders, chest, and stomach until it was my turn to grab him by the hips and tug so there was no space between us at all.

Like this, with all of our shared heat, it was so easy to forget he wasn't alive—that he wasn't mine to hold forever.

"Fuck," I panted, dropping a line of kisses along his cheekbone, behind his ear, down the length of his neck. "Do you know how long I've wanted this?"

"Probably not as long as I have," he panted, before gripping the collar of my shirt and pushing me backwards so I was the one retreating, all the way until the backs of my knees hit the bed and I tumbled down, knocking into the window.

"Not possible," I growled, gripping his hips when he climbed onto my lap to straddle me.

Charlie blanketed over me, burying his face in my hair, neck, and chest. "Possible..." he breathed. I would've argued some more if he hadn't continued, "Hold me, Reece? Don't let me disappear."

The request was so needy, so vulnerable, like admitting he wanted to stay, that he wanted something beyond what he'd never thought he'd have again, cut him open, too.

In answer, I banded my arms around him and yanked him close.

We were both hard. Feeling the stiff length of him through our joggers had me crying out to reach down and pull us both out for some much-needed relief, but he trembled and flickered, face hidden in the crook of my neck.

"Hey," I whispered, pressing kisses into his hair. "Are you okay? We can stop. I'm sorry if it was too much."

"It's not too much," Charlie answered, glassy eyes finding mine. "It's just overwhelming. Even before I died, I never thought I'd get to have this. And then you showed up. I *want* things now, Reece. I want to find my family and go places with you and kiss you and make love to you, and it's terrifying, because you're going to leave."

His words punched me in the gut. "I'm not leaving," I answered reflexively.

"Of course you will." He said it with such sad gentleness —there was no blame in his voice, only heartache. "You have a life. I *want* you to live your life, and you can't do that holed up in this lookout with me, when I'm not even sure how long I'll be here for."

My fingers dug into him, clinging on. "I'm not leaving, and neither are you. We'll figure something out. I'll figure something out."

He stopped trembling and smiled at me again. "I used to curse whatever it was that kept me here all those years. I don't anymore. Not even a little. Even if this is all we ever have, I'm happy we had it."

Hot tears splashed my cheeks. "This isn't all we have, Charlie," I said, voice rough. "I don't know how I know that, but I do. In my bones, I *know* that."

Charlie searched my face before nodding. "I'm not letting go." The tight band wrapped around my chest eased just a touch. "I'd go with you anywhere, remember?"

I nodded, unable to find more words. "C'mere," I whispered.

Slowly, I pulled him back down to kiss him again. He melted into me, and for what felt like ages, we exchanged languid, open-mouth kisses, hands running along each other's skin in heated touches. Gingerly, he began grinding his hips into mine, pressing our cocks together.

I gripped his waist with one hand to guide his unpracticed movements. He exhaled the softest *"Oh,"* into the space between us with each rocking motion and leaned into where I bit and sucked at his neck.

He smelled like cotton sheets and sex, and I'd never wanted anything more.

"Reece," he whined. "This is... I don't know what's going to happen, I don't know whether I *can,* but it feels—it feels like—like I'm going to come."

He sped up, knees digging in on either side as he ground his still-clothed cock into mine at a frantic pace.

"Take what you want from me, baby, please," I begged, enraptured by the way his eyebrows bunched in pleasure, eyes glazed and soft. "Use me to feel good."

He threw his head back and braced his hands on my shoulders for leverage so he could thrust harder into the movement.

"Fuck," I said, holding back my swiftly approaching release. There was something so hot, so forbidden about letting go and existing only for Charlie's pleasure, especially when he was too needy to even stop and take our clothes off. "I'm close."

"Me—too," he choked out. "It's—*oh, fuck!*" Charlie's hips kicked into mine, spasming uncontrollably while he shuddered and pulsed against me. To my surprise, a wet patch formed on the front of his joggers, and the thought of Charlie being so overwhelmed, so turned on just from dry-humping that he came in his pants had me coming in *my* pants.

I panted and groaned into his neck, squeezing him so tight he couldn't have disappeared even if he tried. By the time my own release soaked through, we'd created an unpleasant, tacky mess between us.

I kissed his cheek and ran a hand through his soft hair. "Alright?"

"Mmhmm," he mumbled, tucking his face farther into the crook of my neck.

I chuckled. "We've gotta get up and change, baby, or we're gonna get uncomfortable real quick."

He peered down between us, that impossible color still high in his cheeks. "Sorry for dirtying your pants."

I pulled his chin up to look at me. "That was the single hottest experience of my life. Don't apologize for coming all over yourself in my arms, because if I have it my way, you're going to be doing that again," I peppered a kiss against his cheek, "and again," his nose, "and again," his mouth.

"You're good at that," he mumbled with a pout on his adorable face.

"Good at what?"

"Smooth-talking me."

I laughed. Deep and full. "I promise you, I'm not. I just know what I want, and I want you. All the time."

He eyed me before shuffling off. I stood too, following his movements a bit helplessly, like a string pulled tight between us whenever we grew too far apart.

I wasn't going to say that weird, needy shit out loud, though.

"Right, I'll warm up some water to clean off," I said.

Charlie grinned at me. "You do that," before he blinked away, reappearing a second later back in his normal clothes, sticky cum pants a pile on the floor.

I glared at him. "Not fair."

CHAPTER FIFTEEN

The day passed quickly, with the sun melting away most of the ice and snow by mid-afternoon.

We received an updated weather forecast that the warm air that'd finally pushed the snowstorm out of the mountains would usher in a tailwind of potentially severe thunderstorms. We'd need to prepare for overtime during the evenings and this coming weekend.

I didn't mind. With Charlie and me tag-teaming the hourly passes and logs, it didn't feel monotonous, and I didn't resent the extra time on the clock.

I also didn't mind finally being able to touch him all the time.

And kiss him.

And feel the way he melted beneath my hands when I teased along the small of his back.

"*Mmph...*" he moaned, leaning into where I pressed a kiss into the soft patch of skin behind his ear. I turned him to face me, and he easily folded into my arms, breathing each other in.

"Reece?"

"Hmm?"

He tucked his head more solidly against me. "Remember when you said you could find people on the internet? Like, look them up so you can talk to them?"

"I remember," I said quietly.

"I think I'm ready for you to look for my family, now."

I pulled away just enough to look at him. "Depending on how private their information is, it might be hard to find, or not possible without the help of someone like a private investigator. But I'll try for you."

He nodded. "I understand. If anyone's still alive, it's probably my sister. Maybe." He swallowed. "Frances Randolph is her full name. My parents are Charles Sr. and Carey."

"Do you want to look with me, or would you rather I tell you what I find?"

He fingered the collar of my shirt. "I think I need to go and rest for a bit. I'll try to be back this evening for dinner. Could you look while I'm away, and tell me what you find?"

"Of course, baby," I said, dropping a kiss into his hair. "Go. I'll be here when you get back."

I found his dad's obituary first.

Charles Randolph Sr. passed away peacefully on February 12th, 2013, in St. Luke's Memorial Hospital. He was preceded in death by his loving wife, Carey. He leaves behind his beloved son and daughter, Charles Jr., and Frances. In lieu of flowers, please make your donations to the National Center for Missing and Exploited Children.

With tears streaming down my face, I opened a new tab and began the search for Frankie.

By the time Charlie reappeared in the cabin, I'd prepared dinner—ground beef burritos with a not-so-fresh tomato pico and a spicy lime crema—because I didn't know what else to do while I waited for him to return, and I wanted him to have something to eat if it'd make him feel better.

He took one look at my face and put a hand over his mouth to stifle a sob. Wrapping him up tight in my arms, I guided him to where I had my laptop open and ready.

"Who?" he asked through his tears. "Just tell me who, first."

"Both of your parents have passed away. Your mom went first, twenty years ago, and your dad passed twelve years ago. I'm so sorry, Charlie."

He shook his head. "It's stupid to be s-so upset over it, isn't it? It was twenty years ago," he sobbed.

I held him close, gently rocking. "It's not stupid. For you, they didn't die until today. You need to let yourself mourn that."

He cried for a long time, leaning heavily into me. "Frankie?" he asked eventually. "What about Frankie?"

I grimaced. "I couldn't find anything about her, other than she was still alive at the time of your dad's passing. She and your parents gave a handful of interviews back when you first went missing, but none of them spoke to the press after that."

He wouldn't look me in the eye. "So they think I did it, then," he said gruffly, trying to pull away.

I took his hand to stop him. "I think you should read your dad's obituary for yourself."

Charlie only hesitated a second before he agreed; the trust that I wouldn't make him look at something that would hurt him was heady.

He cried all over again after he read it. "Beloved son..." A sob cut off his words.

"I looked up their interviews, Charlie. They did not believe you were the killer. They were treated pretty badly by the press after their last few interviews; I think that's why they stopped. But I don't read this as the obituary of a man who lost hope his son would come home."

Grief poured out of him. We spent the rest of the night huddled in bed, where he picked at dinner and then curled up, falling into whatever version of sleep he was capable of while I held him.

Days passed that way. Eventually, Charlie asked to read

the interviews his family had given, which upset him almost more than the obituary.

"It's not because it's bad," he whispered into the scant space between us, late one night. "It's not that I would've preferred they believe something awful about me. It's that they were hurting, too. All that time, some part of them hoped I'd come home."

He said he wasn't ready to try contacting Frankie. "She clearly doesn't want anyone to talk to her about when I went missing. What if she's moved on? I'm sure she's married, probably has a family. It would be cruel to insert myself back into the peace she may have found."

"I understand," I replied. "I won't try to find her if you don't want me to. But if you do, I will. I can't promise it would go well, but I think she'd want to hear from you. I think she'd want those answers, maybe the chance to talk to you again. Even if it's only once."

He tucked himself farther beneath the blankets, scooting as close to me as possible before pressing a chaste kiss to my lips. "I'll think about it."

My next resupply trip quickly approached.

Sitting at my desk with weeks of observation logs scattered in front of me, begging to be organized, I dropped my head into my hands and rubbed my temples. "Do you remember if we have any onions left?"

I'd never been a very creative meal planner, and my skills were already stretched beyond their limits. Coming up with dinner ideas felt like more and more of a chore as the days went on.

"I think so? I'll go check," Charlie replied, standing from the bed. He ran a hand along my shoulders as he passed, a soft smile on his face.

My phone rang, and I hit the ignore button.

"Tate again?" he asked, his brow furrowed in displeasure.

"Mmhmm."

"Why don't you just answer it?"

I sighed. "Because I really don't want to talk to him. I check in with Dad and Bobby every day. If he wants to know whether or not I'm alive, he can ask them."

Charlie trailed his hand from my shoulder down across my chest and leaned over to kiss me. I turned my whole body into it, twisting in the chair to face him for a better angle.

"*Mmm*," he hummed when I deepened the kiss with my tongue. Throwing both arms around my shoulders, his fingers dug in. "I was going somewhere," he breathed, tipping his head back to allow my searching mouth to taste the column of his neck.

"Onions," I said, palming his ass.

He laughed. "Oh my, talk dirty to me."

I pulled away a bit to watch the way his laughter made him glow. "Onion *rings*," I said with a grin.

Charlie laughed harder, his head thrown back and dimples on full display. "Only you."

His words held such fondness, such warmth, I thought I might be glowing, too.

He was mourning, yes, and there were times I didn't know how to be there for him or what I could do to make him feel better, but then he'd just ask me to hold him again, and the squirmy feeling of not being enough during his time of need fled.

We hadn't gone any further since that first time, but it somehow deepened the intimacy between us when all he needed from me at night was to be held. Just being in each other's presence was enough.

I still thought about him all the time, though. I still *wanted*. But only if he was ready, only if he also wanted that with me again, too.

With one more chaste kiss, he walked toward the door.

"Please be safe," I said.

He grinned at me through the glass, blinked away, and then re-materialized at the bottom of the tower, right in front of the utility shed.

I couldn't even pretend to roll my eyes at the sight of those dimples reappearing.

With a sigh, I returned to the tedious chore of sorting our weather data records and field observation logs by date. An easier task now that Charlie and I had both filled out the forms—his chicken scratch was slightly more legible than mine.

Squinting between two forms, attempting to decipher which was from the thirteenth and which was the eighteenth of the month, movement outside caught my eye.

Far in the distance, a truck trundled down the only

stretch of park service access road visible from this lookout's vantage point. I stood and snagged my binoculars from the windowsill, brow furrowing when I caught a glimpse just before the road curved and the truck drove out of sight.

It wasn't extraordinary to see cars on the road, but Forest Service or other government vehicles were the only ones legally allowed in the park, and this was clearly privately owned.

Even more confusing, however, was that I knew exactly who it belonged to.

Bobby.

It was a 1986 Chevy Silverado, blue with a bold white stripe down the body. I knew that, because he'd bought it off my dad when he'd sold our house in town and moved out to the cabin. It'd been Dad's back when it was new, and he'd always planned to keep it maintained, but when Mom moved and he got busy with work and solo parenting, it'd fallen into disrepair.

Bobby was good with cars; he'd loved flipping through restoration magazines as a kid, and he'd done a great job fixing the old truck up.

I thought back on our conversations over the last few weeks and couldn't remember him ever mentioning he'd be out this way. If so, I'd have invited him to come up to the lookout. Of all the people in my life, I'd want Bobby to meet Charlie first. He'd probably struggle with the idea of ghosts and be worried for me, but he'd also be the most understanding of how I felt.

So, why hadn't he told me?

What caught my attention the most, though, and twisted

my stomach into knots, wasn't the truck at all, or the road it was on.

It was the camo-colored ATV strapped onto the bed.

Before I could even process what I'd seen, loud barking followed by angry, raised voices startled me so much I nearly dropped the binoculars. I tossed them onto the bed and rushed outside as fast as I could.

The utility shed door was wide open, creaking in the wind. Charlie stood in front of it, hands in the air, the groceries he'd collected sprawled on the ground in front of him. Rocky the dog was a few feet away, squared up and barking ferociously. Next to Rocky, stood Tate.

Pointing a gun right at Charlie.

Fear so acute I couldn't breathe gripped my chest like a vice. "What the fuck do you think you're doing?" I yelled, crashing down the stairs two at a time. "Put that away!"

"Stay back, Reece! I caught him sneaking into your utility shed," Tate yelled. "Call the station. We can get a helicopter out here in thirty minutes if there's a pilot available."

I ignored him, my large strides carrying me down the last flight and over to them.

"Reece, don't!" Charlie yelled.

I ignored him, too, and stepped in front of him, shoving him behind me to block Tate's shot. "Put the gun down!"

"What the fuck are you doing?" Tate yelled.

"Put that down, and we'll talk," I repeated. "I know him. He's supposed to be here."

Eyes darting between me and where Charlie peeked

around my shoulder, Tate dropped the gun. "Fuck. I thought—"

"You didn't think, you hot-headed dick," I interrupted, still shouting. "Is that how you greet everyone you don't know? Barrel first?"

He swore again and flicked on the safety before holstering it to his hip. "Only the ones who might be murderers," he threw back. "Rocky, heel."

As obedient as ever, Rocky ceased his barking and sat at Tate's heel, tongue lolling and looking quite pleased with himself.

"Hello, puppy," Charlie cooed. I wanted to knock him upside the head for having no sense of time and place.

Although if I'd gone nearly forty years without seeing a cute animal, I'd probably be asking, "*Can I pet that dog?*" too.

Charlie's canine affection didn't ease Tate. "Who are you?" he asked, tone accusing.

"*Um...*" Charlie looked at me, eyebrows raised.

I shrugged. *Why not? He can't arrest a ghost.*

"My name's Charlie."

"Hold on a second," Tate said, stepping closer, brow furrowed. "Have we already met? You look familiar."

Charlie cringed. "No?"

Tate squinted at him a second longer before turning as pale as a, well, a ghost. "Holy fucking shit. That's not possible," he breathed, eyes darting back and forth between us. "Holy shit. Holy *shit*. Tell me that's not who I think it is. Tell me I'm seeing things."

"Well, you're probably seeing things just fine," I grumbled. "It's your decision-making that needs work."

Charlie shot me an exasperated glare.

"What?" I said. "It does."

"You're not helping the situation."

"*Can* this situation be helped?"

"Who are you really? What's going on here?" Tate interjected. He looked ready to pass out.

"I told you, my name is Charlie. Charlie Randolph."

Tate mouthed the name silently, dazed, before he swore for a third time. "That's not possible."

Pinching the bridge of my nose, I sighed. "You can say it as many times as you want, but it doesn't make it true. He really is Charlie Randolph."

"Charles Randolph is dead. He died almost forty years ago." It sounded like Tate was trying to convince himself more than us.

"Yes, that's true," Charlie said.

"This is some kind of fucked up practical joke, isn't it?"

"It's not a joke."

"Do you really expect me to believe *this* guy," he pointed at Charlie in disbelief, "who is very much alive, is Charles Randolph, *the* Charles Randolph, responsible for killing six people thirty-nine years ago before disappearing off the face of the planet?"

"He did *not* kill those people," I growled.

Tate looked incredulous. "*That's* the detail you take issue with?"

"It's about time someone fucking does," I spit back. "Maybe people wouldn't be disappearing all over again if someone with more than two brain-cells to rub together had considered Charlie might not have been the killer."

Tate's eyes flashed to Charlie, then back to me. "I don't believe you. Whatever game you're playing, I want no part of it. I thought you were a better person than this, Reece. Your dad calls me almost every day, asking if you're safe out here. Bobby won't leave me alone about this case. I hauled my ass all the way out here to talk to you, *again*, because you won't pick up your goddamn phone, and you pull something like this? It's a slap in the face to everyone who cares about you."

"He's not lying," Charlie cut in, angry and defensive. "I am Charlie Randolph, and to my great dismay, I'm not alive. And I'll fucking prove it, you asshole."

And then he disappeared.

The clothes he'd been wearing, *my* clothes, fell to the ground in a lifeless heap.

I smirked at the stunned expression on Tate's face, his mouth hanging wide open. "Believe me now?"

"But—he—that's not possible. I'm hallucinating. He just —he was right there," Tate rambled, spinning in circles to peer around, as if Charlie could've undressed and streaked away to hide in the trees in the blink of an eye. "Where'd he go?"

Right then, Tate's ball cap lifted off his head seemingly of its own accord, twisted around, and plopped down again, facing backwards.

He spun around, hands going up to hold the hat in place. "What the—"

Charlie materialized right behind him, grinning like the Cheshire Cat. "*Boo.*"

"*AHH!*" Tate screamed, skedaddling away from him. "What the fuck?"

Rocky had lain down a while ago. He cracked an eye open just long enough to watch Tate's distressed retreat before closing it again, entirely unbothered.

That's what happens when you don't give them enough cheese, I thought.

As much as I wanted Charlie to keep going, if only to see his playful side return, Tate looked one more fright away from a heart attack, and I wasn't prepared to explain a ghost *and* a dead cop.

Schooling my grin, I said, "Now that we've cleared that up, will you stop shouting and accusing me of being a shitty person?"

Eyes following Charlie as he returned to his place next to me, Tate put a hand to his chest, breathing hard. "I need to sit the fuck down."

Back in the lookout, Charlie earned Rocky's trust nearly immediately through several offerings of cheese and ear scratches. Then, the dog curled up by the fire and promptly fell asleep.

Tate sat in the desk chair, finally calm enough to have a coherent conversation after gulping down a cup of instant coffee. Charlie and I sat side-by-side on the bed facing him.

"So you're, what? A spirit? An apparition?" Tate asked, looking like he, too, was confronting the beaded curtains.

"I honestly have no idea," Charlie answered. "A ghost, maybe? I think I've been here, in the lookout, since I died. I don't know how or why. No one could see or hear me before. Or if they did, it was a passing glance. Not the way Reece can, anyway."

Tate's brow furrowed. "Are you a medium?" he asked me.

I shook my head quickly. "Nope. Charlie is a once-in-a-lifetime thing." *In more ways than one.* "I'm no ghost whisperer."

"My grandmother is going to have a field day with this..." Tate mumbled lowly before turning back to Charlie. "If no one could see you before besides him, why can I see you now?"

Charlie blushed a bit, but shook his head. "I'm not entirely sure. I have theories." He fussed with the blanket sprawled next to him. "I think it's helped me to be seen. To *feel* alive again, even if I'm not. But I'll probably never know for sure."

I wanted to hold him, kiss the blush from his cheeks, and tell him I'd do anything and everything to make him feel seen, to feel alive.

Tate dragged a hand down his face. "I don't even know where to begin asking questions. I still feel like maybe I tripped and fell into a ravine on my way out here, and this is all a hallucination."

I grimaced, feeling a bit bad for teasing him. "This is really happening. You aren't lying dead in the woods some-where. But I sort of thought the same thing had happened to me the first time I saw Charlie, too, so I get it."

"You're handling this surprisingly well, actually. Reece

screamed like a banshee and nearly chucked himself over the railing."

I turned to glare at Charlie. "I was startled. And I didn't chuck myself off, you yelled at me and nearly killed me."

"*What?*" Tate asked, eyeing Charlie warily. To be fair, though, he'd looked at him like that the entire time.

"He's being dramatic," Charlie answered with an exasperated sigh. "I didn't try to kill him; I assertively asked him not to close my window. I wasn't aware he'd actually hear me. Or see me, for that matter. And then I saved his life by *preventing* him from going over the railing."

I hid a smile at his put-out expression and opened my mouth to continue, but Tate interrupted. "Can you stop bickering like an old married couple for two seconds?" he begged.

Charlie blushed again.

Tate heaved a sigh before shifting into cop mode. I had to give him credit for rolling with the punches, even when faced with a reality so far out of the norm. "So. Say I believe you really are Charles Randolph, and you really are... dead. It doesn't make you an innocent man."

"I didn't kill anyone," Charlie responded angrily. "The same thing that happened to Reece happened to me."

Tate's eyes narrowed. "Really? Did you see who, then? Who killed you?"

"I don't remember," Charlie answered, a tremble in his voice.

"You don't remember?" Tate parroted, his tone making it clear he didn't believe him.

Charlie's outline flickered, and I reached out and took

his hand. He squeezed back before taking a deep breath. "No. I remember seeing a light outside and following it into the woods. I don't remember anything after that."

Tate's gaze was skeptical. "Do you think you could if someone helped you?"

My turn for skepticism. "What do you mean, 'help him'?"

He sighed. "I was a few years younger than you in school, so you probably don't know, but my parents were pretty shitty people. They were in and out of jail for a lot of my childhood. Mostly drugs. My grandmother is the one who raised me. She's... different. Quirky."

"Okay..." I said, not understanding the connection.

"My whole life, she's been into stuff like tarot cards and hypnosis, and reading people's auras. She runs a small business out of her house. She says most of it is just observing people and guessing at what they want to hear. But she's also talked about other stuff, too. Communicating with *the other side*. She wouldn't even let me stay in the house when those clients came calling—she said she didn't want my young, open, vulnerable soul to be taken advantage of if something went wrong. I never knew what she meant, but..." he trailed off, glancing at Charlie again warily. "If it's true you can't remember what happened to you, maybe she could help."

"If you were raised by a woman who says she can talk to ghosts, why are you so shaken up by me?" Charlie asked.

Tate shrugged, looking a bit chagrined. "I've always believed she believes she can communicate with the dead, and I've never had a reason to challenge her on it. But seeing it for myself is different."

I didn't like any of this.

First, would Charlie even want to remember? Was the identity of the killer buried somewhere in his subconscious? What would happen to him when he did remember? Would it hurt him?

Suddenly, I couldn't get the question he asked me the other night out of my head.

Do you think it's why I'm still here? Because I haven't fully faced what happened?

I squeezed his hand tighter.

On the other hand, if there was anyone who could explain why Charlie was still around, wouldn't it be her? Or maybe she could at least point us in the right direction for answers.

What if she can help bring him back?

I couldn't look at that tiny flame of hope head-on, afraid it would snuff out the moment I wanted it too much.

Charlie peered over at me, his hand still firmly linked with mine. I felt like he could read every thought I'd ever had. Even that tiny, hushed flicker of an idea.

"I don't want anyone else to get hurt," Charlie began uncertainly, turning back to Tate. "So if there's something I could remember that would help, I want to try. But I'm not going anywhere with you until you tell me why you think I did it. If I disappeared, how could they have been so certain it was me?"

Tate paused, weighing Charlie's words. Probably calculating the risk of divulging information to the one and only suspect in the murders of six people, with the benefit of his restored memories.

He turned to me. "No one else, remember? By some miracle, this hasn't been leaked. If it happens now, I'll know it was you."

I nodded. "Not a word."

He sighed heavily. "They searched the lookout top to bottom. Tore the place apart. They never found you, or any indication you planned to leave. But they did find the murder weapons—covered in the victim's blood."

CHAPTER SIXTEEN

Stunned, I stared at Tate for a moment. "*Weapons?* As in plural?" I asked.

He nodded. "I won't say more than that. Not until you meet with my grandmother."

Charlie looked shell-shocked, his gaze distant. "I didn't do this," he said softly, as though the weight of defending himself grew too heavy.

"I know," I said vehemently. And then I remembered. "What about that police officer who came to see you?" I turned to Tate. "Don't you have those reports? Surely more questions would've been asked if someone had been here only hours earlier and didn't notice anything odd?"

His eyebrows lifted in realization. "*That's* what you were going on about at the ranger station. I thought you were hallucinating."

"What?" I asked, confused.

"You talked about Charles Randolph like you knew him.

You said a police officer came to visit him, but that's not real. I checked. There's no record of anyone coming out to the lookout that day. You looked like death warmed over, though, so I thought it was all nonsense. *Uh*, sorry," he added in Charlie's direction, cringing.

"It wasn't nonsense," I cut in, angry again. "Someone came to see him."

Charlie focused on Tate. "It's true. A police officer came out to ask if I'd seen anything unusual."

Tate eyed him suspiciously. "Do you remember their name? What did you tell them?"

Charlie shook his head. "I don't remember his name. He was young. Twenties, maybe? Said he was the sorry deputy saddled with hiking all the way out here to talk to the lookouts." He shrugged. "He wasn't here very long. I gave him my observation logs, and that's really it. He said he'd pass them on to the ranger station for me unless there was something necessary for the investigation."

"You gave him your logs?" Tate asked, tone sharp.

"Wait," I interrupted, holding up a hand. "There's no record of this at all? How is that possible?"

Tate made a non-committal noise. "It's been almost forty years. Some information gets lost in the shuffle."

If smoke could come out my ears, it would've. "Fuck that," I snarled. "Lost in the shuffle? A cop was here *hours* before he disappeared and didn't notice a goddamn *murder weapon?* And that was somehow overlooked when they decided to wrap this up and put a pretty bow on it? Sure, blame it all on the missing guy, who isn't around anymore to defend himself!"

I stood and paced, gesticulating with my hands. "Get the fuck out of here with that. His family suffered for years because of that lazy excuse of an investigation. More people are going missing, now! And let's all be transparent for once—they're dead. I saw what he did to that bobcat. What if it wasn't a cop that came to see Charlie, huh? What if it was the killer? Did no one look into this *at all*?"

Tate looked cowed. Rocky perked up from his nap, whining softly.

"We're trying to do the right thing, this time," he said softly. "*I'm* trying to do the right thing. I don't know for sure who was responsible for the murders in eighty-six, and I don't know who's responsible for the ones in the last few months. Maybe it's the same person, maybe it's a copycat. We don't know yet, but we are trying."

He looked at Charlie. There was less hostility in his gaze, now. "If..." he took a deep breath. "If you're not the one to blame, your memories will help. Even if you didn't see the killer's face, there could be details you don't realize are important."

Charlie nodded. I sat back down next to him and took his hand again.

"I'll do it," he whispered.

I squeezed our linked fingers harder than I should've.

"Alright," Tate said. "Thank you. If I can arrange it, would you be able to come to my grandmother's house? Are you able to leave the lookout?"

Shit. I hadn't even considered that.

"For short periods, I've been able to manage it. It's much

easier with Reece. If I'm with him, I think I can go. Or we can try, at least."

He nodded. "When's your next supply run?"

"In a couple of days," I answered. The band around my chest tightened even more. I wasn't ready for it to be that soon. What if it went wrong? What if Charlie disappeared forever? I needed more time. *We* needed more time. There was still so much I wanted to do with him, to say—

We can't lose him, the Thing wailed. *We can't, we can't, we can't—*

It's not my decision.

It bared its teeth at me and slinked off.

"I'll see if I can swing it," Tate said. "Work's hell right now, obviously, but I'll talk with my grandmother and ask her about seeing you."

"Is that okay with you?" I asked Charlie, hating every single word of this conversation.

He nodded and squeezed my hand back. "Sure. Yeah. Great."

Rocky's loud bark cut through the cabin. He leaped up, front paws on the windowsill, and continued to huff and growl even after Tate's command to hush.

"What are you hollering at?" he asked as we all stood to see for ourselves.

Randy sat on the railing outside, chattering back at Rocky as if scolding him for all the racket.

Finally, she'd found someone besides me to be angry at.

"Oh, it's time for her hot dogs!" Charlie said.

He pulled one from the package on the counter and stepped outside, ripping it into pieces. His dimples appeared when she ignored Rocky in favor of washing her tiny paws in the water bowl he kept out for her, before reaching for the first piece of hot dog he left on the railing.

"You two seem... close," Tate said, keeping his voice low.

I cleared my throat and turned back to him, realizing I'd been caught staring. "Yes."

He raised an eyebrow. "How do you know you can trust him?"

"You didn't see how broken and angry he was when I told him he'd been blamed for murdering six people in cold blood."

Tate sighed. "I hope you're right, for your sake. And be careful. Not just because of that, but... He's a *ghost*, Reece. That will never end well—for either of you."

My mouth set in a hard line. "We'll see."

He sighed, shaking his head. "You're a stubborn ass."

"And you're just an ass."

He laughed, hearty and deep. Something shifted between us, like the walls of pretend cordiality finally fell. For the first time, I thought that maybe, someday, we could be friends.

Charlie came back inside, his gaze darting from me to Tate before he slipped Rocky the last bit of hot dog with an ear scratch. Wordlessly, he went to fill the water kettle.

"Alright, buddy, time to go," Tate said to Rocky, strapping the hands-free leash across his shoulders. "I'll give you a call to sort things out. Pick up this time, please," he added with a raised eyebrow.

I waved him off one last time before he disappeared into the trees, then turned to Charlie. "Making tea?" I asked.

He nodded without turning around to face me. "It helps. To ground me, like you said."

I walked up behind him and wrapped my arms around his shoulders, squeezing as hard as I could. It only took a few seconds before he softened, set the kettle down, and turned around to mirror my tight embrace.

"You're tense. I know you're worried about—" he began, but I interrupted.

"Can we not, for a little bit? Please?" I whispered. "I just want to hold you right now."

He sighed deeply. "Yes."

We were quiet for a few minutes, breathing each other in. "Tate likes you," Charlie said after a while. "Or liked you, maybe, before he saw you holding hands with a ghost," he mumbled into my chest.

I hummed. "To be fair, I think the part where he thinks you might be a murderer is the bigger hill to climb."

He huffed out a short laugh and squeezed tighter. "You skipped the first part of what I said."

"I did, because it doesn't matter. It didn't before you, and it certainly doesn't now."

"He's alive."

"So are billions of other people. I don't want them, either."

"He's handsome."

"You're more handsome."

"*Josh* was more handsome," he replied testily.

I'd told Charlie about how I was diagnosed, and everything that'd happened that day and shortly after. He'd asked to see a picture of Josh, and scowled at my phone when I showed him an old one of us.

I kissed Charlie's cheek and pulled back to look him in the eye. "One of the first thoughts I had about you was how shockingly beautiful you are. I was deeply upset the scary ghost pushing me over the railing was so hot."

He rolled his eyes. "I did not push you. I *saved* you, you—"

I kissed him, slow and deep. I loved the way his body reacted to my touch—muscles loosening and leaning in for more.

"Yes, you did," I whispered when I pulled away. "In more ways than that, Charlie. And I don't want anyone else."

Ever.

"*Reece.*" His fingers danced up my spine, clinging to my shoulders.

"Let me help," I said, voice low and gruff between nips along his jaw line.

"With what?" he breathed.

"Grounding you. Keeping you here, with me. I bet I can do a pretty good job. At least as good as the tea."

He smiled, guiding me to suck at his exposed collarbone. "What did you have in mind?"

"Well, I could use my hands," I palmed him through his joggers. "Or maybe my mouth."

He sucked in a sharp inhale.

"Or whatever else you'd like."

"Anything else?" he asked, voice cracking halfway through.

I took his mouth again, relishing in the warmth I found. *So real. So mine. Please be mine.*

"Something you have in mind?" I asked, nipping his full bottom lip once more before pulling away to gauge his answer.

He fidgeted with the elastic waistband of my pants, bringing our hips flush. "You know I've never been with a man before you. I have with women, though. Do you ever..." he hesitated.

"Do I bottom?" I asked.

He blinked and then nodded.

"I have before. It's not my preference, but if it's something you want to try, we can."

That skiff of pink dusted his cheekbones. "And if I wanted to try?"

"Do you?"

"Would that be okay with you?"

I pushed forward, crowding him up against the counter. "I'm asking what *you* want, Charlie. I've told you what I want—you. All of you. However I can have you. So, tell me how to make you feel good. Tell me how to ground you."

He gripped my collar. "I want to feel you inside of me," he whispered.

My breath shuddered out. "Okay," I answered, voice tight. "Did you ever try on your own?"

Charlie buried his face in my chest. "Yes. With my fingers."

"Did you like it?"

"Yes," he said, voice muffled. "Sometimes I could reach this spot..."

I groaned, pulling him away from the counter and backing him up toward the bed. "Yeah? And how did it make you feel, baby?"

"*Good.*"

"I'll give you that again." I laid him back on the sheets and watched his eyes go molten. "I'll make you feel so, so good."

He yanked me down on top of him. "I don't want anyone else, either, you know," he said, kissing me roughly. "Even if I had billions to choose from. I'd find you all over again."

"*Charlie.*"

There was little talk after that. I couldn't get over how *alive* he felt beneath me, shuddering under my fingers as I pulled off his shirt, dropping kisses down the planes of his chest.

Stretched out, his belly pulled tight, and I couldn't help but use my teeth and tongue to taste the soft skin underneath his navel. He reacted beautifully, shivering and jerking at my touch like a live wire.

He nearly squeaked when I lunged up to suck a nipple into my mouth, flicking it with my tongue. Clawing at the back of my Henley, he pulled it up as far as he could and shoved his hand down the seat of my pants to grip my ass.

"Wanna feel you," he whined.

I sat up, straddling him, and tugged my shirt over my head, tossing it away. Usually, I avoided this part with Josh and others before him. We'd either fuck in the dark or I'd leave my shirt on because I didn't like to feel analyzed or exposed. Seeing the comparison of our bodies in their eyes burned.

But there was only raw hunger in Charlie's as he drank me in, gaze darting across my hair-covered chest and following my prominent happy trail down to the soft pouch of my belly that I'd never been able to get rid of. "C'mere…" he mumbled, tugging on my torso.

I scooted further up until my knees were tucked into his armpits. His hands ghosted along my chest and belly, as if testing how firm I wanted to be touched. "I can't stop looking at you," he breathed, digging his blunt nails in. "Since the day we met. I wanna—"

Pupils blown so wide his eyes were nearly black, he shimmied backwards to brace his shoulders on the wall behind him, elevating his head.

"Wanna what?" I prompted, voice reedy.

He groaned, as if frustrated he couldn't find the words, and buried his face in my stomach instead. With a deep inhale, he breathed me in and reached up to scratch his nails through the dense hair across my pecs. "I wanna taste you here," he said, so needy and wanting it made my cock pulse. He rubbed his cheek against my chest, his hands, lips, and tongue dragging across every inch he could reach.

I leaned into it, nearly purring. "God, Charlie," I moaned.

"I wanna know what you feel like, everywhere," he continued, biting at the soft swell of my belly, and again at the sensitive skin under my nipple. "I wanna know what it's like to be covered by you, to drown in you."

Fucking hell. I'd never felt more seen, more wanted, more *worshipped* than by him in that moment.

"Yes," I replied. To all of it. "Yes, baby. Whatever you want. I'll do whatever you want."

He flicked my nipple with his tongue and pulled away to peer up at me, grinning feral and wide. "*Whatever* I want, big guy?"

I nodded dumbly. I was a dog on a leash, ready to beg for the scraps of whatever he gave me.

Ready to grovel, if it made him happy. "*Uh-huh.*"

Wasn't I the one meant to be taking him apart? And yet there I was, silly putty in his hands.

"Good. Because I want you to show me how to suck your cock."

I swore, unprepared to hear such unfiltered need in his voice. My dick pulsed again, still trapped in my pants, and I helped him along in yanking them down until it bobbed free, the thick length fully hardening inches from his wet mouth.

Charlie watched in rapt fascination as a bead of precum formed at the tip. For a second, I worried he had second thoughts. "It's alright if you'd rather not—*uh!*"

Charlie leaned forward and flicked his tongue over the head. I slammed a hand onto the glass above him to brace myself; even that tiny touch made me lightheaded.

Alright, so the man knew what he wanted—who was I to argue?

"That's really good, baby," I gritted out, eyes wide. I couldn't help but kick my hips forward once, twice, tagging him on the mouth with the head. "Keep going."

Charlie might hold my leash, but he bloomed beneath my praise. Growing more confident, he wrapped one hand around the shaft, thumb slotting into the sensitive *V* on the underside of the tip, and dug his other hand into my meaty backside.

"I love how hairy you are," he mumbled, massaging my ass cheek. "Here. Everywhere."

"*Uh-huh*," was all I managed in reply before he yanked me forward to lick off the next drops of precum that formed, one after the other.

My hips stuttered with each teasing touch, blunt cockhead dragging across his perfect, pouty lips before he captured it again with his tongue.

My brow furrowed. "Baby," I ground out, both hands up on the glass now to keep from gripping the back of his head and feeding him my cock the way I wanted. "You gonna get a move on? I'm dying, here."

He laughed, deep and throaty, before slurping down as much of me as he could at once, both hands gripping the backs of my thick thighs.

His mouth felt neither warm nor cool, like an exact match to my own body temperature. But it was wet, sloppy, and whatever he was doing with his tongue nearly had my eyes rolling back.

"Oh, God," I croaked. "I love the way your mouth feels. So good."

He peered up at me. Tears clung to his long lashes, and his throat fought to keep me inside.

Fucking. Hell. "Such a pretty fucking crier."

He pulled off with a soft *pop*. "Call me pretty again."

And then he swallowed me back down, the muscles of his throat working overtime to fight his gag reflex.

I stopped protesting my own urges and tangled my

fingers in his hair. With a proper grip, I gave a tentative rock of my hips, just enough to suggest, to ask for permission to thrust deeper.

He palmed my ass in assent, a wicked gleam in his eye when he burrowed his fingers between my cheeks and traced around my rim.

I jerked forward. "Pretty baby likes to tease? That's a two-way street."

He groaned and swallowed.

With a shout, my back bowed like he had my soul in his throat and not my dick. I couldn't shift my hips very much with my pants still wrapped around my knees, but I made do, cradling his nape while I surged forward and claimed his mouth.

"I wanna watch your throat take me all day," I panted, dragging my thumb over his Adam's apple. "You're doing so good."

He whimpered.

My other hand left wet condensation streaks on the window as I moved, slipping along the fogged-up glass. Release barreled toward me. My cock swelled, and I pulled out roughly, blinking heavily and trembling from the intensity of stopping right before the point of no return.

Below me, he gulped down air, chest heaving. "I like doing that," he panted and grinned, cheeks wet with tears.

"I like you doing that, too," I replied when I caught my breath.

He laughed. "More. Let's do more."

I scrambled up, kicked off the rest of my clothes, all sense of self-consciousness gone, and helped him out of bed so we could switch places, with me sitting on the edge and him standing in front of me.

Shifting from foot to foot with a pair of my joggers still cinched around his waist, all of his earlier bravado fled, and he looked uncertain in a way he hadn't before. The pent-up tension from my near-orgasm relaxed, and I gently reached out to bring him forward, wrapping my arms around his middle and resting my chin on his stomach.

I peered up. "All good, baby?"

His eyes went from hesitant to trusting in a blink, and I knew I'd sketch him like this later.

"All good." He wiped his face and cleared his scratchy throat. "You?"

I quirked an eyebrow at him. "I'm not actually sure you are a ghost. Judging by what you just did to me, I think a succubus is a more apt description."

He flashed me his dimples.

"Yes, I'm very good, Charlie. And now it's your turn." I dipped my fingers into his waistband. He was still hard, tenting the front of the soft cotton in a way that was so erotic I knew I'd sketch that, too. "If you want?"

He nodded, resting his hands on my shoulders.

I placed kisses up one side of his stomach, burrowing my face in the heady scent concentrated in his underarm—*sunwarmed cotton*—before kissing back down the other side, stopping right below his navel.

Slowly, I tugged his pants down in increments until just the tip of his cock peeked out, glistening and begging for attention.

He wasn't wearing any underwear, so precum leaked all

over. I rested my thumb just under the head, gently teasing up and down. "Oh, pretty baby. Look at you. Did you like sucking me so much you made a mess all over yourself?"

He whimpered, fingers bunching in my shirt. "Yes."

Charlie was sharp and witty most of the time, but this version of him, soft and needy, might become my favorite.

Because it was mine.

I leaned forward and licked the tip, teasing him just as he'd done to me.

"Holy shit, Reece." His hands scrabbled along my shoulders, fingers rooting in my hair. I tugged his pants down the rest of the way, supporting his weight as he kicked them off each foot until he was bare before me.

I sucked in a breath. He was pale and lithe, all lean and toned with narrow hips. His cock jutted out of a nest of dark curls, angled slightly to the left with a soft pink tip I wanted back in my mouth.

Now.

"Beautiful," I breathed. "You're beautiful."

Warmth flickered in his eyes. "You make me believe that."

I guided him to stand between my legs again and looked him in the eye when I dragged my tongue from base to tip, fully tasting him. He groaned, and I reached between his legs to cup his balls, tugging gently to see if he liked it as much as I did.

"Oh, that's—"

"Good?"

"Mmhmm."

Enough teasing. I took him down to the root, relaxing my

throat and swallowing around his cock in a way I knew would send him through the roof.

He hunched forward, nails digging into my back. "*Guh.*"

I pulled off, but kept fondling his sack. "You're usually so eloquent. What's the matter?"

"Fuck you."

"We'll get there, pretty thing. Patience."

And I took him to the back of my throat again.

We repeated this dance a few times until I was sure he was seconds from blowing his load. Pulling off one last time, I wiped my mouth and peered up at him.

He looked completely, gorgeously wrecked, with swollen, parted lips and gleaming eyes.

"C'mon," I said, shuffling back so he could lie next to me on the bed, chest to chest.

On Bambi legs, he tumbled down, rolling onto his side and tucking into me so there was nothing between us. I hooked his leg around my hip so our cocks slid together and kissed him back into awareness.

"*Mmm...*" he moaned, blinking owlishly when I pulled back.

"Still up for more?"

"Obviously. You?"

I pressed my smile into his cheek, nuzzling him. "Obviously."

Reaching over him, I snagged the lube from the nightstand drawer and flicked the cap up. Fingers slick and warm, I leaned in to kiss him again while at the same time reaching down and around, searching, until—

He gasped, clinging to me.

I massaged the lightest, most teasing circles around his rim, gauging his reaction.

"Good?"

"*Uh-huh.*"

When he relaxed beneath my touch, I pushed a fingertip in. He bit my shoulder, wrapping his arms so tightly around my neck I nearly choked. "More. Keep going."

He liked one finger, but came alive at two, writhing next to me. Three was a stretch.

"Wait," he panted. "Just wait."

"Wanna stop?"

"I said wait, not stop," he grumbled, before kissing the tip of my nose.

I nipped his back and waited until he nodded, then twisted and searched until his hips jerked forward.

"That's it," he gasped. "There."

"Mmhmm."

"Smug isn't your best look."

"Squirming on my fingers is *absolutely* yours, though."

I pressed into his prostate again, ripping the reply from his lips. I'm sure it would've been brilliant.

"Turn over," I said once he was soft and pliant, pulling my fingers out.

A flash of vulnerability crossed his face, and I kissed him soundly. "We'll start like this, then we can shift however you want. I've got you."

I scooted until my back was flush with the wall, giving him plenty of room to roll and nestle into me. "I, *uh*, should've mentioned earlier. I don't have condoms up here."

"That's okay," he said, waving me off.

"No, I should've thought about it before. I can make you come on my fingers, baby. We don't need to keep going."

He half-rolled, so he was looking right at me. "Reece, get inside of me before I die of old age."

We stared at each other for a beat and then burst out laughing. I dropped a kiss onto his shoulder when he turned back around and slicked up my cock. Hooking his top leg open over my hip again, I nestled my dick between his cheeks and notched the head against his hole. My other arm snaked below him, wrapping around his chest and holding him close.

"Kiss me," I said.

He turned his head toward his shoulder, and I thrust my tongue into his mouth, pushing into him at the same time.

"Fuck," he huffed, reaching back to grip my hip.

"Tell me when to move," I ground out, doing my best to breathe deeply and think about anything except how tight that first ring of muscle was squeezing my cockhead.

"Okay. Move," he said after a few breaths, tapping me.

I surged into him again, punching a tiny whine from his lips. His outline flickered, but his arms and torso were still firm against me.

"Right here, Charlie," I said, placing a hand over his heart. "Right here with me."

"Yes," he breathed, canting his hips back into my thrusts.

Out, and in. Out, and in.

The drag on each slide made my eyes cross. I didn't have the greatest leverage in the world, but his belly tensed and twitched, and he half-moaned my name every time I bottomed out, so I must've been doing something right.

Zeroing in on his nipples, peaked and begging for attention, I tweaked one with my fingers and sucked a mark into the back of his neck until he cried out.

"It's—" his fingers flexed against my hip before clawing at me again, pulling me into him with more force each time. "It's so good."

"I'm not gonna last," I moaned, embarrassed at being reduced to a one-pump wonder at the ripe age of thirty-four.

He looked close, too, though, with the way precum drooled from his cock. He just needed a bit more to spill over the edge.

I pulled out and sat up so I straddled his lower leg. Encouraging the one that'd been draped over my hip forward, I folded it up toward his chest. He tried to turn and lie flat on his back to face me, but furrowed his brow when I stopped him, keeping him on his side.

"Hold yourself open for me," I huffed.

"Wha—?" he began to ask, but hooked a hand around his knee and did as instructed when I sat back on my heels, lined up, and pushed into him again, hard.

"Reece!" he cried out, scrambling to brace himself against the mattress with an elbow so he wouldn't slide up the bed on every thrust.

I leaned over, bent his leg further forward with my torso so he could let go, and buried myself inside him, the position allowing me much deeper. "Better?"

Mouth slack, he could only nod, eyes glazed and staring at me as though I'd hung the moon, just for him.

I stilled deep inside and stayed like that until our breaths synced. With my heart in my throat, I couldn't tear my eyes away from his. He saw everything; all the angry, grumpy, rough parts of me, and still wanted me anyway. As if I'd opened my chest and invited him in to peer around, I'd never felt more vulnerable in my life than in that moment.

And I didn't want it any other way.

Only this. Only with Charlie.

Slowly, I began grinding into him again. He made the tiniest, sexiest involuntary noises with every rock of my hips, eyes widening when I moved just so.

"Kiss me again," I begged, desperate for it. He lunged up and shoved his tongue into my mouth. With equal fervor, I began thrusting, aching to be impossibly closer to him. Adjusting the angle of my thrusts, I pulled away from the kiss just long enough to search his face, waiting for—

"Oh my God," he sobbed, eyes rolling back as he shoved a hand down to fist his cock. "Right there!"

I pistoned into him relentlessly after that, mindless in my need to throw him over the edge before me. Thankfully, I didn't have to hold back for very long. He tensed and shook when ropes of cum flew out all over his hand. With my own release barreling down, I threw my head back, fingers digging into his thigh to hold him tight against me when I spilled deep inside him.

Hips rocking in a few more aborted thrusts, I slowly pulled out when he shivered from overstimulation. Using whatever strength I had left, I rolled him onto his back and collapsed on top while we breathed through the come-down.

Eventually, we shifted so he was sprawled over me, with one leg hooked around my hips and his cheek resting on my chest. He softly scratched his fingers through the hair there, giving me goosebumps.

I studied the soft contentment on his face and the way his long lashes smiled at me when his eyes were closed.

"Well?" I eventually asked, peppering kisses into his hair. "Was that *grounding?*"

He cracked an eye open and laughed, low and husky. "Consider me tied down forever."

Hope fizzed and bubbled in my chest, and for once, I didn't want to look away from it.

A little while later, we cleaned up, slapped dinner together, and snuggled back into bed to watch the sun set, disappearing over the far mountain range until the lookout was once again plunged into darkness, lit only by the glow of the twinkle lights strung above.

"I know you're thinking about the visit to Tate's grandma," Charlie whispered into the space between us once we'd settled in for the night.

"Mmhmm."

Of course I was. I'd barely stopped thinking about it. But in the end, it was Charlie's decision, and I'd never been good at voicing my fears.

He tangled his fingers through mine, lifting our linked hands into the air. "I don't think I could live with myself if I don't at least try."

"I know that."

"Reece?"

"Hmm?"

"Tell me what you're feeling, please."

His eyes were open pools of warm whiskey, and I'd never been able to deny him anything, even the things I wasn't good at.

"What happens if you're not able to get there?" I started, opening the valve that was so much easier to keep shut. "What if you disappear before we arrive? What if we do make it, but you need to rest? Won't you just appear back here at the lookout when you return? Then you'd be alone. I'd be without you. What happens if you can remember everything? Would that be it? Is that the reason you've stayed? I don't want to let you go. Not yet. Not *ever*, Charlie."

His eyes gleamed, and he leaned forward to kiss my forehead. "I haven't felt stuck in this lookout since you arrived," he whispered. "You've set me free and bound me, in every way I want to be bound. When I think of where I want to go when I come back from that other place, I don't think of the lookout anymore—I think about you. Just you. I'm pretty sure as long as we're together, I'll make it to town just fine. And I think I'd be able to find you anywhere."

Tears rolled down my cheeks. "We should test that first," I sniffed. "Do some practice runs before we go."

He smiled. "Yes, my man of science."

I laughed and wiped my face. "You know, when Josh and I broke up, he wanted to try couples therapy."

Charlie tensed next to me.

"I couldn't even fathom it. It confused me. I didn't understand why I'd put in the effort to fix it when there was nothing to save."

I pulled him closer, right up against my chest. "I'm terrified that going to see Tate's grandmother and helping you remember what happened will take you away from me. I can't stand it. But... If there's even a remote possibility she can help us, that she can explain how you're here, how I can keep you here, I'll do it. I'd do anything to keep you, Charlie. I'd give everything I have. You say you'd follow me anywhere, but I'd go to the ends of the Earth for you."

He rested his forehead against mine and breathed deeply. "I can't put words to how much I hope for that, no matter how impossible it seems. But if anyone can do it, I know it's you. My grumpy, stubborn, irritatingly perfect man."

"*Perfect?*" I asked, my chest swelling three sizes at being called *his*. "I'll remind you of that the next time I burn your grilled cheese."

He flicked my ear. "I prefaced that with irritating for a reason."

I chuckled, nuzzling into the bend in his neck. "You love it."

He smiled, eyes soft and twinkling in the dim glow of the fairy lights all around. "Yes," he said quietly. "I think I do."

My chest cracked open. I pulled away, just enough to look at him—to *really* look at him. I wanted him to feel the weight of the words on my tongue.

Before I could say them, though, a slight movement just

over his head caught my eye. I peered up, blinking as my eyes adjusted to the pitch black darkness, only to find the outline of a man standing right outside the window, staring at us.

CHAPTER SEVENTEEN

I shot up, fumbling for the gun I kept in the nightstand. The sound of boots hitting the deck jarred Charlie upright as well.

"What the fuck is that?" he yelled, confused.

I slammed the clip into the gun and made for the exit. "Stay inside!"

"Wait!" he yelled, just as I opened the door. Judging by the sound of the man's steps, he was already on the stairs. "Don't!"

His voice was desperate enough to make me pause. "He's getting away!"

"He wants you to follow him, you idiot!" He untangled himself from the sheets and lurched forward to grab my arm. "*Don't.*"

I shook him off and ran out onto the deck just in time to hear a loud metallic *bang,* followed by a pained shout. The whole tower shook.

"I think he tripped on the stairs," I hollered back to Charlie. "I'm just going to go—"

Charlie's nails dug into my arm. "It's a trap," he snarled. "If you go out there, he'll kill you."

Just then, the beam of a flashlight lit up a small strip of the ground below, erratically bobbing back and forth as it moved away from the tower and into the trees at a fast clip.

"He's getting away again! I could catch up, I could—"

Charlie yanked me by the nape of the neck back into the tower and slammed the door, throwing the lock into place. He strode over to the solar light panel and flicked off the switch, plunging us into darkness.

Then his hands were on my shoulders, holding me fast. "You *could* catch up, because he *wants* you to catch up. He's been luring you and me and Janine and probably every other poor, naïve hiker he's killed into a trap. He's a predator. He knows those woods better than you, and he's hunting you. Don't let him."

I breathed through my rising panic long enough to see the sense in Charlie's words. "You're right," I said, voice scratchy. "I'm sorry."

"Of course I am," he said, and then he threw his arms around me, clutching on as if his life depended on it, trembling violently.

I shuffled backward to where I knew the bed would be, keeping an eye on the door and holding him close with one arm until we tumbled down. Setting the gun on the nightstand, I tucked Charlie under my arm.

"We'll sit here together," I whispered. "And we'll watch

—all night long. If he comes back up those stairs, I'll shoot him."

Charlie nodded.

"I should call Tate," I said, reaching for my phone.

He picked up on the fourth ring. "This had better be an emergency," he said with a yawn.

"He was just here."

"*Fuck.*"

I put him on speaker so Charlie and I could fill him in on what happened, and I swore I heard a faint "*Who is it?*" whispered in the background before Tate prompted us to continue.

He sighed once we finished. "And he's not trying to get in? He ran off?"

"Yeah. Not sure if he's still out there waiting or if he left. I didn't follow."

"It's probably best that you didn't. Stay in the tower, I'll call the station and have a response out to you in—"

"Wait," Charlie cut in, a hand on my arm. "Let's think about this."

"What do you mean?" Tate asked.

"Other than the three of us, does anyone else know about me? Have you said anything about having a guest up here with you? Maybe that someone hiked in to stay?" he asked me.

"No. I didn't want to lie, I'm just not sure how to approach that conversation with Dad or Bobby."

He soothed his hand along my arm. "I understand that. What I'm saying is, he saw... us." He shuddered, and my blood boiled that such a tender, intimate moment had been tainted and violated.

"Tate is the only other person who knows you're not alone," Charlie continued. "Tate, and *him*. If we are the only ones who know, the killer could slip up and admit to knowing something only the three of us do."

Tate hummed, considering. "Did you see him? Or what he was wearing? Is there anything more you could identify him by than the first time he lured you into the woods?"

"No. I only saw an outline, and then he ran."

He sighed. "I need to think about this. If you can't help, it might be beneficial to keep it to ourselves for now. Even the information that he was out there at all, never mind Charlie, would be a secret. I'll talk it over with Waters, see what he thinks about divulging this more widely."

"You two working better together now, are you?"

I could hear the scowl through the phone. "I don't know what you mean. I've always been perfectly cordial."

There was a whisper of a chuckle in the background.

We decided that, given a response would be at least a half-hour out by helicopter and the killer had already fled, Tate would consider what was shared more widely in the morning. For now, Charlie and I would hole up and hike out at first light.

After we hung up, I ran a hand through his hair, tangling my fingers in the soft strands. "That was a good idea. You're so much smarter at all this than I am."

He kissed my shoulder. "And you're hellbent on charging into danger to protect the people you care about."

"You sound irritated by that."

"I am irritated by that. *Irritatingly* perfect, remember?"

How could he make me want to laugh in a moment like this?

"I love you," I whispered, voice warm and adoring. The confession just slipped out, and it was shitty timing, but I'd never felt more sure about something in my life. Judging by the way the emotion swelled in me, sudden and overwhelming, I knew I'd felt it for far longer than I realized.

Charlie scoffed but leaned in to kiss me, hard and quick. "I'm not saying it back until it's romantic again. Huddled in the dark with a serial killer outside is not how I want my first real love confession to go."

I grinned even though he couldn't see and kissed his temple. "Alright."

"But I do, you know."

"Mmhmm."

"I'm just not saying it until my twinkle lights are back on."

"Whatever you say, baby."

"And maybe you should roast me another chicken."

"I'll spatchcock for you, any day."

"Okay, now I'm not saying it until you promise to *stop* saying spatchcock."

"I'm afraid that one's a deal-breaker for me."

He huffed and linked his fingers through mine. We sat in silence that couldn't ever be called peaceful, ears strained. My hand was at the ready to reach for the gun again. But even with all of that, it wasn't anywhere near as horrible as the last time I'd sat frozen in this lookout, afraid of the killer waiting for me in the shadows.

And that was entirely because the man I loved was right beside me.

Charlie and I left shortly after dawn the next morning. I packed light, shoving only the essentials into my backpack before strapping the firearm to my shoulder holster and departing. I'd called and left Leonard a message that I'd be hiking out early, citing a shortage of groceries. It left the entire west side of the national park unmonitored, but Tate was anxious for Charlie to meet with his grandmother, and neither of us wanted a repeat of last night.

I turned back just before entering the tree line and peered up at the lookout. Sunlight poured through the eastern-facing windowpanes, casting a glow inside the tower, almost like magic.

A part of me wanted to climb back up and live with Charlie in that ethereal light forever.

We couldn't, though, and nothing was more of a stark reminder than the darkness that waited when we stepped under the thick canopy of trees.

A monster had robbed me of the joy I felt beneath the pine-laden branches of this forest, and while small compared to his other transgressions, it was one I personally resented him for.

I took Charlie's hand, linking our fingers together, and stepped into that darkness.

"How are you feeling?" I asked once we'd walked for a bit.

"Good. No different than I do at the tower."

I nodded, thankful for that at least. I had many worries about what awaited us in the next few days, but it was a relief to know Charlie wasn't trapped inside the lookout anymore.

"Let's practice for when you go to rest, and see if you really can find me."

He squeezed my hand. "Alright. Be right back."

And then he blinked away.

I slowed my pace, already mentally preparing to hoof it back to the tower if he didn't appear in the next minute or two. Without him next to me, the reality that I now hiked through the same woods a serial killer disappeared into last night slithered into my mind.

What if he were still here? Watching? Waiting until I was alone?

My breath shortened, and my gaze darted around, looking for any sign of movement. How long had it been since Charlie disappeared? Ten seconds? Twenty?

He should be back by now.

"Charlie?" I called. My voice carried through the trees, dead pine boughs and twigs crunching under my boots as I turned. "Charlie—*ooph!*"

I toppled to the ground, weighed down by the man who'd suddenly appeared out of thin air nearly on top of me.

"Found you!" Charlie said, coughing.

"You certainly did," I wheezed.

He cringed down from where he sprawled over me, limbs a tangled mess and covered in dirt and leaves. "Sorry. I was in a rush to get back; it's usually easier to tell what's going on around me before I fully show up."

"As much as I don't hate this," I said, picking a twig out of his hair and shifting my hips into his, "your elbow is somewhere in my abdominal cavity, and I stopped romanticizing outdoor sex years ago."

He scrambled up and brushed himself off before offering me a hand. We both grunted with the effort.

"What if *I* wanted to try outdoor sex?" he asked when we were both upright again, grinning.

I raised an eyebrow at him. "Do you?"

"Maybe I'd like to be a little adventurous one of these days."

I huffed a laugh and swung my arm over his shoulder, moving us along. "Fine. But you'll need to rub Biofreeze all over my back for a week afterward."

He smirked. "I'll take care of you, old man."

I tried not to focus too much on that flicker of hope his words ignited, a brief glimpse of a future we might have together.

Even if it involved dirt in places I'd never be able to scrub clean.

If he wasn't trapped in the tower, if he could exist the way he was now, indefinitely, didn't that mean we had a shot at something close to a normal life?

He'd have to start over in a town that wasn't so familiar with his face, yes. I'd happily go with him, though. Our lifestyle would be unconventional and probably very isolated, but if he were content to have that with me, to *live* with me...

I'd go to the ends of the Earth for you.

I would snatch that future with him in a heartbeat. Absolutely.

Would he want that, though?

I shook my head, focusing back on our surroundings. Charlie and I kept our heads on a swivel for the rest of the hike, but it was becoming increasingly clear to me that for whatever reason, the killer wasn't going to confront us in broad daylight.

Actually, I didn't think he wanted to confront us at all. His modus operandi appeared to be luring unsuspecting people into a situation where he had the upper hand, where he was in control.

I shuddered. He couldn't keep going on forever. With modern technology and testing, it was only a matter of time before he slipped up or was backed into a corner.

I just hoped no one else was around when he lashed out, the way cornered and wounded animals would just before they were caught.

We stopped off at Lake Sapphire on our way down. As beautiful as ever, she greeted us with stunning views and a nice, cool breeze. Charlie was quiet as we rested in the shade, peering out at the wide stretch of glacial-blue water.

Seeing the wonder in his eyes, I realized... This was the first time in thirty-nine years he'd gazed at something other than what could be seen from the lookout.

"Is it different?" I asked quietly.

He merely shook his head no. A single tear tracked down his cheek.

I wanted this moment to last forever. Under any other circumstance, I would've thrown my nonsense about disliking outdoor sex out the window and taken him skinny dipping, before laying him out to dry in the warm sun while I drew as much pleasure from his body as possible.

As it were, we were technically in a public space, and I was not an exhibitionist. *Especially* for a serial killer.

So I clung to his hand, instead, until it was time to depart.

Another two hours later, Charlie and I stopped about a hundred yards away from the small dirt lot where I parked my truck.

"I'll be fine," he said, reading my mind. "I need to rest, and so do you, Reece." He brushed a thumb across my cheek, probably noting the dark circles that'd formed from another sleepless night.

I could sense a migraine in my very near future.

"I'll find you later when you're alone at your Dad's. Don't worry about me."

I pulled him into a fierce embrace and pressed my face into his hair. "Promise?"

He kissed me. "I promise."

I released him, not ready to part but acknowledging it

was time, when his eyes caught on something over my shoulder. His brow furrowed.

I spun around, hand going for my gun, ready to confront whatever waited behind me.

But there was nothing.

"I saw something in the leaves over there," he said, pointing just off the trail. "It looked shiny."

"Shiny?"

"Like a reflection."

My stomach twisted and tumbled, already sensing something was off. He softly tread over with me just behind him, looking all around us. This didn't feel right.

Charlie tilted his head this way and that, as if trying to catch the light again, picked up a stick, and began scratching around in the leaves and dead pine needles.

"Baby, we should go. I don't like this." I stood behind him, head on a swivel, afraid someone would sneak up behind us. My skin prickled like we were being watched.

Charlie gasped, the stick tumbling to the ground. He quickly backed away, bumping into me.

"What?" I asked, frantic. "What is it?"

"I saw *hair*. Someone's hair." He bent over, dry heaving even though there was nothing in his body to expel.

I didn't want to look. I didn't.

But I had to see. I had to know.

Without releasing him, I took a few steps toward where he'd moved the debris around, squinting, trying to make sense of what I saw...

I picked out her hand first.

Then her skull, beneath a waft of white hair matted with blood and decomposition. Her face was unrecognizable, whether from the elements or scavengers or the monster who'd murdered her, I wasn't sure, but I knew who she was based on the glasses that still sat askew on her nose, and the sleeve of the light blue zip-up hoodie from the missing persons posters.

We found Janine.

CHAPTER EIGHTEEN

"And you're sure you didn't touch anything but the stick?" Tate asked.

The scene was organized chaos. I'd met him in the gravel parking lot only a few hundred yards from where we'd found the body. Over his shoulder, a team of evidence technicians milled around, zipping themselves into full-body jumpsuits and roping off the trailhead with yellow crime scene tape.

They'd pulled up in large, unmarked vans that looked entirely too expensive to belong to the Ponderosa Sheriff's Department.

Apparently, the FBI was a little more than *casually involved.*

"Yes," I said. It was the third time I'd given my account of what happened, and it'd be so much easier if I didn't have to remember to leave Charlie out of it. "I saw something shiny, used the stick to scrape at the ground, and dropped it when I saw the body."

He nodded, but Special Agent Sunglasses didn't look convinced. "Tell me what you thought you saw again," he said, frowning.

I sighed. "Look, *um...*" *Fuck, I forgot his actual name.*

"Special Agent Waters."

"Right, Agent Waters. I was hiking to my car, saw a reflection of something off the path, and felt weird about it. I can't explain any more than that."

"Have you seen anything suspicious in the area in the last few days? Any hikers or vehicles?"

I raised an eyebrow at Tate, very aware that it was illegal to lie to a federal agent. I'd already toed the line a little too much for comfort.

He pinched the bridge of his nose and motioned for us to follow him further down the gravel path, away from everyone else.

"He knows," he said once we were out of earshot.

"About..."

"All of it."

"You told him about Charlie?" I asked, shocked. I couldn't imagine trying to explain a ghost to a federal agent, let alone *that* federal agent.

"He explained you've had a... *surprise guest* staying with you at the lookout. I don't believe Officer Morris to be a dishonest person, so I've chosen to accept what he's told me until I confirm it for myself."

"I also filled him in on what happened last night," Tate said, going a bit red in the cheeks.

Agent Sunglasses smirked.

Ah. So he was the mysterious voice in the background when I called Tate. "Is that right? You *filled him in?*"

Sunglasses coughed, and Tate looked ready to turn me into another crime scene. I couldn't decide if Charlie would've batted me upside the head or high-fived me for that one.

Probably both.

"*So,*" he continued, voice dripping with venom, "now that we're alone, other than finding an unknown male staring at you through your windows last night, have you seen anything else odd in the last few days? And is there anything you'd like to add to your account of how you found the body?"

I clarified it was *both* Charlie and I who'd made the gruesome discovery, and reiterated that I hadn't seen anything else out of the ordinary.

"Oh!" I said as we began to walk back toward the gravel lot. "I did see Bobby's truck on this road yesterday. There's a stretch farther into the park that's visible from the tower. He would've had to come by this way; maybe he saw something?"

I'd completely forgotten about it after everything that happened when Tate showed up at the lookout.

Tate blinked.

"How do you know who it was?" Sunglasses asked.

"I saw the truck through my binoculars; it was the old Chevy he bought from Dad. It's the only one like it in the area, unmistakable. And it—"

I stopped, warring with myself on whether or not to

share the next detail. Certainly, it was a coincidence. Nothing to get worked up over. I'd already given a DNA sample when Tate arrived, so they could rule me out. They'd ask Bobby a few questions, clear everything up, and rule him out, too.

Right?

"It's what?" Sunglasses prompted.

"*Um,* he had an ATV in the bed of the truck."

Tate grew very still, while Sunglasses waved me off. "Thanks for letting us know. We'll give him a call."

Now that I'd remembered, I couldn't shake it from my mind. Why was he out here in the first place? And what a coincidence, that it was the day before I found Janine's body in a *very* discoverable location—one that absolutely would've been searched when she first went missing.

Back in my truck and finally ready to depart, I weaved through the gravel lot, dodging the crammed government vehicles. Before I could leave, though, Tate broke away from what appeared to be a heated conversation with Sunglasses and motioned for me to stop and roll down my window.

"I spoke with my grandmother," he said lowly, casting a look around for listening ears. "If Charlie can make it, she wants to meet him tonight."

The rubber band squeezing around my chest doubled, then quadrupled. "Tonight?"

He nodded. "We've never found one of the victim's bodies before, Reece. Why now? Why this one? Why here?" He shook his head. "Whether or not it's the same guy or a copycat, this is big. It's a lot harder to avoid being caught in 2025 than it was in 1986, especially now that we have more evidence to work with. You two should... prepare yourselves. If he can remember anything, we need to know now."

"Okay," I said, clearing my throat. "He's resting, but should be back later. I'll tell him."

"Good. I'll give you a call when we're ready."

Dad's truck was gone when I pulled up to the cabin. I hadn't told him about the man outside the lookout last night and only warned him of my early arrival once I'd left the trailhead.

He replied a few minutes later.

DAD

No problem. I'm on two twenty-fours this week, staying at the base in town to sleep in between. I'll be back in a few days. Keep in touch and take care.

Oh, I banged up my knee pretty good splitting wood before my shift, and left some first aid supplies out on the bathroom sink. No need to worry.

I frowned down at the last text before digging around in the front pocket of my backpack for my keys. Stepping through the front door, I was struck by how odd it was to be there alone. In such a small space, Dad's absence was noticeable, and despite being able to lock myself inside four solid walls that weren't made of glass, I still felt vulnerable. Unsafe.

Almost as if the killer could watch me still, even now.

I wish Charlie were here.

Shaking my head, I tossed my bag by the couch. He needed to rest. *I* needed to rest, too. I could feel the brain fog and muscle tension that preceded a migraine setting in.

I stepped into the small bathroom to take a piss, but backpedaled at the mess I found.

Blood-soaked tissue and gauze filled the sink, with dried droplets splattered all over the counter and tile floor. A pack of bandages was left open, along with disinfectant and various tools used to stitch wounds closed.

"What the fuck did he do to himself?" I mumbled aloud. He must've been hurt badly if he'd needed stitches, and rushed out for work before he cleaned up the aftermath.

I sighed heavily. It wouldn't be the first time he'd avoided going to an emergency room when he really should've, and it didn't bode well for future conversations about safety and taking care of himself as he aged.

Shaking my head, I piled the soiled tissue and dressing into the trash and cleaned off the counter and floor, clearing enough room to set my toiletries. Then, I stepped into the small, stand-up shower and let the hot water wash away the tension in my neck and shoulders.

A few minutes later, clean, dry, and changed into a fresh set of clothes, I crashed onto the sofa, threw an arm over my eyes to block out the light, and tried to nap.

Except all I could think about was Charlie, and that the day or two of buffer I thought we had before we met with Tate's grandmother was gone.

Tonight. It was all happening tonight. I could lose him tonight. I could figure out how to keep him tonight.

I already missed him, and we hadn't even been apart for a full day. What would I do if—

No.

No. I couldn't go there, not even hypothetically.

I rolled and pressed my face into the cushions. The dichotomy of possibilities was impossible to manage—to actually feel. The muscles that'd loosened under the hot shower spray tensed again, pulling my neck and shoulder tight.

Ding.

I patted around for where I'd set my phone next to the couch and pulled up the incoming message.

BOBBY

Are you back in town? Heard something happened up at the trailhead. Everything alright?

I frowned. How did Bobby know about that so quickly? And hadn't he been the one to call me when Janine was reported missing, too?

It was time to nip those questions in the bud. Besides, seeing Bobby was infinitely better than spiraling about what might or might not happen later with Charlie.

Yeah, can I come see you?

Sure, come on over. Molly just went down, though, so if you ring the doorbell, I'll murder you.

"You look like shit," I said.

Bobby waved me through the front door. He had a scrub brush in one hand, a sudsy baby bottle in the other, and it smelled like he hadn't changed his shirt in seven to ten business days.

Or showered.

"Yeah, well, you don't look like you're gonna be on the cover of *Men's Health* anytime soon, either."

I chuckled. "Is she doing okay?" I asked, pointing at the closed door to Molly's room.

"One ear infection turned into three this month, and I've resorted to bargaining with demons to get her to sleep, but otherwise, she's fine. I don't know how Jade or I are alive, though."

I cringed. "That sounds awful. Can I help with anything? Sit here and make sure she stays asleep while you shower, maybe? Or nap?"

He set the half-washed items down on the kitchen counter and crashed onto the sofa. I settled into the armchair opposite.

"No," he sighed. "Other than Jade, I feel like I haven't had a real, normal adult conversation since you've been at the lookout. I'd rather do this, if you don't mind the smell."

I smiled as wide as I could. "I never have."

He flipped me the bird and grinned back. "So, what happened at the trailhead?" he asked.

"How do you know about that?"

He shrugged. "I've got a police scanner. Keeps me entertained when I'm stuck inside taking care of the baby. Makes me feel like I'm still up on what's going on around me."

I grunted. That just sounded like extra anxiety no one needed, but to each their own. "Well..." I sighed. "We, that is, *I* found a body on my hike out this morning. I called Tate, and now the place is crawling with law enforcement. I'm pretty sure the FBI's involved."

"Holy fuck," he said. "Oh, my God. Do you know who it is?"

"I mean, I'm not positive, but from what I could tell, I think it's Janine."

"Fuck," he repeated, shaking his head. "I'm sorry. Can't believe they finally found one of the bodies."

"Mmhmm." I studied his face some more. "How are you? Really?" I asked.

He dragged his fingers through his hair. "Stressed. Really stressed. Jade's job has been crazy the last few weeks, so I've been up with the baby most nights, and it's killing me. I need sleep, but I'm so delirious I'm not even sure I *could* sleep, ya know?"

"Not really, but I can imagine how hellish that is."

He grunted. "And I didn't tell you before now, but Mom and Dad are getting a divorce, and it's not going well."

"What?" I asked, baffled. "I just talked to your dad the other day; he seemed fine."

"They're both being difficult about assets and who gets what in the split. Dad won't budge on a few pieces of land that really should just be sold off," he finished with a wave. "It's tough feeling like I'm in the middle."

I nodded. "I'm sorry."

"Meh, you went through this as a kid, that's gotta be worse."

"They weren't consulting me on who I thought should get the house and shit like that, though. You've already got enough going on."

"Yeah..." he sighed. "So, what did Tate say about the body when you talked to him? Do they know anything? What's the FBI's involvement?"

I shrugged. "He didn't say much, really, other than they don't know if it's a copycat or the same guy as before."

Bobby's eyes sharpened. "You mean they think the same guy's still around? And he started killing people again after all these years? Why? I thought they'd pinned the last ones on that lookout who went missing."

"It wasn't him," I said, the words falling out of my mouth on instinct.

"Did Tate tell you that? How do they know? Do they have DNA or something?"

Fuck, it wasn't the right time to tell him about Charlie. I wanted to, but my head was beginning to throb, and we were both exhausted.

Besides, I wanted to get through tonight first. If Tate's grandma had answers for us, it would make a conversation with Bobby and Dad easier. Maybe.

"No, he didn't, just that they hadn't ruled out that it could be the same killer," I answered.

And in the most obvious, fumbling segue imaginable, I continued, "Oh, that reminds me. I saw you yesterday driving on the park service road, near the trailhead. I told

Tate you'd been in the area recently, so he may give you a call to ask if you saw anything suspicious. The body's only a few hundred yards away from the parking lot."

He stared at me for a second, face blank. "What are you talking about?"

"Yesterday?" I asked. Had that been yesterday? Everything was happening so fast. "I saw you driving into the park."

He shook his head. "I was home with Molly all day yesterday."

I cocked my head. "I'm certain it was your truck."

He peered out the window at where it was parked, no ATV in sight. "I didn't leave the house yesterday, Reece."

What the fuck?

"I'm not trying to argue with you. Maybe it was someone else. I just thought I saw you."

He frowned, looking shaken. "I'll tell Tate it wasn't me if he calls."

Something in his gaze made my skin itch, like it was suddenly two sizes too small. "Yeah, sure. Hey, I should get going. I've got plans tonight and need to catch some sleep."

Really, I needed to be alone. Charlie might want to come back soon, and I needed to see him. Needed to hold him. Needed to get myself together and stop reading into whatever I'd just seen in Bobby's face.

"Of course," he said, standing and pulling me into a hug. "I miss you. I'm sorry this was so short. Hopefully, the next time you're back, we can go to dinner. And maybe then you'll be comfortable enough to introduce me to whoever it is you've been shacking up with in that lookout without telling me."

My entire body tensed, and I quickly pulled out of the hug. "What?"

"Shit, I told myself I'd wait for you to talk to me about it first," he said, looking at me oddly. "It's just, I'm your best friend. I thought you'd tell me something like that. You've sounded good the last few weeks—really good. I want you to know that if you've met a guy, I want to know him, too. I know I wasn't the greatest around Josh. Not that he was particularly *easy* to be around, either, but—"

My blood ran cold. "How do you know that?"

He looked surprised at the interruption. "What do you mean?"

"How do you know I've had someone staying with me?"

Bobby blinked and opened his mouth to answer, but a loud banging on the front door interrupted him.

"Fucking hell…" he mumbled, striding over to yank it open. "I just got the goddamn baby to sleep, you asshole. Who the fuck are you to—"

Sunglasses stood on the porch, stoic. "Bobby Mandich?"

"Yes? Who are you?"

"I'm Special Agent Waters with the FBI," he said, pushing his way inside and handing Bobby a piece of paper. "We have a warrant to search your home for items connected to the murder of Janine Wallace, including both the vehicles in your name and the outdoor structures on your property. Please step outside."

CHAPTER NINETEEN

"What the fuck is going on?" I roared into the phone, pacing back and forth in Bobby's front yard.

Police were crawling all over the place, loading giant totes filled with God knows what from Bobby's house into the back of those same unmarked vans from earlier.

"Calm down, and I'll explain," Tate shouted back.

I took a deep breath and shook my head. "It's not him. It's not," I said, my voice catching. "Whatever you think you have, you're wrong."

I looked over at Bobby, currently having his own frantic phone call. Hopefully with a lawyer. He had one arm around Jade's shoulders while she bounced Molly on her hip. She'd rushed home after he'd called and told her what happened.

"He's not under arrest yet," Tate said warily. "But there was enough for the search warrants."

"My friend is not a murderer," I hissed.

A few of the evidence technicians glanced over at me, faces hidden behind their goggles and masks.

"Reece..." Tate sighed.

He couldn't be. Bobby was kind and gentle and stopped to help turtles cross the road. He'd cried when he accidentally stepped on a snail when we were seven.

He'd cried the day he married Jade, too, and again when Molly was born. He'd held her so gently, so tenderly, like all of a sudden the whole world rested in the palm of his hand, and he couldn't do anything but stare at her in awe.

Bobby was there for me on my lowest fucking days, when the Thing squatting on my shoulders told me I didn't deserve his friendship anymore because I could never be a good enough friend in return.

It wasn't him. It couldn't be him.

"What about tonight? Why couldn't you have waited, huh? What if Charlie remembers something important? Something that could change everything?"

"I still want to hear what Charlie remembers, but that was thirty-nine years ago. He may not be able to remember anything at all, and I couldn't keep ignoring the evidence we have for the most recent murders."

"What evidence?"

"You're not the only one who's seen his truck in the area. Janine logged it, too. She also logged a camo-colored ATV driving on restricted park trails near her tower the day before she disappeared."

My heart skipped a beat. "Well, that's... I mean, that

doesn't mean anything, though. Just because he was nearby—"

"The ATV is new, Reece," he said, frustrated. "There's no evidence of transportation in the first six murders. The FBI profilers say the first guy wouldn't change how he kills—he liked it too much. Everything points to it being a different suspect. I know you don't want this to be your friend. I know you want to make it right for Charlie. And maybe he will have something important to say, maybe not. But I can't tip the scales of justice for you in the meantime."

"You're an asshole, Tate. A real fucking asshole."

His voice hardened. "I'm trying to do my goddamn job and hold the right people accountable. You can't have it both ways. You can't defend a past injustice and hate me for pursuing the person who should be held responsible in the same breath."

"Bobby isn't the one responsible!"

Tate sighed. "I'm not going to argue with you anymore. Wait for my call, okay? I've gotta go."

He hung up, leaving me ready to throttle someone.

Fuck him, and fuck his justice. Too many people I loved had been hurt by it.

I turned just in time to see that Leonard and Joan had arrived.

"Reece," Bobby said when I walked over. Frazzled, his attention snagged on every box carted out of his house. "We've gotta go meet with the lawyer. Are you good to drive home?"

"Yeah, of course. Is there anything you need? Anything I can do for you?"

He shook his head. "No. Mom's going to take the baby for the night. I can't think of anything else right now, but I'll let you know if I do."

"Sure. Okay. Whatever you need." I turned to Leonard. "I'm not sure when I can get back out to the lookout, maybe a couple of days? I want to be here in case I can help."

He patted me on the shoulder. "No problem at all. Just let me know when you need a ride back out. Hopefully, this is all over by then."

Before I could go, Bobby grabbed my arm, eyes pleading. "I didn't do this, Reece. Please believe me."

I searched for a killer in his eyes, but all I found was my friend. "I know. I believe you."

At least, I wanted to.

Lost in thought and exhausted, it was easy to ignore the eyes I felt following my every move when I stopped off at the drug store on the way back to Dad's.

I wasn't sure whether news of Bobby's house being searched had already spread, or if I just looked rough enough to earn Ponderosa's suspicious gaze.

Light blue shirts dotted in with the pink ones now, and another poster, not as weather-worn and crinkled, joined the others all over town. I wished I'd been able to know Janine more in life, and not the version of her that was reduced to a handful of facts.

It was dusk when I arrived back at Dad's cabin, and I

plodded through the door, chucked my keys on the coffee table, and crashed onto the sofa, dropping my head in my hands.

This can't be real. This can't be happening.

My migraine had fully kicked in, so once I was able to stand, I washed down my usual cocktail of drugs with a glass of water and went searching for an ice pack in the freezer.

"Hey, I remember that truck."

I slammed the freezer door shut and spun around. Charlie stood in the living room, staring at a photo hung on the wall.

"*Charlie.*" All at once, my fight and rage fled. Here, alone with him, I didn't need it anymore.

His gaze immediately found mine. "What's wrong?"

I strode over, wrapped my arms around him, and buried my face in his hair.

"Hey, it's alright," he cooed, rubbing my back. "I'm here. What happened?"

I took a deep breath. "I saw Bobby's truck yesterday, hauling an ATV not far from where we found the body," I began, the words tumbling out. "But when I went over to talk to him this afternoon, he denied it. And now the FBI is searching his house. He *knew*, Charlie. He knew about you. He asked why I didn't tell him I had someone staying with me at the lookout. How? How did he know? There has to be an explanation. He's my best friend. My *only* friend, until you. What if—what if he—"

I cut myself off, unable to even finish the thought.

Charlie's fingers bunched in my shirt, tucking my head

beneath his chin. "*Shh,* it's going to be okay. I'm sure there's an explanation."

"But... He *knew.*"

Charlie pulled back and looked me in the eye. "You know your friend. Don't give up on that. I don't know how he knew, but I'm sure you can find out. Should we go talk to him?"

I shook my head. "We can't," I said, voice breaking. "He's meeting with a lawyer, and Tate is going to call soon. He wants us to meet with his grandmother tonight."

Grief flashed across Charlie's face, and I realized just how much we'd both hoped to spend a few more precious nights together.

Just in case.

No. No, I wouldn't lose him. I'd do anything to keep him with me, and she would have answers for us. She would help.

I'd *make* her help before Charlie told them anything useful.

"Oh," he said. "I thought—*tonight?* Already?"

I took his hand. "Tate said if there's something you can remember from the previous murders, he needs to know as soon as possible. They could arrest Bobby at any time."

Charlie cleared his throat. "Of course. I don't want Bobby to be blamed for something he didn't do. Of course, we'll do it tonight."

Shit. I shook my head, crowding him over to the sofa until he sat down. "No, that's not how I meant to say that."

I urged him to lie back and followed him down, so that I

lay angled over him on the narrow cushions. "It's not a trade. It's not a compromise between the time we deserve to have together versus information that could help him." My lip curled. "If Tate had just fucking *waited*, instead of rushing into this like an idiot..." I sighed, ghosting my mouth over his. "I'm sorry. I just wasn't prepared for any of this. I have a massive fucking headache, and all I really want to do is hold you."

Charlie ran a thumb along my cheekbone. "I understand. And Tate's decisions aren't really why you're upset," he whispered.

I buried my face in the crook of his shoulder. Of course, he was right, but if I didn't have the wind of my anger keeping me up, what was there left to face?

My best friend was under investigation for murder, and Charlie and I had precious few hours left before we confronted the fears we'd avoided for weeks.

"I just don't know what to do," I whispered. "I don't know how to help Bobby, and I don't know how to help you stay."

Charlie kissed me on the forehead. "One thing at a time, baby. Have you eaten anything?" he asked.

I shook my head, cheeks warming. He'd never called me that before.

He shifted until I was the one pressed against the back of the couch, and stood. "It's been a few years since I've tried, but I'm confident I can make a better grilled cheese than you."

I snorted. "You distracted me. It won't be a fair comparison."

He smirked, but there was only soft care in his eyes. "We'll see about that."

He did make a better grilled cheese than me, the stinker.

"It's all about layering the cheese properly," he sniffed, slurping up a spoonful of tomato soup.

I mirrored him, rolling my eyes. "I think you're full of shit."

"If there's one thing I am confidently not full of, it's shit. Been about forty years, actually."

A laugh rumbled up from my belly. "I think that means you're *extra* full of shit. You should go see a doctor."

"If I showed up in an emergency room, they'd have more immediate concerns than my bowel movements," he said, shoving another bite of crispy, toasted bread and cheese into his mouth.

Once we'd finished, we curled back up on the couch in each other's arms. "I do feel a bit better after that, thank you," I whispered.

"Mmhmm."

I peered down at him. "Tell me what you're thinking?"

"That's my line."

"It's a good one."

He smiled. "I'm thinking... This is all I need. This is all I've ever needed, Reece. And no matter what happens tonight, I just want you to know—"

"No," I cut in firmly. "No. We're not doing that."

He pressed his hand against my heart. "I'm afraid," he whispered. "I'm afraid we'll push whatever's keeping me here too far. Or that remembering will wear me out again, like when we first met. I'm afraid I won't be able to come back for days or weeks. I told you, time is different there. What if I come back too late? What if you've left? Or moved on? What if I come back and something's happened to you, or it's been another forty years, and—" his words broke off in a sob.

I wiped the tears from his cheeks and kissed his temple, a few of my own escaping. "I love you."

When he looked ready to reply, I cut him off. "*Shh*, no. Not yet. You don't get to say it back yet, because we don't have your twinkle lights on, and I want to spatchcock another chicken for you first. But I need you to know I will do everything in my power to carve out a life for us, whatever that looks like. There is no moving on from you. I'm not going to let you go, no matter what happens tonight."

He pressed his trembling lips to mine. "I promise I'll always be able to find you. Wherever you go, I'll be there, too."

I kissed him, and it was different than all the others we'd shared. It burned, and time slowed, like Charlie and I were all that remained in the world.

"Reece..." he breathed, fingers finding the hem of my shirt and lightly scratching through the hair on my belly. "Do you feel okay enough? Your head—"

"Yes," I panted, gripping his waist and moving over him. "Please."

We were a match lit too soon.

Rushed and immediate, our hands raked over each other like we only had seconds before time ran out. He wrestled my shirt over my head—a considerable feat, seeing as I didn't want to stop touching him. I straddled him and shoved my tongue back into his mouth, one knee slipping between the cushions and digging in painfully to the frame of the pull-out bed below, but I didn't care.

I needed to have him close to me. Needed the reassurance that we were both still there. Still together. Still real. He did too, judging by the near-feral gleam in his eyes when he nipped and tugged my bottom lip, like he wanted to consume me before it was too late.

"Fuck," I said, trying to pull out my cock in the tight squeeze of bodies and clothes and stuck limbs. "I need to feel you."

"Up. Get up," he said, hands moving over me just as frantically. I stood long enough to kick off my pants and grab the lube I'd stored in the front pocket of my backpack.

This wasn't supposed to be a rushed fuck. We should've had more time.

"Stop thinking, Reece," Charlie commanded, lifting his hips to slide off his pants until they dangled from one ankle. He flung his own T-shirt across the room. "Come here. Now."

Stretched out on the couch, cock already half-hard and beckoning me closer with open arms, I could do nothing but obey.

I covered him again, grinding my pelvis down into his

until I saw stars. He shifted beneath me, eyes rolling back from the friction.

"Keep doing *that*," he panted, palming my ass with both hands. I couldn't tear my gaze away from him, and the way that impossible dusting of pink flooded from his cheeks all the way down to his chest drove me wild.

When I looked back up, his eyes were already locked on mine, full of something needy and desperate. My chest tightened, and the urge to be inside him grew overwhelming. "Charlie. Can I—"

"Yes. Now. I want you, now," he said, hooking one leg around my hip. He kissed me, pouring gasoline over the fire in my blood.

Too impatient to let me prep him as thoroughly as I should've, he barely took my searching, slick fingers before rushing me along. Still, I secretly enjoyed watching him gasp and shiver beneath me when I lined up and pushed every inch of my hard cock inside.

"God, I'll never get used to how tight you are," I said through gritted teeth.

Maybe we'd *both* been impatient.

Unable to help rocking into the hot squeeze of him right away, I stuttered to a halt when he made a sound that wasn't entirely pleasure.

"Too much?" I panted.

"I like it," he rasped.

I knocked my forehead into his. "That's not a no."

"I'll be better once you pick up the pace," he snarked, swatting my ass.

I bit his shoulder in answer, braced a hand against the arm of the sofa overhead, and drove into him, hard.

"Better," he gasped.

He didn't sound better, though. He sounded... Frantic. Not in an *I need you now* kind of way, but in a rushed way. I buried my face in his neck, because even though I was literally inside of him, it still wasn't close enough.

"Reece," Charlie said after a few thrusts, patting my side. "Reece, hold on."

I stopped and quickly pulled away to look at him. "What's wrong?"

He shook his head, eyebrows narrowed in concern. "Nothing, but it feels like I should be asking you that. Are you ok?"

I blinked at him, willing the tightness in my chest to ease. "Yeah. I'm fine. Just uncomfortable," I said. "The angle's wrong. I keep jamming my knee into the bed frame."

His eyes searched mine, and he brushed a thumb across my cheekbone. "Then let's move."

I pulled out and stood. Quickly, he sat up and twisted so he was on his knees, facing the back of the sofa. The muscles from his neck to his hamstrings were one long line of tension, and he eyed me over his shoulder. "This good?"

Tongue-tied, I could only nod. Aching to be back inside him, my cock throbbed at the sight of his plump ass presented just for me. The arch of Charlie's back belonged in a painting. I wanted to bite the meaty, soft part of his inner thighs and spread his cheeks to watch while I tunneled inside.

He was the most beautiful man I'd ever seen, and he was real. He was mine.

For now.

"What are you waiting for?" he asked with an impatient huff, almost irritated.

My brow furrowed. I took a deep breath and sidled up behind him, bracing one knee on the sofa. My weeping cockhead tagged the cleft of his ass, and I pressed my thumb into the sticky wetness, smearing it across him.

Gently, so gently, I traced my fingertips along the swell of his bottom and up the planes of his back to soothe those tight muscles, trying to find the words to describe that squeezed feeling in my chest. "I don't want to take you like it's some quick back-alley hookup."

Close. But not quite.

He blinked. "What's wrong with that?"

"With you? Nothing. But that's not what I want right now."

He shrank away from me. "You don't want me?"

I leaned forward and laced my fingers through his on the back of the sofa, cradling his entire body with mine. "I love you, Charlie," I whispered into his cheek. He pressed his face into my words, his body melting into mine. "I want you so much. But I don't want to hurt you, and I don't want to be inside you when you're looking at me like it could be the last time."

Bullseye.

He looked away. "That's not—I wasn't—"

"Because it's not," I said, bucking against him.

He moaned and arched his back, pushing his ass into me. "Reece, please. Come back. I need you."

Desire consumed me again. I swiped even more lube over my dick and pulled his cheeks apart, lining back up. "Say it's not the last time."

Charlie dropped his head forward. "*Reece...*"

I banded an arm around his middle to hold him up. "Say it."

"I'll always find you," Charlie breathed.

Close enough.

I drove back inside him in a powerful thrust. He gasped at the intrusion, his whole body adjusting to how big I'd feel like this, but there was no pain in his voice this time.

Setting a steady pace, I leaned over and wrapped my other arm across his middle to keep him close. I fit one hand around his throat, holding his face to the side so I could kiss away his tears between the vows I breathed into his skin.

"Don't be afraid," I rasped. "I love you. There's only you. We'll figure something out, I promise."

A promise for him, and a promise for me.

He arched into me. "More. *Please.* More."

I obliged.

We were both too emotional, too overwhelmed for it to last long after that. I sucked and nipped along his neck, and his fingers dug into my thigh and ass, clawing at me to go harder, to give him more.

I'd pour all of myself into him if I could.

Once I found the angle that made him cry out, I didn't let up, hurtling us both toward the edge.

"Reece. Reece, I'm close," he croaked, arms braced to push back into each of my thrusts. His cock bobbed in front of him, but he didn't seem to care, only tilting his hips so I tagged his prostate over and over.

"Me too. Come for me, baby," I begged.

I couldn't hold back anymore, and let each one of his breathy "*Oh's*" shove me right off the cliff into oblivion. I gasped, coming deep inside him.

Claiming him.

All it took was one pump of my fist before he came too, spilling into my hand. I leaned on him heavily while we breathed through the come-down, until I gathered my wits enough to realize I was probably crushing him.

"C'mon," I whispered, dropping kisses along his shoulders. "Let me take care of you, this time." I gingerly pulled out and offered a steady hand to help him off the couch.

Once we faced each other again, Charlie wrapped his arms around me. We stayed like that for a long time, before he eventually tilted his head back to kiss me, slow and deep. "Thank you," he whispered when he pulled away. "I know it's difficult for you to open up like that."

"I don't mean to keep things from you. I just get caught up in my head. But I'll try, for you."

He kissed me again, and a spark of that sly wit I loved so much peeked through. "For the record, I would thoroughly enjoy a quick back-alley tryst with you."

I laughed and ushered him into the bathroom, forever buoyed by the way he could lighten any burden. "The Biofreeze probably applies there, too."

Upon seeing the shower, he groaned. "A *shower*? Oh, fuck yes."

"I can leave you two alone, if you'd prefer privacy."

He tugged me into the stall by the wrist. "Not a chance. Soap me down while I sizzle under the hot water."

"Yes, Chef."

My phone rang an hour later.

Lying on the couch with Charlie on top of me, I carded my fingers through his soft, still-damp hair, and contemplated turning the ringer off and letting it go to voicemail.

Along with the next call, and the next.

I thought about living out what half the town had accused Charlie of doing nearly forty years ago, and driving out of Ponderosa, with him right next to me in the passenger seat. We could start over brand new, somewhere we'd never be found.

It'd be enough just to have each other, wouldn't it?

As if in answer, Charlie propped his chin on my chest to look up at me and whispered, "You should answer that."

I thought of Bobby. And Mom, Dad, Keith, and everyone else who loved me. Everyone who would love Charlie, too, if given the chance.

He pressed his hand over my heart, lightly scratching the hair there.

I'll always be able to find you.

I reached over, answering just before the call went to voicemail. "Hello?"

Tate's somber voice crackled through the line. "It's time."

CHAPTER TWENTY

Viola Morris's red brick house was unremarkable.

Sitting on the corner of a quiet street on the outskirts of Ponderosa, the lawn was manicured and flowerbeds were weeded, lit by a few solar lanterns staked into the ground.

It didn't look like the kind of house where paranormal dealings occurred. There were no creeping vines, crumbling and decrepit walls, or unsettling silhouettes peering out of third-story windows.

But then again, who was I to judge what the paranormally inclined looked like? I was in love with a ghost.

I clutched Charlie's hand as we followed Tate up the walkway.

"My grandmother is... quirky. She can be a bit abrasive, but she means well."

"Like you?" I asked before I could stop myself. To my

surprise, it sounded less like an accusation and more like something I'd say to Bobby.

Charlie gave me a look, anyway.

Tate shook his head. "I know you're not my biggest fan right now, but I swear, before we die, I'll get you to call me your fucking friend, West."

I sighed. "Let's just get this over with. Are you ready?" I asked Charlie.

He squeezed my hand. "Not really, but there's no sense in prolonging it."

"That's the spirit," Tate quipped, before knocking.

A minute or so passed before the door creaked open, revealing a stout woman with long, white hair, wearing half-moon glasses attached to a beaded chain and a flowing, gauzy, colorful dress.

"Hello, my boy," she said warmly, embracing Tate. "You've been away too long."

He eyed her. "I saw you on Tuesday."

She waved off his reply. "Too long. Now, show me... *Oh.*"

The second she laid eyes on Charlie, she stepped back, a hand over her heart. "My God..." she mumbled, before making the sign of the cross over her forehead and chest. "What have you brought to me?"

Tate cringed. "*Uh,* well, this is Charles—*Charlie*—Randolph. And I'm pretty sure he's not a serial killer. He is dead, though. I think."

"That's quite the introduction," Charlie mumbled. "Hi, Ms. Morris. My name is Charlie, and I am most certainly *not* a serial killer. I am dead, though. I don't understand what's happened to me, with, you know," he gestured to his corporeal body, "and Tate said you might be able to help."

He offered his hand to shake, which she stared at before making the sign of the cross again and stepping back. "Come inside, the neighbors already have enough to gossip about."

We all followed her into a living room draped in faded brown, mustard yellow, and gaudy orange. The plastic sofa cover squeaked when Charlie and I sat down, and I made the intentional effort to tuck my elbows in, hoping to avoid knocking over one of the many lamps and trinkets cluttered atop every available surface.

All of her decorative items were displayed on white, delicately crocheted doilies, and judging by the way my nose itched, I'd hazard a guess she hadn't dusted since the moon landing.

"Tea?" she asked.

"No," I replied quickly, fearful of what would be *in* the tea. "*Uh*, thank you, though."

"Yes, please," Charlie said with a smile.

I side-eyed him, and his responding shrug said, *"What? I'm already dead."*

She shuffled into what I presumed was the kitchen, through a doorway adorned with, honest to fucking God, *beaded curtains.*

"Your grandmother is... something," I whispered to Tate, confident she wouldn't hear me over the still-rattling doorway.

He unzipped his jacket and peeled it off. It had to be at least eighty degrees inside, no fan in sight. "Yes, she is. But she's a saint and set me right before I could fuck up my own life irreparably, so give her any of your usual shit and I'll punch your teeth in."

As if to tempt me into testing what I was certain wasn't an empty threat, a hairless cat jumped up onto the sofa cushion next to me and began rubbing itself against my arm, purring.

Charlie covered his laugh with a cough.

Tate looked like a kid at Christmas, gleefully pulling out his phone to take a picture. "That's your contact photo now, by the way," he said, grinning.

"This is the first time I actually wish I had one of those, so you could mail me that picture," Charlie said, chortling.

"I'll have a print made for you." He turned to me. "She usually growls at everyone, so you two are made for each other."

I frowned down at the little creature, who looked more like a raw chicken with eyeballs than a house pet. "If I get punched in the face, it's your fault."

She scowled back and began purring louder, kneading her paws into the sticky plastic covering and head-butting my shoulder, as if pleased to have chosen the person it would bother the most.

The curtains rattled again, and Viola Morris's return brought me back to the matter at hand, the rubber band around my chest squeezing impossibly tighter.

She placed the tray carrying four cups of tea on the coffee table before sitting across from us in a brown recliner that was probably older than me. "I see you've met Sunshine."

On cue, the cat stepped across the table and sniffed at the mugs before curling up in her lap.

I raised an eyebrow. "Sunshine?"

Charlie coughed again.

Tate shot me a look that said, "*Go ahead, one more.*"

"Yes," she cooed, petting the cat. "She's such a joy. Now, tell me again why you're here."

Charlie glanced at me and then at Tate. "Well, *um,* my death was... sudden. I remember bits and pieces, but not all of it. Not the end. I'm the lookout who—"

"I know your story," she cut in, not unkindly. "Is that it? You want to remember the moments before your death?"

"I want to help stop more people from dying. I don't know if what I remember can do that, but I'm willing to try," he answered, looking over at Tate again.

She hummed. "Most who come to me with questions aren't looking to relive that, especially if it was traumatic. It could affect you in ways you're not prepared for."

"Will it..." Charlie began, before clearing his throat. "Will it make me disappear for good? Will it force me into, I don't know, *passing on?*"

I took Charlie's hand and squeezed, my heart in my throat.

Glancing down at our interlocked fingers, she raised an eyebrow. "I doubt that very much, considering how strongly you're clinging to your anchor's life force. But it will be taxing for you both—you might not be able to sustain this form again for a while."

Charlie blanched. "What? What do you mean, *life force?*"

She eyed him warily, assessing. "Intentional or not, I can't tell, but you're feeding off his energy to sustain yourself in this form."

The three of us gaped at her.

"I still don't understand," I said, feeling Charlie's hand begin to tremble in mine. "He's been stuck in the lookout for almost forty years; he couldn't have been doing that this whole time, it's not possible."

"Spirits that haven't let go of this world are usually drawn to a place or thing that has significance to them. Sometimes, where they died; other times, where they felt the safest. But what's happening between you two now is more than that. He's attached himself to you, like an anchor, to mimic being alive in a way I've never seen before."

"*Mimic being alive*, what does that mean?" Tate asked, with apparent disgust in his voice.

She turned to me. "Possession, Mr. West. He's possessing you. And any attempt to sever that connection won't just harm him, it could hurt you, too."

I stared in disbelief. "*Possession?*"

"What do you—ean hurt—im? I—not—*p—essing* him!" Charlie cried, his words cutting in and out like they hadn't in weeks.

I tugged on his hand until he faced me. "Hey, it's alright. You're here. Deep breaths."

He inhaled, following my breathing, and exhaled, already looking steadier. "What do you mean, hurt him?" he repeated quietly.

She peered at Charlie, and then at me. With a little more softness in her voice than before, she said, "I think I understand, now. It's clear that you two... care for each other. It's not something I've ever seen, but you may have accidentally tied your presence to him through that connection."

"Is it harmful?" he asked again, panic returning in his voice. "Am I hurt—im?"

Her face turned grim. "Right this moment? Probably not. But any extreme emotion or use of energy will be taxing on you both. I'm not sure what the long-term effects of possession are, even if it's voluntary. It could hurt him—especially if he gets sick or overly tired."

Charlie looked ready to throw up.

"Can you help us, then?" I asked, desperate and pleading. I'd beg on my knees if I had to. "I love him. He deserves a life. A real life. Can you help us get it back?"

An eternity of silence stretched before us.

"Is that possible? For me to be alive again? To be real, without hurting Reece?" Charlie asked into the quiet, voice so small I wanted to wrap him up and hide him from everything that'd ever hurt him, forever.

Briefly, I saw a flash of possibility in her eyes, a thought almost spoken aloud, before it flitted away. "The dead don't come back to life, Mr. West. I'm sorry."

I gritted my teeth. "Don't, or can't?"

Her gaze sharpened. "What you speak of requires great sacrifice, one of which I will never help you in achieving. Any attempt to make him stronger at this point will only make you weaker. I wouldn't recommend it, lest you wish to join him in death."

Charlie released my hand like it burned. "I'm going to be sick," he said, shooting up from the sofa and heading for the front door.

I jumped up too, following him. The tightness in my chest had grown unbearable. "Charlie, wait."

The mugs of tea rattled against the serving tray, and one of the lamp lights popped, shorting out as he passed by. "Sorry," he said, voice full of despair. "I'm sorry."

His outline flickered. He scrambled for the front door handle, but his fingers kept slipping through, unable to grip the knob. "I *can't*," he said, choking back emotion.

My hand fell through his shoulder when I tried to steady him. "It's okay," I said, reaching around to open the door.

He stumbled out onto the front walkway, startled at the sight of a passing car before darting around to the side of the house, tucked away in the dark.

"Charlie!" I called, jogging after him. The pounding in my head had increased significantly since we'd arrived. "Hold on!"

I turned the corner to find him dry heaving into the bushes. "Baby, it'll be alright." I soothed my hand over his back, firm again under my touch. "It's going to be fine."

"I didn't know," he croaked, straightening to look at me. "I didn't know, Reece. I would never, *ever*—"

I gripped both of his shoulders. Desperation burrowed into my chest and squeezed. "I know that. I know you wouldn't do that. *I know you*, Charlie. But I don't resent this.

I told you, I'd do anything to keep you here. I'd give you anything. If you need to be tied to me, so be it! We'll figure it out—"

Charlie shook his head, fingers digging into my shirt. "Reece."

"We'll ask someone else," I continued, ignoring him. "I'm sure Viola knows more than she's saying—"

"*Reece.*"

"I'll extend my sabbatical, or get permission to work remotely. We'll stay at the lookout through winter. Or, you could come live with me in Missoula, and we'll find someone there who can help—"

"Reece!"

"What?" I hollered, unable to bear the way he kept shaking his head.

His face was marred with an emotion I refused to name. "You can't do that. You can't give up your life like that."

Anger found me again, heating my cheeks and wetting my eyes. "Yes, I can. It's mine, and I want to spend it with you. I don't care if you need my energy, or life force, or whatever the fuck that quack was talking about. *I don't care!*"

Charlie pushed forward, hands braced against my chest. I took a step back. His eyes were filled with fat, angry tears, too. "You're so goddamn stubborn! I refuse to be the reason you spend your life chasing impossible things. I refuse to take so much from you; you deserve better than that. You say you're fine with it now, but what happens in the future? What if you get sick, or resent me? I won't tether myself to you like this. I would've never done it if I understood what was happening. Especially not to stay like this," he thrust out his see-through palms, choking on a sob. "Not for this farce of an existence."

I grabbed each hand in mine. "You haven't taken anything from me," I growled, dragging him into my chest and wrapping my arms tight around him. "I *gave* it to you. You've brought me back to life! You've made me want to *live*, Charlie, and I gave you my heart freely. Take it. It's yours. It will always be yours. No matter the cost."

He didn't hug me back. The pit in my stomach yawned open, like I could already feel him slipping away.

"Reece..." he said, pulling back. His eyes were deep and endless and broken. "I care about you far too much to ever accept that. I lo—"

"Stop," I snarled through my tears, cutting him off. "Stop it. Don't say that. You don't get to say that yet. *Not yet.*"

Charlie covered his mouth and looked away. "I wanted to stay with you so much," he finally choked out. "Even like this. Even if it meant I could never have a normal relationship with your friends or family, or we couldn't go places together, or someday you'd pass away like everyone else, and I'd still be stuck here, like this. Even then... I would've snatched up that life with you, because you're worth it. You're so worth it. But not like this. Not at the expense of your life or your health. I won't take that from you."

I shook my head. "No." I reached out, begging, and when he fell into my arms and held me back, something inside me snapped.

No longer did I plead alone for Charlie to stay, but the Thing did, too.

Together, we protested and wailed. We flayed our chest

open so Charlie could see everything—all the bruised and broken pieces. We'd never been two separate entities in the first place, and it'd taken Charlie caring for me, for all of me, to see it. "No, I don't accept that. I don't."

He squeezed me tighter, and I buried my face in the crook of his neck. "It's not fair," I sobbed. "It's not fair you're dead, and it's not fair we couldn't have met like a normal couple. It's not fair everything you wanted in life was cut short, and it's not fair my health got fucked over. But then I found you, we found each other, and now I can't do it without you. I don't accept it without you. I'd take all of it over and over and over again if I could just have you. I'll stay in that lookout forever if it means I get to be with you."

Charlie wept, tears streaming down his face. "I'd endure it all again, too, if only to meet you again. All the injustice in my life can't compare to the gift it's been to know you. To be loved by you."

"Please," I begged. Dropping to my knees, I pressed my face into his stomach. How could he feel so real when everything else was falling apart at the seams? "Don't give up. This isn't the end. You said you'd stay—you promised me. You promised."

Charlie brushed the hair back from my face, fingers gentle despite their trembling, and landed the final blow. "If I loved you any less, I'd keep that promise."

I sobbed into his shirt. "Don't. Don't."

"I'm sorry to interrupt," a voice cut in behind us. I quickly stood and turned, wiping at my face. Tate was there, shuffling from foot to foot, looking more uncomfortable than I'd ever seen him.

He held out his phone. "I just got a call from Waters—there were traces of blood found in the bed of Bobby's truck. They've confirmed it's human. DNA results won't be available for another couple of days, but they're going to move forward and arrest him for Janine's murder."

CHAPTER TWENTY-ONE

The ground slid out from beneath me.

"You can't," I said, shaking my head back and forth. "It's not him. It can't be him."

This isn't happening. This isn't real. None of this is real.

"I'm so sorry, Reece." Tate truly looked it.

I wanted to wake up in Charlie's arms back in the lookout and find the last twenty-four hours had all been a horrible nightmare.

No one had interrupted what should've been a beautiful moment between us. That truck I saw belonged to a perfect stranger, and it was their life currently being flipped upside down, instead of my best friend's.

Viola Morris had given Charlie and me an easy solution to being together. A simple incantation or ceremony, and *poof.*

Everything was fixed.

Charlie could stay, and we'd be happy. Forever.

Instead... My shoulders dropped, arms limp at my sides. All of my anger and fight fled. It washed away in those last fleeting, precious moments we'd spent together, leaving me raw and exposed.

Charlie took my hand, fingers cold against mine. "I want to remember," he said, voice scratchy.

My heart seized. "Charlie, she said it would—"

"I'm doing this, Reece. I want to help your friend before it's too late."

Tate's gaze darted between us. He nodded. "Okay. We have to do it now, though. I should already be at the station."

Now.

Now.

Now.

It was happening *now*, and I wasn't ready. There was so much left unsaid between us. So much life ahead of us, unlived. There was way too fucking much meaning in the way Charlie squeezed my hand before he released it.

He strode forward, confident and sure as he went with Tate back into the house.

Stumbling along, I could only follow. I refused to let him out of my sight. "*Charlie*, please," I begged. "Please."

He turned to face me and cupped my cheeks between his hands. "You're not the only one allowed to give everything for the people you love."

My chest cracked wide open.

"And this isn't goodbye," he continued, looking similarly dismantled. "I'll try to come back before... Before that. But I need to do this for you."

I felt like I was trapped inside a car that'd broken down

across a set of railroad tracks. I could see the train quickly approaching and knew it would be the final blow to this horror of a day, but I was powerless to stop it.

Charlie kissed me once, hard and devastating. Then he pulled me through the door, back into that awful room to do the thing that could take him away from me forever.

It could also save my friend from a murder conviction.

I didn't have room anymore to even hope for the best in either scenario. I just wanted it to never happen, and to already be over, all at once.

Still in the recliner, Viola and Sunshine were where we'd left them. Unfortunately, so was the sweat imprint of my ass and thighs on the sofa cover, which made it less sticky and more slippery when I sat back down.

Of all the tragedy today had wrought, that might've been the final fucking straw.

Charlie sat next to me on the squeaky couch, with his back straight, shoulders squared. "I'm ready. I want to remember."

I'm not ready, I thought selfishly.

"Alright," she said, voice soft. "I'm going to take you through a few calming exercises first, before we attempt to access those memories."

She reached for a small remote and pointed it at a wireless speaker sitting on the table next to Charlie.

The soft pattering of rain began to play, accompanied by the slow, quiet musical cords I imagined one would find in a massage parlor.

"Close your eyes," she said, "and breathe. Inhale," she acted out her instructions along with Charlie, "and exhale."

He did as she asked, stoic and dutiful in his mission, until a peacock cried out over the sound of the rain. His eyes popped open, looking around with concern. "What was that?"

"Just the music, dear. Focus on your breathing."

If I felt less like the world was ending, I'd have commented that being lost in a jungle seemed like the complete opposite of *relaxation*. As it were, I could only concede this psychic, new-age bullshit was the appropriate soundtrack for the worst day of my life.

Once the breathing was done, she began coaching Charlie to visualize his mind and where those memories were stored.

I glanced at Tate, who stared at his feet, avoiding eye contact in a way that felt intentional to prevent us both from bursting into crazed, hysterical laughter.

"Now, find the day you wish to remember. Where were you when you woke up?"

"I was in the lookout," Charlie answered, eyes closed and voice distant. "It had rained the night before, and the air was humid. I went to open the windows for a cross breeze, but... Someone was there. Someone was walking up to the lookout."

Tate looked up, eyes narrowed. My attention honed in on Charlie's words.

"He introduced himself as a police officer investigating the disappearances," Charlie continued. "Ted? Ned? I can't remember his name. He was nice. Polite. He asked if I'd seen anything unusual in the last few days, and if he could see my observation logs. He said he had to stop off at the ranger station on his way back anyway, so he'd drop them off for me."

His fingers twitched where they rested on his lap.

"And then what?" Viola prompted.

"I was preparing to go to bed, but I hadn't even finished taking my boots off yet. Something outside caught my eye."

"What did you see, Charlie?" she asked quietly.

His eyes darted behind his eyelids, and his breathing picked up. "I saw something through the window, down below. Someone's out there, with a flashlight. I think they need help."

He began to flicker and tremble. I grabbed for his hand on instinct, and he clutched my fingers close, body solidifying again.

Now that I knew what was happening, I could feel his presence, his energy, gently tugging on my own. He wasn't demanding or too much. It was more like a request, maybe?

Like someone holding out their hands over an open flame, he soaked in the warmth I freely gave him. If only I could convince him I'd happily burn for him for as long as he needed; I'd burn for him forever.

"I'm down there now, by the trees. I call out to them, but they aren't responding. Why do they keep getting further away?"

His tone shifted. "I ju—ant to make sure you—okay!" he called out, voice echoing through time as if he were actually speaking with them, all those years ago.

I wasn't sure if the shaking of our hands came from him or me.

"I think I'm lost now," he whispered, his outline shifting

and blinking. "It's darker under the canopy than I thought, and my flashlight doesn't carry as far as it did out in the open. I need to get back to the lookout."

The genuine fear in his voice was hard to listen to. I wanted to pull him out of the recollection, to protect him from what was about to happen, but...

Charlie wanted to do this. He wanted to remember, to help.

I squeezed his hand tighter.

"*Something's there,*" he said, voice a hushed warning. His head turned sharply to the left, and I felt him pulling on that connection more forcefully, now, like he struggled to remain in the present. "Someone's running at me. I turn to get away, but..." he gasped. "I—tripped. I d—t have m—light. It's so *dark*—can't see."

"It's okay," I whispered, taking his other hand in mine, too. "Stay here. Stay with me."

He listened, and all of a sudden, I understood what Viola meant when she said our connection could be dangerous. My eyes grew heavy as he pulled energy from me, and my head throbbed. I wasn't sure if my nausea was migraine-related or from the realization that Charlie *could* take too much.

"Do you see anyone, Charlie? Do you see their face?" Tate asked.

Charlie shook his head rapidly, eyes squeezed tight. "No. I can't see anything. I just hear—behind me. Running. I can't st—if they—catch me, and—*AHH!*"

He let out an inhuman scream and flinched, doubling over in pain. Tears rolled down his cheeks before disappearing completely, and nearly his entire body turned translucent.

I could feel how much of a struggle it was for him to hold on. He clung to me, both physically and through our shared connection, doing everything he could to stay.

"HELP!" He wailed. The knick-knacks on the table beside him shook and spun around, clinking against each other. "I can't get up!"

"Charlie?" I called. The room tilted when I knelt in front of him and took him by the shoulders, shaking him. "Charlie! It's okay. It's just a memory. Please, baby, he can't hurt you again. You've gotta let go of it. You can't stay there anymore. We can't stay there. Come back here, please."

"I can't," he cried again, fighting me, fingers scrabbling at his lower body. His leg? Or his foot? "I—stuck—*hurts*."

My heart broke. He was reliving the worst moments of his life, and I couldn't help. I couldn't stop it. No matter how hard I tugged, I couldn't pull him back.

"H—lp! P—se! Wait—*no*—don't!"

He inhaled sharply. His eyes flew open with a gasp, blinking rapidly and casting around the room until they landed on me. "R—ce," he tried, words nearly inaudible, "you—n't—go—ack. No—afe!"

Dread pooled in my gut at the stark terror and pain etched into his expression, but even more so at how pale he was. Barely there at all, wavering and patchy, nearly his entire lower half was gone.

"What happened?" Tate asked, voice urgent, probably sensing Charlie had seconds left before he let go. "Do you know who killed you?"

I didn't want to know. I didn't. As much as I longed for retribution, as desperately as I needed justice for what happened to him, the knowledge of how the man I loved had died would haunt me for the rest of my life.

Charlie gripped my hands tightly, truly hanging on by a thread, now. He'd become entirely see-through, a hazy, shimmering suggestion of a person, at most. Only the vague outline of the man I'd held in my arms and made love with remained, and I was so exhausted from keeping him in the present that I could barely hold my own body upright.

He shook his head again, frustration and fear yanking him from me.

"I—uck—ap!"

"What?" Tate asked. "I can't understand you."

Another lightbulb popped behind Charlie when he tried to speak, dimming the room further. I couldn't hold onto him anymore, my grip falling right through the pieces that were still there.

"It's okay," I whispered. I could feel that he needed to let go. "It's okay, Charlie."

He gritted his teeth, sheer determination pushing his final words through with a shout. The baubles surrounding him flew into the air, and glass shattered all around us. "—BEAR TRAP!"

And then Charlie was gone.

CHAPTER TWENTY-TWO

BEAR TRAP

    BEAR TRAP

    BEAR TRAP

I couldn't remember how old I was when I first found the bear traps Dad kept hidden in the basement closet.

Charlie's gone.

They weren't illegal in Idaho, but there were strict regulations on how, where, and which types could be used. The ones dad had found and brought home, though—big, old, rusted things with giant serrated teeth that looked ready to snap clean through a shin bone—hadn't been legal in decades.

He'd hung them in the shed once he built the cabin.

Charlie's gone.

The fact he'd found *one* out on a public trail was odd enough to begin with, let alone half a dozen over the years. For one, it was illegal to set them in protected grizzly bear territory, but even folks who still used foothold traps to prevent livestock predation wouldn't place *that* where someone might accidentally step on it.

So, who'd set them?

The question had bothered me for as long as I could remember.

Charlie's gone.

Dad claimed he didn't know. The whole thing was weird as fuck—I knew that. He'd grow tense and closed off anytime I brought it up. "I keep meaning to turn them in at the ranger station and never get around to it," he'd say, brushing me off.

I'd let it go and eventually stopped asking, because I never really wanted to think about it, either.

I knew he'd never use them. He respected wildlife too much and was incredibly passionate about protecting natural areas. Besides, he'd removed the pin and spring mechanism in each, essentially making them useless.

Macabre decorations, at worst.

Right?

LEAVE

LEAVE

LEAVE

"Reece?" someone called. It sounded like they were underwater. Or maybe I was?

Charlie's gone.

Dad had never wanted me in that lookout. He fought Leonard hard on my placement, nearly demanding a closer posting.

"Reece! Are you okay? We may have to call an ambulance..." the voice trailed off again.

I banged up my knee pretty good splitting wood before my shift, left some first aid supplies out on the bathroom sink. No need to worry.

It looked like a fucking crime scene when I walked into his bathroom earlier that evening. Had he really hurt his knee chopping wood? Or had he fallen down a flight of slippery stairs, tripping over himself in the dark while he sprinted away?

"*Reece!* Can you hear me?"

No, I can't, because Charlie's gone.

Blearily, I opened my eyes. Tate leaned over me, hands brushing through my hair.

I winced when his finger caught on something sharp. "*Ow*, what the fuck are you doing?" I groaned, batting him away.

"Thank God. He's awake!" he hollered over his shoulder, before turning back to me. "You have glass in your hair. Hold still."

LEAVE

LEAVE

LEAVE

"Charlie's gone," I responded. Had he asked me a question?

"I know. I'm so sorry."

Time blurred. Tate's frantic fingers were replaced by smaller, more gentle ones.

"I think he just needs to rest a bit," their owner said.

Viola.

That's right, I'm at her house.

"I need to get to the station," Tate said. He was far away

again. "I'll call his Dad and let him know what's happened. He can come pick him up."

No. Wait, I think I need to tell you something.

"Did it change anything? What he remembered?" she asked, dabbing at something on my head that stung.

"No. That probably was the killer who came to see him, but if he can't remember details, we have nothing to go on. And we already knew about the bear traps. Found six of them covered in dried blood in the lookout after he disappeared."

His name is Charlie. And he's gone.

"And you're sure it's this Bobby? What about the old murders?"

"It'sssnot Bobby," I slurred, trying and failing to open my eyes again. It was too fucking bright.

Tate sighed. "I'll call you later, Grandma."

Time slipped again. I was lost in a hazy liminal space, searching. Searching.

What was I looking for? Oh, yeah.

Charlie's gone.

"Okay, great. We'll see you soon. I think he's alright, he's just had quite a shock," I heard Viola say. Who was she speaking to?

"We've called your Dad, sweetheart." She was closer now. "He said he'll be able to pick you up in half an hour or so, after they fly back to the base here in town."

No, that's not right.

The plastic couch under me creaked when I tried to sit up. "I need to go," I mumbled.

I lost Charlie in this house. I can't be here anymore. And I need to tell Tate something.

"He shouldn't be too long," she reassured. "Then you can go home and rest."

LEAVE

LEAVE

LEAVE

I shook my head and winced. "No. No, where's Tate? I think I need to tell him something. He needs to come and see."

"He left for the police station a few minutes ago. Just rest. Everything will be fine."

It won't be fine, because Charlie is gone.

"It's not Bobby."

She shushed me and pushed on my shoulder to lie back down again. "I'm very sorry about your friend. Tate told me you've had a rough go of it. I know how much he wanted to do right for you, and for your Charlie."

"No," I said with more force, heaving my body into a sitting position. I was so tired. "No. I'm not in denial. *It's not Bobby.* Please," I said. "I need to show Tate something. I can't—I can't explain it. I just need to show him."

She sighed and handed me a glass of water. I gulped it down gratefully, ashamed I'd turned my nose up at her hospitality before.

"That was far more intense than I imagined," she said. "You need to rest. Your Dad will be here soon to pick you up, and then you can talk to Tate."

That buzzing, itchy feeling under my skin grew nearly unbearable. "I can't wait," I said, nudging her away to stand.

My head went fuzzy, and my vision blacked out for a moment. I braced myself against the back of the sofa until the feeling passed.

"Where are you going?" she asked, voice raised. "You can't drive!"

"I'm sorry," I said before stumbling out the front door.

Later, I'd be ashamed I'd driven home in my delirious state and endangered myself and others, but I had to get back to the cabin before Dad.

I had to see. I had to know.

Charlie's gone.

After skidding into the circular drive, I stumbled up the steps and fumbled with the keys before I found the right one.

The cabin looked like a stranger; unwelcoming and cold in a way it'd never been before. As if it sensed I knew the secrets it kept, and would no longer allow me entry.

Behind me, the trees leaned in and whispered to each other, trapping me here.

He knows. He knows. He finally sees.

I was clearly fucking delusional.

Crashing through the front door, I yanked open drawers and threw the contents all over the floor. Pictures, pamphlets, instruction manuals, old notebooks, scribbled recipes, and work schedules fluttered through the air.

What I actually searched for among the clutter, I had no idea.

I paused and sucked in several deep breaths to steady the throbbing in my skull. Looking up, I saw the picture that'd caught Charlie's attention earlier.

Charlie's gone.

Taken when they'd brought me home from the hospital after being born, Mom held me in her arms while she and Dad beamed in front of a 1986 blue and white Chevy Silverado.

The very same truck he'd sold to Bobby.

Hey, I remember that truck.

Charlie hadn't been up in the lookout with me when I spotted Bobby driving down the service road; he'd been searching for dinner scraps in the outbuilding just before Tate arrived.

Charlie remembered that truck from when it was *new,* not from forty years later.

He knew it from when it belonged to Dad.

What if Bobby hadn't been driving the truck, after all? What if it'd been someone else—someone who'd merely borrowed it from him, instead?

LEAVE

LEAVE

LEAVE

I ripped the picture off the wall and threw it across the room with a roar. It didn't make me feel better to see it shatter all over the back of the sofa—Charlie had sat there with me only a few hours ago.

He'd whispered my name and pulled me close, and we'd made love on that piece of furniture. He'd trusted me and cherished me and put me back together in this room, in this cabin, built by the man who'd—

My brain short-circuited.

No.

No.

I was wrong. I had to be. This cabin was built by my *Dad,* not some faceless monster.

He was a good man. He'd raised me with care and support and unwavering love; he'd been there for me during some of my darkest days, always, *always* showing up right when I needed him most. He'd never failed to ensure I knew how much he and Mom loved and cared for me.

It was all a coincidence. It had to be.

I blinked and found myself standing at the back door, the handle gripped tightly in my fist. I thought I wasn't sure what I searched for when I came here, but that was a lie.

It's not him. It's not him, I chanted in my head, tears streaming down my face as I stepped out into the pitch-black night air.

The motion-sensor floodlight flared to life, casting long, harsh shadows into the trees beyond. They cradled the small yard, forming an amphitheater around the tragedy about to unfold.

A stoic audience to my worst nightmares.

Despite the artificial light, the hair on my arms rose, just like when I'd first arrived at the start of the season.

A predator is near.

Looming before me, the shed stood dark and foreboding, with the garage door flung wide open.

Beckoning.

It's not him. It's not him.

The shadow cast by the floodlight made it impossible to see inside from this distance. I crept across the yard, my heart racing and breath coming shallow and quick as I slowly placed one foot in front of the other.

I wished I could turn around and never look inside, but an overwhelming, impending sense of doom drove me forward. A breeze blew through the trees, rustling the pine needles and ruffling the sweat-drenched shirt stuck to my back.

I heard them before I saw them.

Creeeak. Creeeak.

Squinting, I stopped my approach just outside the door.

If I don't go inside, it's not real.

It's not real.

My dad's hugs were gentle, but firm. He had a warm laugh and kind eyes, and he couldn't possibly be the man who'd done *this.*

Four huge bear traps, coated in a flaky, red-brown substance, hung from the rafters, gently swaying in the wind.

Snap

My stomach dropped. Every muscle in my body tensed.

I whirled around, alarm bells screaming at me to *run, run, run!*

A man stood a few feet behind me, silhouetted against the harsh motion sensor light, his face hidden in deep shadow.

Voice shaking so much my words were barely discernible, I said, "I know who you are. Get the fuck away from me."

He chuckled, low and without feeling.

And lunged.

I threw myself backwards to avoid the heavy object he swung right at my head, and tripped on something crinkly and plastic covering the floor of the shed. The air in front of my face whistled with the force of his swing—he'd missed by a hair's breadth.

Still wielding the blunt object, he lunged again. I took another step back. Desperately, I reached out for something, *anything* I could use to defend myself.

I'm bigger. If I can disarm him, I'll be able to—
SNAP!

The shock hit me first, and then an overwhelming pressure, like I'd shoved my entire lower left leg into a vise. I looked down, uncomprehending what I saw.

A bear trap, quintuplet to those hanging from the rafters above, clamped around my left ankle. Giant, serrated teeth ripped through skin and muscle and lodged firmly into what could only be bone.

Then, pain.

I screamed. And screamed. And screamed.

Collapsing onto the plastic-covered floor, I cried out when it jostled my leg. I reached out with shaky hands to where the trap chewed through skin and viscera, as if I could simply pry it off.

My vision grew spotty before I even touched the wound, and I fell backwards, writhing and groaning.

Heavy leather boots stepped over to where I lay on the crinkled tarp. Dazedly, I followed them up. He carried a large MAGLITE flashlight in one gloved hand and wore dark clothes. His face still hid in shadow, but it didn't matter.

Whoever he was, he wasn't human anymore.

He was a monster.

His head cocked to the side. Chest rising and falling rapidly, he relished in watching me bleed out on the floor of my father's shed.

As if it *excited* him.

"Gotcha."

And then he swung that heavy flashlight at my face. I didn't even have time to try to dodge the blow before the world went dark, and there was nothing at all.

CHAPTER TWENTY-THREE

"*Y*ou *have to wake up, Reece.*"

I blinked my eyes open to find Charlie standing in front of me, his hands gently cupping my face.

I smiled at him. "You came back."

Something was wrong, though. He didn't return my smile, and he looked... Sad? No, that wasn't right. Angry, maybe? Determined?

He shook my shoulders. "You have to go back. I'll do what I can to help them find you, but you need to hold on for just a little while longer."

"I don't understand. What's wrong? Why are you so upset?" I looked around.

We weren't in danger. In fact, we were back in the look-out, tucked away high above the forest. Except, all the color and life we'd brought to it was gone. Instead, everything was cast in deep shadow.

Diminished.

Charlie's twinkle lights didn't glow, and the stove was cold.

But nothing hurt in this place, and we were together. What else was there to want?

"You shouldn't be here. Not yet. Wake up, now. Please," he implored, pushing me backwards toward the door.

An echo of pain, distant and muted, made my whole body throb. I took one of his hands in mine, shaking my head no. "I don't think I want to go back there, though. It hurts a lot, and you're not there."

Tears ran down his face. "I know, baby. I'm so sorry. But you need to try."

"Will you come with me?"

He sobbed. "I can't. I need to help them find you."

My brow furrowed. "But I'll see you again after that, right? You promised."

"Reece," he said, frantic. "We're out of time. You need to wake up."

"But—"

"WAKE UP!" he shouted and shoved me out.

The world tilted and rocked beneath me.

I blinked, and it hurt. So did breathing. I whipped my head to the side just in time to vomit without choking, and gasped as pain bolted up the side of my skull, searing and sharp.

Coughing, I tried and failed to wipe my mouth, unable to lift my hands. Why were they stuck behind my back?

I tugged again, and the world rocked more fiercely. Wait. They weren't stuck; they were *tied*. Blinking some more, I groaned and struggled against the bindings.

"Stop moving," a voice growled from above.

A heavy boot connected with my leg, and I gasped in pain, ears ringing as stars danced behind my eyelids.

Gotcha.

My heart raced as memories flooded back. Charlie's pained cry just before he left me echoed along with the ringing. With horrific clarity, I now understood just how terrible that had been to relive.

The shed, wide open and inviting. *Luring.*

The bear traps.

That haunting, raspy voice. *Gotcha.*

It didn't sound like Dad, but he'd said so little, I honestly wasn't sure if my mind merely protected me from a truth that would destroy me.

I tried to peer down at my ankle, certain I'd only find a bloody stump remaining where my foot used to be. Only, I couldn't see anything at all.

Oh, no, no, no!

After everything that'd happened in the last twenty-four hours, I hadn't thought about my MS once. I'd only worried over Charlie, and Bobby, and *Dad...*

I blinked again, eyes darting back and forth, and caught a dim flash of light, almost as if—

Scratchy fabric pulled at the hairs on the back of my head, matted and clumped together.

I was blindfolded.

For once, being able to explain my lack of vision wasn't reassuring.

My ears quit ringing. In its place, I heard loud, steady sloshing noises, and the ground rocked and tilted in time with each *swoosh*.

Suddenly, the sound stopped, and ambient noise crept in all around. Insects hummed, frogs croaked, and water lapped at the hard surface beneath me.

Am I in a boat?

Ever so faintly, I heard a fast, low, *thrum, thrum, thrum,* like distant drumming.

The man cursed under his breath before what I assumed was paddling picked up again, almost frantic.

I could still hear that rhythmic sound, though. It burrowed into my ears and rooted deep in my soul. It was so familiar, its origin on the tip of my tongue, playing hide and seek in my broken and bruised peripheral thoughts, yet I couldn't place it among the night song all around.

Still, if I could hear whatever it was, maybe it could hear me. "Help!" I shouted over the splashing of the oars. Or tried to, anyway, with my wrecked and hoarse voice. "Help me!"

The boot connected with my stomach, this time. "Shut up."

Wheezing, I gasped for breath and tipped onto my stomach, landing in the puddle of my own sick. I retched, rolling again so I was on my back, and inhaled a few shallow breaths.

The thrumming metronome grew louder.

"Impossible," the monster muttered lowly. "They'll

sweep the roads first. There's time. There's time." Then, his voice switched to something disturbingly neutral, as if he were simply teaching me how to tie a knot. "Alright, far enough. Up and over you go."

And that was when I finally recognized it.

The reason his voice sounded like someone instructing me on how to tie a knot was because he *had* taught me how to tie knots. He'd also helped me set up my first tent, locate the best kindling to start a fire, and navigate through the forest without a compass.

I'd slept in his house countless nights as a child when Dad had to work, blissfully unaware of the predator that lurked down the hall.

In my brief moments of clarity between pain and unconsciousness, I'd ignored how familiar his voice was, unwilling to even consider my Dad could also be the man trying to murder me.

But as the real killer's nonchalant words washed over me, I understood with sharp clarity who the true monster was, and just how far he was willing to go to hide in the shadows —even sacrificing the ones closest to him in the process.

Rough hands grabbed my shoulder and yanked me upright. Every functioning survival skill I possessed kicked in, and only one thought raced through my mind.

Up and over.

We were in a boat because I was being *dumped,* and if I didn't act right now, it would be too late.

If it wasn't already.

I used the momentum to throw myself forward, knocking him back with a heavy grunt. Still unable to see through the blindfold, I rammed my shoulder out indiscriminately, connecting with a soft, fleshy part of him. My thigh landed hard on something bony.

I screamed when he stumbled away, stomping on my injured leg in the process. In a blink, I was flat on my back again after what could've only been an elbow hit me in the cheek.

Stars circled around and around and around.

Except this time, it wasn't just stars. There were trees, too, and the moon, far, far, away, beaming down like a distant spotlight onto the forest below.

Dazedly, I noted my blindfold must've fallen off in the scuffle, unless I was hallucinating.

But... No. I couldn't be, because even in my worst nightmares, I wouldn't conjure something so evil.

Leonard struggled to his feet, his face dimly lit by the glow of a headlamp and twisted in a grimace. He gingerly prodded at his bloody knee, which he must've landed on hard for it to be soaked through the tan material of his pants.

Unless he'd already been injured, and our tussle had only reopened the wound. Maybe by falling down the stairs, fleeing the lookout last night?

"Fuck," he growled, limping and readjusting the light strapped across his forehead.

I couldn't stand. With my hands still tied behind my back, I barely had enough strength to inhale, let alone fight him, but I tried anyway, kicking out with my one good leg.

He caught it in both hands, his eyes empty, hollow sockets of shadow cast by the harsh headlamp he wore.

"Let go of me," I snarled, trying and failing to kick him off balance.

He chuckled, placed one heavy boot on my shattered leg, and *pressed*.

My vision blacked out again. If I screamed, I couldn't hear it.

"You have to hold on, Reece."

"Charlie?"

"Just a little longer, now. Please. Just a little longer."

"I can't. I can't."

"You can." The force of his words rumbled through my murky thoughts like thunder. *"We're coming for you. We'll find you. Hold on."*

Was it really him? Was he with me, somehow? Still latched onto the life force I'd so freely share with him, if he'd let me? Or was I only imagining he was there, so I wouldn't die alone?

If I could choose the face death wore as it lulled me into that peaceful goodnight, it would be his.

"No!" he snarled. "Hold on!"

I came to as I was heaved up by the shoulder into a sitting position. Leonard grunted from the strain of lifting me with his injured leg and propped me sideways against the edge of the boat.

Even though I didn't have the strength to look up and read his expression, I knew he drank in the sight of me so close to death, vulnerable to his every whim.

It was the most disturbing thing I'd ever experienced.

"Why?" I croaked before coughing up bloody spittle all over my shirt. Charlie's words echoed through my mind.

Hold on, hold on, hold on!

Leonard knelt in front of me so I could finally see him. I wasn't sure what I'd expected to find in his face, but I had expected *something.*

Instead, it was like staring into a void. He didn't sneer or grow defensive. He merely cocked his head and furrowed his brow, those dead shark eyes giving away nothing.

"Because I wanted to."

Then he reached behind him and pulled a gun from the waistband of his pants and shoved the barrel right underneath my chin. "Now, get in the water."

The boat had drifted while we fought, and the moon hung over his shoulder now, even closer and brighter than before. I could feel the *chop chop chop* of that strange thrumming in my chest.

That's not the moon.

Moonlight didn't zig-zag across the tree tops, as if guided by a—

"Helicopter," I breathed. *They're searching for me.*

Leonard did snarl, then, briefly looking over his shoulder before turning back. "Hurry up. In, before they come this way."

"*I need to help them find you,*" Charlie had said. Or was that a dream? "*We're coming for you.*"

Not fast enough, though.

The helicopter passed over the forest, back and forth, coming closer and closer. It was almost as if someone guided it, pointing the pilot in the right direction to search without knowing an exact destination.

This way, this way, this way.

Was Dad flying that helicopter?

There's nothing I wouldn't do to be there for you, Reece. Please remember that.

Was Charlie with him, serving as a compass?

Suddenly, like a part of him really was with me after all and heard my thoughts, the spotlight dancing back and forth below the helicopter swung forward, pointing straight over the lake.

I squinted against the glare, the light reflecting brightly off the glacial-blue water.

Sapphire blue water.

Oh, no. We were on Lake Sapphire.

One of the deepest, coldest bodies of water in the whole country, my academic-fact-filled mind added unhelpfully, like a doll with dying batteries repeating the same phrase over and over.

If I tumbled over the side of this boat now, I'd never be found. Not even by the body recovery SCUBA team.

Leonard swore again, his calm, collected facade breaking as we both realized the helicopter wasn't searching anymore.

Its pilot knew where to go.

Leonard yanked me by the shoulder. "Let's go!" he shouted. I fought back, half-wondering why he hadn't shot me already, but it was obvious that standing grew more and more difficult for him with his busted-up knee.

Maybe he couldn't lift me overboard if he shot me while I was still in the boat?

I kicked out one last time, jamming my foot right into his bloody kneecap.

He groaned, and something wild came over his face. "It

doesn't matter anymore, anyway," he said, detached, before he aimed the barrel right at my face.

"REECE!"

The yell came from the woods, distant, but echoing across the water.

"REECE! H—D ON!"

Charlie. That was Charlie's voice. Was he in my head, still? Or was I hallucinating? Or maybe Leonard had already shot me dead?

He swore, attention pulled away to scan the trees surrounding the lake, swinging the gun around wildly. The helicopter closed in, nearly to the break in the trees.

"REECE?" Charlie yelled again. I could barely hear him now over the sound of the blades.

"CHARLIE?" I yelled back.

And then I saw him.

If he were alive, I wouldn't have. In his ghost form, though, he glowed a faint, opaque white and appeared on the shore, just ahead of us.

"What the fuck?" Leonard asked, shaken.

Charlie blinked away, reappearing right in the middle of the boat, protectively standing over me while he faced off with Leonard.

He was barely visible at all—the outline of his body more of a suggestion of a person than anything else, and his face twisted in anger, flickering in and out of view.

Like this, standing face-to-face with his killer, he looked like a true harbinger of death.

Leonard went still. "It's *you*," he said, pointing the gun at Charlie.

"Charlie!" I yelled, struggling to stand on my one good foot.

The helicopter bore down on us, propellers spraying water outward in waves from where it hovered above.

A loud, artificially amplified voice echoed across the lake. "Leonard Mandich, drop the weapon and put your hands in the air. You're under arrest."

Tate? He'd come with Charlie and Dad, too?

Leonard didn't react to the arrival of the helicopter or the order; his attention still focused on Charlie. He shuffled back, heels knocking against the edge of the boat. "I thought I had to be seeing things, but it really is you. How'd you get on this boat?"

Charlie still didn't reply.

"Drop the weapon!" Tate hollered over the speaker again. "We won't give you another warning!"

Shaking his head back and forth rapidly, Leonard ignored the order again. "It's not possible. You're dead. You're rotting at the bottom of this lake."

"So will you."

And then Charlie rushed him.

Leonard tried to back away, lifting the gun to shoot, realizing too late he was already at the edge of the boat.

A shot rang out. With stunned surprise, he tipped backwards, a bullet hole in the center of his forehead.

He was dead before he hit the water.

"Charlie!" I yelled, lunging for him.

Except something was wrong.

Very, very wrong.

As exhausted as I'd been just a few seconds ago, it was

nearly impossible to move now. In fact, it was difficult to breathe at all.

My one good foot collapsed beneath me. I barely caught myself in time to sit on the edge of the boat, rocking it violently.

I looked down, perplexed, still noting my oozing, bloody, shattered ankle.

Huh. Why couldn't I feel it anymore? And where'd all the blood on my shirt come from?

"Reece?" Charlie turned toward me, sounding more horrified than I'd ever heard him.

He had every right to be scared. There was a perfectly round hole in his stomach, exiting out the back of his see-through jacket, shot right through the center of him.

Leonard must've fired at the same time he was gunned down by someone in the helicopter.

Charlie's hands hovered over the hole, shocked, before he looked up at me, and his face morphed from stunned terror to downright devastation.

"*Reece!*" Charlie screamed, anguished.

I didn't have time to ask what was wrong before I, too, tumbled over backwards into the cold, blue water.

With a gunshot wound ripped straight through my chest.

CHAPTER TWENTY-FOUR

I was back in the lookout.

Shadows hung over everything, hiding all of the happy memories I'd made in shades of gray. The shutters were closed, blocking out the view of the world outside, and where the door used to be, the wall and windows continued in one long line, erasing the exit entirely.

Somewhere far, far away, I was aware my body sank deeper into the lake. Someone followed right after me, though, diving in headfirst.

Charlie.

His strong arms wrapped around my shoulders, trying and failing to swim us both back to the surface. He couldn't keep a solid enough form to hold on.

"You shouldn't be here," he said to me again. He was right beside me in the lookout, now. Sadness marred his beautiful face, and a tear escaped down his cheek.

I sighed heavily. "I know. I'm sorry. I tried to hold on."

Mom's smile, full of laughter at something Keith had said, flitted through my thoughts. Dad's quiet joy at spending slow days out in the forest together made the backs of my eyes burn. I thought of Bobby, laughing so hard water came out his nose.

I wasn't able to say goodbye to any of them.

I wiped away the tears tracking down Charlie's cheeks and the ones on my own. There was so much life we hadn't had the chance to do, so many things we hadn't been able to say.

I wanted so badly to give those things to him; to bring him into the land of the living. There was nothing I wouldn't do to accomplish it.

Death was greedy, though, and in the end, stole us both.

I took his hand, needing the reminder I wasn't alone, but instead of feeling the soft brush of his fingers against mine, the oddest thing happened.

Colors, bright as the sunsets he loved so much, glowed from our joined palms. An amalgamation of soft oranges, pinks, and purples slipped through our fingers, shining brighter and brighter the longer we held on to each other.

Back in that faraway place, someone else dove into the water above us, backlit by the beaming spotlight hovering overhead. He hooked an arm through mine and Charlie's, who'd slipped into unconsciousness next to me, and kicked hard for the surface.

I couldn't remember his name, but I knew he was our friend.

Somehow, we made it. Linking an arm through both of ours, he grabbed onto an inflatable floatation device and held on as we were dragged to the shore by a rope attached to the helicopter still hovering above.

"What are you doing?" Charlie asked, panicked by the unexpected phenomenon of our joined palms.

I tore my eyes away from the sight to look up at him, ready to ask the same, only to be distracted by the life I saw in his face.

I didn't have to search for it. The blush on his cheeks was no longer a dusting, but rather a splash of color. His eyes shone clear and bright, and his lips were pink and full.

"Reece, what's happening?" he asked again.

Awed that he could become even more beautiful than he already was, I shook my head. "I'm not sure."

I had an idea, though.

The more alive he looked, the paler I became. Now, my hand was the see-through one. My fingers slipped through his, instead of the other way around.

"Stop it," he growled, trying to sever our connection. "You're giving up. Stop it!"

A second man joined the first once we reached the shore, propelling down after sending a stretcher ahead of him.

"I'll start CPR!" my friend yelled over the deafening sound of the helicopter. "You hold pressure on the wound!"

"What about him?" the other asked, firmly pressing something against the gaping wound in my chest. He wasn't wearing sunglasses in the dark, but for some reason, that was what I wanted to call him.

"He's not alive, remember?"

The pressure let up for a second before returning, hard. "He has a pulse!"

"Then get a second stretcher!"

"I'm not trying to do anything," I told Charlie, squeezing his hand tighter. It felt very important not to let go, now. Like our roles reversed, and I was the one clinging to him for once. Or maybe, we were holding on to each other.

Maybe we always had been.

"I don't know what's happening!"

The colors swirled up our arms, almost tickling as they danced like heatless flames along my skin.

"I don't want this," Charlie said, angry and defiant. He grabbed hold of my nape, bringing our foreheads together and closing the loop, feeding the current of energy flowing into him back toward me. "Not without you."

With the kind of deep knowing that only came from personal experience, I understood exactly how he felt. So, I cupped his cheek with my free hand. "Alright, then. Together."

Whatever happened, we'd face it together.

Color exploded all around us, like a painting poured onto a canvas. Gone were the shadows obscuring our beautiful little home. The windows blew wide open, and the sunset hues swirled and swirled, spilling out into the real sky above.

"He's stopped bleeding!" Not-Wearing-Sunglasses yelled, words nearly drowned out by the sound of the propellers.

"WHAT?" Tate shouted back. He hovered over me, pounding on my chest to force what little oxygenated blood remained through my heart and out to the rest of my body.

"HE'S STOPPED BLEEDING! THERE'S NO WOUND!"

The compressions halted, rough hands pulling the bloody piece of cloth away. "I don't understand—what happened?"

"Maybe the shot missed him?"

"No, I saw it! He's covered in blood!"

Sunglasses shrugged. "The other one's breathing is shallow. We need to get them in the chopper, now."

"You go first, I'll keep working on him."

With the color returned to our lookout, I realized I wasn't see-through anymore. Neither was Charlie. By closing the loop, he fed the energy I gave him right back into me.

Mine, and then his.

Mine again, now his.

Ours.

Around and around and around. All I could do was hold on.

I peered through the open windows behind him. They faced west, overlooking the forest we'd watched over together.

Just a hint of a Mountain Bluebird sky peeked through the brewing thunderheads bathed in warm sunset hues. Over the distant ridge, a hazy, orange glow threatened fire; embers sparking and popping through the air. For a moment, I wondered if that was what came after death, beckoning us both.

But why would it be filled with more hardship and strife? More uncertainty?

I looked back at the storm clouds overhead and the raging fire just out of sight. Those things weren't a finality.

They were a possibility.

A future.

If we decided to leave the lookout, to walk into that great unknown, the blaze might burn out by the time we arrived.

Or, we might have to walk through it.

We could be caught in a storm and left with nothing but each other to brave the elements. Or it could pass us by, merely shading our journey from the harsh sun.

We wouldn't know, unless we tried.

And oh, did I want to try with Charlie. Always with Charlie.

"I think we're meant to go out there," I whispered, still clinging to him. The door reappeared, propped open wide for us in invitation.

He looked over his shoulder at the beautifully foreboding vista, eyes weary. "What's going to happen if we do?"

I kissed his temple. "I'm not sure."

He looked into my eyes. "There's a fire out there, though. And a storm is coming. What if we get hurt?"

I wrapped my arms around his middle, bumping our chests together. "We almost certainly will, but I still want to go with you."

"TATE! WE HAVE TO GO! NOW!"

Sunglasses was already back up into the helicopter along with Charlie. He leaned out the side, beckoning for us to follow.

"ALRIGHT!" Tate yelled, strapping me into the stretcher.

"You hold on, you stubborn idiot," he said to me as we were lifted into the air. "I'm not nearly as open-minded as you are. I'm not gonna be your friend if you show up as a ghost to haunt me."

"I'm scared, Reece," Charlie said. "I don't know if I'm strong enough for this."

Smiling, I tugged him toward the door. "You are. And we'll do it together. I'll never let go."

"Promise?"

"I promise."

He took my hand in his again. The world around us surged, sunset orange and the deepest blue of night smudging together, like bleeding watercolors meeting across the page.

I could see Charlie standing before me, whole and healthy, and lying on a stretcher next to me, soaked through and barely breathing.

Urgency tugged on those blue-black shades all around us, telling me to return to that darker place. It was time to go.

Charlie must've felt it, too. "Ready?" he asked, poised to step out the door.

Movement out of the corner of my eye made me turn.

The Thing appeared just on my other side. He looked right at me, gaze boring into mine more directly than ever before. Something quiet passed between us; a truce. For now, at least.

Together, we faced ahead, toward the possibilities that lay before us.

He was coming along, too.

I stepped away from the small shaving kit mirror propped on the counter and squeezed Charlie's hand.

"Ready."

CHAPTER TWENTY-FIVE

Death fucking sucked.

Everything hurt, the blankets itched, and there was a grating alarm going off somewhere that had about five seconds to quit before I started yelling.

Oh my God, I'm in Hell.

Clearly, making fun of Viola's new-age relaxation music had been the final straw. She was kind, in the end, and really, wandering around in the jungle couldn't be as bad as suffering for eternity with that alarm.

Ding! Ding! Ding!

"Turn that fucking thing off," I mumbled, blinking my eyes open.

My mom's face appeared over me, a halo of light cradling her head. Her brow knit in concern. "Reece? Sweetheart? Are you awake? How do you feel? Are you in pain?"

Mom's here, too?

No, that wasn't right. My mom was a saint; there was no way she'd end up in Hell. But that could only mean...

"Let's let him wake up slow, Pop. I'll go flag down a nurse and ask about getting the med bag changed."

Dad.

Blearily, I looked toward my other side—a great feat, considering my head pounded like it'd been run over by a truck—and found him sitting in one of those horribly uncomfortable-looking hospital chairs.

That's a familiar sight.

I took in the bed I lay in, and the low ambient murmur filtering in through the door. Somewhere down the hall, another machine began screeching.

So, maybe I wasn't *actually* in Hell, but a hospital wasn't far off.

Dad stood, stretched his back, and padded over, gently ruffling my hair. "Good to see you're awake," he said, eyes shining.

Shame kicked me in the chest.

How could I have even considered he was anything other than the patient, gentle, loving father I'd always known him to be?

"Dad, I'm—" I began, before a coughing fit took over. God, I needed water. My throat was parched and scratchy.

"*Shh,*" he said, leaning down to kiss my temple. "Everything's going to be ok. You just rest, now. I'll be right back."

"Want some water?" Mom asked. She offered me a plastic cup with a straw as Dad left the room.

I sipped it gratefully. "Thank you."

She wiped at a tear that'd tracked down her cheek. "I'm

so glad you're safe," she said, trying to contain her blubbering. "I just can't imagine what would've happened if your father hadn't found you in time."

I wasn't ready to talk about it yet.

Not because I was afraid to or didn't want to share things with her. It was more that there was just *so much* to say. So much to ask. I wasn't even sure how I was alive, let alone how Dad found me in time.

But one thing dominated my thoughts more than any other, one thing I desperately needed to know. "Charlie? Is he..."

I couldn't finish my question.

Had I imagined it all? I was on the boat alone with Leonard, and then suddenly, Charlie was there. He defended me. And when I fell into the water, when I was *shot...*

He'd found me in that gray place, too, and he'd saved me. Somehow, by some miracle, we'd seized the chance to live, and we'd stepped into the colorful unknown together.

Were those real memories, or simply my desperate attempts to cling to life?

Mom doesn't even know Charlie, I thought. *She won't have any idea where he is or what happened to him.*

Instead of the confused look I expected, however, she gave me a soft, knowing smile. "He's still asleep a few doors down. And now that you're awake, I can scold you for not introducing us sooner."

I gaped at her. "Asleep? Like, he's... *here?* Down the hall?"

"Mmhmm," she winked. "Officer Morris has been back

and forth between your rooms the last few days to check on you both. Now, he's dreamy, too. Seems to have something going on with that grumpy FBI agent, though."

Torn between gouging my eyes out at my mother calling Tate *dreamy* and clawing my way through the wall until I reached Charlie's room, I tried to sit up.

"Was he hurt?" I asked her, suddenly wide awake. "Has he come looking for me? I need to see him. Now."

Mom gently pushed my shoulders back, and to my great embarrassment, I didn't have the strength to fight against her. Plus, searing pain shot up my entire lower left leg when I tried to move it, halting my flight out of bed. When it abated, I realized it was wrapped in something bulky and heavy.

"He's okay, sweetheart. He's resting, just like you. He wanted to come see you, too, but you've both been through a lot. You need to take it easy."

He's here. He's resting. I hardly knew what to do with the balloon of hope that swelled in my chest.

Charlie's still here.

Then her words caught up with me. "Days?" I asked, confused. "How many days?"

"Four." Every minute of those four days was etched into her face, lined with exhaustion. "Keith's been here every day, too. He just left about an hour ago. He'll be so glad to hear you're awake."

Just then, Dad arrived with two medical personnel in tow. "Hello there, Reece. Good to see you're awake," the one on the left said. She was short, with straight, black hair pulled away from her face, and wearing a white coat over her purple scrubs. "I'm Diya Blake, a Nurse Practitioner. How're you feeling?"

The other person, a nurse, I assumed, pushed a few buttons to halt the machine's awful beeping and wrapped the blood pressure cuff around my arm before she began fiddling with a new IV bag.

"*Um*," I paused, assessing. "Like shit."

She smiled. "Not surprising, given what you've been through. You have a mild TBI—a concussion," she clarified at my horrified look.

I thought back to the force Leonard used when he knocked me out with that heavy flashlight. A mild TBI was probably the best outcome I could hope for. "What about my MS? Is it, I mean, do concussions cause relapses?"

She gave me an understanding look. "You'll have to talk with your neurologist about keeping an eye on things over the next few months, but there were no new lesions when we did an MRI to assess the extent of your concussion."

I blew out a sigh of relief, and Dad patted me on the arm.

"So, overall, it seems your head injury is healing well," she continued. "Our main concern is infection, given the nature of your other injuries and your compromised immune system from the MS treatments. We'll need to keep you a few more days for observation, but so far, you've been doing fine."

"Infection?" I asked. "In my leg?"

She nodded. "You have fairly extensive tissue damage, but no broken bones. You'll benefit from physical therapy to rebuild the muscle mass in your leg."

Again, I was stunned. *No broken bones?*

Images of the bear trap clamped around my ankle flashed through my mind. Could I really have been lucky enough to avoid broken bones from that monstrosity?

"Wait." I reached up, patting at where I'd been shot, and frowned. My hands were clumsy with the IV and oxygen monitor, but still, shouldn't I have felt bandages? Stitches? Something?

"What about here?" I asked. "What about my chest?"

Mom's brow furrowed. "Your chest, sweetheart?"

The nurse practitioner cocked her head to the side. "You had a few superficial scrapes and bruises, but no significant chest wounds."

I gaped at her. That was impossible. I'd been shot. Not grazed—*shot*. Right through the chest. Hadn't I?

Dad's face was grave, as if he remembered the same thing I did. Subtly, so Mom wouldn't notice, he shook his head once, eyes glassy.

I don't understand, either.

"We've got one more round of IV meds for you," the nurse practitioner said, "so you might feel ready to sleep again, soon. You can use the call button to let us know if you need anything."

The room was quiet while the nurse finished with her rounds and left.

How was it possible I'd escaped everything Leonard did to me with nothing more than a mild concussion and a bandaged-up leg?

"I don't want this. Not without you," Charlie had said, before pouring all of that color and life back into me.

I'm a man of science. I don't believe in magic healing. I

didn't believe in ghosts, either, before I met Charlie. And yet, he'd brought both into my life. He'd healed me, he'd *saved* me, over and over.

"I think I'll step out to use the restroom and find some more coffee," Mom said with a yawn.

I wanted to tell her she should rest instead, but my tongue already felt thick and heavy from the medication, and I could barely keep my eyes open.

Thankfully, Dad was on the same page. "You should go get some sleep, too, Pop," he said gently.

"I'm not tired," she replied defensively. "And I need to be here in case he needs anything."

"*I'll* be here, and I'll call you right away if something changes. He's going to be fine. Go, get some sleep."

"I'mfffine," I echoed, trying to reassure her. "Gosssleep."

Her soft kiss upon my brow was the last thing I felt before sleep swept me away again.

"Wow, he really does snore like a wombat."

My eyes flew open.

Tate sat in the chair that Mom had the last time I was awake, arms crossed with a smirk on his face. I rubbed my eyes and scowled. "I do not."

"Told you that'd get him up."

My head hurt less when I quickly looked to where Dad had been—or maybe it was just the sight of the man who'd taken his place that made everything else insignificant. "*Charlie.*"

He smiled, whiskey-brown eyes bright and clear. "Hey there, you wombat."

He hugged me, harder and stronger than ever before. I wrapped my arms around him as best I could and squeezed back.

"Are you okay? Are you hurt?" I asked, breathing him in. His hair smelled like hospital soap, and my muscles ached from holding him at this angle, but I'd never let go again.

I'll never let go.

"I'm okay. More than okay," he whispered, tucking his face into the crook of my shoulder. I probably stank far worse than antibacterial wash.

He pulled away to look at me, settling on the edge of the bed with one leg tucked underneath him. His skin wasn't ghostly pale anymore. He had a warm, tawny complexion, and the dusting of freckles across his nose deepened, as if he'd just come in from lying in the sun.

"Beautiful," I murmured, unable to tear my eyes away. I already missed his warmth.

Wait.

"You're warm," I said, eyes darting up and down, taking him in as fast as I could. He hadn't been cold before, but he hadn't been exactly warm, either. Now, though... Now, he felt alive.

"You're *warm,*" I repeated, my mouth lagging behind my racing thoughts.

Tears spilled down his cheeks. "Yeah. I'm... *here,* Reece. I don't understand how." He lowered his voice, looking toward the door. I realized Tate had stepped out to give us privacy. "But I'm alive. Like, *alive*, alive."

I gaped at him. "You mean—wait. What do you mean?"

He laughed, and I brushed my thumb over the tear that settled in one of his dimples. "I mean, I have a heartbeat. My lungs work like they're thirty years old, not almost seventy. The doctors didn't look at me like I was a talking corpse when they hooked me up to all those machines. The paperwork was a nightmare. I'm not sure what Tate and that FBI guy said to convince them everything was above board, but Reece. I'm *alive*."

"You're... alive?"

He beamed, nodding. "*Uh-huh.*"

I blinked. "You're alive."

"Yes, and if you clarify it one more time, I'll start doubting whether or not you're happy about it."

I yanked him down by the collar and slammed our mouths together. I pulled back quickly, though, when I remembered I'd been asleep for days and didn't even want to know what sort of morning breath situation that created.

"I'm happy about it," I whispered. "I just... Did all of it really happen? Did we really come back?"

Resting a hand on my chest, he brushed his fingers over the ghost of a gunshot wound. "The very first time I saw you through the window, you were bright—like the sunset. You were scowling," he said with a tear-soaked laugh, "but so full of color and life. You yanked me out of that gray world I was in for so long. And then you closed the window."

He paused with a hand gently pressed over my heart. "When you opened it back up, all I could think was I didn't want to be lost in the dark anymore. I wanted to follow you out, follow you anywhere. I didn't want you to shut me inside again."

Charlie leaned down and brushed a wet kiss on my forehead. "I told you, I think we were always meant to meet, Reece. I had no idea I was using your energy to gain strength—all I knew was with every day that passed, I wanted to *live* more and more. Not for some ambiguous future, but for you. *With* you. I don't know how we did it. I don't know how we're alive. All I know is if there was anyone in the world who could stubbornly will it to be so, it's you."

I knocked my forehead into his. "I've hoped for the impossible for so long, it's just hard to let myself believe it. I feel like you're going to disappear again, or I'm going to wake up and this has all been a dream."

He cupped my face between his hands. "Believe it. I'm really here, Reece. We're here, together. For as long as you still want me."

I hugged him again. "I'll always want you," I growled.

"Good," he said, voice turned playful. "It would be terrible to find out you were only attracted to me because you have some weird ghost thing. I'm fully flesh and blood now, baby."

A laugh rumbled up from my chest. "First, you say I snore, *which I don't,* and now, I have a ghost fetish? What else are you going to falsely accuse me of? Smelly farts?"

"Well, I can confirm that one."

I quickly looked toward the door, again so caught up in Charlie I hadn't realized someone else had entered the room.

Bobby stood there, shuffling from foot to foot, holding a bag of *Reese's Pieces*.

He tentatively offered up the candy, as if unsure of whether or not I'd accept. "I, *uh*," he cleared his throat. "I brought you these. I knew flowers would irritate you. *What the fuck am I meant to do with a fern? This needs to be planted in at least a fifteen-inch pot. It's a chore, not a gift,*" he said, imitating my voice. "So, ya know. Something to snack on."

I stared at the bag of candy. My parents had called me *Reese's Pieces* since I was a child, because of the obvious shared name, but also because I'd have eaten them by the fistful if they'd let me.

And while he hadn't used the nickname in many, many years, there was a time growing up that Bobby called me *Reese's Pieces*, too.

The dark circles under his eyes were much deeper than they were the last time we spoke, and there was a cautious brokenness in the way he carried himself I'd never seen before. He looked like he'd aged ten years in just a few days.

"Bobby," I said gruffly. "I'm so sorry."

He dropped the bag onto the side table and strode forward, leaning down to hug me just like Charlie had. "I didn't know," he said, voice choked with tears. "I swear, I didn't know. I'm so, *so* sorry, Reece."

I shook my head, gripping him tight in return. "It's okay. It's okay."

He pulled away. Over his shoulder, Charlie gave me a soft smile and joined Tate in the hallway.

"I understand if you'd prefer I go," Bobby said, avoiding

eye contact. "I mainly just wanted to check in and see how you're doing. I get it, if it's too hard to talk to me right now."

I shook my head hard enough to make it throb again. "No. Stay. I want you here. You're my best friend. He can't—he can't have that, too. He can't take that away."

Bobby finally looked at me, a swirling mix of grief, betrayal, and devastation in his eyes I understood all too well. "I really didn't know," he repeated quietly. "He's been weird and distant lately, but I thought it was the divorce. Or work. I honestly never questioned his absences. He argued with Mom a lot over who got the cars, the house, the land, everything. Lawyers were involved. It was exhausting."

He shook his head. "When he'd ask to borrow the truck to get away, I didn't think twice. Not until you said you'd seen it out on the park road. I didn't understand why he'd take a personal vehicle out there when he has his work truck for that. But then the FBI showed up, and shit hit the fan so fast."

"You can say that," I replied darkly. "How are you, though?" The image of Leonard's lifeless body falling backwards into the water flashed through my mind. "I mean, with... Everything?"

Bobby looked at his feet, stoic. "I don't think I'll be okay for a long while," he said gruffly. "I don't know what to do with any of it. How am I supposed to grieve my dad and be glad he was killed before he could do the same to my best friend? How are Jade and I meant to raise Molly in a town that mourns people her grandfather murdered? How do I separate who he was to me from the monster he was to everyone else?"

"I don't know," I whispered. "I haven't really thought about any of it, either. Or what comes next. It's easier not to."

Bobby nodded. "Probably going to be messy, once we do."

I looked over at where Charlie stood in the hall, still within sight of me. "Yeah, it will be. But we don't have to do it alone. And you don't have to do it without me."

"Now who's the Hallmark card?"

I huffed a laugh. "C'mon, there's someone I want you to meet."

Introductions were awkward as fuck, but Bobby and Charlie did their best.

"Hi," Charlie said with a small wave. "Nice to finally meet you. Reece talks about you all the time. I'm Charlie." He stuck out his hand, which Bobby shook.

Shoulders tense, Bobby ignored Tate's greeting, but flashed Charlie a weak smile. "Yeah, *uh,* nice to meet you, too. I mean, I've heard of you, but..." he trailed off.

I felt awful for them all. What was Bobby meant to say? *"So sorry my dad killed you, but glad you're alive again. By the way, thanks for also saving my friend from my dad!"*

And that wasn't even considering the elephant in the room that Tate may have been the one to kill Leonard.

They were trying, though. Hopefully, once we all had a chance to process the unconventional circumstances of, well, *everything,* they'd get to know each other better. Bobby clearly wasn't ready to discuss details, though, and he excused himself shortly after, never once looking at Tate.

"He's going to have a hard road," Tate murmured once he'd left.

Yeah, he would. But I wouldn't let him go it alone.

I cleared my throat. "So, how did you find Tate?" I asked Charlie. "I thought you could only appear wherever I was or at the lookout."

He shrugged. "Same way I found you. I thought about him, concentrated, and" he snapped his fingers, "there I was."

"Scared the absolute shit out of me," Tate grumbled. "I was driving, for fuck's sake. On my way to find *you,* because you were a stubborn idiot, *again,* and left my grandmother's house even though you were already knocking on death's door. And then he popped up in the passenger seat next to me!"

"You still handled it better than Reece the first few times," Charlie said. "I know I was a few close calls away from getting bear-sprayed in the face."

I scowled. "I thought *I* was the only one you could find."

Tate raised an eyebrow. "Please don't tell me you're jealous?"

"I'm not *jealous,*" I said, willing my face to go back to normal.

Charlie sat back down on the bed, scooting in close. "*Aw,* baby, don't be jealous. You know you're the only one I *want* to haunt."

Tate made a face. "You know he saved your life, right? If he hadn't found me when he did, I wouldn't have known to intercept your Dad on his way home. We would've lost a lot of time trying to figure out what happened and where to find you."

That sobered me. I'd be at the bottom of a lake by now, had Charlie not reacted immediately.

"How did you know something was wrong?" I asked quietly.

As if haunted by the memory, he looked away. "I didn't. You came to *me*. You walked right through the lookout door."

By his expression, I knew he wasn't talking about *our* lookout, but the one we'd left behind when we chose life with each other.

I squeezed his hand.

"I can't figure out why he'd try to kill me at Dad's, and not the lookout," I said.

Tate sighed. "He got away with framing someone else once; he may have been trying to do the same to you, or your Dad. I think that's why he left Janine somewhere she was so easy to find. That, or he didn't want to dump her body on the side of the lake you could see from the lookout, just in case."

"Why kill Janine, though?" Charlie asked. "If he wouldn't be able to hide her body like the rest of us? And why go after Reece?"

"Maybe he thought you saw something," Tate said. At Charlie's furrowed brow, he continued, "He was spiraling. I don't think he was in control anymore. He wanted the thrill of the kill as many times as he could before getting caught. These kinds of people can't hide who they are forever."

Like a cornered and wounded animal, I thought again.

"Right. Waters and I have a truckload of paperwork to finish, so I'm gonna head out," Tate said with a yawn.

"Are you gonna *fill him in* once you get there?"

He pointed a finger at me. "No one will notice if I add

another black eye to your already fucked-up face, West. Watch it."

I grinned before growing serious again. "Thank you," I said, looking at my hands. "For helping Charlie find me. For saving us both. I'm glad to have you as a friend."

Tate blinked and shuffled on his feet. "You're welcome. Me too." The room was quiet for a beat before he continued, "That was weird, right?"

I sighed. "Thank God. Yes. Can we never do it again?"

He chuckled on his way out the door. "Sounds good to me. Oh, I almost forgot." Pulling a small square of paper out of his back pocket, he handed it to Charlie. "For you. Once you get a phone, I'll text it to you."

Charlie flipped the paper over, revealing a photograph of me and Sunshine, Viola's hairless cat, sitting on that horrible mustard brown couch. Grinning, he looked back at Tate. "This is *awesome*. Thank you."

"You're welcome," Tate said with a smile, and left.

Eyeing the picture, I said, "You can't hang that up."

"Oh, I can, and I will. It'll be the focal point on our picture wall."

Our picture wall.

The words tucked into my chest, warm and cozy. "Lie down with me?" I asked, shifting over to give him room.

With a smile, he joined me, wrapping one arm around my middle and scooting in close.

"Where have you been staying?" I asked, fingers carding through his soft hair. It was a rich brown, even darker than before, with a subtle hint of auburn. I couldn't wait to see it catch in the sun.

"I've only been out since yesterday. Your Mom let me sleep in their hotel room for a few hours earlier, but I mostly just wanted to be here."

I pressed a kiss into his hair. We'd have to think about where to stay once I was discharged. Could we go back to the lookout? Who was in charge now that Leonard was dead? Was I even strong enough to do all of those stairs on crutches?

For now, I was content to hold Charlie until one of us had to move.

I opened my mouth to ask if he'd given any thought to what he wanted to do with the future spread out before us, only to be jostled when he sprang up next to me, as if startled.

"Oh, no! I have to pee!" he exclaimed, scurrying out of bed and making for the door.

I laughed so hard my whole body hurt, and it was the most wonderful thing in the world.

CHAPTER TWENTY-SIX

"I think the physical therapist is trying to kill me."

Sweaty and out of breath after fighting with a resistance band for half an hour, I sat back on Dad's couch with my ankle propped up on an ice pack.

"It might be too soon to make that joke," Charlie quipped, sitting in the chair across from me, a smile on his face. He didn't look up from the book in his lap.

I chuckled. "Where'd Dad go?" I asked, looking over my shoulder into the kitchen.

"He went out back halfway through your grunting and cursing."

Alright, so maybe I was a bit dramatic with the calf raises, but *fuck*, rebuilding my strength after being off my left ankle for two weeks sucked. Snagging the crutch propped on the arm of the sofa, I stood.

The pain in my ankle was mostly gone, and the stitches

were removed, but I'd have a gnarly scar for the rest of my life.

Which was okay, because I *had* a life, and so did Charlie.

"Good," I said, bending down to press a kiss against his neck. "Because I need to tell you how fantastic you look in that shirt."

His eyes flicked up, sultry and heated. "You already have. Several times."

He'd finally ordered some clothes of his own, and as much as I loved seeing him in mine, this particularly fitted shirt did things to me.

"Let me clarify." I trailed my lips up behind his ear. "I need to tell you how fucking hot you look in that shirt. You're packing it, right?"

He turned to capture my lips in a heated kiss, fingers tugging on my collar to yank me closer. "As long as you pack those hiking pants of yours."

Sorting through laundry the other day, I found an old pair of pants I'd left at Dad's after visiting with Josh a while back. They fit tighter in the ass and crotch than I was used to, and I hadn't felt good in them.

The way Charlie stared, though, dragging his eyes over my body in a way that had me all sorts of hot and bothered when I tried them on, made me feel good.

Very good.

"Already in my bag," I said, breaking the kiss before we got carried away.

Dad had taken off work to be there for me and help settle us both in after I was discharged from the hospital, which I was so, so grateful for. He'd embraced the weirdness of how Charlie and I met better than I could've hoped for.

The fact that he was thrown into the deep end with the whole ghost thing via Charlie magically knowing where to fly the helicopter to save me, helped.

Starting off on the right foot, and all that.

However, in the two weeks we'd stayed at Dad's, we shared the pull-out sofa mattress in the living room while he slept in the open loft upstairs.

It had not been conducive to any activities that required privacy. Or for great sleep at all, really.

"I'm looking forward to tomorrow," I said, dropping a kiss into his hair and straightening up.

He snagged my hand and smiled. "Me too."

I squeezed once and let go, making my way out the back door. I could limp around now without a crutch, but I wanted to give my ankle a rest after the strength exercises.

Daylight filtered through the trees, a stark contrast to the harsh floodlight illuminating my nightmares of that night. Despite the warm sun on my back, a chill ran down my spine as I made my way over to the open shed where Dad rummaged around.

"Hey," I greeted, noting the tension in his back.

He dropped an armful of tools into a box and straightened to face me. "Hey there. How was PT?" he asked, wiping his sweaty brow.

"Hard. But fine," I said, scuffing my foot through the dirt at the entrance. We both knew why I didn't come inside.

Dad joined me in the daylight, skirting around the spot Leonard had trapped me. "I, *uh*, I can't stop picturing it," he said gruffly. "The police came and went while you were still in the hospital, and I've tried to go back inside ever since, but I just can't. I'm moving everything out now to tear it down."

"Can't you rearrange instead? Maybe throw a rug down?" I asked, attempting a joke.

For as long as I could remember, Dad and I had danced around the subject of the bear traps. In the weeks since I was released, we'd danced around that night, too.

Maybe it was time we finally talked about it.

He chuckled, but it didn't reach his eyes. "No, a rug isn't going to cut it. I can't be in there, knowing what happened to you. What he did to you."

I stared at my feet, unable to look at him. "After Charlie remembered stepping on the bear trap... When I came back here and saw them in the shed..." I shook my head. "I'm sorry." The words had choked me for too long and needed out. "Everything had gone to absolute shit that day, and I was so confused, and I thought—I wondered if you were the one who—"

I couldn't finish, but it didn't matter, because Dad was already hugging me. "Oh, Reece, no. It's okay. It's okay. *I'm* the one who's sorry."

Shame colored his words, emotion swelling as he spoke. "If I'd listened to my gut, if I'd been a better man and reported what I knew all those years ago, what I found..."

"It's not your fault," I said, stepping back, but he shook his head and interjected.

"It is, though. At least some of it." His eyes were far away, as if remembering things he'd avoided for many years.

"I wondered, back then. Before the lookout—before *Charlie* —went missing. I found a few traps on the trails Leonard and I hiked together. I knew they were his favorite spots to go when he wanted to be alone."

His voice grew angry. "I confronted him about it. Our job was to protect nature and the wildlife in it. How could he do such a thing? Especially with something so cruel?"

"What did he say?"

"He denied they were his. He was having a hard time with Joan. They weren't married yet, but they were fighting. She wanted him to commit, he said he wasn't ready. He told me he'd been outside more because he needed to let off steam, that's all. He said he'd never seen them before in his life."

"Why did you keep them?" I asked. "Why not turn them in?"

Dad sighed heavily. "Those crimes are reported to the Forest Service. I'd have turned him in *to him*. Plus, what if I was wrong? He'd lose his job if he were cited for something like that, and the fines aren't cheap. Then Charlie went missing. They didn't tell us much, but they stopped requesting the use of the helicopter. The searches ended. The hikers weren't labeled as missing persons anymore; they were officially declared deceased. Clearly, they believed they knew who'd murdered them, and it wasn't Leonard. The killings *stopped*, Reece," he repeated, as if pleading for me to understand. "And I never knew the traps were related to the murders. At worst, I thought he was selling hides he poached on the black market. If I had known..."

He shook his head. "So I held on to them. I think a part of me always wondered, even if I didn't want to believe they were his."

I thought about my absolute refusal to accept that Bobby was a murderer. "I understand," I said.

It wasn't for me to forgive him; those were his wounds to mend, his actions to reflect upon. But I didn't hold it against him. It wasn't natural to assume the absolute worst of the people we cared about.

We stood in the quiet, listening to the forest all around.

"I'm happy for you," Dad said after a while. "That you found Charlie. I don't understand how it's possible he's here, or what happened that night, but I know he saved you. I know he loves you."

I smiled. "I don't understand any of it, either. He was there, at the lookout, when I arrived. Scared the shit out of me. But we got to know each other, and," I shrugged. "I've never felt more at peace than when I'm with him."

Dad chuckled. "Only you would find someone all alone up in a fire lookout tower. Are you packed and ready to go back?"

"Yeah, we both are. We'll hit the grocery store this afternoon and drop everything off at the ranger station. Looks like Angie is taking over for Leonard, at least for now."

Leonard had been her direct supervisor, and she'd called me a few days ago to ask if I was open to resuming my lookout duties once I healed. She'd apologized for even asking, but was having a difficult time filling posts after everything that'd happened.

I'd asked Charlie, and he was happy to go. Excited, even, now that the danger was over. It would be good for us to have some time before we decided what to do next.

Plus, all my shit was still out there.

"You're not hiking out on your leg, are you?" Dad asked.

"No," I said, relieved. "There will be room in the helicopter for us both."

"Good. Angie already did half of Leonard's job for him, anyway, I'm sure she'll shine. And I know things are better, now, but if you need anything—"

"You're only a phone call away," I finished.

He gave me another one of those familiar hugs. "Always will be."

Returning to the lookout felt like a dream.

When the tower first came into view, I nearly told the pilot to turn around and fly us back to Ponderosa. I was afraid of discovering we really were living in that gray place all along, and I'd only imagined the colorful life we'd fought for.

Upon landing, though, we were greeted by a beautiful, sunny sky, birdsong, and the rustling trees.

And of course, Charlie stood right next to me, happily chatting away with the helicopter pilot—who had no idea who he was—while we unloaded our supplies.

A few people had stared a little too long while we

grocery shopped, but I wasn't sure if they were focused on me or him.

Word had spread I was *almost* one of Leonard's victims, and it was funny how so many flocked to form search parties and hold candlelit vigils for the tragically murdered, but skirted around those left alive like they were cursed.

Charlie received a few double-takes, but who would actually believe he was *the* Charles Randolph, and not someone who shared an unfortunate resemblance?

The divers never found any of the others.

Lost to the deep blue of Lake Sapphire, each would be memorialized and remembered by their family, who finally knew where their loved one rested.

Except for Charles Randolph, of course.

He remained a mystery, forever a ghost in the minds of those who'd comfortably blamed him for something he didn't do.

"Have the stairs grown since we were last here? I think they have," Charlie groaned as we made our way up.

"There are at least two more flights than I remember," I wheezed, pausing to take a breath on the second landing.

I had my backpack on for the trip up, but otherwise Charlie and the pilot did all the heavy lifting. Thankfully, other than groceries, there wasn't much to unload since all my things were still there.

By the time we waved goodbye to the pilot from the deck, I was a sweaty mess and needed a lie down. "Two weeks away, and every bit of stamina I built up on these goddamn stairs went out the window. How's that fair?"

Charlie strode into the lookout ahead of me. "I miss

being able to disappear and reappear at the bottom. This whole being alive business is not what it's cracked up to be."

Chuckling, I closed the door behind us and turned to find he'd thrown himself onto the bed like a star-fish, face pressed into the pillows.

My sketchpad full of him lay open on the desk, ready for a lifetime more. His stove sat in the corner, with a chair placed in front and a blanket thrown over the back. No longer would it wait for his return.

No longer would I wait for his return.

I swallowed thickly. In that moment, more than any other in the past two weeks, it hit me. "You're not going to disappear again."

"Unfortunately," he grumbled, rolling to look at me before he stilled, eyes soft. "Come over here," he quietly beckoned.

I crawled onto the bed and draped myself over him, face buried in the crook of his shoulder.

Sun-warmed cotton and *Charlie*.

"No, Reece. I'm not going to disappear," he whispered, throwing his arms around my neck. "I'm going to stay right here with you. I'd follow you anywhere, remember?"

"Remind me?" I begged, overwhelmed with emotion.

Like an oxygen-starved fire igniting in a howling wind, all the pent-up tension between us boiled over. His fingers dug into my back, one leg hooking around my hip to pull us flush. Our mouths met in a clash of hot need and teeth, and contrary to his words, Charlie led.

My breath stuttered when he rolled us until he straddled my hips and pushed my shirt up. The caress of his calloused hands across my belly made me shiver. Sliding down my body, he dropped hot, wet kisses everywhere he went, fingers scratching through the hair on my chest like he couldn't get enough.

"Have I told you lately how gorgeous you are?" he asked, lightly biting at the meat of my pec before sucking a nipple between his teeth.

I tried to answer. "*Um...*" but then he switched to the other, flicking it with his tongue while he tweaked the overly-sensitive one between his fingers. "Oh, God," I moaned.

"Because you are," he continued, trailing kisses down to my navel. He exhaled a hot breath over my soft stomach, nuzzling his cheek into the coarse hair. "And I can't believe I get to keep you."

Nimble fingers fumbled with my belt buckle and zipper. He pulled my cock out, heavy and thick and already leaking, begging for his attention.

"I get to keep you," he said again, almost to himself. Then, he wrapped his lips around the head and sucked, tongue cradling me while he bobbed up and down.

My eyes rolled back, and I dug my fingers into his hair to hold him steady. "Charlie," I huffed. The beginnings of an orgasm bloomed low in my stomach.

In my defense, it'd been two whole weeks of waking up next to him, hard, only to dart into the bathroom for a cold shower before I embarrassed everyone. "I'm gonna come in about two seconds if you keep doing that."

With a low hum, he pulled off, watery eyes peering up at me. "I love all of this," he said, planting his hands firmly on my stomach. "All of you," he breathed, dropping kisses on every bit of exposed skin he could reach before dragging his tongue up the underside of my dick.

Eyes locked on mine, tears clinging to his long lashes, he swallowed me down again once he reached the tip.

"You're so pretty," I cooed, desperate to return the compliments. I cupped his face between my hands, cradling him while he pleasured me. "Too good at sucking my cock. Too good," I said, tone pleading.

For what, I had no idea.

He moaned and pulled off, using his hand to pump me while he caught his breath. "I wanna ride you."

My brain went offline at his words, only rebooting when he released me and slid off the bed.

I scrambled to rip the rest of my clothes off while he rooted through my bag.

Before I knew it, he'd tossed the bottle of lube onto the sheets next to me, perfunctorily undressed, and climbed back on top, this time on his knees, facing away from me.

"Open me up," he said, bedroom eyes peeking over his shoulder like the sweetest fusion of bashful and seductive.

God, the sight of him was enough to make me think maybe I had died and gone to heaven, after all. If he'd asked me to fly him to the moon, I would've figured out a way to make it happen.

This, however, would be much more fun.

I heaved myself upright and palmed the soft flesh of his ass, presented just for me. Familiar and yet new, just like the rest of him, I cupped the meat of his cheeks and spread them.

"So fucking *pretty*," I praised.

Trailing kisses across the hot expanse of his shoulders, I

reached around to run a soothing hand across his stomach, purposefully avoiding his hard and flushed cock.

"Reece, please," he begged, pushing his ass into my lap.

"Pretty baby doesn't wanna tease, this time?" I asked, brushing the back of my hand against his weeping cockhead.

"*No,*" he whined, voice catching.

That sound did things to me; it made me want to pin him down and make him come, over and over, until he cried those pretty, pretty tears all for me.

I squeezed lube onto my fingers and teased at his rim instead, still neglecting his needy cock. "*Shh.* Alright, no teasing."

I wrapped my other hand around his neck, gently holding him still while I gave him one thick finger. "Sit back on it. There you go."

Reduced to an obedient mess, he did just as I asked, breath hitching when I crooked it inside him. His back muscles bunched and shivered, and his head fell back, loose and pliant. "I missed this," he sighed.

"Me too, baby. You're doing so good. How about another?"

He nodded and gasped at the stretch of a second finger, but took it beautifully. I watched, gaze razor-focused on the way he practically sucked me in. In reward, I closed my fist around his cock and pumped once, twice.

"*Shit.* I want more. Give me more," he begged, thrusting forward into my hand and then back onto my fingers. I tapped on that sensitive spot inside him, just to make him jerk and whimper, before I pulled out to slick up my cock.

I lay flat on the sheets and steadied him with a hand on his hip. "Ready?" I panted, desperate for him.

Hands braced on my thighs, he peered over his shoulder again. "*Uh-huh.*" He groaned when I breached him, head dropping forward.

His shoulders and back tensed, relaxed, and twitched with each inch that disappeared inside him. "*Fuck,* that's good," I said like the uncouth, hairy mountain man I was. "You take me so well. The best. Such a pretty thing," I groaned.

My mouth hung open, near delirious, as I watched his ass stretch and give until I was fully seated. He cursed and shifted, swiveling his hips with my cock buried deep, nestling in. "You're so big."

I liked to pretend I was above such a compliment, but the way my cock throbbed inside him said otherwise. "Yeah, you like it though, don't you?"

His fingers dug into my thighs, and he nodded. "I like the way you make me ache."

That was the limit of my dirty talk. Any more, and I'd blow my load inside him way too soon. I dragged my palm down his back, overwhelmed by the hot grip of him. "Charlie," I replied. "*Charlie.*"

When he tried to bounce on it, I gripped him by the waist and held him in place. "Hold on," I panted. "Don't wanna come yet." My orgasm burned at the base of my spine.

Obediently, he waited until our breaths evened out and I cooled off a bit. My fingers danced light patterns across his skin until he batted me away. "Ticklish," he said with a huff, clenching around me.

I took hold of his hips again and rocked him, slowly, before he caught on and leaned into each movement, speeding us up.

He arched his back and cried out when I found the right angle to tag his prostate. Nonsense poured out of his mouth, a litany of jumbled curse words, praise, and delicious moans.

I could've come just like that, but the need to kiss him grew overwhelming. "Turn around," I growled with a light swat on one cheek. "I need you, baby. Need to see your pretty face when you come."

As hot as it was to watch his ass swallow my cock, I wanted to kiss him and stare into his eyes while I made him feel *everything*.

Clumsily, Charlie pulled off and spun around to face me. Our limbs jumbled together until he braced his hands on my chest and straddled me again.

I yanked him down by the neck and kissed him, demanding and thorough. "There you are."

Eyebrows knitted together, we breathed each other in while he slowly sank back down. He grunted when I bottomed out, the angle just new enough. "You feel so good inside me," he moaned before he swiveled his hips again.

Oh, I was in danger, now.

"Not gonna last long like this," I grunted.

The hazy pleasure-induced fog in his eyes cleared a bit, and he smirked. Leaning forward, he braced a hand against the window above us, and rode me. "You won't come. Not yet," he huffed in answer.

"*Fuck*," I growled, squeezing my eyes shut tight, desperate to obey. The sight of him moving above me was too much, the heat of him around my cock tugging my orgasm to the surface.

"Look at me."

My eyes popped open at his command. Despite his attitude, he looked wrecked, flushed cock bobbing with each bounce of his hips. Neither of us would last this first time in each other's arms after what we'd been through.

Charlie's breath shortened to match mine, and he sped up, grinding down in the same repetitive motion.

"I love you. I love you," I chanted, wrapping my arms around his neck and yanking him close so his cock ground into my stomach.

His jaw tensed, teeth gritted. "*Reece*," he cried, before he clenched around me, shuddering as he spilled hands-free. I thrust into him a few more times and followed, squeezing him tight in my arms.

Boneless, he sprawled on top of me. His nose scrunched when my soft cock slipped out, and I couldn't help but chuckle. "No more leaving me with the clean-up."

He groaned and buried his face in my armpit, inhaling deeply. "Worth it," he sighed, before propping his head in his hand, the other toying with the hair on my chest. "That was so much more intense than I remembered. I didn't realize—I didn't know how much I was missing, before. How much you can make me feel."

I brushed a sweaty curl behind his ear. "We've got a lot of time to make up for, then."

"What do you suggest we try next?" he asked, waggling his eyebrows.

SCRITCH   SCRATCH   SCRITCH   SCRATCH SCRITCH SCRATCH

I heaved a sigh and palmed my face. "Absolutely nothing, while that mangy thing is outside listening in."

Charlie shimmied off me. "She's hungry, it's been too long. Let me give her a hotdog."

"You do that, and I'll start dinner. Then we can make our plans," I said, gaze focused on his retreating backside.

"No grilled cheeses, please," he threw over his shoulder.

I winked. "How about a roasted chicken? With the crispy skin?"

Glassy-eyed, he grinned. "I'd love that."

"This is so delicious," Charlie groaned from his spot beside me on the bed, stuffing mashed potatoes and roasted chicken into his mouth. "Food was dull, too. God, I missed out on so much."

I forked the last piece of chicken into my mouth. "I can show you how to spatchcock next time, if you'd like."

He looked at me with disgust. "You can't be serious."

"It's not hard. It's how you get the skin really crispy while the meat stays tender."

Charlie grimaced. "That's wonderful, and I appreciate your efforts, baby. I really do. But I won't be doing that."

He smacked a kiss on my cheek to soften the rejection and scraped his plate clean.

I narrowed my eyes. "I see how it is. I'm just your spatch-cocker. A means to crispy chicken skin, that's all."

Despite the heavy meal I'd just devoured, the look he gave me went straight to my dick. "Not *all* you're good for."

Want pooled low. "Weren't we meant to be planning all the ways I can make you *feel*? I have ideas."

He blushed, but his face grew serious. "Speaking of plans, what are we going to do after the season ends?"

I blinked, caught off guard by the change in topic. "What do you want to do?"

He shrugged. "I don't know."

I cocked my head. "Is there somewhere you want to live? Do you want to stay here and apply to be a ranger? Or go back to school to do something else?"

He took both our empty plates and stood, placing them on the counter. "No, I'm serious," he said before turning back to me. "I really don't know. Is that bad?"

I followed him over and crowded him against the counter. "Of course not. You deserve time to decide. And I'd follow you anywhere, too, you know. We'll choose those things together."

He cupped my cheek. "Honestly, I just want to be with you. I want to go wherever you go. I want time to figure out what to do with my life, now that I have it back. I was just wondering if you already had plans for after this. I never wanted to ask, before..."

His eyes drifted. I kissed him, pulling him back into the present before he was lost down a road that wasn't ours to take anymore. "Well, actually, I emailed my department chair and asked if it would be possible to cut my sabbatical short. I thought about returning for the spring semester, instead of taking the whole academic year off."

At his surprised look, I hastily explained, "It'd still give us through the end of the year to plan, and I was just inquiring whether it would be possible. I don't have to go back if we decide we want something different. I just... I teach a dendrology class every spring, and I realized the other day that I miss it. I'm looking forward to it again."

Charlie smiled. Of course, he'd understand what it meant for me to want some part of my career back. "Spring in Missoula," he said, cautious hopefulness in his voice. "I bet it's beautiful. Let's do it."

"It's cold," I said with a laugh. "Most of the semester is still winter. But are you sure? If you want to stay in Ponderosa, we can figure something out. I don't want you to follow me just because it's what I want to do. I want you to be fulfilled."

He kissed me, long and slow. "I want to be with you. The rest we can figure out as we go. And who knows," he continued with a wink. "I hear the University of Montana has a great forestry program. Maybe I'll enroll. Someone said there's this really swoony, grumpy tree professor who works there. I think I'd like to meet him."

I threw my head back with a laugh. "I'm far too ethical to ever be your professor, but I think I could be persuaded into holding special office hours, just for you."

"Good," he said with a gleam in his eye. "Because you're

mine. I'll stake my territory so those wide-eyed twenty-some-things know to keep away."

Just then, his twinkle lights flicked on in the fading light. He smiled up at them before looking back at me, their warmth reflected in his eyes. "You roasted me another chicken, and my lights are back on," he whispered. "You know what that means."

I cupped his face in my hands and stepped backwards until I sat on the bed again. Peering up at him, I marveled at the magic that'd brought us together. There were moments I'd doubted whether or not we'd make it, but we had, and I'd never take it for granted. "I seem to have forgotten, you'll have to remind me."

Tears pooled in his eyes. "We're here because you didn't give up on me, Reece. You didn't give up on us. Not once. I may not know yet what I want to do with this beautiful life I get to live, but I know I want to spend it with you. Just you. And I know I love you so, so much."

The sun dropped below the far horizon while we spoke, casting the lookout in a wash of soft pink light that high-lighted the hidden auburn hues in Charlie's hair. I stared, committing the moment to memory.

"I love you, too," I said through my tears. "And I can't wait to live my life with you."

I pulled him back into bed, and we spent the rest of the evening under the glow of his twinkle lights, our kisses and slow touches coated in happy tears as we planned, hoped, and dreamed. We'd sleep peacefully, knowing no more ghosts lurked in the shadows, and no more monsters crept through the woods.

Still, the storms of life surely brewed, and if anything, our time at the lookout taught us that fire could come at any moment to sweep away everything we thought the future held.

Certainly, we hadn't yet faced all the hardship and strife life had in store. But as long as we held on to each other, we could weather the strongest tempests.

And so, hand in hand with Charlie, always with Charlie, we did the scariest thing of all.

We lived.

EPILOGUE

On a cold Tuesday in January, Charlie and I flew to Maine.

"I bet it's beautiful here when the leaves change," I said conversationally, creeping the rental vehicle down a snow-packed lane. My hands were cold and stiff, but the strengthening exercises I was recommended really helped.

"Mmhmm," Charlie replied, eyes glued to the window. His foot bounced anxiously against the clean plastic mat. Reaching over, I laced my fingers through his and squeezed once.

Quaint and darling even in the dead of winter, I quietly hoped today went well so we'd have a reason to visit Ogunquit again and see for ourselves how the town changed throughout the seasons.

"This it?" I asked a few minutes later, signaling my turn off Main Street.

He swiped up on his phone, pecking at the screen like it would bite if he hit the wrong button. There were some aspects of modern technology he still hadn't adjusted to. "The Coastal Cafe," he read aloud, checking the sign. "Yeah, this is the place."

I pulled into the small gravel lot and parked. As with all the other buildings in town, the inn was a mix of rustic pine, cedar, and coastal cottage.

The view of the marina would be breathtaking from the outdoor patio in summertime, with a cool ocean breeze blowing in over the water. It was still beautiful now, of course, but I wasn't keen on freezing my ass off outside.

"How are you feeling?" I asked gently, noting Charlie's gaze hadn't left the front door of the cafe. We were half an hour early, but he'd barely slept last night, and nearly wore a rut into the floor pacing around the Airbnb, so I'd suggested we go for a drive around town.

He finally pulled his eyes away to look at me. "Like I want to crawl out of my skin and run in the opposite direction."

I chuckled. "Do you really want to leave? I can tell her something came up."

"No," he said quickly, looking back toward the front entrance. "I'd always wonder. And I don't want her to be left waiting. Not anymore."

I kissed the back of his hand. "It's beautiful here. Seems she's done well for herself."

He nodded, rubbing his palms along the tops of his jean-clad thighs. Sometimes I still marveled to see him in modern clothes that actually fit, instead of my oversized T-shirts and sweatpants.

Somehow, though, through whatever magic had brought us both back to life last year, his flight jacket came along, too. He zipped it up against the chill creeping into the car. "Do you think I'm doing the right thing? Coming to see her?"

He'd asked me that many times over the last few months, but I didn't mind reassuring him again. "I don't think she would've agreed to meet you if she didn't want to see you. Or at least see if you are who you say you are. There's only one way to answer that question, though."

Tate was the one who finally found Frankie Hart, formerly Frances Randolph. She owned a small bed and breakfast, the Coastal Cottage, that served brunch on the weekends out of an attached cafe.

She married Robert Hart over thirty years ago, who ran his own recreational sightseeing business, sailing tourists up and down the coast during the summer months.

I assumed he was the stone-faced man who stepped out of the cafe upon our arrival, arms crossed and feet planted wide, barring entry.

"Right. Time to convince *him* we aren't con artists or scammers claiming her dead brother is sending us messages from the beyond."

"I *was* sending you messages from the beyond," Charlie quipped.

I smiled at the return of the wit I loved so much. "Yes, dear. I've got the beaded curtains to prove it. Now, let's go before he gets angry."

"Or *angrier*," Charlie mumbled under his breath.

Even in his seventies, Robert Hart was every bit as intimidating as I was sure he'd been at forty. It actually made me grateful Frankie had found a protector, hopefully a kind one, after all she'd been through.

Tate had a hell of a time getting her on the phone, and it was even more difficult to convince her to let the young man claiming to be her long-lost dead brother visit. Frankie and Robert made it very clear neither actually believed Charlie was who he said he was, but somehow, Tate—or maybe Sunglasses, I wasn't sure—talked them into meeting us.

So, we left our home in Missoula and flew all the way to Maine.

When Charlie stepped out of the car, Robert's arms fell limp at his sides, mouth agape. "Holy shit," he mumbled just over the sound of our boots in the snow.

I took Charlie's hand again and angled him behind me as we approached. I didn't want Robert to lash out in anger if he suspected Charlie was an imposter.

"Are you Robert?" I asked, halting several feet away.

"How is this possible?" he asked Charlie, ignoring me completely. His eyes scanned up and down as if looking for the sleight of hand.

"Is Frankie here? I'd like to explain everything to you both, if that's okay." Charlie asked. He unzipped his jacket and held it out to Robert. "You can show her this."

Awe morphed Robert's face into something much softer and kinder. "You can give it to her yourself," he said gruffly, opening the door and waving us in. "Come inside. She's been stress-baking since four this morning."

The mouth-watering smell of cinnamon rolls greeted us

first, along with the pleasant warmth of a crackling fire. Most of the chairs were still on top of the tables in the empty dining area, except for one.

A woman sat with her back to us, facing the fire. She'd wrapped her cardigan tightly around herself, as if to shield from what was to come.

She turned at the sound of our entry. Charlie stopped in his tracks next to me with a sharp inhale, his tight grip on my hand going lax.

Frankie's hair was a beautiful, dark shade of salt and pepper. She wore the years of her life on her face, both in laughter lines and in the deep, endless amber of her eyes. But even with forty years separating them, the resemblance was striking.

"Charlie?" she breathed. "Is that really you?"

He swallowed through his tears. "Hi, Frankie."

She stood at the same time he stepped toward her, meeting in the middle of the empty room in a hug so fierce, so long overdue, I almost felt like Robert and I should look away.

The stoic man from five minutes ago was gone. Together, we wept for the people we loved most in this world, who'd finally reunited with each other.

Explanations would come, along with more tears and promises to meet again soon. Time wasn't easy on either of them, and yet there they were, on the other side of decades of grief.

I hated when people mindlessly parroted the old saying, *"Everything happens for a reason."* Sometimes, terrible things happen to good people, and there is no explanation for it.

They didn't deserve it. In fact, life may have been easier if the bad thing hadn't happened.

I understood better now, though, exactly one year after that fateful day I was left in an airport, the day my life changed forever, that even when life wasn't fair, it could still be beautiful.

It could still be endlessly full of love, joy, and celebration, as mine was every day I woke up next to Charlie.

It could still *be*.

Would I have agreed to take the lookout job, had a life-changing diagnosis not forced me to grapple with a future I was never promised to begin with?

What would Charlie's life have looked like, had it not been tragically cut short?

We'd never know. But in the aftermath, we'd found each other. We'd fought for each other. And if given the chance, I would never go back.

I'd choose him. Over and over.

And wasn't that the most beautiful thing of all?

ACKNOWLEDGMENTS

When the idea for Reece's story first came to me, I had no idea it would turn into something so personal. Scrolling TikTok one day, I came across a video of someone who lived out in the middle of a national forest and worked as a fire lookout, all the way up in a tower on top of a mountain. I thought to myself, *that would be an incredibly cool setting for a spooky murder mystery.*

Except, let's also make it a romance, because, *duh.* But how does a lonely fire lookout meet someone to fall in love with all the way out there? And why is he out there to begin with? Well... What if a ghost also lives in the tower? And what if our MC feels a bit like a ghost, too?

And so the plot of this book was born.

I was diagnosed with MS in April 2024. Much of Reece's diagnosis, symptoms, thoughts, feelings, and journey to accepting that part of himself mirrors my own real-life experience. I'd considered that our lookout also had an MS diagnosis that prompted him to move out to the tower while brainstorming this story, but it wasn't until I wrote the epigraph (before I'd even finished the Prologue) that I knew I was ready to look the Thing in the eye and dive into the deep end with Reece.

Writing this book opened wounds I didn't know I had, forced me to confront and put a name to the things I felt, and then helped heal them. As with Reece, that journey is still ongoing, but I'm so grateful for the people around me who help on that journey.

Which brings me to all the people I want to thank!

I'm so grateful to my alpha and beta readers. This book is much better because of your feedback, comments, and edits!

Thank you, Jen, for your incredibly helpful and hilarious beta comments and feedback, and for helping me get out of my own head by talking through plot points with me!

Thank you, Emory Winters, for reading those early vulnerable chapters and motivating me to keep going, and for your friendship and constant support!

And thank you, Milo de Moss, for your beta and sensitivity reader feedback, cheerleading and support, all the creative and plot brainstorming, and friendship!

To my parents and friends, thank you for being there for me in the ways I needed during those dark days. I can't express enough how much it means to me.

And finally, thank *you* for reading *The Lookout's Ghost*. It's an honor to share it with you! Reece and Charlie's story is done for now, but I'm never one to fully close a book. They deserve so much happiness after what they've been through —who knows what that might inspire in the future. Also, I was fighting for my life to keep Tate from stealing some of those scenes. I don't have any plans yet, but we might just have to come back to Ponderosa someday and see what he's up to, and what's going on behind those Sunglasses.

ABOUT THE AUTHOR

A. Knightley lives in the wilds of the Midwest with her dog. She loves to crochet, watch scary movies, and of course, write cozy and swoony paranormal romance stories. To stay up to date with what she's working on next, you can connect on Instagram @author.aknightley.